Glowing Revie... Y0-AWG-080
JEANETTE BAKER

IRISH FIRE

"Using the beautiful Irish countryside as a backdrop, gifted writer Jeanette Baker delivers an engrossing tale of treachery and secrets." —*Romantic Times*

"Ms. Baker has brilliantly blended the powerful horse racing industry with a stunning tale of romance and personal rebirth. She has crafted a true champion."

—*Rendezvous*

NELL

Winner of the RITA Award for Best Paranormal Romance 2000

"Baker is a forceful writer of character and conflict."
—*Publishers Weekly*

"Jeanette Baker spins an eloquent and intricate story that combines the lives of two extraordinary women. *Nell* is yet another shining example of Ms. Baker's exceptional gift for storytelling." —*Romantic Times*

"Ms. Baker has put together a breathtaking novel that has the reader eagerly turning the pages. All the classic themes, including an innovative time travel twist, combine for an explosive read. Ms. Baker waited for the right moment to pack on the sensuality. And it was certainly worth the wait."
—*The Literary Times*

"*Nell* is rich in the Irish history of a couple of time periods, and Ms. Baker's prose draws her readers right in. Blend this with not one but two love stories, and readers will cherish this creative masterpiece that spans two decades and the past." —*Rendezvous*

IRISH LADY

"*Irish Lady* grips the reader from the first page to the last! A wonderful mix of past and present comparing the griefs and tragedies of ancient Ireland with the heartbreak and passion of present-day Ireland, and an exploration of divided loyalties and discovered destinies."

—Diana Gabaldon, author of the Outlander series

"A delicious yet poignant read. Truly one of the best and most touching books I have ever read—a true love story complete with a host of emotions."

—*The Literary Times*

"The pride of the Irish and their struggle for freedom from the British is brought to life with outstanding skill. Add two amazing heroines, one in the present, the other in the past, but each with a love that outlives time, and the reader is ensured of hours of joy."

—*Rendezvous*

"Inspired writing! Splendid! 4½ BELLS!"

—*Bell, Book, and Candle*

CATRIONA

Books by Jeanette Baker

Legacy
Catriona
Irish Lady
Nell
Irish Fire
Spellbound

Published by Pocket Books

JEANETTE BAKER

Spellbound

POCKET BOOKS
New York   London   Toronto   Sydney   Singapore

This book is a work of fiction. Names, characters, places and incidents are products of the author's imagination or are used fictitiously. Any resemblance to actual events or locales or persons, living or dead, is entirely coincidental.

An *Original* Publication of POCKET BOOKS

POCKET BOOKS, a division of Simon & Schuster, Inc.
1230 Avenue of the Americas, New York, NY 10020

Copyright © 2001 by Jeanette Baker

ISBN: 0-671-03458-8

First Pocket Books printing April 2001

10 9 8 7 6 5 4 3 2 1

POCKET BOOKS and colophon are registered trademarks of
Simon & Schuster, Inc.

Front cover illustration by Vincent McIndoe

Printed in the U.S.A.

Spellbound

1

$\mathcal{I}$n the small bedroom of her thatched cottage, Kerry Tierney struggled to give birth to her third child. Sleet, thick and dangerous, slanted sideways, pounding against the windows, seeping under the door, leaving great wet puddles on the flagstone. Outside, the driveway glittered like glass under the falling ice and snow.

Wind roared from the north, dislodging stones from unmortared fences, uprooting stunted trees, ripping through power lines, overturning boats in the harbor, sweeping away henhouses, pony carts, street signs, everything not securely tied down.

Lashed to the mooring, the ferry dipped and rose, a twig helpless in the endless cresting of the Atlantic's mighty swells. The airport had been closed since early morning, all flights to the mainland canceled, throwing the island into an isolated darkness not seen in twenty years.

Kerry had been pushing for nearly six hours with little progress. The child wouldn't descend beyond the pubic bone. The midwife, Mabry O'Farrell, knew that her patient belonged in a hospital. She knew also that there was no hope of getting her there in this weather.

"Come, lass," Mabry urged, paying no attention to the white face and trembling hands of the young man by her side. "You can manage it. It won't be long now."

"Why won't he come?" Kerry moaned, writhing with the pain of another mounting contraction.

Mabry ignored her question and moved between the woman's legs, pushing them apart. This was the third time she'd been summoned to bring a child of Kerry's into the world. It should have been easier than this.

Suddenly Kerry cried out and her legs went slack. Her husband screamed. Alarmed, Mabry moved to the woman's head, checked her pulse, and listened for a heartbeat. There was none. Immediately, she knelt down and breathed air deep into Kerry's lungs.

"What's happening?" Danny shouted.

Mabry inhaled and fastened her mouth over Kerry's, breathing deeply, pushing down hard with the heel of her hand over the woman's heart, once, twice, three times, four times . . . ten times. She breathed in again, twice, and pressed again and again and still again, repeating the cycle over and over. Mabry was crying now. There was little time left. If she didn't act soon, the child would die as well. "Breathe, Kerry," she begged silently. "Breathe." Crucial moments ticked by.

Finally she straightened. "Fetch me a knife, Danny, a sharp one, and see to your daughters."

The knife he brought to her was a carving knife, twelve inches long and serrated, with a brown handle.

Mabry hesitated before taking it. "She's gone, lad. You know that, don't you?"

Danny nodded.

"I'm going to save your child."

Again Danny nodded. Mabry lost precious seconds waiting for him to leave the room. Her hands shook. Kerry was dead. There was no reason to disinfect the blade. She pressed the knife into the dead woman's skin and watched the line of blood spread. Then she cut again, exposing the round pink uterus, mindful of the child so close to the blade. Feeling carefully to determine exactly where the baby was, she pricked the skin with the knife and slowly, delicately tore open the womb. Her hands grazed the baby's cheek, his forehead. She reached in, found a leg and an arm, and lifted him from his lifeless mother. It was a boy, just as she thought.

She suctioned the mucus from his mouth, heard his first strangled gasp of breath followed by the unmistakable mewl of a newborn, and watched gratefully as the blue tint of his skin turned to pink, heralding life.

After wrapping him in a blanket, she laid him in the wooden cradle that had once belonged to his sisters, the cradle with the handstitched blanket. Then she covered Kerry Tierney with a sheet, sat down in the straight-backed chair near the bed, buried her face in her hands, and wept.

Seventeen days later, Mabry stood on the bluff in front of her cottage, narrowed her eyes against the rare June sunlight, and focused on a spot in the distance where the unbroken expanse of sky met the sea in a blurred, slate-gray horizon line. It settled her, this communion with the distance, a place the ancients once called the summerlands, a place one could go for peace and meditation before time and progress had forever removed them from the path of humans.

Above her, gulls circled the ancient Celtic fort of Dun Aengus. Below, a turbulent sea crashed against treacherous cliffs, reshaping, rounding, wearing away, one centimeter at a time, year after year, the island that for three millennia had seen the births of her ancestors.

She knew the island better than anyone. She had always known it. It was part of her, the pulse of it beating through the soles of her feet in perfect harmony with the blood thudding in her throat, her temples and wrists. Ocean tides matched the ebb and flow of the life force within her, low, stretched out, calm in the morning, churning, energized, moon-touched as night deepened.

Mabry was old, the oldest woman on Inishmore. She couldn't remember how old. Once she'd known the details of her birth, but that was long ago. All who could have told her were dead now, buried beneath Celtic crosses and rich limestone turf, behind small, white-washed, thatched-roofed churches dotting the lush green of the island, an island three miles wide, eight miles long, an hour's ferry ride from the mainland, an island where in winter time stood still and its eight hundred inhabitants reverted to the old ways, ways the mainlanders, with their computers and their cell phones and their trendy flats in Dublin, called primitive.

With hushed voices, her neighbors whispered behind her back. A witch, they called her, *cailleach, an ealain dhubh,* one who practices Wicca. Mabry opened her eyes, looked directly into the friendly face of the spring sun, and laughed. Perhaps she was. Perhaps she did. Voices spoke to her, urging her to keep the sacred trusts, to ease suffering with her herbs, to counsel the sorrowful, and still she continued to live, long past the time when others had closed their final chapters.

If that was witchcraft, so be it. Mabry had few illusions. Superstition had no place in her life. Experience and wisdom did. If others were too blind to see that living a long time gave a woman insights, she would make no attempt to educate them. Their superstitions brought her chickens, potatoes, and carrots for her pot. It gave her respect in the villages, something that came rarely to the old and feeble no longer able to earn their own keep.

Only once had she doubted herself, and the doubt had cost her a moment in time, a moment when her common sense was suspended, replaced by a desperate fear that held her frozen, until sanity returned and she was able to practice her craft.

It had been too late for Kerry Tierney but not for her unborn son. The woman's life had already been predetermined, but the child was another matter. Mabry had done what was needed to avoid two deaths that day. Danny Tierney was another matter. The Sight had evaded her completely when it came to Danny.

He had been a borderline alcoholic when times were good. The loss of his wife sent him over the edge of his already precarious control. Following her death he drank around the clock. Not two weeks after Kerry was laid to rest under the green limestone of Inishmore, Danny's boat foundered aimlessly on a flat sea beneath skies as cloudless and blue as a spring morning. His body was found tangled in his nets.

More than likely he would have come to a tragic end no matter what. Danny was born difficult, no matter how one turned it over. There was no polite way around the truth. The lad had few redeeming qualities. There were reasons, of course. Poor little lad, growing up with no mother, never mind a father who spent his life closing down the pubs. Normally Mabry didn't torture herself with what-ifs. But she'd known Danny Tierney all his life, and she couldn't help wondering if he'd taken another fork in the road, would it have turned out differently for him?

She sighed. If only Kerry had gone to Galway with her brother. Perhaps she would be alive today. But the girl was stubborn. She'd wanted Danny Tierney with the single-mindedness of a migratory bird whose instinct guides her, mindlessly, south, without the slightest notion of what awaits her once she lands. She was a woman island-born, island-locked, unlike her brother, Sean.

Despite Kerry's coaxing ways and her sweet, blue-eyed face, pretty where Sean's was rugged, she hadn't dreamed the dreams that moved her brother forward. There was a fineness in Sean, a quiet resolution, an honor where so few had any memory of honor. The essence that surrounded her brother and made him stand out from the rest had escaped her completely, and so she'd found her fate.

Mabry, a woman with little patience for organized religion, crossed herself and muttered a quick prayer. Later, when the moon was high, she would come back here to this same spot. She would stand upon sprinkled salt, light a candle, and with water and wine anoint her eyes, her nose and mouth, her breasts, loins, and feet, while reciting the ancient invocation for health and healing. *Bless me, Mother, for I am your child. Blessed be my eyes, that I may see your path. Blessed be my nose that I may breathe your essence. Blessed be my mouth that I may speak of you. Blessed be my breast, that I may be faithful in my work. Blessed be my loins, which bring forth the life of men and women as you have brought forth all creation. Blessed be my feet that I may walk in your ways.*

Perhaps it would be enough. It never hurt to offend either of the deities.

She shivered despite the sun. There was no help, no prayer, no invocation, no spell to prevent what would come. Sean would return to the island for Kerry's children, but there would be no peace. They were Danny's children, too, and Danny had a mother, an outlander, an American, a sun-worshipper with lacquered nails and a laugh like music, a woman who'd stayed long enough to bear a man's two children, long enough to break his heart.

Her mouth twisted. Foolish were the sons of Adam to think they could alter the course of destiny. Mabry was forty-seven years old before she knew that she would never leave the island, never sail down a canal in a gondola with a dark-eyed man, never feel the heat of a brilliant sun on that spot on her head where the hair parted. She was ten years older before she realized it didn't matter. Nothing mattered but the sky and the sea and the spring coming in after the long, gray, wet months of winter.

2

Sean O'Malley loosened his tie and sat down in his favorite theater seat, the farthest one to the left in the first row. He stared down at his program with unseeing eyes. The debut of his play, the one the critics had praised for its "uniquely Irish voice," had come and gone, as had the audience, the musicians, the lighting crew, and the janitor, leaving him alone in a fog of numbing darkness. Three weeks ago his success would have meant everything. Now the attention was no more than a nuisance, an obligation that took him away from the island and Kerry's children, his two nieces who had lost everything, his nephew who would live his life without knowing his mother.

Sean had been connected to his twin as he had never been to another human being. Kerry's death had been a severing, a shock of such horror and magnitude that for days he'd been unable to work, to write, to think or even speak. He'd walked around the spacious, light-filled home he'd bought for himself in Salthill's exclusive residential area in a myopic daze, scattering his belongings around him, setting down a pencil, a tea cup, a fork, a manuscript page, the turf bill, forever lost in a clutter as hopeless as the condition of his mind.

People died. Sean knew that as he knew the sun rose in the east and that the ride to Inishmore from Rossaveal on the morning ferry was so choppy a hesitant sailor frequently lost his breakfast. What he had not known, what he could not accept, was that it was Kerry who died. Kerry with three small children, a husband, and all of life ahead. Kerry with her welcoming hearth and her lovely pirate's smile and her voice that when lifted in song put the sirens to shame.

Sean dropped his head into his hands, the emptiness of his loss too great for tears, his future looming before him. He had little experience with caring for children. But he had a reasonable income and a housekeeper. Quite simply, there was no one else.

If it meant a bit of inconvenience on his part, so be it. He would take a leave from the university, concentrate on his plays, and stay on the island until he could win the girls over to the idea of relocating with him to his house in Salthill. Meanwhile, he would tie up loose ends on the mainland and try his best to get through the funeral and wake.

Newport, California

Mollie Tierney sat on the bar stool of her mother's newly remodeled kitchen and stared out the window. Life had a way of flattening out the highs, of putting things into perspective, of reminding a person not to expect too much or run the risk of grave disappointment. Murphy's Law, Kerry would have called it if she had been able to communicate at all. But Kerry, Mollie's sister-in-law and pen pal of nearly six years, her link to her family in Ireland, was dead.

Three months ago, with Kerry's encouragement, Mollie had accepted a teaching fellowship on Inishmore. Her eyes filled with tears. Now she would never meet the gentle young woman who had been her friend.

Mollie's mother, Emma Reddington, stood at the counter and nervously rubbed a nearly nonexistent water stain marring the gloss of the cobalt blue Mexican tile. Near her elbow, a glass of Cakebread Winery's finest chardonnay sat neglected, false courage for a dreaded journey.

Mollie broke the silence. "What does Dad think about Danny's will?"

Emma flushed. "I haven't told him yet."

"I thought you were going to tell him weeks ago. Did you change your mind?"

Emma's lips tightened stubbornly. "Weeks ago Danny and Kerry were still alive. The situation wasn't urgent."

"Mom, you have to tell him." A thought occurred to her. "You are going to bring them back here, aren't you? You wouldn't give up Danny's children, not when he left them to you?"

Her mother stared at her with a look Mollie had never seen before. It frightened her, as did the words that came from her mother's mouth. "I will never give up Danny's children, not even if it means I lose everything else. That's the least I owe him."

"What about Dad?"

"I haven't figured everything out yet. When I do, I'll tell Ward. There are legal issues to consider. I'm not sure I can bring Irish citizens out of Ireland into America, no matter what their parents' will stipulates. I've discussed all of this with an attorney. He's working on it, but I may have to come home for a while after the funeral." Emma bit her lip. "I hate to leave you there all alone, Mollie. You have no idea what it will be like, all by yourself, on Inishmore."

"I won't be alone, Mom. People live on the island."

"Yes," Emma said woodenly. "I suppose they do."

Mollie sighed and gave up. There was no point in interrogating her mother. She was upset enough. Her reasons for keeping the contents of her son's will from her second husband were her own.

Mollie knew that the provisions of her brother's will had mystified her mother. Emma didn't understand why he would choose her in the first place. For years, when he'd come to visit in the summers, she tried to reach out to him, to overcome the wall that months of separation erected higher and higher every year. But Danny was stubborn, his father's son, Emma said, immune to the lure of the California promise. He preferred the island, his father, and the life of a fisherman.

When Emma received her copy of the will drawn up by a Galway attorney, signed by her son and his wife three months before their third child was due, she'd shared her misgivings with Mollie. Three small children. She was fifty-six years old, no longer young, and she hadn't seen Danny in nearly ten years. He refused to come to California, and she was not welcome on Inishmore. But then she realized it was nothing more than a technicality. People didn't die young anymore, not both parents, not even on Inishmore where the conditions were still terrifyingly primitive, wet, cold, and Third World.

Kerry's death had shaken her, as did the cavalier way she was informed, a week too late for the wake, one week before her son was lost forever in a deceptively calm Irish Sea.

Inishmore, Ireland

Mollie turned up the collar of her calf-length coat with one gloved hand and stuffed the other deep into her pocket in search of warmth. With the exception of her mother and Ward, she knew no one, not even the young man whose funeral she had traveled eight thousand miles to attend, her brother, Daniel Tierney.

On the other side of the casket she recognized Caili, her five-year-old niece. The child clutched the hand of the man who, Mollie sensed instinctively, was not an islander. He stood motionless, his face carved into hard, grief-pulled lines, staring at the freshly dug grave. The older girl, Marni, her face pinched with a look that tore at Mollie's heart, leaned against him.

Patrick Tierney, the stranger who was her father, stood on the other side of the closed coffin, facing the black-garbed islanders who'd braved the icy winds and driving rain to pay their last respects. A woman Mollie didn't know held Kerry's new baby, the baby who had cost his mother her life.

The world was gray. Mollie stared helplessly at the horizon line, her eyes straining to separate sea from sky.

The only color her frozen, gray-locked mind could distinguish was the green of the hills, rolling grasslands dotted with gray stone walls surrounded by gray ocean, suffocated by gray sky, pelted by gray rain. How could they bear it, these solemn islanders with their chapped, wind-red faces, their fingers blue and numb with cold, their hair wet and lanky, pasted to their skulls by the relentless weather?

She closed her eyes and prayed, not for her brother and sister-in-law, long beyond the rain and bitter cold, but for the children they had left behind and the silent, stoic islanders who had come to bury one of their own, despite the cold, the wind, and the water penetrating their dark wool clothing, seeping down upturned collars, loose cuffs, and low-cut rubber boots, drenching them to the bone.

Mabry O'Farrell, the island healer and midwife, was the only one who appeared unaffected by the weather. To Mollie she looked like a pagan goddess. She stood apart from the others, somehow more substantial, more connected to the rest of them than the ineffectual priest whose voice was lost in the maelstrom of nature's clashing elements. She wore a black cloak that billowed about her figure like wings, and her long gray hair streamed out behind her, drawn away from her skull as if a powerful hand had combed it back. She stood motionless, hands at her sides, her body braced against the wind force pressing against her, her eyes leveled on the priest.

Raising his right hand in the sign of the cross, he uttered the closing benediction, "In the name of the Father and the Son and the Holy Spirit." Then he stepped back and Mabry stepped forward.

Three times she circled the coffin, sprinkling first red powder, then blue, then gray in three linking circles on the face of the wet wood. Where the powders touched, they crackled and smoked. Sulphur filled the air.

Mollie wrinkled her nose against the smell, tried to wring out her hair, and gave it up. There wasn't a dry spot on the island. The smoke thickened. The lines ignited, forming three glowing circles on the coffin. As if on cue, the women began to wail, a lonely, piercing, inhuman keening, calling up voices from the past, from other centuries, other lifetimes, voices that pierced the wet wool of Mollie's coat to burrow deep beneath her skin, wrap around her heart, and squeeze until she gasped for air.

Then it was over, the coffin lowered into the ground, the obligatory shovels of earth thrown in, and the weary, heart-sore survivors marched back to town, to life, to aged whiskey and dark beer, to hot food and sincere toasts, to long stories, tears, memories, and finally laughter, reluctant at first but more enthusiastic as the night grew older until it was finished and Danny Tierney had been laid to rest with the same ritual that had passed through so many generations of islanders that no one living knew its source, except, perhaps, Mabry.

3

$\mathcal{F}$inely drawn. The words leaped into Sean's mind the moment he saw her, and with them came an awareness of how understated she was compared to her mother.

No one had to tell him that Mollie Tierney was an American. It was her skin that defined her nationality. Nowhere in Ireland could a woman have acquired that gold-touched look, that subtle luminous color that exposure to months of perpetual sunlight could bring. Even more than her accent, it was her skin that gave her away, that and her teeth.

She had those American-girl teeth, even and perfectly straight, very white, as if she'd spent a lifetime in braces and fluoride. Americans cared about those things. They knew nothing about their ancestors and even less about their history. Few could go back more than two generations if asked to compose a family tree, but they all had the kind of teeth that would feature well in a mouthwash commercial.

He absorbed it all in those first seconds. Straight hair,

expensively cut—brown, some might call it, yet brown wasn't the right word for the shades of tobacco, honey, and wheat that skimmed her shoulders. Other than a hint of violet on the lids of her eyes, she was cosmetic-free. A pretty girl, especially pretty, and determined. Sean would grant her that. She had the kind of confidence that comes from warm air, unconditional acceptance, and a lifetime spent in the pursuit of recreation. She'd been on the island for nearly two weeks now, ever since the funeral. Her mother, after a few obligatory visits to her grandchildren, had gone home with her husband. Why was the girl still here?

The baby squirmed in his arms. Sean shifted him from one shoulder to the other. "What can I do for you, Miss Tierney? The girls aren't home. They're with your father."

"Yes, I know," she said crisply, flashing the full power of her smile. "I came to talk to you. You're very hard to pin down, you know."

Sean's stomach churned. It needed only this. He couldn't very well refuse to allow her in the house. After all, she was Danny's sister. "What did you want to talk about?"

Again she smiled, two rows of even white pearls. "I'm cold. May I come inside?"

She was standing on the doorstep, the wind playing havoc with her hair. So much for Irish hospitality. Ashamed of his manners, Sean rallied and stepped aside. "Will you come inside, lass? I'm not much of a house-keeper, but I can manage a pot of tea." It would be just his luck if she planned on a lengthy visit.

"I'd love a cup of tea, Mr. O'Malley."

"Sean," he corrected her. "Call me Sean. We're family, after all."

She held out her arms for the baby. "I'll take him. You can make the tea."

He handed Luke to the stranger who was his aunt. "Kerry never mentioned whether you had children of your own."

She nuzzled Luke's little neck and followed Sean into the kitchen. "No. I'd like to be married first."

Sean grinned and measured out the tea. "That's the best way, I think." His smile disappeared. He wouldn't wish a Tierney on anyone on the island. "I hope you're not thinking to find someone here. There aren't many who would suit you."

Resting her lips on the baby's downy head, she looked up at him. "How would you know who would suit me?"

He shrugged and kept his eyes on the kettle. "You're an American, a city girl. Most of us haven't the kind of education you have."

"You do," she countered.

Over the baby's head, their eyes met. He couldn't resist. "It isn't that I'm not tempted, lass," he said evenly, "but I'm not in the market for a wife and I've children enough at the moment."

Was he mistaken, or did those eyes she so quickly veiled with her violet-tinted lids dance with mischief?

"It doesn't matter whether you're tempted or not, Sean O'Malley, because you aren't my type."

"No?"

"No."

"What is your type?"

"Someone who returns my phone calls."

Her eyes were blue, vivid against the warm gold of her skin. The kettle whistled. "Well, then, Miss Mollie Tierney, how will you be taking your tea?"

"Milk, please, and sugar."

He shook his head. "Americans don't drink milk with their tea. They like lemon and honey."

Expertly, she lifted Luke to her shoulder, mindful of his head. "You have a great many notions about Americans. Were you there long enough to know us so well?"

"I've never been there," he admitted.

"I see."

He waited for a caustic remark. Tierneys were never short on words. Instead, she handed him the baby. "He needs his diaper changed. I'll pour the tea. Will the girls be home soon?"

"Soon enough, but not for tea." Cradling Luke in the corner of his arm, he disappeared into the bedroom. A few minutes later he came out again, alone.

Mollie had poured the tea, added milk and sugar, and found a tin of biscuits he didn't know they had. She arranged all of it on a tray and carried it into the living room.

"Where's the baby?"

"Napping, I hope. I was about to put him down when you arrived."

"I'm sorry." For the first time she looked contrite.

"It's not a problem," he assured her. "Luke sleeps whenever he's tired. Nothing stops him."

"Good." She gestured toward the tray she'd assembled. "I hope you don't mind."

He sat down across from her. "Not at all. You're a take-charge sort of person, aren't you?"

Without the slightest twinge of self-consciousness, she considered his question. "Probably," she admitted. "I'm a teacher. We're accustomed to being in charge. I'm sorry if I've been presumptuous."

Presumptuous. How many on the island even knew what the word meant? "Don't be. It was just an observation. I suppose it's natural for me to compare you with Danny."

She lifted her cup halfway to her mouth and stopped. "Are we alike?"

"God, no."

She looked startled.

Hastily, he regrouped. "I haven't noticed a resemblance, but you haven't been here long."

"What was he like?"

He stared at her, and the rage he'd kept fairly bottled up spilled over. "What do you want to know, Miss Tierney? Danny the fisherman, the drunk? Danny the father? Danny the husband, Kerry's husband? What was marriage like for the two of them? Did they ever, in their years together, have a meeting of minds, a communion of souls where their thoughts overlapped? I can't imagine it. But then I can't imagine a man who drowns himself in drink and forgets about his three children who need him."

She was staring at him with those eyes that saw more than he intended her to see. He looked down at his hands. He'd worked the biscuit into crumbs. Shrugging, he smiled, a quick twisting of his mouth. "That was uncalled for. Your father is the one to ask about Danny."

Mollie changed the subject. "Have you always lived on Inishmore?"

"Until I went away to university."

"Were you and Kerry close?"

"Yes," he said shortly, swigging down his tea, wishing it were something stronger. Were all Americans this casual about personal matters, or was it a particular characteristic of this one?

"Tell me about the girls."

Sean relaxed. That he could do. "Marni is eight," he began. "She's smart, smarter even than those two levels above her." Pride surged through him. Marni was a love, responsible, bright, perceptive. His only worry was that she took too much on herself. "Caili's turned five," he continued. "She'll be in school next term. She's a charmer, fey-touched, we call her."

"Fey-touched?"

He thought a minute. Such a common term for an islander, but for an American, an outlander, something else entirely. "It means to be filled with a different kind of understanding from the rest of us. I suppose you might call it a powerful intuition."

"Like having the Sight?"

Sean looked surprised. "Now where would a woman like you learn of the Sight, Miss Tierney?"

She tilted her head. Sean watched her hair, the shining mass of it, swing against her cheek. Her hands, one holding the saucer, the other the handle of her teacup, were completely steady.

"My mother lived here for eleven years. I was born here. It would be a remarkable thing, don't you think, if I knew nothing about this part of my heritage?"

"Your mother hated it here," he said bluntly. "I wouldn't have thought she would bring up the subject of Ireland at all."

Mollie set the cup down on the tray and carefully wiped the corners of her mouth with a napkin. "You have a great many misconceptions, Sean O'Malley," she said quietly. "Is it me, or are you always like this?"

He expected fireworks, tears, a setdown at the least. Mollie Tierney's poise shook him. Apparently, dignity wasn't completely extinct in America, or perhaps there was more to her mother than the gossips had repeated.

"I've had a bad few weeks," he confessed. "I'm sorry, lass. It's a poor sort of welcome I'm offering you. Forgive me."

"Tell me about it."

"I beg your pardon?"

"Tell me about your bad few weeks."

She took him aback. That directness again. "It's nothing for you to be worrying over."

"Tell me anyway."

He frowned, exasperated. "You're persistent, aren't you?"

"Yes. I am."

"I've lost my sister and her husband. Three children including a newborn infant have no parents except me. That would give any man a few sleepless nights."

"Isn't there anyone else to care for them?"

Sean bristled. "No one else they know and trust, except for your father. Patrick loves them, but he could never manage on his own. Besides—" He stopped. Out of loyalty to Patrick, an islander, he wouldn't refer to his weakness for the drink.

She surprised him. "How are you managing? Kerry told me that you taught at the university."

"When did you meet Kerry?"

"I didn't. We wrote, regularly. She was a lovely person."

Reluctantly, Sean warmed to the American girl. "Aye," he said softly, "she was."

"Are you still teaching?"

He shook his head. "I've taken leave for the term." No need to mention that he would be working at his writing.

"Will you continue to write?" she asked, again surprising him.

Kerry would have told her. "Aye. I've a few things in the works."

She smiled. "Thanks for the tea. I should be going now."

"Where are you staying?"

"I've rented a cottage just beyond Kilronen. It's lovely. The windows look out on the ocean. I wanted something special. I'm going to be here for a while."

Sean nodded, confused. "I know the place. A couple from Dublin lease it out. Still, I suppose it's not what you're used to."

She laughed. "I hope not. Why would I travel eight thousand miles to live in a place exactly like home?"

Could Danny and this woman really share a gene pool? "Why, indeed?" He frowned. "I believe I may have missed something. Are you paying us an extended visit?"

"I'm the new primary school teacher on the island. I thought you knew."

"No. Isn't this rather sudden?"

"Not really. It's an exchange program."

"Who's being exchanged?"

The red rose quickly in her cheeks. She had Irish skin after all.

"No one," she admitted. "Ordinarily someone takes my place and I take hers. There wasn't anyone here to spare, but I wanted to come to the island. Besides, Alice Duncan needs the help. I have the advantage because I was born here."

"When did this come about?"

Her blush deepened. "I've known for a while that I wanted to come."

"For how long?"

"Five years," she confessed, "ever since Kerry started writing to me."

Sean's head spun. *Five years.* Kerry had known her five years and never said a word. Why?

Without warning, the door flew open and a small girl threw herself into Sean's arms. Panting, she forced the words past her lips. "I ran all the way, Uncle Sean. Mabry O'Farrell was on the road. Marni says she's not wicked, but she scares me."

Sean settled the little girl on his knee. "Mabry O'Farrell is an old woman, Caili. She's no more wicked than I am. She's never hurt anyone." The child's dark curls felt silky under his hand. "Where's your sister?"

Caili's finger found its way into her mouth. "She's coming," she mumbled, staring with wide green eyes at the stranger who sat in her mother's chair.

Sean kissed her head. "Will you welcome your Aunt Mollie, lass? She's come to spend some time with us."

The child sat up. "With me?"

"Aye, and Marni and Luke."

Caili slid from her uncle's lap and approached Mollie. "I've a bunny," she confided. "Uncle Sean won't let me keep it in a cage, but he comes at night. I watch him."

"Do you?" Mollie appeared suitably impressed. "What color is he?"

"Brown," said Caili. "Are bunnies not brown in America?"

"Some are white. I've seen black ones and spotted ones."

Caili clapped her hands, setting in motion the springy curls around her head. "May I go to America, Uncle Sean? I want to see the spotted bunnies with Aunt Mollie."

"Aunt Mollie isn't going to America for a long time. She's come to be the new school mistress."

Caili's eyes widened. She moved closer to Mollie and leaned against her knee. "Will you teach at my school, Aunt Mollie?"

Sean watched Mollie's arm settle naturally around his niece's shoulders and pull her close for a quick hug. The two had met before, but only briefly, at the wake. Mollie had kept to herself since then.

"Yes, love," she said. "We'll see each other every day and be great friends."

Caili shivered with delight. "I like you," she decided. "Even if Marni doesn't like you, I will."

Mollie's eyes warmed. "That's a relief. Is Marni difficult to please?"

Sean stood and walked to the window. Coming up the rise was his older, more serene niece. "See for yourself."

Keeping Caili's hand in her own, Mollie joined him at the window.

Marni was nearly at the door when she looked up and saw them. She grinned, and Sean's heart turned over.

Where there were once two perfect teeth was now a large irregular gap. He waited until she walked through the door. "You pulled it out," he accused her.

Shaking her head, Marni dug into the pocket of her jumper, pulled out an envelope, and handed it to her uncle. "I didn't have to. It fell out, and Grandda gave me this to save it."

Sean groaned and peered inside. "I suppose you'll be expecting a fortune for a tooth of this size."

Marni considered the matter. "It's my best one," she said after a minute's deliberation.

"I'll take the matter up with the tooth fairy." He gestured toward Mollie. "Your Aunt Mollie is here for a visit. She's come to teach primary school on the island."

"We've met before," Marni said. "You're Da's sister."

"She is," broke in Caili, "and she's going to teach at our school."

"Welcome," Marni said formally. "I hope you'll like it here."

"Thank you, Marni. I like it very much already. I'll like it even more if you and Caili come to visit me often."

Marni relaxed. She looked at her uncle. "May I, Uncle Sean?"

"You may, if it's convenient for everyone. Run in and check on Luke. He's been asleep for a while now."

"She must be a tremendous help to you," observed Mollie when Marni left them.

"How do you mean?"

"She's very mature for an eight-year-old."

"Aye, that she is," Sean said proudly. "Marni has been more adult than child from the day she could walk."

"Does she have many friends close by?"

"A few. She prefers to be by herself or with her family. She's not much for friends."

"I see."

Again that simple, uncommunicative phrase that revealed nothing of her inner feelings. *I see.* What did it mean, anyway, when spoken from the lips of a woman like Mollie Tierney? Perhaps he should borrow some of her directness. "What do you mean?"

"I beg your pardon?"

"Do you think it's wrong that Marni doesn't prefer friends her own age?"

"*Wrong* is a very strong word. I don't think it can be used to describe an eight-year-old girl who's probably done nothing *wrong* in her entire life."

"Then why did you say it?"

"What?"

"You said 'I see' in that way you have."

"What way?"

"You know what way."

Her glance moved to a place behind him. Suddenly she smiled. "Let's play another game, shall we? Caili doesn't understand this one."

Caili. He'd forgotten her. Quickly he turned around. The little girl was staring at Mollie with her thumb in her mouth and that look about her eyes that he'd seen too often lately. He groaned. Mollie Tierney was stretching the edges of his temper. Danny had affected him the same way.

He held out his arms to his niece. "Don't be frightened, *a stor.* It isn't what you think."

First she looked at Mollie and then at Sean. "Are you angry at Aunt Mollie, Uncle Sean?"

"No, love. Look at her. She's smiling at us."

Bless the woman. She really was smiling.

Caili relaxed, and Sean released his breath. She'd shamed him. His instincts were right the first time. Mollie Tierney was nothing like her brother.

$\mathcal{F}$or the third time, Mollie read the instructions for running the dishwasher, filled the soap dish, and turned on the tap full force before pushing the start button once more. What had Sean meant when he said the cottage was probably not what she was used to? It had every amenity she could ask for—a modern kitchen, four large bedrooms, two bathrooms, an upstairs loft, and floor-to-ceiling windows with sweeping views of the sea—all for one-third the cost of a tiny studio apartment in Newport, California.

Sean O'Malley wasn't what she'd expected. His sharp wit and pointed teasing had drawn out her laughter a number of times this afternoon, and yet every instinct warned her that under his polite veneer simmered frustration, the kind that festered and turned into anger. Clearly the man adored his nieces and his tiny infant nephew. So much for her mother's worries on that score.

Mollie looked at things squarely, without excuses, and her innate honesty told her that guilt was a large part of the reason she'd agreed to come to Inishmore. If she'd been Emma Tierney's firstborn, it might have been Danny with all the advantages. It wasn't the only reason, of course. Kerry's letters, so warm and accepting, had fueled her desire to know her family, her brother and his wife, her nieces, and most of all her father, the father who'd stubbornly refused to give up one child while making no effort, not even the most superficial, to contact the other.

Patrick Tierney lived on the other side of the island, near the town of Cill Einne. Mollie knew that much from her mother. But she knew little else. Emma was remarkably close-mouthed about her life in Ireland. Mollie knew that after her mother's marriage to Ward Reddington, she had been discouraged from returning to the island first by her ex-husband and later by Danny, who harbored an understandable resentment toward the mother he felt had abandoned him.

That same resentment couldn't possibly apply to a younger sister, Mollie had reasoned when first planning her visit to the island, a sister who had no part in the chain of events that caused her brother to grow up with a mother he knew only in the summers, a mother who was another man's wife.

Now it didn't matter. Danny was dead, and so was Kerry, changing Mollie's position completely. The children were being cared for by a caustic stranger who, although he was Kerry's brother, was definitely not welcoming. Her image of a happy family reunion was rapidly fading.

Mollie flipped off the kitchen light and walked into the living room. Blocks of peat glowed in the open fireplace, and a steady flame licked at the few sticks of wood she'd thrown in to give the silent turf a familiar crackle. She glanced at the books stacked on the coffee table. School was two weeks away. She would share thirty students from six different levels, ages five to twelve. Alice Duncan, her teaching partner for the older children, a cheerful, no-nonsense kind of person, had stopped by earlier in the day with a parcel of textbooks.

Stretching out on the couch, Mollie picked up the first-grade primer and flipped through it, but her mind wasn't on her job. She had hoped to learn something about her father before she approached him. She'd seen him only once, at the funeral.

Mollie didn't want to knock on his door and demand entrance without some kind of warning. A phone call would have been much easier. Three days had passed since she'd officially leased the cottage. To wait any longer to approach him was out of the question. Inishmore was a tiny island. Mollie wanted to be the one to tell him that she would be staying. Unless she did it first thing tomorrow, that option might very well be taken from her.

Lightning flashed across the sky. She counted to ten, smiling when the rumble of thunder followed. Even in Ireland, eight thousand miles away from everything she knew, nature behaved predictably.

At first she thought the hammering at the front door was the fierce island wind her mother had warned her about, but when it stopped suddenly and then started again, she knew it for what it was. Setting the book aside, she walked quickly to the door and opened it.

Rain-drenched and shivering, the woman standing on

her doorstep was unusual enough to stop traffic in any cosmopolitan capital of the world. Everything about her reminded Mollie of moonlight—silvery rain-wet hair, pale skin, gray eyes framed with thick, water-starred lashes. She was slender and straight, with haughty carved features and a face so ageless that at first Mollie was fooled into thinking she was a much younger woman. She recognized Mabry O'Farrell from the funeral.

"Will you know me the next time you see me?" The voice, coldly sarcastic and heavily accented, didn't match the woman's appearance.

Mollie stepped aside. "I'm sorry. Please, come in."

After shedding her coat, Mabry hung it over the heating pipes and walked into the living room. She turned so that her back was to the fire. "Have you anything to drink?"

Mollie frowned. "What would you like?"

"Spirits, if you have it."

"All I have is wine."

"It will have to do, won't it?"

Mollie hesitated and decided to ignore the woman's rudeness until she found out the purpose of her visit.

"What are you staring at?" Mabry demanded.

Mollie ignored her question. "Are you hungry? Can I get you anything else?"

"Wine will be good enough."

Mollie disappeared into the kitchen, returning with a bottle of chardonnay, two glasses, and a plate of fruit and cheese. "I didn't have much for dinner. You're welcome to join me if you like."

Mabry shrugged and took the chair nearest the fire. "I don't suppose you're accustomed to waiting on people."

"Waiting on people?" Mollie poured a glass of wine and handed it to the rain-soaked woman with the sharp tongue.

Her shrug was a quick, surprisingly graceful lifting of the shoulders. "Fixing a plate, pouring drinks. I would imagine the daughter of a fine plastic surgeon would have a houseful of servants."

Mollie forced a smile. The woman was impossible. "In California I have my own apartment. A teacher's salary doesn't cover servants."

"But at home with your mother, you must have had them."

"Mother takes care of the house herself. Occasionally a woman comes in to clean and wash windows, but not on a regular basis."

"I know you're rich, Mollie Tierney. There's no sense in sweeping it under the carpet."

Carefully, Mollie spread the creamy cheese on an apple wedge. Taking her time, she chewed and swallowed it. "Not that it's any of your business, but my stepfather is a doctor. Where I come from, doctors do very well. I'm a teacher. I support myself on a teacher's salary without help from anyone."

"Are you his heir?"

"Whose?" Mollie leaned forward to refill her unwelcome guest's wine glass.

"Your stepfather's, of course."

Mollie bit her tongue, stifling her natural inclination to send the woman on her way. A year was a long time. It wouldn't do any good to offend the natives. "I have no idea," she said. "It doesn't matter either way. Ward is only sixty years old, and California is a community property state. My mother would inherit everything."

"And you're her heir."

Mollie looked over the rim of her glass at this. She was tired of cooperating. "What does any of this have to do with you?"

Mabry leaned back in her chair. The heat from the fire had dried her hair. It fell in loose ash-colored waves around her face. "I've more right than you know. You drew your first breath in my arms, lass, and so did your brother. There aren't many I lose sight of the way I lost you. I blame Emma for that."

Mollie frowned. "I don't understand."

Mabry's eyes were hard and bright, ice on metal. "No. I imagine you don't. Emma should have come back."

The unfairness of such a remark spurred Mollie to defend her mother. "She wasn't welcome. My father didn't want her here. She told me so."

"Emma always went her own way."

Mollie fell silent, uncomfortable with the obvious, the unspoken criticism that hung in the air between them.

Mabry's profile was edged in golden light. "So, lass, why are you here?"

"To teach school."

Mabry waved her hand in dismissal. "Why are you really here?"

Mollie released her breath. "To know my father and my nieces. They're the only ones left."

Mabry's eyes narrowed to slits of cool silver. "Is that all?"

"Yes."

Mabry leaned forward. "Don't lie to me, Mollie Tierney. You're no good at it."

"I'm here to see my father," Mollie insisted. She'd

read somewhere that it was possible to fool a polygraph. It required a complete relaxing, a hypnotic detachment from the issue at hand. She tried it now.

Mabry searched her face for a long moment and then turned away and stared into the fire. When she spoke, her words were husky, smoke-choked. "Wanting can be a curse, lass. Don't want so that your judgment is impaired and you can't see the truth in front of you."

Mollie's head reeled. "I want to find my father. Can you help me?"

"You might be disappointed."

"Why is that?"

"He can be—" Mabry hesitated. "Difficult."

"Does he still drink?"

"He's dry now, but he'll go back to it. He always does. There isn't a family on the island that's escaped the curse of a pint all around."

"What about the O'Malleys?"

"Sean is the only O'Malley left on the island, and he rarely touches the stuff. He never had the taste for it, nor the stomach, not even as a lad."

Mollie's impression of Sean O'Malley rose. "Will you tell me where I can find him?"

"Who?"

"My father."

Mabry stood, a small, satisfied smile on her lips. "You'll do, Mollie Tierney. I'll send someone for you tomorrow morning."

Mollie smiled. "Thank you."

"Don't thank me until it's happened." Mabry walked past Mollie toward the door and took her coat from the peg. "I'll see myself out."

*   *   *

It was Sean who appeared at her door the following morning. "Mabry sent me," he explained. "She said you needed a ride to Patrick's cottage."

Mollie recovered quickly. Pushing her doubts aside, she smiled. "Thank you for being so accommodating. I'm nervous enough to accept who I can get."

He grinned, and once again she noticed the extraordinary blue of his eyes, ocean-colored, light-filled, clear.

"Who are you, Miss Mollie Tierney, to be insulting the only escort you're likely to find?"

"I intended it as a compliment."

"Warn me, please, before you give me another one."

She looked around. "Are we walking?"

He nodded toward the bicycle leaning against the house. "Americans walk only for exercise, not to get anywhere."

"Really?"

"Aye." His face was serious, but his eyes were not.

She decided to ignore what she thought was a slight. "I don't have a bike."

"We can ride the one together, as long as you're not too heavy and you can hold your balance. Can you manage that?"

"I suppose I'll have to." She looked down at her navy skirt. "Shall I change?"

"There's no need. You'll be riding sidesaddle."

"I really don't think—"

He lifted a mocking eyebrow.

Challenged, Mollie reached for her small backpack, slipped her arms through the straps, braced herself on the crossbar, and hopped on. Sean's hand, steady on the small of her back, prevented her from falling backward.

"That wasn't so bad, now, was it?" She could hear the laughter in his voice.

She gripped the bar like a lifeline. "Ask me when we get there."

The ride to the village of Cill Einne was surprisingly smooth and uneventful. Mollie relaxed enough to appreciate the rare, jewel-bright blues and greens that sunlight brought to the island. She knew something of flowers, and amidst the crags and crevices of human-looking boulders, purple milk-vetch, the island's rarest plant no longer found on the mainland, flourished. Yellow hoary rock-rose, blood-red crane's-bill, and white vernal sandwart covered the rocks in brilliant profusion. Long-haired sheep hugged both sides of narrow twisting roads. Cows munched on limestone-nourished grass behind low stone walls. Smoke swirled from chimneys, soft spirals, white against blue, caught on the updraft. Men grinned, lifted wool caps, and called out the traditional island greeting, "Dhia Duit." Women nodded politely, looking away before making eye contact, and children stared.

Mollie knew that strangers were a common enough sight on the island, especially during the summer months. Either they knew who she was or her mode of transportation wasn't as typical as Sean led her to believe. She wished he would say something. The tune he whistled over and over again just behind her ear began to grate on her nerves. "Are we almost there?" she asked.

He braked suddenly around a sharp bend and turned down a fractured limestone footpath. "Nearly," he said cheerfully, and resumed his whistling. The lane narrowed, rutted, disappearing almost entirely. Sean's pace never lagged, nor did he lack for breath as he maneuvered the bike up the gradual incline. "There it is," he said at last.

Mollie straightened. "What?"

"Your father's cottage, just ahead of us."

Her chest hurt. She'd forgotten to breathe. Inhaling deeply, she took her first long look at the house where she was born. This was her beginning, the place where it all started so hopefully, changed direction, and came to a final crashing halt. Divorce spared no one, not even an adult daughter who had no memory of her father. There was something about knowing your parents had once been in love and no longer were, that something permanent had been severed, and no one, not even two small children, could keep them together.

The friendly thatched-roof, whitewashed cottage with its fading red door was nothing like she'd imagined. It was smaller, warmer than her mother had described it, with tiny windows, a clearing in front, and a comforting spiral of smoke escaping from the chimney.

Sean pedaled the bike to the yard and stopped. Mollie slipped off the bar, unbuttoned her jacket, and smoothed her hair. "Do I look all right?" she asked anxiously.

He looked startled, as if she'd caught him off-guard. "I suppose so," he said guardedly.

Mollie raised her eyebrows. "A simple yes or no will do."

His eyes glinted the same blue-green as the water around him. "The thing is, your hair is a bit mussed, and there's something black across your right cheek."

Mollie's hand flew to the spot. She rubbed it briskly with her fingers.

"Now you look like you've seen the worst of a bee stinger."

Nerves turned her voice brittle. "There's nothing wrong with my cheek. You're teasing me, and I don't appreciate it, not now, anyway."

"At least it brought back your spirit," he said cheerfully. "No more than a minute ago you looked like a spring pig on her way to slaughter."

"I feel like one," Mollie muttered.

"What's that you said?"

She looked back over her shoulder. There was that eyebrow again, quirked at a forty-five-degree angle. He knew exactly what she'd said. He probably knew exactly what she was thinking. Maybe all of these islanders had the Sight. "Never mind. Are you coming in with me?"

"I don't think so. Patrick and I never did see the world from the same side of the fence."

Mollie attempted the eyebrow quirk, gave it up, and asked instead, "Is that your fault or his?"

He balanced the bike against one leg and narrowed his eyes. "You are a direct lass, aren't you?"

She was spared from answering. The red door creaked open, and a voice, not at all feeble and surprisingly steady for a man addled with drink, called out, "What have you to say for yourself, the two of you, to greet the morning in such a way?" A tall man in clean but faded clothes and a wool cap stepped out into the light. "Is that you, Sean O'Malley?"

"It is, Mr. Tierney," replied Sean promptly. He grinned. "I've brought your daughter from America to visit you."

The man squinted into the weak sunlight. "Is that

so?" he said amiably, as if daughters from America appeared on his doorstep every morning. "Tell me your name, lass."

Mollie's throat felt like steel wool. She cleared it and attempted the words. Incredibly, they came out. "Mollie," she croaked, "Mollie Tierney."

Sean straightened his bike. "I'll be leaving you to get acquainted."

He couldn't really mean to ride away and leave her with this stranger. Mollie panicked. "When will you be back?"

"Patrick will take you home. He has a pony trap. It's the best way to see the island."

Mollie stammered. "I don't think—"

"Come now, Mollie," Sean mocked her. "Don't tell me you're afraid of horses."

She watched helplessly as he turned the bicycle around and swung his leg over the bar. "Not afraid, exactly," she mumbled.

He had ears as sensitive as a fly trap. "What is it, then?"

She swallowed and lifted her chin. "Nothing. Don't worry about me. I'll be fine."

He winked at her, and this time his smile was warmer. "I never doubted it, lass. If things don't work out, I'll be down at the Silver Seal for an hour or so. Just follow the road. You can't miss it."

Relieved, Mollie straightened her shoulders and turned to face the man who was her father.

5

*P*atrick Tierney was still handsome, with fine sharp features, brown skin lined from weather, and eyes the piercing aquamarine common to men who live on water-locked land. Under the wool cap, his hair was thick, wavy, the hairline young, the color white without a hint of its former darkness. Lean, clean-shaven, and spare of flesh, he showed no evidence of the alcohol her mother said he drank to excess.

"Will you know me when you see me again?" he asked softly.

The words were the same ones Mabry had used, but the tone was different. Mollie smiled. "I would have anyway. I've seen pictures."

"Your mother still has them, does she?"

"Yes."

"Ah, but I was younger then."

"Some things don't change," Mollie said simply.

He looked at her, this time more closely. "What do you know about change, Mollie Tierney?"

She shrugged. "I'm here."

"Why is that, I'm wondering?"

She wrapped her arms around herself and clamped down on her lip to stop the shivering. "May I come inside?"

He frowned. "Of course. Come in, lass. The shock of seeing you here in the flesh after all these years has made me forget my manners."

Patrick Tierney didn't look shocked. He didn't look particularly pleased, either. Mollie preceded him through the Dutch door he held open for her and looked around at the snug cottage. It was small but clean, with white-washed walls, tiny windows, and a slate floor. A fire smoldered on the hearth. Suspended from a hook over the open flame, a blue cauldron bubbled, throwing off a meaty, appetizing smell. Two chairs stood on opposite sides of a low table, and shelves heavy with books lined the walls. The fire, the food, the warmth of the tiny cottage, and the anxious restless night she'd spent took their toll. Her eyes felt heavy.

"Would you like a cup of tea, lass?" Patrick Tierney asked.

Mollie sat down in one of the chairs. "Yes, thank you."

She watched her father move about his kitchen, scouring the teapot with water from the kettle, shaking in loose tea leaves, assembling milk, sugar, cups, and spoons. It was all so comfortable, so familiar, and yet it couldn't possibly be. She ran her fingers over the carved wood of the chair and breathed in the essence of the cottage. It was cozy and clean, with handmade furniture and everything in its place. Once her mother had crossed this floor, cooked at the old-fashioned stove, eaten at this very table. Mollie thought of her glass-and-chrome kitchen in Newport and couldn't imagine it.

When the tea was ready, Patrick sat across from her. He kept his eyes on her face. "You look tired. Have you had enough rest, or shall I turn down the bed for you?"

Mollie rubbed her eyes. "I've been poor company. I'm sorry."

Patrick smiled. "You're not accustomed to the air here. Would you like milk in your tea?"

"Yes, please."

He poured milk and steaming tea into a china cup and passed it to her. She stirred a spoonful of sugar into her cup and sipped it.

"What brings you to the island, lass?"

Mollie swallowed and looked directly into her father's eyes. Her well-rehearsed story of the teaching exchange, her fellowship, and the desire to try life away from Southern California disappeared.

"All my life I've wanted to meet you," she said honestly. "The opportunity arose, and I took it."

"Was it that important?"

"Yes."

"Why?"

Mollie considered his question. She knew it would be asked, but she hadn't really formulated an answer. "Where a person comes from determines who they are," she said at last. "I don't really know who I am, not completely, anyway. I think that's because I don't know you."

"You have your mother."

"We aren't alike. Surely you can see that."

Again he smiled. "I wouldn't say that quite so vehemently. There are qualities you both share. But maybe that's due to where you were raised rather than genetics."

"Why didn't you ever come to visit?"

His answer surprised her. "I did, once. I made it to your stepfather's front door. But then I changed my mind. It was clear I didn't belong in California. Heat addles the brain, and the air—" He shook his head. "I couldn't breathe there."

"I could have come here."

He shook his head. "For a long time you were too young to come alone, and having Emma here would have been difficult."

Patrick's answers weren't particularly evasive, but they weren't telling her what she wanted to know. "Why did she leave?"

"Emma wasn't happy here. After a while we didn't get on."

"Why couldn't Danny have gone with us?"

Her father's lips tightened. "Losing one child was difficult enough, lass. Would you have begrudged me two?"

Mollie was frustrated. Patrick Tierney was either obtuse or an expert at manipulation. She would come out and ask him, and if he told her she would know. If he didn't, she would have lost nothing. "Why didn't you ever want to see me? Weren't you the least bit curious?"

The eyes that looked at her across the low table were kind and blue and completely veiled against her. "It wasn't like that," he said gently. "I'm sure your mother told you how it was. Don't go making me recall events that happened a lifetime ago, events I'd rather not sort through again. It's enough that you're here now. Perhaps we can start again."

She leaned forward and spoke passionately. "You've missed my whole life."

His lips twitched. "Surely not your whole life, Mollie Tierney. After all, you're still very young."

For a long moment Mollie stared into the blue eyes twinkling at her. Finally she laughed. It wasn't enough, but it would have to do for now. She wasn't one to dwell on missed opportunities. "You're right. I suppose there's no point going over what can't be changed. What would you like to know about me?"

Now he was looking at her as if she pleased him very much.

"How long will you be staying on Inishmore?"

"For the school year. I've accepted a teaching fellowship."

"Are you set for accommodations?"

"Yes."

"That's all right, then. Will you be staying for supper? The lamb stew is nearly finished."

Two hours later, filled up on tender stew and milk-sweet tea, Mollie sat behind her father in the pony trap, a rug tucked in around her legs, while he pointed out the sights of the island, the lighthouse, the fields of limestone coloring the island green, the three tiny towns clustered together among the verdant hills, the Celtic crosses, the jagged cliffs, the artists' haunts, and, above it all, hovering like a protective sentinel, the ancient Celtic fort of Dun Aengus, half gone now but no less impressive than it must have been to the ancient Celts thousands of years ago.

The Norman marcher lords had bypassed this land entirely. There were no stone towers, no granite castles, no history of recorded battles and stolen land, no enmity between Gael and Sean-Ghall. This windswept coastline stood alone, a limestone rock that few wanted and where fewer stayed, a land of men with eyes like blue glass who made their living from the sea and women whose faces had the permanent mark of too many hours squinting at the horizon wondering, always wondering, when tragedy would fall.

It was early fall, and the weather was already cold. Seasons on Inishmore were determined by sunlight. The green limestone turf was green in both winter and summer, and clouds, giant powder puffs, hung suspended in the heavy, rain-wet air, white with the sun behind them, gray-black in the rain. The terrain was treeless, with an endless spider-webbing of rock walls, their stones uprooted from the fields and piled on top of each other without mortar, without gates.

Listening to her father's melodic voice, watching him expertly ply the reins and guide his Connemara pony around precipitous turns, Mollie stared at the back of his white head and wondered why, in all that long sun-drenched afternoon, she had seen no evidence that he had a drinking problem.

She had little experience with alcohol abuse. Her stepfather was fanatically health-conscious, and her mother never had more than two glasses of wine at a time on any occasion. Could a man who drank excessively go an entire afternoon without touching a drop? Could a man as pleasant and gentle as Patrick Tierney really be an alcoholic, as her mother called him?

"Do you see Danny's children often?" she asked, her voice carrying through the wind.

"I saw more of them when Danny was living."

Mollie mulled that one over in her mind. Surely he couldn't object to Sean. Sean O'Malley was educated, intelligent, and employed in a capacity unrelated to water and weather conditions. No. It must be the other way around. It must be Sean who objected to Patrick.

"We're nearly there, lass." Patrick broke into her thoughts. "It looks as if you've got company."

She hadn't locked the door. Alice Duncan told her it wasn't necessary. Now it stood ajar, and through the long ocean-facing windows, Mollie could see movement. Patrick pulled back on the reins, stopping the trap, and Mollie jumped out and walked through the open door.

Eight-year-old Marni sat on the couch holding her baby brother. Caili sat beside her, her thumb wedged into her mouth. In the middle of the room, his hands clenched and a wild look on his face, stood Sean O'Malley.

Something was terribly wrong. Mollie sat down beside Caili and wrapped her arms around the child. "What's the matter?" she asked Sean.

"Did you know?"

"Know what?" Mollie was bewildered.

A thin white line appeared around his lips. "Did you know about Danny's will?"

"I don't know what you mean."

He reached into his pocket, pulled out a crumpled piece of paper, and threw it at Mollie. "Read it," he ordered.

With shaking hands, Mollie smoothed out the note

and read. Then she read it again. Caili snuggled closer, burrowing her face as far as it would go into her aunt's shoulder.

Wetting her lips, Mollie tore her eyes away from the note and forced herself to look at Sean's face. "If you'll explain to me what it is that's bothering you, maybe I could—"

"Are you simple, Mollie Tierney?" he flung at her contemptuously. "Does it need spelling out for you? You come here with your fancy clothes and your American manners and your bank account, and you tell me you're here to find your roots? Do you really think I don't know what your purpose is?"

Mollie's face whitened, but her chin was up and her words were firm, deliberate, carefully chosen. "Your sister and my brother made a decision that has nothing to do with me. Don't blame me because they didn't choose you or anyone else on this island to raise their children. And don't blame me because my mother wanted to be sure you were fit to raise her grandchildren."

She watched the tide of red wash across Sean's cheeks.

"It won't be as easy as that," he muttered. "I won't give up without a fight—" He stopped, looked at the bewildered expression on Caili's face and the haunted one on her sister's, and caught himself. A strained smile replaced his own murderous look. "Don't worry, Marni. It's all right, lass. Don't pay any attention to me. A day or two with a solicitor in Dublin will sort everything out."

The baby began to fuss. Sean lifted him from Marni's lap.

"Grandda's here," Caili announced, slipping from the couch and running to Patrick's side.

Her grandfather scooped her up in his arms as naturally as if he'd done it every day of his life.

"What do you think, Patrick?" Sean's voice carried a desperate note that rubbed Mollie's heart raw.

Patrick shook his head and smoothed the dark head resting on his shoulder. "Shall I help with the girls tonight, or can you manage on your own?" he asked, ignoring Sean's question.

"If you're going to Dublin, they can stay here," Mollie said quickly. "There are more than enough rooms."

Marni rose from her place on the couch and tugged on Sean's arm. Bending down until her lips nearly touched his ear, he listened to her whispered confidence. Then he straightened, finally sure of himself. "Thank you both for your hospitality, but the four of us will be sleeping at home as usual."

Mollie reached for the backpack she'd dropped on the floor and rummaged inside for her wallet. She tore off a piece of paper from a pad and wrote down her mother's phone number. "I don't know all of the legal ramifications, but it wouldn't hurt to call my mother. You're not really on opposite sides, you know."

"No, thank you." Sean's mouth was a tight angry line. "It won't be necessary. I'll leave the details to an attorney."

"It doesn't have to be like this," Mollie said.

"Leave it, lass," her father broke in. "This has nothing to do with you."

Mollie cleared her throat. "Have the children eaten?" she asked Sean.

He looked surprised and then embarrassed. "Luke's been fed, but I didn't even think of the girls."

"Never mind." Mollie stood and walked toward the kitchen. "I have soup that Alice Duncan brought over yesterday and bread and cheese. I'll make grilled cheese sandwiches. They're fast, and everybody likes them." She smiled over her shoulder at her nieces.

"Have we ever had grilled cheese, Uncle Sean?" Marni asked her uncle.

"Aye," her uncle said absently. "It's toast with cheese in the middle."

Marni sighed with relief. "That's all right, then."

"Will I like it?" Caili asked.

"Well enough," said her sister in a voice low enough for only Caili to hear. "It's plenty for tea, I suppose. Maybe she'll have some biscuits to go with it. Remember to say thank you, Caili, whether she does or not, and don't be a bother to her always asking your questions."

"I'm not a bother. Aunt Mollie likes my questions."

"How do you know?"

"She asked about the bunnies."

"She didn't. Really?" Marni appeared suitably impressed.

Caili nodded. "Aye, she did. There are spotted ones in America."

"She told you that, did she?"

Again Caili nodded.

Marni stood and walked to the bookshelf. From there she could peek into the kitchen without anyone knowing she had a purpose other than to glance at the selection of books. Her aunt was slicing cheese on the breadboard, humming as she worked. Marni remembered her mother humming just so when she'd prepared meals. Not that she would ever compare Aunt Mollie to her mother. The woman was friendly and kind, but she wasn't Marni's mam. If only Mam would come back. There would be no need for Aunt Mollie to cook for them anymore.

6

𝒯he unfamiliar single ring of Sean's international phone call sounded three times. A man's voice, pleasant, warm, very American, answered.

Sean exhaled and spoke quickly. "This is Sean O'Malley. May I speak to Emma Reddington, please?"

A moment's hesitation. Then, "I'll see if she's home."

Could a house be big enough that a person was home and the others not know it? Or perhaps it was a polite way of warning him that Emma might not want to accept his call.

The minutes ticked by. Sean looked at his watch. Four in the morning. Eight o'clock in the evening in California. The last thing he wanted to do was talk to Emma Reddington. Damn all solicitors, anyway. If clients could work everything out among themselves, where did the lawyers earn their fees?

"Hello, Sean." The woman's voice was lovely, friendly and welcoming, like Mollie's. The blood left his head. He felt faint. "Hello, Mrs. Reddington. How are you?"

"Fine, thank you. Is everything all right?"

"Aye. The children are well." He drew a deep breath. "I was wondering if we could settle this matter between us, without lawyers."

"Oh?"

"I'd rather not drag this out, for everyone's sake."

"Is there a problem?"

Was there a problem? He couldn't sleep, his appetite was nonexistent, he hadn't written anything worth reading in weeks, and she wanted to know if there was a problem.

"Sean?"

"There's no problem, Mrs. Reddington. I think it might be better if the only family left to Danny's children aren't feuding amongst themselves."

"I agree."

"Then you'll come."

"Come?" Her voice turned wary. "To Inishmore?"

"Aye."

"I don't think I can do that right now."

"Why not?"

She hedged. "It might be a bit difficult."

"For whom?"

"For me."

He couldn't help himself. "It's difficult for my nieces, Mrs. Reddington. They've lost their parents. It's difficult for your daughter, who's enduring a bit of culture shock living on an island no bigger than a postage stamp with people very different from those she's accustomed to. It's also difficult for me, a man caring for two little girls and an infant all alone. For you, it would be merely inconvenient. Surely a bit of inconvenience isn't too much to ask of a woman considering taking on the task of raising three young children."

The silence was thick between them. Finally, she sighed. "I see what you mean," she said at last.

He waited.

Again, the silence. "There's more opportunity for them in California," she said at last.

"Undoubtedly. My home is in Galway. Inishmore is only temporary."

This time he heard her surrender. "I'll discuss this with my husband and call you back."

"Thank you."

The warmth returned to her voice. "How is Mollie?"

"Enduring, Mrs. Reddington. That's all there is to do here. I'm sure you already know that."

"Good night, Sean."

He stared at the phone. She didn't like him. He hadn't intended her to. Children were a serious matter, particularly these children. They'd had enough disruption in their lives. Once she took them away, there was no turning back.

Papers were strewn across the bed in disorganized piles. If he left it until morning, he might get three hours of sleep. After sweeping aside the mess, he stretched out and closed his eyes. Sleep brought relief. For a few brief hours he wouldn't have to think.

The alarm had bleeped its series of three a dozen times before Sean groggily lifted his head, reached out, knocked it over, swore, found the right button, and turned it off. With eyes at half mast he looked at the time in disbelief, groaned, and threw back the covers.

The girls would be late to school again. Christ, how had Kerry done it all? Three well-scrubbed children, a clean house, meals on the table at regular times. Were women born to it, or was there some secret society that kept the smooth workings of a home exclusive to the feminine gender?

Sean splashed water on his face and pulled on a pair of frayed denims. Peering into his nieces' bedroom, he called softly, "Caili, Marni, time to get up. Hurry. It's late."

Marni was up in a flash. "Oh, no," she moaned. "Did you oversleep again?"

Guilt sharpened his voice. "My night didn't end until a few hours ago, Marni. You're old enough to be waking by yourself."

"I would if the alarm clock was in my room," she mumbled under her breath. "Never mind, Uncle Sean," she said placatingly. "I'll make oats while you take care of Luke."

Sean breathed a sigh of relief. Thank God for Marni. Maybe he would put the alarm in her room. It certainly wasn't doing him any good.

Luke smiled at him and chewed his fist. Sean's throat closed the way it always did when he saw Luke first thing in the morning. He lifted the baby from the crib and buried his face in his chubby neck. Poor little tike. He had no idea of the drama being played out around him, no idea that his world wasn't a normal one. "I'm sorry, Luke," Sean murmured against the baby's cheek. "It's a poor sort of life I'm providing for you. Don't hold it against me."

The baby smiled, batted his incredibly long eyelashes, and pressed his open mouth against his uncle's shoulder.

Sean grinned. "Come along, lad. I'll fix you up and then we'll have some breakfast."

Caili walked into the room. "Marni says the oats and tea are ready."

Sean finished diapering the baby and lifted him to his shoulder. "Are they now? Isn't Marni a grand girl?"

"I lit the fire all by myself," Caili announced proudly.

Sean grinned and ruffled her hair with his free hand. "You're a clever lass. What would I do without the two of you?"

The oats were perfect. Another woman thing, Sean thought ruefully. His own were too watery one day and too dry the next.

"We've been late to school three days this week," Marni observed. "Aunt Mollie doesn't like it when we're late."

Swallowing the last of his tea, Sean pulled two pieces of toast from the toaster and buttered them. "I'm sure she doesn't."

"She says it disrupts the class."

Even toast didn't taste the same. "I'm sure she's right."

"Aunt Mollie says we should go to bed earlier."

Sean gritted his teeth and glanced guiltily at the mountain of paperwork on the counter. "So, we'll all go to bed earlier."

Caili piped up, "Aunt Mollie says—"

It was too much. "Caili." His voice was strained. "Shall we put what Aunt Mollie says to rest for the morning?"

Caili's green eyes widened. "Don't you like Aunt Mollie, Uncle Sean?"

"Of course I like her."

"Why can't I talk about her?"

Two pairs of eyes, one green, one gray, looked at him accusingly. He sighed. "Just for this morning, give it a rest. That isn't too much to ask, is it?"

Caili sulked. "I was going to ask you when you would work late again. You said we could stay with her when it happened again."

"Tonight," Sean promised automatically, wondering if it were possible to love three human beings as much as he did and still wish himself rid of them for a time. "I'll ask her if you can stay tonight. Hurry now. Leave the dishes and go on to school."

Both girls brightened visibly. Gathering their belongings, they opened the refrigerator, pulled out their lunches, kissed their uncle, and ran out the door and down the path.

Mrs. Harris took Luke in her arms and nuzzled his cheek. "How are you this morning, love?" She set the baby down on a blanket on the floor and returned to Sean. Her smile faded. "I know it hasn't been easy for you, but I can't be keeping them here after five, not with the boys home. My house is too small to have three more children underfoot. Perhaps Patrick can manage them when you're working late."

"I'm sorry for your trouble, Mrs. Harris. Patrick would be glad to keep them, but it's a long journey from the school. I'll see what I can do."

"He has the pony cart."

"Patrick Tierney won't be doing me any favors."

"It's the girls he would be accommodating, Sean O'Malley, not yourself."

"I'll see what I can do," he repeated.

She handed him a covered plate. "I made a bit of extra for tea. There's no sense wasting it."

He lifted the cloth and grinned. "Shepherd's pie. My favorite." Bending down, he kissed her cheek. "How would I manage without you?"

She blushed and waved him away. "Go along now and be back by five."

Sean walked down the winding road bordered with stone fences toward his sister's cottage, the cottage that he now shared with her three children. It was the soft season on the island, when all the tourists had gone and Inishmore was left to the Irish, when the skies were in constant transition and clouds hung low to the earth, when yellow grass fringed the limestone hills and the sea changed from turquoise to silver and the days were soft with lonely mists. This land where his ancestors had climbed the jagged cliffs, shouted their warnings, weathered the elements, and survived was part of him, wrapped around his heart with ties that bound no matter how he tried to escape them. Without Kerry, it wasn't nearly the same. If he lost the children, and when his mother passed on, there would be no reason for him to return.

Did Emma, a woman approaching her sixtieth birthday, really want to raise her grandchildren? The question haunted him. He passed the last red fuchsia of the season, swaying in the wind, and the yellow gorse blooming on a green hillside above Curwin Sound. It stayed with him as he sat down at his desk in the bedroom that doubled as an office to work on the same scene that had eluded him for weeks. He pushed it aside while he finished, but it was with him again later when he walked to the dock where he stopped to speak with local fishermen who'd caught their limits and come in early.

Sean was so caught up in his dilemma that he nearly forgot his promise to the girls. It was three o'clock before he called the school office and left a message for Mollie that he would stop by after her students had gone for the day.

When he showed up at the door of her classroom, she was seated behind her desk with a pair of wire-rimmed glasses perched on her nose. Like Kerry, she was pretty, but warmer, more golden—sun-touched, he would have said if he was of a poetic turn of mind, which he wasn't lately, and if he ever was again it wouldn't be this woman who inspired him. Mollie Tierney was a potential trouble source. It wasn't easy jumping into the fire the way he had, taking on the care of two little girls and a baby. He wondered how much of his fumbling she reported to her mother.

Ashamed of his uncharitable thoughts, which he knew even in his worst moments were a stretch at best, he spoke before he lost his nerve. "Good afternoon."

She looked up and smiled. She always smiled, a lovely separating of her mouth revealing those perfect teeth. Were women from California always happy, or was it just a characteristic of this one?

"I got your message," she said. "How can I help you?"

An innocent question, if only he dared answer honestly. How could a beautiful young woman the children adored help him? She would fall on her face if he told her the truth. "You said the children could stay with you for a night if I was in a tight spot."

"Are you?"

"Am I what?"

"In a bind?"

"In a manner of speaking. The thing is, the girls would like it very much, and I could use the time. I'm a bit behind. It's Friday, and I thought—"

She didn't wait for him to continue. "I'd love to have them. Luke, too. Shall I pick them up?"

He shook her head. "I'll deliver them with their things and Luke's carriage. Will tomorrow afternoon be soon enough to collect them?"

"Tomorrow afternoon will be fine," she assured him. Her voice gentled. "How are you managing?"

He stuffed his hands into his pockets and looked everywhere but into her eyes. "Fine, thank you."

She stood and walked around her desk to lean against it. She wore something that was long, below the knee, and softly flattering, blue, the same color as her eyes. She crossed her arms. "Kerry was a lovely person. You must miss her very much."

Her sympathy tore at his insides. He couldn't speak of Kerry. Not yet.

He changed the subject. "Your mother thinks the children would be better off in California."

"California can be very tempting," Mollie said slowly. "It has everything—mountains, deserts, recreation, restaurants, wonderful stores, entertainment. My mother never cared for Inishmore."

"And what of you, Mollie Tierney?" he asked softly. "Do you think they would be better off in California with your mother?"

In the background he heard the ticking of the clock.

The children were gone, but the room was still warm from their bodies, and this woman who looked too much like the one who had driven Patrick Tierney to drink stood across from him with something in her eyes that was very close to pity.

Her answer surprised him. "I'm not sure."

His eyes burned, and he felt the tension in his neck. That was the only explanation he could think of for what he said next. "I don't want to lose them."

"It hasn't come to that."

"And if it does?"

"California isn't that far away. People write plays and teach in California."

Her cheekbones were high and carved like Danny's had been, but her mouth was different. Mollie Tierney had a generous, lovely mouth. He clenched his fists. He wouldn't go there. He would never go there. He turned to leave.

He couldn't remember the walk back home or the people who greeted him. Once again Mollie had managed to shock him. *California wasn't that far away.* Was she insane? His life was here. His work was here. Reason told him that California was the land of the screenplay. Still, he couldn't imagine living in such a place. His voice was Irish. The first rule for a writer was to write what you know. What did he know about California? The woman was insane.

Caili's clothing was tumbled together in her bureau drawers. He must remember to help her fold it. Marni's was ordered neatly—socks, underwear, and pajamas in the top drawer, play clothes in the middle, and sweaters in the last. He pulled out what he thought they would need, folded them neatly, and placed them in a knapsack. Luke was easier. Babies had no separate clothing for home and school. Diapers, a few toys, and a container of formula would do it.

Looking at the mountain of clothing, he felt a stab of guilt. Mollie was on her own, a single woman. What was he doing imposing on her this way? He thought back to her smile. She hadn't hesitated, not even for a minute. Perhaps she was lonely. There weren't many young people her age on the island, and those who were weren't in her league. Presumably, Mollie Tierney had come to Inishmore to find her family. Other than Patrick and a few remote cousins, Luke and the girls were it. Besides, he rationalized, the experience wouldn't kill her. It might make her more wary, but perhaps that was a good thing. Perhaps it would teach her to think twice before she wished for something.

Caili was beside herself with joy. "You won't come before tomorrow afternoon, will you, Uncle Sean?"

"No, lass," he promised.

Caili executed the first few steps of a jig beside Luke's carriage. "No matter what, you won't come early?"

She stumbled over a rain-slick rock. "Easy, now." He reached out a steadying hand. "I told you I wouldn't. Have I ever broken a promise?"

Marni frowned and pushed Luke's buggy across a rut in the road. "You don't make many promises, Uncle Sean."

"All the more to trust me."

"It's just that I want to stay for as long as I can," Caili explained. "Aunt Mollie is lovely. She makes lovely food, and she tells stories and sings songs."

"A veritable saint," Sean murmured.

Marni looked at him sharply. "We're nearly there, Uncle Sean. Are you sure you want us to go? We don't have to, you know."

"Marni!" Caili wailed.

"Enough of that," Sean interrupted. "Your Aunt Mollie is expecting you. I wouldn't dream of disappointing her so by telling her I've changed my mind. Besides, I've work to do. You'll be asleep by the time I'm finished."

Mollie's cottage was at the end of a long unpaved road. A black-and-white dog pricked up his ears and watched their approach from a hill dotted with shaggy-haired sheep. Smoke curled up, smudging the darkening sky with feathers of white. Against the slate-gray sky, the cottage welcomed them, a beacon of yellow with a thatched roof and red door. Something meaty-smelling and delicious wafted through the air.

Caili sniffed appreciatively and broke away from Sean's hand, running ahead. "She's cooking something grand," she shouted back over her shoulder.

Mollie saw her from the kitchen window, opened the back door, and called out to them. "Hello. I hope you're hungry."

She was wearing something different, dark slacks and a turtleneck. How odd to be noticing a woman's clothes. Sean couldn't recall when he'd ever done so before. Her hair looked very gold against the black wool of her sweater.

"I won't be troubling you for a meal, Mollie," he said, handing her the bag containing the children's clothing. "You've done enough already."

She smiled. She was always smiling. Were there ever two siblings so different on the face of the earth?

"It's no trouble," she said, "but I understand if you have things to do."

He chastised himself all the way home. Why hadn't he accepted her invitation? He had to eat. Now he was facing a meal of scrambled eggs and brown bread in a lonely kitchen. Pride was the culprit. It wasn't the first time it prevented him from doing what he really wanted. Even though something told him that Mollie Tierney wasn't one to keep score, he couldn't help thinking he should have something to offer her in return.

"Mrs. Harris was out of sorts today," confided Caili. She pushed another fried potato into her mouth and attempted to get the words out from around it.

"Stop it, Caili," Marni said, disgust wrinkling her nose. "You know you're not supposed to talk with food in your mouth. Mam would scold you."

"Mam isn't here." Caili had finished her potato. "She hasn't been here for ever so long. I don't think I can remember her."

Marni's face whitened. Her fork stopped in midair. "Don't say that," she choked. "Don't ever say that. She's our mother, and we'll always remember her." She appealed to Mollie. "Isn't that so, Aunt Mollie?"

Anything, she would say anything, whatever it took, to wipe the terror-struck look from the child's face. "Of course you will," Mollie replied heartily. Please, let her answer be the right one.

Marni relaxed. "I told you," she said in a superior voice. "Aunt Mollie knows."

Caili continued eating. "This is good," she said. "What is it?"

"Taco burgers," replied Mollie. "They were supposed to be tacos, but the grocery store here hasn't heard of tortillas."

"What's a tortilla?"

Another reminder of how far away Mollie was from home. "Round flat pieces of cooked flour or corn meal. They're filled with meat, lettuce, tomatoes, and cheese, folded and eaten with your fingers. I decided on burgers when I couldn't find them. Do you like them?"

"Aye." Caili nodded. "I do."

Luke waved his arms from his infant seat on the floor. Mollie cooed at him. He laughed back at her. She picked up his rattle and shook it. Luke was diverted.

"Who's ready for ice cream?" Mollie asked.

"Me, me!" the girls shouted.

She carried bowls of ice cream into the living room and was returning for Luke when the phone rang. With a rush of pleasure she recognized her father's voice.

"Would you care to come tomorrow morning for a hike in the hills and, later, stay for a bite to eat?"

She was touched. "I'd love to, but I have the children."

"All the better. Bring them along."

"I'll have to check with Sean."

"Do that. I'll be waiting to hear back from you."

Sean was surprised but agreeable. "Patrick doesn't usually extend himself. You must lead a charmed life, Mollie Tierney. How are you holding up?"

"How do you think?"

There was a grin in his voice. "I think you're regretting the invitation."

"Not a bit."

"You're an amazing woman."

The warmth of his approval startled her. She couldn't resist asking. "Why amazing?"

"I would have thought you could manage the girls, but Luke—"

"Luke is a wonderful baby," she protested loyally. "I wonder if you realize how lucky you are."

His voice was low, fervent. "Of course I do."

"I'll let you get back to what you were doing. We may not be home until late tomorrow afternoon. Shall I drop off the children?"

"Only if it's convenient for Patrick. I don't want to set his back up."

Mollie couldn't help herself. "What is it between you and my father?"

"The Irish are always feuding, Mollie. We've never invaded another country because we're always fighting among ourselves. Don't concern yourself. It's ancient history."

"He seems so kind."

"Most likely it's my fault." That edge in his voice was back again.

She could be just as cool. "I'm sure you're right. We'll see you tomorrow." She hung up the phone.

What was it about Sean O'Malley that raised her hackles? Mollie rarely lost her temper. She was like her mother. Nothing seemed quite worth reaching those levels of passion. It was much better to remain logical, think things through, compromise.

Why then was she so ready to throw away the habits of a lifetime because a man she barely knew, with only the slightest provocation, brought out emotions she had previously reserved for major crises?

The sight of the two little girls in their long white nightgowns tucked into the double bed in her spare room brought a smile to Mollie's lips. She sat down on the edge of the bed and smoothed the feather comforter. "Luke's sleeping. Shall I read you a story?"

"Tell us one, please," said Marni.

Mollie was at a loss. "I'm much better at reading."

"You could tell us about when you were a little girl," suggested Caili. "Mam did that."

"All right." She patted Marni on the knee. "Move over."

Marni rolled to one side of the bed, and Mollie climbed over her to lie in the middle. Caili curled up against her side, molding her body to fit Mollie's. Marni rested her head in the dip of her aunt's shoulder.

"Where shall I begin?"

"Tell us about the bunnies?" Caili suggested.

"No," said Marni. "Tell us about your friends and your house. Was it like ours?"

"Houses are very different in California," Mollie explained. "The weather's warmer, so the rooms are larger and there are more windows. I lived near the ocean just as you do, but it's very warm and the sun shines nearly all the time. The beach is all white with soft sand that can be very hot under your feet. When I was younger, my friends and I swam and surfed all year long."

"Even in winter?" Caili asked.

"Even in winter, although sometimes we wore wet-suits."

"What's that?"

"You know what that is, Caili," Marni interrupted. "Our harbor master has a wetsuit when he has to go under the water."

Caili's thumb had worked its way into her mouth. "What else?"

Mollie continued. "Every day in the summer we would wake up early, rub lotion all over our bodies, and lie out in the sun until we burned."

Marni looked surprised. "Why?"

Mollie laughed. "I have no idea. It was ridiculous but fun at the time. We swam and sunbathed and ate popsicles."

"What's a popsicle?" Caili asked around her thumb.

"Frozen fruit juice. It comes on a stick, and you suck on it."

"Is it good?"

"Very good."

"Will you make us a popsicle?" Caili begged.

Mollie hugged the little girl. "Of course I will. I'll do it tonight before I go to bed, and we'll have them when we come home tomorrow."

"Will you take us to California?" Marni whispered.

Mollie hesitated. "That's a bit complicated. If your uncle agrees, I'll be happy to take you when I go. But it's really up to him, Marni, and it would be much better if he came along." She kissed both girls and climbed out of the bed. "That's enough for tonight. Sleep well." She turned off the light.

"Aunt Mollie?" It was Caili.

"Yes?"

"Mam said a prayer with us."

Mollie's religious instruction was spotty. Her mother

was a lapsed Catholic. She walked back to the bed. "I'll listen while you say it."

The little girl's hands came together like a pyramid. Marni folded hers and closed her eyes. In their sing-song, Irish Gaelic, they recited the unintelligible words. When it was over Mollie was strangely comforted. "Go to sleep now," she whispered again before leaving the room.

7

Newport, California

*E*mma sat outside on the deck of her patio and stared at the panoramic view before her. The sun had just dropped into the Pacific, and coppery light spilled across the water like a melted penny. She had known this moment would come, had anticipated and dreaded it for three decades, the reckoning for leaving her son, for placing her own needs, her own sanity, before what was best for her child. She was an unnatural mother, a mother who had abandoned her young and left him unprotected.

"Emma," Ward's voice called out to her. "I'm home."

She forced a smile to her lips. Ward liked to see her happy. It worried him when she thought too much, especially about the past. The years of therapy, Ward's contribution, the confusion, the self-doubt that had plagued her for nearly a decade after she'd left the island, belonged to a time that neither of them cared to remember.

Her husband walked into the family room, smiled when he saw her, and joined her outside. She reached out a hand; he clasped it and leaned down to kiss her. If it hadn't been for Ward, she might have lost Mollie, too.

"You look comfortable," he said. "Are we eating in tonight?"

"I think so. There's something I need to discuss with you."

He walked back to the bar, poured himself a scotch, added water and ice, and came back to sit beside her. "What's on your mind?"

She plunged in. "You're not going to like this, Ward. I never told you because it seemed absurd even to think about it." She drew a deep breath. "I'm the legal guardian of Danny's children."

The silence terrified her. Ward was never silent. He was comfortably quiet, reasonably reserved, thoughtful, but never silent. What did it mean?

"I see," he said after long minutes had passed. "How long have you known?"

"Three months or so."

"When were you planning to tell me?"

"I wasn't."

"Why not?"

Emma felt the stirrings of exasperation. "Young people rarely die, Ward, not both of them. Up until a few weeks ago, the odds against our raising my grandchildren were very small."

"And now?"

Emma sighed." I don't know. Kerry's brother has the children. I know nothing about him."

"For God's sake, Emma." Ward's voice was harsh. "Two young children and an infant. Do you have any idea what that would do to us?"

"I can't abandon them, Ward. They're my son's children."

"What about their grandfather?"

Emma's lips thinned. "Impossible. You know what Patrick's like."

"He's familiar to them, far more than we are."

Emma's hands shook. She folded them tightly in her lap. "Are you telling me I can't bring them here?"

"Of course not."

He was angry, and for the first time since she'd known him, Emma didn't attempt to placate him.

"I just want you to consider your options carefully," he said. "The brunt of all this will fall on you. What about the uncle they're living with now?"

"Kerry's brother is a bachelor, a playwright. I'm not sure that's the best place for them. They might be better off here with us."

Ward shook his head. "If you're thinking this will make up for losing Danny, you're wrong. Danny isn't your fault. We gave him every opportunity to live with us. Look at what you've accomplished with Mollie. She's a wonderful young woman."

"I'm going," she said flatly.

Ward stared at her. "Going where?"

"To Ireland."

"Emma—"

"I'm going to see my grandchildren. I want them with

me. I need to do it because of Danny." She swallowed and looked directly at her husband. "I would very much like your support, but I'm going either way."

"Oh, Emma." Ward sighed, reached out, and pulled her close to his heart. "Of course you have my support. I'll even go with you if you want me to."

Emma hummed under her breath and stood back to survey the contents of her suitcase. Surely she'd packed enough. She wouldn't be gone long, a day to fly into Shannon Airport, rent a car, and spend the night outside Galway. Another day to catch the ferry from Rossaveal, stay a few weeks with Mollie, become better acquainted with the children. She would stay just long enough to persuade them to come home with her.

She refused to consider the ramifications of a fifty-six-year-old woman caring for three children, one of them an infant under three months old.

Marni was the responsible one, Mollie had told her over the phone last night. She would be a tremendous help with Caili and Luke. Emma smiled. In less than forty-eight hours she would be with Mollie again. The thought of it warmed her heart. The bond had always been strong between the two of them. Watching her go about the smallest task, hearing her laugh, sharing conversation over a cup of coffee, and smelling the clean, floral scent that clung to her hair and skin was pure pleasure. Mollie had never given her a moment's worry, not until she announced that she'd accepted a fellowship to teach on Inishmore.

Emma's first reaction had been shock, followed by dismay. But after Mollie had explained, she felt better.

Mollie had always been sensible. It wasn't a lack in her childhood or a sense of resentment that prompted her decision, but rather a natural curiosity to meet her family and learn something of her Irish heritage. Emma recalled their conversation. Curled up in opposite chairs in the airy living room decorated with seascapes and van Gogh prints, Mollie had gently and characteristically coaxed her out of her initial gloom until Emma was nearly as excited about the trip as she was.

She had a way about her, as her father had. The thought popped, unbidden, into Emma's mind. Patrick also had that beguiling Irish charm coupled with the words of a storyteller. She remembered the way his friends had described him that first night in O'Meara's pub. *Patrick Tierney can tell a man to go to hell and make him look forward to the trip.* He'd certainly charmed her in no time at all. Charmed her enough so that she gave up her life and her dreams to marry him and live for ten long years on the bleakest, loneliest spot on earth.

She had made mistakes. There was no getting around that. Her dreams of taking the art world by storm had amounted to nothing more than a hobby she dabbled in now and then. More than anyone, Danny had suffered. Emma couldn't turn back the clock, but she could make it up to him through his children. Tucking a pair of boots into the side pocket of her suitcase, she smiled, happier than she'd been in years. There was a slight possibility that her entire family would be nearby for the first time.

Ward parked the car and pulled her suitcase from the trunk of the claret-colored Infiniti he had purchased only last week. He insisted on escorting her to the gate and waiting by the window until he saw her plane soar into the air.

"I'll be fine," she chided him. "You don't have to do this."

He squeezed her hand. "I want to," he assured her.

"Be careful," she said. "Watch your diet. I don't want anything to happen to you."

"Don't worry."

Her heart melted. Ward was her love, her savior. Except for his gray hair, he was as handsome and fit as he'd been twenty-five years ago. More important, he was the most decent man she'd ever known. "I love you."

"Emma, Emma." Ward wrapped his arms around his wife. "Promise me you won't stay any longer than you have to. I miss you already."

"I'll be back before you know it."

"Give Mollie a kiss for me. I miss her."

"I will."

The voice over the intercom was loud and garbled. "First-class passengers for Flight 441 to Shannon may board now."

Emma kissed him lightly on the lips. "Remember, only egg whites for breakfast, and cut out the beef."

"My cholesterol is perfect."

"Only because I take care of you." She handed her boarding pass to the woman at the gate. "I love you, Ward," she repeated.

He stroked her cheek. "I love you, too, darling. See you soon."

He stood there in khaki-colored Dockers and a navy polo shirt, smiling benignly, waiting for her to turn down the gangway and out of sight.

Emma faltered, unable to take the steps that would block her husband from view. She had the oddest sensation in her stomach, a moment of sheer panic, disturbing enough to change her mind, nearly, but not quite. Drawing a deep breath, she cleared her throat, threw Ward a final bracing smile, and walked around the corner onto the plane.

Inishmore, Ireland

Rare November sunlight colored the land in the crisp, gilt-colored way particular to autumn, blue ocean, green hills, gold fields.

After a breakfast of French toast and ham for the girls, formula for Luke, Mollie bundled the children into their coats and waited on the porch for Patrick to collect them in his pony trap.

Marni heard the *clip-clop* of his Connemara pony before anyone else. "He's here!" she shouted, and raced down the road to meet her grandfather with Caili at her heels. Mollie waited on the steps with Luke.

The pony cart appeared over the rise in portions, like a ship at the edge of the horizon. At first Mollie didn't notice the small woman sitting behind her father. When she did, her eyes widened. Mabry O'Farrell was old, older than anyone Mollie had ever seen outside a rest home, but her body swayed in the cart with the grace of a much younger person. Long white hair was pulled away from her face to form a sizable knot at the back of her head. Her skin was unusually brown and very wrinkled, and her clothing—a long dark wool dress, a woolen shawl, and sturdy shoes—was the kind seen on the island a century ago. She stood and held out her arms when Patrick stopped the cart in front of Mollie.

"I'll take the bairn while you climb up," she said in her strong island voice.

Mollie handed over the baby and pulled herself up into the trap. "Good morning," she said.

The woman studied her carefully before speaking. "Good morning to you, too, Mollie Tierney. Patrick tells me you're doing a fine job with the schoolchildren."

Mollie smiled. She didn't notice the woman catch her breath. "Thank you. I like it here." She hugged her nieces to her. "I especially like it when these two visit me."

Mabry smiled. "Well said."

The old woman was different but interesting. Everything about Ireland was different and interesting. Mollie laughed out loud, and once more Mabry stared at her curiously.

"We're dropping Mabry at the village," Patrick said. "Then we'll be on our way back."

"What do you have planned for the wee ones, Patrick?" Mabry asked.

"A family of sea lions swam up on O'Callough's beach. There's a white one with them. I want them to see a silkie firsthand."

"I've seen one already," Marni announced smugly.

"You did not!" cried Caili.

"Aye, she did," Patrick broke in. "I brought her to the very same beach when she was a wee mite, not even as old as you, Caili. That was her first."

"What's a silkie?" Mollie asked. She couldn't call him Da, not yet, not in front of a stranger.

Mabry answered. "A seal who takes on the body of a human and returns, after a time, to the sea."

"How do you know which one is the silkie?"

"The white one is the silkie, lass." Patrick looked as if he would say something else but changed his mind.

Mollie held out her arms for her nephew. "Thank you for holding him, but I'll take him back now." She left no room in her voice for refusal.

The baby was warm and pleasantly heavy in her lap. She kissed the top of his head.

"You're like your mother," Mabry announced.

Surprised, Mollie stared at the old woman. "Did you know her?"

"I've never been off this island, child. I know everyone, but I wouldn't say I *really* knew her. I doubt if anyone did. She kept to herself."

She still did. Mollie didn't say the words, but she thought them all the same. Emma had always preferred her husband and daughter's company. "How am I like her?"

"The resemblance is in your laugh and in your face."

"She moves like Emma," Patrick spoke up.

Mabry cocked her head to one side and studied Patrick Tierney's daughter. "Does she now?"

Embarrassed at the careful scrutiny, Mollie brushed the words aside with her own question. "What about Danny? Who was he like?"

Mabry's eyebrows lifted. "Danny was an islander, lass. He was like Patrick. It was that way from the beginning. That's why he was the one to stay and you to go."

Mollie's lips tightened rebelliously. How dare they be so certain? How could they possibly have known she was not an islander? "I was six months old. How could anyone know that?"

The old woman tilted her head. "I'm not often wrong, but it's possible. I've often thought—" She hesitated, smiled, and tapped Patrick on the shoulder. "Never mind. Drop me at the Superquinn, Pat. I've a bit of shopping to do before I stop in at the Cleary house."

"It's still a ways off."

"A walk wards off the stiffness." She winked at Mollie. "Let me down now, or I'll die young."

Mollie bit back a smile. *Young* had passed Mabry O'Farrell decades ago. "Goodbye," she said politely. "It was a pleasure seeing you again."

The old woman rested a ropy-veined hand on Mollie's knee. "Come and see me, lass. Bring the children if you've a mind, or come alone, but come."

"I will," Mollie said, and realized that she meant it. The tension that had characterized their first meeting had completely disappeared.

Patrick clucked to his pony and turned the trap around. "We'll drive down as far as we can and walk the rest of the way to the beach."

"How do you know they'll still be there?" Mollie asked.

"Grandda knows everything," said Marni smugly. "Don't you, Grandda?"

A smile lifted the corner of Patrick's mouth. "Not quite everything, lass, but thank you for the confidence."

The road was empty except for a few art students perched on top of fences or abandoned lorries sketching madly to catch the last of the morning light. Mollie looked out over the loose stone walls to the Atlantic where the untamed sea rolled like a boiling cauldron beating at the wind-carved hills and jutting cliffs. In the valley the last of summer's honeysuckle and blackberry bushes pushed their way through cracks in the boulders. Footpaths twisted across the limestone burren, disappearing behind the hills.

Patrick pulled up the trap and jumped down. After lifting the girls to the ground, he reached for Mollie and the baby. Then he took Luke from her and began making his way down the rocky path to the sea. Mollie watched the girls pick their way as nimbly as mountain goats down the steep path. Using both hands to cling to the rocks, she scrambled after them.

He stopped at a flat boulder large enough for all of them and put a finger against his lips. "Hush now, and watch for a minute."

They squatted down to wait. Minutes passed. Luke had drifted off, and the girls were as still as morning mist. Mollie's calves ached. Carefully she shifted position and nearly missed them. There, on the morning tide, four sea lions frolicked, and one, effectively camouflaged by the churning sea foam, was white.

Caili sucked in her breath, her quick gasp the only sound in the silence except for the lapping waves, the crying gulls, and the joyful bark of the sea lions cavorting on the beach.

"It's truly a silkie, isn't it, Grandda?" Caili whispered.

"It is, lass."

"Can we take a photograph of him?"

Patrick shook his head. "You know that no one has ever photographed a silkie. It can't be done."

"Why?"

"Because they're fairy creatures, Caili. Fairy creatures have no reflection. Your photo would show no image at all."

Mollie stared at him in disbelief. He was serious. This wasn't a Santa Claus or tooth fairy story that benignly disappeared as a child aged. Her father, a fifty-something adult, actually believed his silkie tale. She couldn't imagine her practical mother ever relaying such a story. Believing it would be unthinkable.

Luke stirred against Patrick's shoulder. Mollie swallowed and looked at her father holding his grandson, her mother's grandson. Then she looked at the white sea lion among the brown ones. For an instant she willed herself to suspend her beliefs, the sensible Southern California reality she'd acquired over twenty-eight years of living in the midst of a sophistication so planed and polished and brittle that childhood was the merest blip on the road between infancy and adolescence.

Her imagination took flight. She shivered and rubbed her arms for warmth. Caili leaned against her, tilting her chin so that Mollie could see her face. "Silkies are good luck, Aunt Mollie," she whispered. "Once you see one, nothing bad can ever happen to you."

"It isn't fair," Marni said in low tones. "We've all seen one, even Aunt Mollie."

"What isn't fair?" Mollie asked.

The child bit her lip. "Da lived here all his life and never saw a silkie, not even once." She looked at her grandfather. "Why is that, Grandda?"

The life left Patrick Tierney's face. He looked tired and old. "I don't know, lass. Some things are meant to be."

A chill seeped through Mollie's bones, as if all joy and promise had passed out of the morning. Marni was right. It wasn't fair at all.

8

*E*mma stifled a yawn and glanced out the window at Ireland, a brilliant green dot swimming in blue ocean below the boiling clouds. The seatbelt sign flashed above her as the plane began to descend. The dot was a mound now, looming larger by the second. Various shades of lime, emerald, jade, and forest green separated into distinct patterns. Her breath caught. Soon, very soon, she would be on Irish soil once again.

The soft lilting voice of the Aer Lingus flight attendant interrupted her thoughts. "Please return all seats to their upright positions and remain seated until the seatbelt light has been extinguished. On behalf of the captain and crew, I would like to thank you for choosing to fly Aer Lingus. *Slán go fóill*, and enjoy your stay in Ireland."

Customs hadn't changed. For Americans visiting Ireland it was a mere formality. Emma hadn't bothered to check her suitcase. Bypassing the luggage carousel and the elevator, she walked briskly down the stairs to ground transportation, rented a late-model English Rover with Limerick plates, adjusted to the left side of the road, and was on her way west on the N4 within the hour. Jet lag hadn't yet set in, and she was able to appreciate the beauty of a rare sunlit November afternoon.

Even the endless number of roundabouts outside Galway City proved no trouble to negotiate, and, sooner than she expected, Emma found herself driving through the sweeping hills and desolate boglands of Connemara. Her heart ached and her breath came quickly when she saw, once again, the shattering beauty of winter light settling over the Twelve Pins.

Ireland was still a country of contrasts, from the bustling streets of Dublin to the warm smoky pubs of Galway and the remote loneliness of Connemara. A terrible beauty, Yeats had called it. The rocky limestone burren, the thickly forested glens of Antrim, the lush green plains of Kildare, the stone fences of the Arans, and surrounding it all was the sea, relentless, pounding, gulls crying, waves lashing, flooding her senses until her blood beat in a symbiotic rhythm with the beauty around her.

The small guesthouse where she'd reserved a room for the night was located on a remote stretch of beach in the prestigious Salthill area outside Galway. Nora Logan was as famous for her hospitality as she was for the delights of her late-afternoon tea tray and her sustaining meals. Emma sank back into the comfort of an elegant and slightly shabby wingback chair, closed her eyes, and lifted the steaming cup of Queen Anne's tea to her lips. She sampled her hostess's lemon scones and moaned with pleasure.

Nora chuckled. "You'll be wanting more, I think, but not too many more or you won't eat your evening meal."

"What time are you serving?" A wave of fatigue washed over her. She didn't think she could manage a late dinner.

"Whenever you like. You'll be the only guest this evening. I think it's best to feed you now and keep you awake for a bit. That way you can go to sleep at a normal hour and get a full night's rest. Those that travel through the night and arrive in the morning too tired to do anything but sleep are at sixes and sevens with their schedule for days."

Emma nodded.

"I'll show you the room and have your meal on the table in the corner by the fire in twenty minutes or so. Will that suit you, Mrs. Reddington?"

"Perfectly." Emma stood and followed her landlady down the hall and into a room decorated in floral prints and dominated by an elegant four-poster, a desk, and an easy chair that took up most of the room.

Nora opened the armoire and set the suitcase inside. "You'll be comfortable, I think. The noise from the street won't bother you, not that there's much in winter except for the normal traffic and we've not much of that. I'll see to your dinner now. Try not to fall asleep before you've eaten." With that she left the room, closing the door behind her.

The bed looked more than inviting. Emma dared not risk even sitting on it. She walked into the bathroom and filled the claw-footed tub. The water was surprisingly hot for Ireland. After shedding her clothes, she tore open the package of bath salts, sprinkled it in, and stepped into the foam.

Thirty minutes later she walked into the sitting room and sat down before a repast elegant enough for a five-star restaurant in Corona del Mar. Spring lamb chops, pink in the center and crisply brown around the edges, nestled against tiny red potatoes seasoned with rosemary. A fresh green salad, a small sourdough bread loaf with rounded balls of ice-flecked butter, and a glass of excellent French merlot rounded out the meal.

Emma was ravenous. She'd no more than picked at her meal on the plane. Airline food didn't appeal to her. She ate slowly, enjoying every savory mouthful. When she couldn't possibly manage any more, she set down her fork, leaned back in the chair, and closed her eyes. Tomorrow she would meet her grandchildren and see Mollie.

The nagging worry, so easy to ignore in the sunny splendor of Southern California, rose again. This time she couldn't push it away, not here, not when she was so close. Patrick Tierney would be on the island. Patrick with his lean, blue-eyed good looks and his crooked smile and that way he had of telling a story. His stories and those blue eyes had kept her hoping it would get better for far longer than she should have, long enough to conceive and give birth to Mollie. She couldn't be sorry for that. What was the middle-aged Patrick Tierney like, and why had he never married again? Emma wasn't so taken with herself that she thought for a minute the reason had anything to do with missing her. More likely his memories were so painful he wouldn't risk another marriage. She would be very relieved when tomorrow was over.

From Rossaveal, the ferry left at nine in the morning for the hour long ride to Kilronen Harbor. The day was typical for Ireland, brisk and cold, the air stingingly pure. A bitter wind forced the few passengers to huddle in silence against the wall to wait while the ferry refueled. Cupping a mug of coffee between her hands, Emma pulled the hood of her parka over her head and resigned herself to the cold. This was Ireland, and it was November. No one who waited with her had come for the weather.

At last the queue moved slowly up the gangway. A man with a mauve muffler wrapped around his neck and chin took her ticket and pointed her toward the cabin. "You'll stay dry inside, Miss, but the seas are rough today. If you're one to be seasick, you'll want to spend most of your time outside."

Emma heard the rumbling of the engines. The ferry lurched, started off slowly, and picked up speed. Traveling west, it moved against the current, and the seas heaved and rolled. Soon those with weak stomachs left their seats to stand outside and brave the elements, only to be rewarded with a thorough drenching from the six-foot spumes that swept across the deck.

Inside the heated cabin, Emma looked around. She was one of nearly twenty passengers, a few tourists, but mostly islanders, on their way home after a day or two of holiday in Galway. The natives were easily identified, their sharp-cheeked Celtic bones and odd, light-struck eyes evident in their weathered faces. Unlike the tourists who periodically consulted their watches and stood often to stretch their legs, the locals, hearty souls, born before the cozy glow of gaslight had been replaced by electricity, who lived with seventeen hours of winter darkness, who knew television as recent technology, and who believed that a handshake carried the same weight as a signed contract, sat patiently without moving, waiting for the eventual docking of the boat.

It was Tuesday. Mollie would be teaching, but she'd left directions to the cottage. Emma vaguely remembered it. Thirty years ago the Nolans had lived there. Now they lived in Dublin and leased it out. It wouldn't be more than a two-mile walk, something she did often in the mild climate of Southern California. Attempting it in the rain with a suitcase was something else entirely.

Gritting her teeth, Emma clipped on the shoulder strap of her bag, hoisted it to her shoulder, and stepped out onto the weathered planks of the pier. She looked around. A gray pelican sat on a guano-stained piling. Gulls circled overhead. Two miles wasn't far. At a reasonable pace it should take her no more than three-quarters of an hour.

Ahead of her the road twisted and climbed. Behind her she heard the steady *clip-clopping* of a horse's hooves. She moved to the side and waited for the trap to pass. It stopped beside her, and an unmistakable voice asked, "I'm sorry I wasn't on time, but the boat docked early. Would you be needing a lift, Emma?"

She brushed back her tumbled hair and looked up. Rain blurred her vision and ran in rivulets down her cheeks, her neck, and the front of her parka. "Patrick?"

"Aye. Did you not recognize me?"

Emma wiped her eyes. Mascara rubbed off on her hand. "I'm a mess."

"That you are," he said agreeably, reaching down to pull her into the trap. He waited until she'd settled back into the seat, then tucked a woolen blanket around her from head to toe. "Now you look like an Aran woman again," he said, and picked up the reins.

She stared at him. Just like that, no awkwardness, no preliminaries, just a continuing from where they'd left off nearly thirty years ago, as if all the bitterness and despair over Danny had never occurred. Emma was in no mood to be friendly. Patrick had kept her from her son. There was no going back. She wouldn't forgive him, no matter how pleasant he pretended to be.

"How are you getting on?" he asked when they were on their way again.

Emma hesitated and then decided there was no point in deception. "I'm here for the children," she said at last. "I'm sure Sean O'Malley resents me, but I'm taking them anyway."

"That's to be expected. I wouldn't lose any sleep over it."

Stung by his insensitivity, she asked the question she'd promised herself she wouldn't ask. "Why didn't you tell me when Kerry died?"

Patrick chirruped to the horse until he rounded a bend. Emma waited, but he didn't answer. Sighing, she leaned back in the trap and tried not to feel the rain seeping through the thick wool.

"I did."

The words, bitter and unforgiving, came out. "Not until it was too late to come for the services."

"Danny would have called you if he'd wanted you here. He never did after you'd gone."

Rage boiled to life within her and erupted. "Danny didn't have much of a home with you. You buried yourself in drink and hardly knew he was there."

Patrick shrugged. "I've made mistakes, Emma. But there were good times, too."

They were silent for a while. Finally he said, "You've done a grand job with Mollie. She's a taking little lass."

Disarmed, Emma softened. "Thank you. Everyone feels that way about her. Mollie would have been the way she is no matter who had raised her. She's like bottled sunshine."

"I thought as much." He nodded at the smoke swirling from the chimney of Mollie's yellow cottage. "The rooms should be warm enough."

Jumping to the ground, he unloaded her suitcase and held out his hand to help her down. "If you need anything, call me."

"Thank you, Patrick," she said formally, vowing never to ask him for anything.

Tipping his cap, he climbed back into the trap and drove away.

Emma found the tea canister and a pan of freshly made coffee cake in the oven. After setting the kettle to boil, she unpacked her suitcase in the room with the turned-down bed, changed into dry clothing, and returned to the kitchen. Then she cut herself a generous slice of coffee cake, poured herself a cup of tea, and carried them both into the living room to wait for Mollie. She turned on the television. There had been no television on Inishmore thirty years ago.

*　　*　　*

Sean woke in a cold sweat. The ache in his chest was nearly unbearable. He'd lived the dream again, the one where he learned that Kerry was dead. In painful, lurid detail he remembered the knock on his door and saw the terrible grayness of Patrick's face. Danny's father had chosen his words carefully, compassionately. Sean couldn't have done it, but then he was nothing like Patrick Tierney. Sean wanted to shout his rage and pain to the world. Everything he'd done, all he'd worked for and dreamed of, meant nothing in the face of this loss. Kerry was gone. Danny was inconsolable. He heard Patrick say that someone would need to tell the girls. That someone was Sean. He was closer to them than anyone. They would need him, especially Marni.

He was at home in Galway when Patrick came with the news. The room he'd converted into an office was remarkably neat, stark even, with its wood floors, its single desk with a computer, two chairs, and a reading lamp. Sturdy shelves lined two walls, and books filled every available space. Sean was seated at his desk staring at the computer screen when he first heard the knock.

He'd opened the door thinking it was his housekeeper reminding him of a forgotten appointment. He remembered the tiny surge in his brain, signaling alarm when he saw who it was. Patrick Tierney rarely left the island.

"Welcome, Pat. What brings you here?"

"I've bad news, lad."

He waited.

Patrick nodded toward a chair. "I'll sit if I may."

Sean knew the man was functioning on nerves alone.

Without a word, he motioned Patrick to the only extra chair and sat down across from him. "It's Kerry, isn't it? There's something wrong with the baby."

Patrick shook his head. "The baby survived."

Dawning awareness crept through Sean by degrees. First he heard the words, then his mind understood them. The room swayed. He leaned his head back until he felt the wall. "What happened?"

"Blood clot in the brain. The birth brought it on."

The lines around Sean's eyes deepened. "Was she at home?"

Patrick nodded. "Mabry did all she could. She managed to save the baby after Kerry stopped breathing."

Sean dropped his head into his hands. "Holy God, Patrick. What happens now? What about the children? Danny can't—" He stopped. Even at the high point of his grief he remembered that Danny was Patrick's son.

Patrick reached out and gripped Sean's shoulder. "We'll tell the girls together, and then we'll sort out what to do."

Why did it haunt him so, over and over, the same dream never changing, never reaching its conclusion? Kerry had been laid to rest. He'd taken in the children. Why did he never dream of that?

He turned the alarm to see its illuminated face and groaned. Luke would be up soon. Damn Susan O'Meara. The last thing he needed was a housekeeper for a vacant house. If she wouldn't come to the island and help care for the children, he would find a replacement. Sean hadn't the knack for making a home. Unbidden, the image of Mollie's cozy cottage came to mind. It was a woman thing, the making of a home. Perhaps it was time to look around for a wife, a woman who required little attention, who would take on three children and make no demands. The very thought brought a smile to his lips. Such a paragon didn't exist, and, if she did, no one would want her.

9

Sean stared down at the freshly hewn headstone, the dark soil indicating a new grave and the two small bouquets laced lovingly at its base. For a thousand years O'Malleys had been buried here, first in family crypts and then individually, in single plots with markers gone black and thin with age. Danny was buried on the other side of the church with the Tierneys. Blood, according to the traditions of the islanders, had always been thicker than water or marriage. A man could have many wives but only one mother, one father.

Sean closed his eyes, shutting out the sight of Kerry's name etched on the pale gray stone, "Kerry Tierney, beloved wife and mother." *And sister.* The words leaped to his brain. Kerry had loved and been loved deeply. Who could ask more of life than that?

Opening his eyes again, he looked out at the ocean lapping at all sides of the island, swallowing the land bit by bit. Geologists said the island would disappear in three thousand years, gone the way it had come, a volcanic accident supporting an ecosystem. This was where Kerry had wanted to raise her children, an unfulfilled dream left to him, or perhaps not.

Perhaps they would go to Danny's mother. What had they thought, Danny and Kerry, to leave their children to strangers? What could have possessed them?

Mollie stopped abruptly in the middle of the path, telling herself it was to give him a moment to collect himself. But it was more than that. She wanted to look at him when his emotions were honest and undisguised.

It was too late to turn back. He would see her and know she'd retreated, and he would think the worst. She knew enough about him to know that. Minutes passed. Gulls screeched above her. Waves lapped at the shoreline. And still Mollie stood there, silent, waiting. Finally she could wait no longer. "Hello, Sean."

He turned quickly, too quickly to mask his dismay at the untimely interruption.

It was Mollie Tierney, elegant and poised, her hair spilling gold over the dark wool of her long coat, carrying an arrangement of flowers.

He nodded. "Good morning."

She smiled. "I didn't want to startle you. Now that you know I'm here, I won't bother you. I just came to bring these to Danny and Kerry." She held out the flowers.

"You're no bother," he said politely.

She didn't contradict him, but he knew what she was thinking, this woman who had on more than one occasion read his mind, who moved in a tireless rhythm, ministering to her mother, to Patrick, to the children, and to him. Where did it come from, that endless reserve of strength and compassion, of knowing exactly when they needed food or rest, conversation or silence?

For a moment Sean allowed himself his fantasy, a woman like Mollie, children well adjusted, cared for, a cottage neat because Mollie was organized, warm because she exuded warmth, loving because she had love enough in her to spare, and if anyone could bring life back into his severed family, she could.

Christ. He rubbed at the headache he couldn't lose. He was insane, weaving hallucinations that were humiliating as well as absurd. He missed having a woman in his life. His stomach clenched. He wouldn't go there, not with this woman, not yet, not ever. He wouldn't take advantage of her, not when she was alone in an unfamiliar place where a woman like her would never be found under normal circumstances.

She was far too accommodating. He wasn't accustomed to caring for children. His mother was too old to be of much help, and as for Patrick, one never knew when there would be a recurrence of his drinking. Mollie would be a habit Sean could fall into far too easily.

Across the space that separated them, he smelled a hint of floral perfume. If only she wasn't an American and Emma Tierney's daughter. Suddenly he was consumed with gratefulness. "Thank you," he said abruptly, "for the flowers and everything."

Mollie looked surprised. "You're welcome."

Just like that. No explanations, no question. Some of the grimness left his expression. He smiled, and she smiled back. The defensive, arbitrary wall he'd built against her because of who she was came crashing down.

She must have felt it, too. Horrified, he watched the tears well up in her eyes, spill down her cheeks, and run into her mouth, an onslaught of them, raining down, bathing her face in salt and warm water.

Unsure of what to do, he reached out. She must have moved, too. Somewhere, at a place in between, they met, arms reaching, bodies straining, blood pounding loudly enough to drown out the words, comforting words, dangerous words, words that neither would remember when the moment was safely behind them.

"My goodness," she said at last, pulling away and laughing shakily when the worst of her outburst had passed. There were no more tears left, and her insides felt like mush. She couldn't look at him. "I'm a mess."

He lifted her chin, and the warmth in his eyes reassured her. "You're a grand lass, Mollie Tierney. But you've too much on your shoulders, and I'm to blame for it."

Mollie shook her head. "I'm worried about my mother. She seems so bitter. I've never seen her like this." Her voice broke.

"Will she be staying on with you?"

"Not for long."

He surprised her. "Perhaps you can convince her. It will give her a chance to know Luke and the girls." *And me.* The unspoken words hung between them. Perhaps if Emma came to know him better, she would leave the children with him.

Mollie's brow wrinkled. Her mother had rarely said anything positive about her life on Inishmore. Still, Sean was right. There was more to consider now. "If only she would."

Sean smiled encouragingly. The bleakness was still

there. Mollie could see it around his eyes. But there was strength, too, and determination. His sister's loss had taken its toll. But he would come about, sooner rather than later. The thought brightened her spirits. "I'll suggest it to her."

"You've held up well under all of this."

She bit her lip. "For now. I do well under pressure. My low points are still to come."

He looked down at her hands, slim, with long fingers. The urge to touch her was strong. He decided against it. "For what it's worth, I think you're the most capable female I've ever met," he said instead.

She smiled. "Thank you. I'll leave you alone now."

He nodded and watched her walk away, a woman out of the ordinary with the manners of a lady. His playwright's mind conjured up the adjectives: a hybrid, sophisticated but warm, a cross somewhere between wholesome and elegant. Once again he was conscious of a fleeting wish that she was someone else, someone other than Emma Tierney's daughter.

Patrick Tierney picked his way through the long grass and around the headstones to where his son lay buried under the verdant soil. Cut flowers, artistically arranged, lay at the foot of the fresh grave. Emma, or perhaps it was Mollie, had already come and gone. In death as in life, Danny was surrounded by women who loved him, a circumstance unfamiliar to his father.

As always, when attempting to reconcile the direction his life had taken, Emma and their last painful years together came to mind. Patrick racked his brain to analyze exactly when it had all gone wrong.

Emma was intelligent and strong-willed by nature, not an unusual combination but a difficult one for a man like Patrick, an islander steeped in the traditions of his ancestors. She thought and moved and spoke quickly—American qualities, he'd thought at first, but he later came to realize that quickness of mind was a personality trait rather than belonging to any particular nationality. When Emma disagreed with him, and she did more often than he cared to remember, she'd fought him every step of the way. Fighting with Emma was like hooking a hundred-pound tuna on twenty-pound test. He would think he had her only to feel her pull away again, take the line and run with it, while he slowly, methodically, worked to reel her in. In the beginning he managed fairly well, but after the first few years he lost her every time.

Patrick was a patient man. Few who searched the seas for schools of fish and boats in distress in the long, dark winter mornings could be anything else. In the beginning he refused to admit his marriage was over. When he could no longer deny it, he braced himself for what he knew would be their final argument, the custody of his only son. His daughter, Mollie, the child born ten years after Danny, would go with Emma.

At first Emma resisted him, claiming that a ten-year-old boy needed his mother. But when Danny flatly refused to consider leaving his father and Inishmore, Emma gave up all talk of leaving the island. But she wasn't the same. Her spirit, that impulsive wild joy that had intrigued him from the beginning, was gone.

His family and friends believed he had fallen in love with Emma for her striking beauty. They were wrong. It was the life force within her that captured his imagination. Never before had he found a woman so lit from within. The simplest of pleasures filled her with happiness. Quite simply, she expanded his heart. Patrick knew what he wanted. He wanted that joy with him forever. He wanted Emma.

For weeks after his refusal to give up Danny, she'd crept about their home like a fearful ghost, lifeless, jumpy, afraid of creaking branches and cracks of thunder. It was as if the wind and rain of that terrible winter had leeched the energy from her body. Patrick believed her restlessness was finished and what he was seeing was a grieving process, an acceptance of the real world to which she now belonged, his world.

For a while he was grateful, willing to take a shadow of the former Emma, a subdued, distant silhouette of the woman she had been. Anything, he'd thought, was better than having her leave him for good. But as the weeks became a month and then two, and the distant, netherworld quality she carried about her continued, he became anxious and then angry and, finally, resigned. She'd turned against him. He had no doubt that she thought of him as the enemy. There were moments when he feared that her mind had become unbalanced.

One morning when she looked across the table at him and said, "This is killing me," he felt nothing more than a quiet relief that it was over.

His relief had been temporary, an anesthetic, replaced by years of aching loneliness, a shortness of breath whenever he happened upon a fair-haired woman of Emma's build, and days and nights of drunken forgetfulness when he could bury himself in a world where pain did not intrude.

Hunching his shoulders, he turned, thrust his hands deep into the pockets of his jacket, and climbed the hill toward the cottage where once his family waited for him. His lungs ached more now that he was older, and the climb was harder on his back. Mabry had warned him. He shouldn't have married an outlander. The price had been more than dear.

Patrick opened the door and stepped inside. He hung his coat near the fire and added several more squares of peat to the flame. What was Emma's life like now with her rich American husband? He searched deeply within himself to see if he cared and found that it didn't matter. Emma had ceased to matter a long time ago.

Oddly, the thought depressed him even more. What had he to live for? He had no woman in his life. His only child left was an American, a stranger, who would leave when the school year was over, and his grandchildren—for an instant Patrick paused. What of his grandchildren, serious, motherly Marni, fragile Caili, and the baby, Luke? Sean O'Malley was a decent lad, despite his differences with Danny, but he'd left the island long ago. With Kerry gone, there would be no reason for him to return with the children.

Patrick was done arguing with himself. He wanted a drink. He wanted more than a drink. He wanted to step back, to bow out of his life for a bit, to forget. If only for a moment, he wanted to feel the ebbing of his pain. Reaching into the farthest corner of the sideboard, he pulled out a bottle of whiskey and poured himself a deep glass. The first swill burned his lungs and brought tears to his eyes. The second went down more smoothly. By the time he refilled his glass, the glow, the familiar glow that colored the air amber, was in full effect.

Mabry O'Farrell couldn't shake the uneasy feeling in her middle. It wasn't a pain or even an ache but the kind of emptiness one feels when hovering on the edge of wakefulness, when the mind knows something is very wrong but the fuzziness of sleep masks the source. Mabry knew it would come to her in time. She would wait and let fate work its own magic on the future.

Meanwhile she would visit Patrick. He had a penchant for soda bread as only she could make it. A pint of her blackberry jelly and a pat of sweet butter would round out their tea.

The day was a fine one, clear and cold but sunny, with a crispness that stung the delicate tissue lining the inside of her nose. Patrick's cottage looked unusually desolate. Although it was mid-afternoon, the window shades were already pulled against the night and no welcoming curl of chimney smoke drifted across the sky. Mabry frowned. Perhaps he wasn't home. But there was his trap in the shed and Brownie chewing on good limestone grass behind it.

She tapped on the door. No answer. She tapped again and this time nudged the door open. He wouldn't mind if he came upon her halfway inside like a thief, but he would mind a great deal less if he was passed out somewhere with a stroke and she happened to find him in time to save his life.

"Patrick." His hat and walking staff were in their usual places. She walked into the sitting room. "Patrick?"

The smell of thick, uncirculated air hit her immediately. She wrinkled her nose. Jesus, Mary, and Joseph, why didn't the man open a window? She pushed aside the curtains, struggled with the sash, and lifted the window, drawing in deep gulps of ocean-fresh air. Reluctantly, she turned back to the stuffy room. Despite the airlessness, it was cold, the fire long dead. Summoning her resolve, Mabry walked through the sitting room, down the miniature hallway into the first bedroom. Patrick lay stretched out on top of the bed, fully clothed, an empty quart of whiskey beside him. Just out of reach was another, barely touched.

Her mouth twisted with pity. Poor man. His body was failing him. She could remember a time when he could empty more than two without passing out. But that was years ago before his self-imposed dry spell of the last decade.

Gently, she pressed her fingers against the inside of his wrist and then at his throat. His pulse was strong. She relaxed. It would take more than a bottle to finish Patrick Tierney. This time she wouldn't wake him. Neither would she search the house for more spirits. She'd lived long enough to know that no woman could stop a man from drinking, not unless he wanted it for himself. After draping a blanket over him, she walked back to the sitting room, found the fire starter and matches, and banked the fire with turf from a wicker basket. She waited long enough for the flame to burn steadily and then closed the door behind her.

Her pace down the hill was filled with purpose. Mollie Tierney had two parents on Inishmore, and the one she was attending at the moment needed her considerably less than the one Mabry had just left sleeping it off in an icy bedroom.

Mollie lifted the hair off her neck, pulled the sides away from her face, and secured the thick mass with a claw clip. Then she looked in the mirror and winced. A week of sleepless nights had taken its toll. Her eyes were rimmed with red, and the shadows beneath looked like giant purple bruises against her skin. She needed a full eight hours of sleep and a decent meal.

She hesitated at the foot of the stairs. Directly above her she could see the door to her mother's room. It was closed. Sighing gratefully, she walked into the kitchen, turned on the kettle, and began rummaging through the refrigerator. A soft knock on the back door startled her. It was three o'clock in the afternoon. Every Irish family on Inishmore would be hungry for their tea.

Through the cut glass, Mollie saw the outline of a woman's figure, small, dressed in black with a colorful shawl around her head, the style worn on Inishmore a century ago. Mabry O'Farrell. She opened the door and stepped aside. "Come in. I was just about to have something to eat. Will you join me?"

Mabry smiled. "Just like your da, a welcome like that. I've eaten, but a cup of tea will do nicely."

The kettle whistled. Mollie felt the old woman's eyes on her as she scalded the pot, added tea leaves, and filled the water. Not until she carried the tray to the table and sat down across from her did Mabry speak.

"Your da is in a bit of trouble, lass." She held up her hand. "Don't get up. It will be more time than we'll take to finish our tea before he knows you again."

"What are you saying?"

"This last week has been a difficult one for him."

"Really? That surprises me."

"Aye." Mabry nodded her head. "To you and your mother and Sean and the children he's been well enough. But he's not strong, and the effort has taken the will out of him."

Mollie felt sick to her stomach. Her hand shook as she lifted the tea cup and sipped the cooling liquid. "What's the matter with him?"

"He drinks," Mabry replied simply, "and when he starts he doesn't stop."

Mollie stared into her cup. "Why are you telling me this?"

"You're his daughter, lass, the only child he has left. You can help him."

The toilet flushed upstairs, followed by the sound of footsteps and the gentle creaking of the mattress springs. Emma was back in bed. She'd slept nearly six hours already. Mollie hoped it was only jet lag and that her mother wasn't slipping into a depression. She hadn't called Ward yet for a completely selfish reason. She didn't want him taking her mother home. "I didn't need this right now," Mollie said.

"He has no one else."

Mollie shook her head. "He didn't have me, either, not for twenty-eight years until I came back to find him."

"He had his reasons."

"Did he? Are there reasons enough to eliminate your child from your life?"

"Your mother was the one who left," Mabry reminded her.

"People divorce each other, not their children."

"He needs you."

"So does everyone else. Besides, what am I supposed to do?"

"You're his daughter," Mabry repeated.

Tears boiled beneath Mollie's eyelids. It was all too much, Ward eight thousand miles away, her mother behaving strangely, the sleepless nights and the guilt. Above all, the guilt, enough of it to burn a hole in her stomach. Her life had been so different from Danny's. "There's my mother," she whispered, "and Caili and Marni and the baby and Sean—" She choked. "I can't be everything to all of them."

Mabry's eyes gentled. She reached over and squeezed Mollie's hand. "Poor little lass. You've lost your chance to know your family, haven't you?"

She didn't know the half of it. But maybe she didn't have to. The understanding in the old woman's voice undid her, and the dam of pain gathering in Mollie's chest broke. Burying her face in her arms, she wept. Mabry was beside her, comforting arms gathering her close, a soothing voice murmuring words she didn't understand, erasing the worst of the ache, leveling the mountain of responsibility until the path seemed smoother again. Laughing shakily, Mollie lifted her head. Pulling a napkin from the holder in the middle of the table, she blew her nose. "I'm sorry."

Mabry smiled. "You're a right one, Mollie Tierney."

"I still haven't the slightest idea of how to go about rescuing my father."

"It will come to you."

"When?"

"Don't be a stranger to him, Mollie. Include him in your life and in his grandchildren's lives. Sean won't think of that."

"This is going to take time, isn't it?"

Mabry smiled approvingly. "Clever lass."

Somehow it was natural to say what was on her mind. "What about my mother?"

"She'll come about. Emma Tierney has spirit. That's plain to all who know her."

Mollie wondered if Mabry had her mother mixed up with someone else. Emma was kind and loving and generous, a perfect wife and gentle parent. But rarely did she have a strong opinion on anything. If Mabry was right, somewhere in the last twenty-eight years, her mother had undergone a complete personality change. Who was the real Emma Reddington, and how did Mollie go about finding her now when she needed her desperately?

Mollie saw the crack of light beneath her mother's bedroom door. "Mom," she called out, knocking softly. "Are you awake?"

"Come in, Mollie. I'm not sleeping."

Mollie opened the door. Emma was sitting up in bed, holding a book against her chest. She smiled and patted the space beside her.

Sighing gratefully, Mollie stretched out beside her mother.

Emma smoothed her daughter's hair back away from her cheek. "What's on your mind?"

"I was thinking about the men I've dated," she began.

"Anyone in particular?"

"Garrett Michaels. A year ago I was convinced that he was the one."

"And now?"

"Absolutely not."

"Any particular reason?"

Mollie rubbed the back of her neck. She could picture Garrett in his starkly modern study, portable phone attached to his ear, hair and nails perfectly groomed, a creamy cashmere sweater knotted around his shoulders, Armani loafers and slacks that broke at the tip of the shoe, slacks that had never come off a rack. What had she ever seen in him? He'd known her for four years, but he was a stranger. "His dreams were different from mine. They made me nervous. He wanted money, nice cars, a boat, early retirement."

"What's your dream, Mollie?"

She rubbed her arms. *Tired* wasn't the right word for the ache in her neck and the heavy weight of her eyelids. "I don't have a dream," she said slowly. "I've never had one."

"Does that bother you?"

She nodded. "It bothers me that I don't want anything enough to fight and sweat and sacrifice for it. I want that. I need to know I want something that much."

Emma leaned over and kissed her daughter's cheek. "I wouldn't worry too much. Maybe you just haven't found it yet."

"Is that a polite way of telling me I'm being overly serious?"

"In a way."

Mollie laughed and sat up. "I think I'll go to bed."

"Good night, love."

"Good night."

Emma turned out the light and stared at the ceiling. Garrett Michaels had never impressed her. He was too smooth, too manicured, and too sure of Mollie. A man like that needed a full bath every morning and night and a valet to manage his luggage. His sweaters alone cost what a fisherman on Inishmore earned in a week. Not that money alone damned a man. Ward had money. The difference was in what he did with it.

Living in an island community with the real world an hour's boat ride away made one realize how connected everyone was to others around him. John Murphy couldn't sink his boat without a dozen men losing their living. Reilley's fishmarket, Tierney's sweater mill, and O'Flaherty's pub were affected right along with them. When the weather was bad and the ferry down, if a family needed milk or flour, someone was always there to lend a hand. The bank was only open on Wednesdays, but when the rain came sideways in sheets as sharp and thick as glass and those who lived on the far side of the island had no cash and couldn't manage the journey, there were places set at fuller tables, and no man or woman ever went without a pint when the urge came over them.

Patrick had never needed money. He couldn't understand a man who worked only for the house and cars it would bring him. And a boat, for Christ's sake. Emma couldn't help smiling. She could still hear his voice. Everyone had a boat. Why did a man need money for a boat? As for retirement, in those long-ago days, Patrick couldn't imagine not working, not facing the day with a sense of purpose, sharing a mug of tea with the fishermen, elated when the catch was good, matter-of-fact when it was not.

Garrett Michaels couldn't be more than thirty, and already he was wishing his life away.

It was her daughter who puzzled her. What was Mollie looking for, this girl who had never wanted for anything, a girl lovely enough to make a man look up from the table where he was eating and stop chewing? What was missing in her world of wealth and luxury and sophistication that turned out a woman like Mollie who longed for something more but couldn't name it?

10

*P*atrick Tierney didn't answer the first time Mollie knocked, or the second. The door was unlocked. She opened it and stepped into the kitchen. Everything looked the same, neat, well cared for, the rag rug on the floor, counters clear, appliances in place. She smelled the turf and walked into the sitting room. Someone had recently stoked the fire. Square pieces of peat glowed cheerily, taking the chill from the air. No one here, either.

Mollie hesitated. It was one thing to walk into a man's kitchen and living room, but invading his bedroom was something else. Still, she was here. Pitching her voice so she wouldn't startle him from sleep, she called out, "Hello, is anyone here?"

No answer. Gathering her nerve, she walked down the hall and peeked into the bedroom. He sat on the edge of the bed, legs apart, head in his hands. Mollie flushed and stepped back, away from the door. "I'm sorry," she stammered from a safe place in the hallway. "I didn't know, I thought—"

Patrick appeared in the doorway, an unsteady Patrick who held on to the frame for support. "What did you think?"

Mollie said nothing.

"Why are you here, lass?"

"I wanted to see if you were all right."

"I was right enough the last time you saw me."

"Mabry said—"

With effort, Patrick removed his hand from the jamb. "Mabry is an interfering old woman." Slowly, he moved past her. She followed him through the sitting room into the kitchen and watched his hands shake as he struck a match and held it to the pilot of a burner on the old cast-iron stove. The flame caught. He filled the kettle, sat down on the wooden bench beside the table, and stared at her. "You're quiet this afternoon." He looked out the window. "It is still afternoon, isn't it?"

"What's the matter with you!" Mollie burst out. "You've never done this before. Why now?"

He frowned, winced, and rubbed his temple. "Done what, lass? Can't a man have a drink now and then?"

In another minute Mollie would be in tears. She couldn't deal with this. This wasn't the reasonable man she thought was her father. "I'll be going now. I just wanted to be sure you were all right." Her voice cracked. She turned away toward the door.

Suddenly he was beside her, vestiges of the Patrick Tierney she knew in his voice. "Don't be losing sleep over me, lass. You've enough on your plate."

His gentleness undid her. Leaning against the door, the tears came, silently sliding down her face. She felt an awkward hand on her shoulder.

"Please, don't cry, Mollie." He sounded desperate now. "It's just a slip. One slip never buried a man. Don't cry, love."

She breathed deeply and wiped her face with the back of her hand. He'd left her. Now he was back, tucking something soft and white into her curled palm, a handkerchief, monogrammed with the letters PT. Gratefully, she wiped her face, blew her nose, and turned to face him. The question needed asking. She had to know. "Do you slip often?"

Behind his eyes she saw his mind sort through different answers, discarding them one by one. Minutes passed. Finally he shrugged. "We've no standard to measure by. To you, it might be often. I've cut back over the years."

"Are you an alcoholic?"

The traces of a smile turned up the corners of his mouth. "You Americans, always wanting to label someone."

She persisted. "Do you drink when something bothers you?"

"Aye, sometimes," he admitted. "But I've been known to tip a pint or two to celebrate as well."

Questions crowded her brain, personal, demanding questions that transcended all semblance of good manners. Instinct told her to leave them, that no good would come of an unprepared interrogation of a man who'd shut her out of his life for twenty-eight years.

She sighed and straightened her shoulders. "Come tomorrow for breakfast. The children will be there."

He hesitated. "What of your mother?"

Mollie bit her lip. What would her mother say to the

regular presence of Patrick Tierney in their lives? "I came here to get to know my family. You're my family. She knows that."

He smiled, and the warmth of it wrapped around her heart. Emma would have to adjust.

"Thank you," he said. "I'll be there."

Desperate for a slice of normalcy, for people going about their ordinary lives on an ordinary Saturday, unfettered by tragedy, Mollie walked into town. Kathleen McVeigh stood on the front steps of her cafe, a broom in her hand, surveying the tide.

Mollie managed a smile. "Are you open, Mrs. McVeigh?"

The woman sighed. "Aye, lass, if you can call it that. I'll go mad if I don't stay busy."

"Is something wrong?"

"The boats are past due. Not long," she added hastily, "but long enough to make me anxious." Wielding the broom like a wand, she shook it at Mollie. "You don't need to hear all this. Come in, lass. I've soup this afternoon and fresh bread." She waved at someone on the other side of the street. "Good afternoon, Sean," she called out. "Your mother stopped by this mornin' with the children. She tells me you're in need of a meal. Come and keep Mollie company."

The band that squeezed Mollie's chest whenever Sean O'Malley crossed her path began its familiar tightening. Attempting a smile, Mollie turned to greet him.

"Hello, Mollie."

"Sean."

"Will you have a bite to eat with me?"

"Where are Luke and the girls?"

"With my mother. I've work yet to do."

Today was not a good day for pretense. Opening her mouth to say she couldn't stay, she happened to glance at his hands, hanging loose and relaxed at his sides. Hands told a great deal about a person. Sean O'Malley was managing. Desperately, she wanted to know his secret. "What kind of soup is it, Mrs. McVeigh?"

"Turnip leek with good-sized chunks of lamb."

Sean followed her into the restaurant. Mollie felt his hand move to her waist and lightly guide her to the small table near the window. Even without sunlight, the harsh winter beauty of the shoreline tore at her heart.

"Lovely, isn't it?"

She nodded. "Spectacular."

Kathleen bustled back and forth with silver, bowls of steaming soup, rough warm bread, and rounds of dewy butter. "I've a bit of ale on hand if you prefer it," she said when the meal was set before them.

"Tea will do for me, Kathleen." Sean nodded at Mollie. "What will you have, lass?"

"The same." She waited for Kathleen to move away, stirred her soup, lifted a spoonful to her lips, and set it down again. "You don't drink much, do you?"

"I've been known to tip a few now and then when the occasion warrants, but not when I've work to do."

"What kind of occasion?" She was finding it hard to look at him.

Across the table she felt his eyes on her face, blue, measured.

"Weddings, *cruínnius*," he said casually, "a celebration where a toast is in order."

The scene at the cemetery came back to her. She'd cried in his arms. Surely she could ask him anything. "What about now? Do you feel like a drink now?"

"I've writing to do, Mollie," he said patiently, as if he hadn't explained once already. "I can't risk an error, and alcohol relaxes a man's mind." He reached across the table and lifted her chin, forcing her to look at him. "What's troubling you?"

Her mouth worked. Why was it so hard to admit? He'd known Patrick Tierney forever. "My father—" She stopped.

Kathleen returned with tea, took a shrewd, observing look at Mollie's face, and wisely left them alone.

Sean's eyes narrowed. Taking over, he poured milk and added a spoonful of sugar to Mollie's tea. "What has Patrick done now?"

She shook her head, lifted the cup to her lips, and gulped the steaming brew. Her tongue burned. Hastily she lifted the ice water to her lips. In control once again, she said, "He's done nothing wrong, really."

"You're near tears. Come now, out with it."

Again she shook her head. Patrick was her father. She wouldn't gossip behind his back.

"Is he drinking again?"

The sudden color in her cheeks betrayed her. She fixed her eyes on the sugar bowl. "Mabry told me the first day, but I didn't believe it. There were no signs, until now."

Sean sighed. "There are so many things you don't know, and most of it you wouldn't understand, you with your American good sense and that air of entitlement all of you bring with you."

Hurt and anger warred within her. Anger won. "Why don't you try telling me? Quite possibly my American mind will figure it out."

He grinned, and suddenly it was impossible to be angry anymore. "Don't get your dander up. It was a compliment." He nodded at her stew. "Finish up, and we'll walk for a bit."

Leaving a five-punt note on the table, Sean called out a farewell to Kathleen and followed Mollie out the door. Tucking her hand in his arm, he led her past the bicycle rental shop, the convenience store that served as a post office, and the bank with the sign that said "Open on Wednesday," to a narrow path that led straight toward the cliffs.

"I'm not wearing hiking boots."

"The path is fairly dry. It's not a difficult climb, and the view is worth it." He smiled down at her and tightened his hold on her arm. "Trust me. I won't let you slip."

She said something. She must have. If only she knew what it was. She hoped it was coherent and appropriate. She pulled her hand away. A strange self-consciousness spread through her. "I won't slip, but the path is too narrow for both of us. I'll follow you."

Apparently unaffected by a similar emotion, he agreed and moved ahead. Mollie waited until he was several paces away before following. Her senses were unusually sharp. With heightened fascination she was aware of the smooth length of his stride as he climbed the hill, the bunch of muscles under his loose corduroy trousers, the easy, confident swing of his arms, and the faint gleam of red where the late-afternoon sun touched his dark hair.

Once more the tears welled, stinging her eyelids, already sensitive from days of spontaneous, unexplained weeping. Pressing her fingers against her closed eyes, she forced them back and hurried after Sean. Ireland wasn't what she'd expected. Everything she'd envisioned had fallen to pieces. There would be no happy family reunion, no welcoming a daughter lost and now regained. Danny and Kerry were dead, and her father— She would never have worried about her father's drinking if she hadn't come here. She pushed the thought away. She would think about Patrick's problem later. A nagging worry formed in her mind. What if she'd taken on too much? She could go home. Her mother wouldn't blame her. In fact she might even be relieved. The strange lethargy that had taken hold of Emma might reverse itself once she was back in California.

"Are you managing, lass?" Sean called back to her. "We're nearly there."

The wind whipped her hair loose. She tugged the stray strands away from her mouth and increased her pace. "I'm fine."

He waited until she caught up, took another long measured look at her face, and frowned. "You're fairly undone, aren't you?" he asked gently. "Shall I take you home?"

"No." The word came out too quickly. She bit her lip and explained. "I don't want to go back just yet."

He nodded and once again reached for her hand. "The path narrows from here. It's called *Bothar na gCread*, the road of the crags. Hold on, and we'll be through in a bit."

The path became a stony track that wound and wove

its way up through a network of stone-walled fields. Bindweed, a native grass, crept across the limestone, and the remains of summer's blackberry bushes lay dormant against gray rock. Looming above them was Dun Aengus fort. He led her past the ancient Viking landmark, around the sound to a stone-spattered cliff. The wind was vicious now. Mollie narrowed her eyes to tiny slits, gave herself up entirely to Sean's direction, and forced herself to push forward against the resistance. Suddenly, he stopped and motioned for her to follow him around a low stone wall.

She looked down and swallowed. Part of the cliff had fallen away, and one side of the path was too exposed for comfort. Sean's head appeared above the wall. He grinned and held out his hand. "Throw your heart over, lass. No one's fallen in yet."

Grasping his hand, she was around the wall in an instant and sighed with relief. The roaring wind had completely disappeared. Rocks, covered with soft green moss were arranged, couchlike, with a spectacular view of a large rectangular hole in a flat terrace below the cliffs. It looked like a swimming pool. "What is it?" she breathed.

"*Poll na bPeist*, the worm hole."

"How did it get here?"

"It's connected to the sea by an underground passage," Sean explained. "The currents surge at high tide to meet the water pouring in over the top. As the tide ebbs, the water inside swirls and boils. Amazing, isn't it?"

"Incredible. It looks like a giant sea monster trapped inside."

He laughed and pulled her down on the rock beside

him. "You've an imagination, haven't you? Rest a bit and feast your eyes. There isn't another place like it."

She looked at him curiously. "Have you traveled much?"

He laced his fingers behind his head and leaned back, closing his eyes. "I've never seen America, but I've been through most of Europe and parts of Asia and Australia."

"Did Kerry go with you?"

He shook his head. "Kerry never wanted to leave the island."

"Do you enjoy traveling?"

He thought a minute. "I do, actually, although it's good to come home."

Again the questions begged to be asked. Again instinct told her to leave them for now.

Streaky orange clouds tinted with black hung near the horizon. The Atlantic, peaceful for a change, except for the great boiling hole below them, lapped at the rock-strewn shoreline. Minutes passed. Mollie closed her eyes. Slowly, by degrees, the ache in her heart lessened.

His voice, lilting, reverent, broke the silence. "My family has lived here forever."

She turned her head and looked down at him resting comfortably beside her. "Nothing is forever."

His eyebrow quirked. "Are you in the mood for a story?"

Mollie smiled. "Always."

With his native brio thicker than usual, he began. "Because of its isolation, Inishmore maintained not only a physical separation from the rest of the island but an economic one. The ruling tribe, the O'Flahertys, developed a lucrative trade between Inishmore, Connemara, and the continent. By the fourteenth century, Connemara and Inishmore with it had become nearly an autonomous kingdom completely free of colonial interference. The O'Flahertys, the O'Malleys, and the Burkes, all island families, had their own fleets of ships and traded regularly with Flanders, Portugal, Spain, and France, while Galway City, the city of the tribes, produced its own governing body and mint.

"This opulence did not escape the notice of Elizabeth, who used brute savagery to squash the region's independence. There arose an island hero, Granuaile O'Malley, the fey pirate queen. Through marriage she united the Burkes, the O'Flahertys, and the O'Malleys to create a united force against the invaders. She managed quite well for many years."

He was silent for a long time. Mollie thought he'd finished, but then he spoke again. "Granuaile wanted to pull away, to have nothing to do with Elizabeth and her ships and wars. But the pull of progress was too strong. She died, a broken woman, on Clare Island."

The words were simple, the moral blatantly obvious. It wasn't a powerful story. But the telling more than the content told her a great deal of the teller. Sean O'Malley was unmistakably Irish, with his sympathy for human suffering, his love of the land and sea, and that uniquely Irish understanding that words are the mightiest weapon of all in their everlasting quarrel with destiny.

He lay there beside her, relaxed, unmoving. She wanted to touch him, the bones of his face, the tips of his fingers. Suddenly she no longer cared if it was safe to ask. "Why did you bring me here?"

She heard the slight, nearly imperceptible change in

his breathing. "Patrick isn't a demon, Mollie," he said carefully. "He's a man who's had more difficulties than most."

"Yours are every bit as hard, and I don't see you drowning yourself in alcohol."

"Times have changed, lass. In Patrick's day it was common for a man to find his solace at the pub or in the confessional."

Again the despised tears rose in her throat. She stared out to sea.

"If you feel you can't be a daughter to him, at least be a friend. You've nothing to lose and more than a little to gain." His hand was on her shoulder, turning her toward him. "Don't cry, Mollie." His voice held traces of humor. "And here I thought you weren't a woman for tears. There's no judgment in what I said."

Light flashed across the sky. Seconds later thunder cracked. Heavy drops of rain fell on her head, her face and arms. Below, the sea boiled threateningly. Sean sat up, scooted back under a sheltering rock, and motioned to the spot beside him. "There's room enough."

Suddenly the thought of touching him terrified her.

It must have shown in her face. Slowly, gently, in the voice he used with Caili, he attempted to reassure her. "The clouds are isolated, Mollie. The storm won't last long. There's plenty of room for both of us to sit here comfortably."

He was unbelievably kind, and she was a fool. If she didn't act soon he would think so, too. Scrambling up beside him, she sat down, pulled her legs up, and wrapped both arms around them.

Again lightning streaked, closer this time. Thunder

cracked. The rain poured down in torrents. Sean had shifted to one side, avoiding her completely. His right shoulder and part of his leg were drenched. Conscience-stricken, Mollie pulled at the sleeve of his jacket. "Move over," she said. "I won't attack you."

He laughed and shifted out of the wet. His left side was flush against her right. "Is that what your panic was all about? I thought you were worried it might go the other way around."

She didn't answer. She couldn't. What was there to say except, this time, he'd gotten it completely wrong?

11

𝓜ollie looked out over the expectant faces of her students. They were amazingly alike, twenty of them, all between five and ten years old, fair-skinned with large light eyes and the sharp, fine features typical of islanders. But it was more than coloring and bone structure that identified them as belonging to the same race. It was something behind the eyes, a quality of patience or, better yet, endurance. Mollie could see it in the lines of their young unformed jaws, in the stillness of their hands and feet as they sat quietly at the wooden desks waiting for her to speak or act, accepting whatever would follow.

That undefinable quality was there in Marni's face staring up at her from the middle row and in Caili's down in front, young as she was. They were her nieces, her brother's children, her mother's grandchildren. They shared her blood, and yet they were separate from her, more like the children around them than they would ever be like her.

Mollie felt her difference. Because of her American

mother she was new blood. For the first time she realized the vastness of what her mother had attempted and failed to overcome.

Mollie cleared her throat and smiled. "Good morning, boys and girls."

"Good morning," they chanted in unison, not a smile or a change of expression among them. It always began this way. Not until mid-morning would she coax a glimmer of a smile from the youngest ones. Eventually, near dismissal time, they would all come around. The following day she would start all over again.

The morning passed quickly. Beginning with the five-year-olds and moving up, Mollie went from one level to the next, explaining assignments, answering questions, writing directions on the chalkboard. The children were attentive and bright. Even the smallest ones showed a remarkable ability to stay on task without fidgeting.

At recess time she pulled on her sweater and followed the children outside. She watched Alice Duncan leave her classroom and crossed the grass to join her. Alice was a wonderful mentor. With her short, no-nonsense hair, sturdy legs, and comfortable shoes, her calling was obvious even to those who didn't know her. Her answers and advice had helped Mollie enormously over the last few hectic weeks.

"How are you getting on?"

Mollie's face lit up. "Beautifully. The children are wonderful. I wonder how long they'll be on their best behavior."

Alice laughed. "You sound experienced. I imagine children are the same the world over." She shrugged, and her smile faded. "You'll have a few challenges as the year moves on but nothing unmanageable. People here take education very seriously. They know it's the only way out for those who want to leave, and most don't stay. Inishmore has had a consistent population for decades. There's no greater nightmare for a parent than to have a child who wants to leave and isn't able to because he can't do anything. That leads to other problems, unemployment, alcoholism, abuse. We've seen it all. You'll have no argument with the parents when it comes to homework and discipline. They all want the university for their children."

"Is that realistic?"

Alice hesitated. "You'll lose a few, Mollie. We always do, and that's the heartbreak. But for the most part, I believe that it is realistic. There's no reason anyone with normal intelligence can't do what he wants if he's willing to work at it." She thrust her hands into the pockets of her jacket. "What do you think?"

"Absolutely." Mollie nodded her head emphatically. "In California, community colleges are nearly free of charge. Everyone goes, but not everyone finishes. There are classes for all ability levels. Those who don't finish are the ones who don't attend."

"So, we agree. I'd not expected that."

Mollie turned to look closely at the woman beside her. Alice stood facing the schoolyard and the white-capped sea, a small, fierce woman, gruff but kind, a woman who groomed herself sensibly, modestly, a woman who had deliberately eradicated all that was feminine about her. It occurred to Mollie that she knew very little about Alice Duncan. "Are you a native of the island?" she asked.

Long seconds passed before Alice answered. "No," she said reluctantly, as if the answer was one she would rather not have given. "I'm not a native, but I may as well be. I've lived on Inishmore for thirty-five years, longer than anywhere else."

Mollie counted backward. Thirty-five years. Her eyes widened. "Did you know my mother, Alice?"

The older woman continued to stare out at the sea, the children apparently forgotten. "Not really," she said slowly. "No more than to look at her. Emma Tierney was something to look at." She glanced at Mollie. "You're very like her, you know." Her mouth turned down. "It was your father I knew. But that's ancient history."

"I don't think I understand."

"There's no reason you should." Alice looked at her watch. "Recess is over. I'll ring the bell."

Mollie gazed thoughtfully at the older woman's retreating figure.

After slipping the last batch of essays into her tote bag, Mollie straightened a desk, pushed two chairs back into place, and stepped outside to lock the door.

"It's almost dark," said a small voice behind her. "I've been waiting for you." Caili sat on top of the playground slide, one hand holding on for balance, the other wrapped around something edible judging from the condition of her mouth.

Mollie smiled and held out her free hand. "If I'd known you were waiting I would have come out earlier. Is there something you needed?"

Caili slipped her sticky fingers into Mollie's hand and shook her head. "I wanted to eat cheese and bread with you and Grandma Emma again." She cocked her head and looked inquiringly at her aunt. "May I?"

"Of course you may, but you'll need to ask your Uncle Sean."

"We're staying with Mrs. Harris until he comes for us. She won't mind," Caili replied confidently.

"We'll ask her anyway, and we'll also ask Marni if she would like to come."

Mrs. Harris was preparing the evening meal for her family. Not only was she relieved to be free of the girls, but she also prevailed upon Mollie to keep Luke as well.

"My son will give you a lift home in the trap with the wee ones," she said. "I'll ring Sean and tell him where the children are." She shooed them out the door.

Once again Mollie found herself in the back of a pony cart with a blanket tucked around her legs. Only this time two small girls were wedged in beside her and she held a baby in her arms. She looked down at Luke contentedly chewing his fist. She loved the smell and feel of him and the plump softness of his baby skin.

"He's hungry," Marni said matter-of-factly.

"Really? How do you know?" Mollie asked.

"He's eating his hands. He always does that when he wants food."

"What shall we feed him? I don't think bread and cheese will do."

"There's baby formula in his bag," said Marni. "Uncle Sean packed it in case he's late coming to fetch us."

Already they'd established a routine without their mother. "Well, then," said Mollie bracingly, "I'll feed him first and then the rest of us will eat together."

"We can help," Caili said, slipping her hand through

Mollie's arm. "We always help at home. Marni fixes food, and I lay the table."

"This time remember that forks go with the napkins on the left," Marni admonished her. "You always forget."

"I don't."

"You do."

"I don't."

"Never mind," Mollie broke in. "I'm sure we'll all remember everything we're supposed to." She looked anxiously at Luke. He smiled gummily at her, and she relaxed. Luke's hunger pangs had not yet reached a level of emergency.

"Sometimes Luke spits his food out," Caili offered, "but not when he's really hungry. You'll have to change his diaper first. Then when he goes to bed you have to change it again."

Mollie laughed. "I'll make sure and do that, but won't your uncle be back before then?"

"He will." Marni nodded confidently. "But sometimes he forgets to look at the time." She looked at her aunt. "You have lots of rooms, more than we have."

It wasn't exactly a subtle request. Mollie's heart warmed toward her motherly little niece. "I have plenty of extra rooms, sweetheart. I'd be happy to have you all spend the night."

"How old are you, Aunt Mollie?" Marni asked unexpectedly.

Mollie considered her answer. "Twenty years older than you are," she said, wondering if the little girl would be stumped over the math.

The child thought for a minute. "Twenty-eight is old not to be married." Yawning, she rested her head against

Mollie's shoulder. "Why aren't you married, Aunt Mollie?"

The child's weight was comfortably warm against her side. The driver, a boy of seventeen or so, was silent, his head turned away toward the encroaching darkness.

"In America it isn't unusual to be my age and unmarried, not anymore."

"You're very pretty," the child observed. "Didn't anybody ever want to marry you?"

Mollie laughed, a lovely clear sound that brought smiles to the lips of both little girls. "No one that I wanted to marry."

"Why not?" This time Caili asked the question.

Mollie bit her lip. How much truth was too much? "Marriage is very important," she said carefully. "Before people decide to spend the rest of their lives together, they should be very sure they won't change their minds."

The answer appeared to satisfy the girls. Luke changed fists and began to chew in earnest. A small growling sound came from the back of his throat.

"We're nearly there, Miss," the Harris boy announced, breaking his silence.

"Thank you," replied Mollie. "Would you like to come in for something before you drive home?"

He pulled back on the reins, jumped down, and, one at a time, swung the girls to the ground before helping Mollie. "No, thank you, Miss Tierney. Mam will have my tea ready. I don't want to be late."

In the kitchen Mollie found Luke's bottle and placed it in the microwave on a low setting. Emma, delighted with the unexpected company, changed his diaper while Caili set the table and Marni sliced bread.

There was something fulfilling about completing homey tasks in the cozy kitchen light with the two little girls. Kerry O'Malley had done a wonderful job with her daughters. The girls were bright, enthusiastic, and unspoiled. There was a great deal to be said for a mother with that kind of influence.

Settling into a corner of the couch to give Luke his bottle, Emma waved Mollie away. "You go ahead and eat with the girls," she said. "I'll manage here."

Marni had poured the tea, set out bread and butter and sliced tomatoes. A delicious smell came from the crockpot Mollie had filled that morning. She ladled three servings into bowls and carried them to the table. Just as she was about to take her seat, a loud knock sounded at the kitchen door.

"Start eating, girls," she said, moving quickly to the door. Before the knock sounded again, she opened it. Sean O'Malley stood on the steps. A lock of dark hair fell across his forehead. His eyes were very blue in the porchlight, and on his face was an expression Mollie couldn't read.

"I understand you have my children with you," he said in formal tones.

His children? Mollie nodded. "We were just about to eat. Will you join us?"

"It's late. I don't want to put you out."

Mollie reached for his hand and pulled him inside. "For heaven's sake, Sean, come inside. Luke is nearly asleep, and the girls have helped with dinner. We were just about to eat. It isn't any trouble to set another place. I'm happy to have the company."

She watched the tension leave his chest first, then his

jaw, and finally his eyes. The first glimmering of a smile appeared on his lips. "All right then, since you've put it that way, it wouldn't be polite to refuse, would it?"

Her own smile appeared. "No, it wouldn't."

He hung his coat up, sat down, and rested a hand first on Caili's head and then on Marni's. "How are my girls?"

"Are you eating with us, Uncle Sean?" Marni asked.

Sean's eyes met Mollie's across the table. "I've been invited. Accepting seemed the proper thing to do."

Marni smiled and applied herself to her stew. Caili stared down at her plate, frowning.

Sean lifted her chin. "Why the glum face, lass?"

"I don't want to go home. Aunt Mollie said there were rooms enough for us to stay."

Mollie set a bowl of stew down in front of Sean. "That was only if your uncle had to work late."

"I still want to stay."

"Your aunt has a busy day tomorrow," Sean explained. "She can't be caring for you and preparing for school at the same time."

"She won't have to care for me," Caili argued. "I'll be sleeping."

"Then it won't matter where you are," Sean replied reasonably. "Eat your supper, Caili. I'm sure your Aunt Mollie has given you schoolwork to do."

"We finished it," Marni said.

Sean was clearly exasperated.

Mollie stepped in. "We've all had a busy day. I'd love to have you spend the night the next time your Uncle Sean has to work late. We'll tell Mrs. Harris, and you can come directly home with me, all of you. How will that be?"

Caili's eyes brightened. "Truly, Aunt Mollie?"

A rush of love for this small green-eyed girl, so powerful it nearly lifted her from the chair, swept through Mollie. "Truly, darling," she promised. "I won't forget."

Sean sent her a grateful look. Later, after saying good night to Emma, bundling Luke against the cold, and buttoning up his nieces' jackets, he thanked Mollie once again. "It was kind of you to take them like this. I hope it wasn't too much of a burden."

"Hardly," Mollie answered simply. "I've waited all my life to have a family. It's lonely being an only child."

He studied her carefully, gauging the sincerity of her response. "I suppose it might be. However, I'm sure you never wished to have a family thrust upon you quite so precipitously."

Mollie nodded toward the children waiting patiently at the end of the driveway. "It isn't that they'd rather be with me, you know. They miss their mother."

Sean glanced at his nieces, and his mouth softened. "I know that. Thank you for helping us through this."

She felt the connection between them, like an invisible thread, strong and resilient enough to withstand the weight of her probe. She braved the question. "You loved your sister very much, didn't you?"

"Aye. That I did."

"Why did you leave the island? Weren't you happy here?"

At first he looked surprised. Then his eyes narrowed. "Happy? Is that what you think is important, Mollie Tierney?" His mouth twisted into the ghost of a smile. "Who told you that life is supposed to be happy? It's enough that we're here. The odds against that alone are nearly insurmountable. Shouldn't a man accept a bit of unhappiness in the exchange? Is anyone ever happy for more than a minute or two?"

She stared at him, astonished. It was such a simple question, no more than making small talk. Obviously she'd pushed a button.

Without waiting for her reply, he turned, carrying the baby, and walked away through the night.

Mollie released the breath she held. Sean O'Malley was suffering, and for some reason it was particularly painful for her to see it.

12

Sean finished reading the report he'd photocopied and frowned. For a long time now he'd toyed with the idea of writing a play set on his native island, something along the lines of Robert O'Flaherty's *Man of Aran*, more modern, of course, with the same stoicism, a bit of romance, and the inevitable twist of Irish humor. His mouth tightened into a grim line. He hadn't counted on dredging up the depressing statistics of life on an island where the sole industry outside the summer tourist season was fishing.

Fish counts were lower this year than last and some varieties close to the blackout the island people dreaded. With emigration to England, Canada, and America, fewer and fewer fishing boats were in competition every year. Normally the take would be better. But the tiny curraghs of the solitary fisherman were no match for the commercial vessels from the mainland, from Scotland and England. Thousands of pounds of fish were harvested from the big boats weekly. Eventually they depleted the waters, leaving the smaller boats dry-docked, men unemployed, and island families on the dole without a good portion of their protein for the year.

He'd seen it all before, but somehow childhood buffered the seriousness of possible disaster. The cycle of feast to famine was a common enough one on the Arans, occurring every ten years or so. The cure was simple enough, allow a fallow season for certain species of fish, but convincing the fishermen was a losing battle. Until the government stepped in and regulated the fish numbers, greedy boats would bleed the coastal waters until there was nothing left for an island man to feed his family and make a bit of profit on the side.

When a blackout went into effect, all commercial fishing within twenty-five miles of the coastline was prohibited. It was the harbor master's task to deliver the unwelcome news, and inevitably, no matter how often he warned them, it was he who was blamed for the fishermen's straitened circumstances. Fortunately, it was seasonal, and all hard feelings were forgotten when the boats went out again. Patrick Tierney had been the harbor master during the years he was married to Emma.

According to Patrick, she'd never understood the love-hate relationship the islanders bore their leaders. She'd resented the hostile mutterings of the island women when they stood behind her in the grocery line. When she left him, Patrick decided the life of harbor master, with its capricious hours and emergency calls, was no way to raise a child, and he turned away from it.

Patrick Tierney had his troubles, but he was a man with a good heart. Sean had witnessed the man's love for his son and his grandchildren in a thousand small acts of compassion over the years. Kerry hadn't seen him in quite the same way, and now it appeared that Mollie, too, had her conditions.

Women, Sean reflected, were hard on a man, no matter if they were wife, mother, or daughter. He wondered how his own nieces would look back on this period of their lives. Would they resent his work schedule, the infrequent family meals, the overall confusion of their home that was no longer a home? How long would it take them to understand that he had no choice?

Guilt consumed him. He looked at his watch. His mother and the children were expecting him. Bless Luke. Poor wee lad had a smile on his face no matter who cared for him.

He was nearly out the door when the phone rang. Debating whether or not to answer it, he swore, turned back, and lifted the receiver. "O'Malley here."

The grim look on his face disappeared. "That would be grand, Mollie. Thank you very much. I appreciate it. I'll be there."

He hung up the phone, looked at his watch, and replaced his jacket on the back of his chair. Thank God for Mollie. She had given him another precious hour.

Eileen O'Malley rubbed her aching wrists, lowered herself into the easy chair closest to the fire, and offered up a brief prayer that Luke would sleep until Sean came to fetch him. If this was what seventy-four felt like, she prayed to God to help those who were seventy-five and eighty.

The years weighed heavily on her face, carving deep

furrowed lines in the fair skin stretched across her cheeks and her forehead and in the fainter ones spidering away from the corners of her mouth. The dourness of her expression was barely relieved by the sparkle in her eyes and the wry wit she sprinkled frugally throughout her conversations. She rarely complained despite the crippling arthritis that afflicted her hands and stiffened the joints of her hips, shoulders, and knees so that every movement, even the simplest, was wrought with excruciating pain.

Sean would be late tonight. He'd warned her in the morning when he dropped off the children, and she'd assured him they would be fine. She should have known better. The girls she could manage, but Luke was too much for her. By noon she couldn't lift him anymore. When Marni was home from school she could cope, but the child had already missed enough. Any more absences would affect her learning.

Eileen's heart ached for her daughter and the man she had married. She hadn't wanted Danny Tierney for Kerry. He was flighty, and he took to the drink like Patrick. Anyone with eyes could see he wasn't husband material, not for a woman's only daughter. But Kerry was fully grown when she'd married and in no mood to listen to a meddling mother.

If only Sean had stayed on the island. He was her youngest, born fifteen minutes after Kerry. From the beginning she'd known he wouldn't be satisfied living on a bit of rock eight miles long and three miles wide. Chomping at the bit was her Sean, straining toward independence.

Sean had been her dreamer, thoughtful, sensitive, the

quiet one, disappearing for hours at a time, coming home rejuvenated by the peace of his own company. Not that he'd been friendless. His striking good looks and infectious smile were magnets for both lads and lasses. Most of his friends were gone now, the ambitious ones, away to jobs in Dublin, London, Chicago, and New York.

Eileen recalled Sean's wanderlust years, when postcards came from parts of the world she'd never heard of. She'd known, even then, that this one would never come home again. Some were born to the call of the island, but not Sean. She'd known the workings of his complicated, searching mind. Because it mirrored her own, she understood his love for the sea and its various moods, for a way of life older than the Viking forts staring down upon them, for a people hardened by time and circumstance and unending battles with nature. But she knew his destiny didn't lie along that path. Sean had buried his father, kissed his mother, wished his sister well on her wedding day, and escaped, permanently, until now.

Eileen stared out the window, and a lump rose in her throat. Marni and Caili were playing what looked a bit like jump rope but with elastic tied around their legs. Poor wee lassies. They would need their tea soon, and she hadn't the strength to turn on the stove. What was to become of them with their mother and father gone, their uncle a bachelor, and both island grandparents unable to keep them for one reason or another? She hated to disagree with Sean, but Emma appeared the most logical choice.

The ringing phone startled her. Wearily she stood and

walked into the kitchen in time for the beginning of the third double ring. "Hello."

"Hello, Mrs. O'Malley." The voice was low, pleasant, not of the island. "This is Mollie Tierney. Would you mind if I came by to pick up the children? My mother would like to see them."

Mollie Tierney. Danny's sister. Eileen hesitated. The temptation was strong, but would Sean approve? "I'm sure the children would love it, Miss Tierney, but have you spoken with Sean?"

"I have," Mollie assured her. "He told me you've had them all day and to give you a break."

Eileen was ashamed of the relief that swept through her. "Well, then," she said heartily, "if your mother would like to see them, that's where they should go."

"I'm leaving now. I'll be there in twenty minutes."

She hung up the phone, summoned new reserves of energy, reached over to the stove, and turned on the burner, watching the instant flame leap into life. Bless Sean. He'd surprised her with a gas stove last Christmas. There was something luxurious about turning a button and watching the flame catch like magic.

She'd said twenty minutes. The lass would be blue with cold by that time. Eileen opened the pantry and pulled out a round loaf of bread studded with raisins. Carefully, painfully, she pulled a knife from a drawer and began to slice. The bread fell away in neat, meticulous squares.

Marni walked into the kitchen. "We're hungry, Gran. Is tea ready?"

Eileen stopped and rubbed her knuckles. "Your aunt is coming to take you home with her. You'll have a bit of something here, but she's already planned the rest of your tea. You'll like that, won't you, lass?"

The child nodded.

She turned back to the bread, sawed through another slice, bit her lip, sighed, and set down the knife. "Would you be a love, Marni, and finish this up for me? My hands won't cooperate."

Obediently, Marni took up the knife and quickly cut the remaining bread. Then she climbed up on a stool and opened the cupboard to take out a platter. After arranging the bread, she pulled a cube of butter from the refrigerator, added it to the plate, and carried it to the table. "I can make the tea, too, Gran," she said.

Eileen smiled at the solemn little girl. "Thank you, love. You're a wonderful helper."

Marni nodded. "That's what Uncle Sean always says."

Sinking into the nearest chair, Eileen glanced down at her swollen knuckles and then over at the child expertly scalding the teapot. Marni was a little girl. What happened to children who were made to grow up before they were ready? Worry deepened the creases in her brow. Most likely they turned out like Sean, always wanting something more than they had.

The door opened, and Caili walked in, her cheeks red from the cold, her hands grubby. She smiled and held up the elastic that had served as a rope. "I did it, Marni. I lasted through the whole of Double Dutch."

"You did not." Marni continued with her task.

Unperturbed, Caili filched a piece of bread from the platter, tore it in half, and began eating out the middle. "I did too."

"You always make it through when no one is there to see you."

"It's easier when no one is watching me." Caili grinned engagingly at her grandmother and held up her leftover crust. "You put in lots of raisins this time."

Eileen laughed and held out her arms. "Come here and kiss me and then wash your hands. Your Aunt Mollie won't want to take you looking like a chimney sweep."

Caili's eyes sparkled. "Is she coming to take us home with her?"

"Aye. But first you'll have some bread and tea."

Caili clapped her hands, crushing the crust between them. Leaving the decimated pieces on the floor, she pulled the stool to the sink, climbed onto it, and turned on the faucet. Eileen opened her mouth to remind her of the bread when she saw Marni reach for the broom and dustpan. Without a word, the child swept the crust into the pan and dumped it into the trash.

Good Lord. Eileen watched in amazement as Marni pulled out the silver, filled the teapot, and carried everything to the table. Was Sean completely oblivious to what was happening with his family? "Caili's old enough to clean up after herself," Eileen said gently.

Marni shrugged. "It's faster when I do it."

"You can't do everything, Marni."

She stared at her grandmother with round eyes. "Someone has to."

The words chilled Eileen's soul. At eight years old, Marni had the uncompromising, fatalistic attitude of an islander. Eileen wanted to lift her twisted hands, grab her granddaughter's shoulders, and shake her, to cry out that a world waited for her, a world outside the limestone perimeters to which she was now confined, a world where life was not defined by the slap of ocean against shoreline, by the docking of ferry boats filled with tourists, by blankets of fog suffocating the land like a shroud, and, least of all, by the fatalistic soothsaying of an old woman who'd lived long beyond her time.

But Eileen did none of those things. Instead she smiled weakly and promised herself she would tell Sean that his elder niece carried the weight of her small family on her shoulders and it was time he relieved her of the burden.

A firm knock sounded at the front door. Offering up a prayer of thanksgiving for her reprieve, she wiped her hands on a towel and nodded at Marni. "That will be your aunt, love. Answer the door and invite her in."

Caili dashed after her sister. "I want to!" she shouted, "Let me!"

Eileen's lips turned up in another smile. There was nothing wrong with Caili, but wasn't it always the way? Where there was a giver, there must also be a receiver.

Mollie Tierney breezed into the kitchen, breathless, laughing, pulled by both little girls. Eileen watched approvingly as she kept one hand in Marni's, extricated the other from Caili's grasp, and held it out.

"Good evening, Mrs. O'Malley," she said politely.

Eileen took the offered hand. "You're welcome to stay for a cup of tea and a bite of soda bread before you take the children. Luke isn't awake yet."

"I'd love to, but my father is waiting outside. He drove me here in the trap."

"Patrick needs no invitation, Miss Tierney." She started for the door. "I'll tell him to come inside."

Eileen returned alone. "He has an errand at the Sheas'. He'll be back at half past the hour. Sit down, Miss Tierney. Luke should be up by then."

Mollie pulled out a chair. "Please, call me Mollie." She looked at the spread set out on the table. "Mmmm, this is lovely. Isn't this lovely, girls?" She slipped an arm around both little girls and pulled them close to her as if she couldn't quite bear to part with them, not even for the meager distance between chairs.

Intrigued, Eileen sat down at the table and, under the guise of pouring tea and passing bread and butter, observed the young American woman weave her spell around the children.

Mollie's charm was subtle, playful, intangible. Within minutes the chill disappeared from the kitchen. The room seemed brighter, and the pinched, worried look disappeared from Marni's face. Even the ache in Eileen's fingers had diminished. Somehow this lovely young American with her glowing skin and perfect teeth knew where she was needed and which child needed wrapping most in the warm cocoon of her love. "How is the teaching coming along?" she asked when the conversation lulled.

Mollie swallowed her bread before answering. "Very well, thank you. I met Mrs. Ryan today. Alice was ill, and she filled in for her."

"Mary Ryan was a good teacher in her day, but it's past time for her to be handling a classroom."

Again Mollie laughed, a warm musical sound that lit her face and poured warmth over them all. "I can't get used to the idea that everyone knows everyone else here. It's nice, isn't it?"

"It can be, but there are disadvantages to living on top of each other. We all know each other's business, whether we want to or not." Eileen sipped her tea. She felt the young woman's eyes on her face. When she looked up they were still on her, appraising, puzzled. She set down her cup. "There's a question hanging on your lips. Ask it, lass. I doubt if there isn't one I haven't heard."

"It's more of an observation."

"Go on."

Caili interrupted them. "May I have more bread, Gran?"

"What of your tea?" Marni piped up. "You'll not be eating that if you fill yourself on bread."

Ignoring her sister, Caili repeated her question. "May I, Gran?"

"Marni's right," Eileen answered. "You need more than bread to last you through the night."

Caili slipped from her chair, popped her thumb in her mouth, and leaned against Mollie. Eileen noticed the way the woman's arm automatically circled the little girl.

"What are we having, Aunt Mollie?" the child asked.

"Roast turkey, stuffing, sweet potatoes, and pumpkin pie."

Marni's nose wrinkled. "Pumpkin pie?"

"You'll love it," Mollie replied. "Everyone does."

Intrigued, Eileen asked, "Where would you be finding pumpkins at this time of year?"

"My mother found them in Galway."

"Pumpkin pie,' Eileen repeated softly. "I can't imagine."

"Please, join us," Mollie said impulsively. "We'd love

the company, and the girls would have their whole family together at once."

Eileen's eyes widened. "Is Patrick coming as well?"

"Yes."

Patrick and Emma sitting down together for a meal? The girl was a witch. "What of Sean? Has he also promised to break away?"

Mollie smiled triumphantly. "He has."

Eileen laughed. "Well, then, Mollie Tierney, I wouldn't miss it for the world."

It wasn't until they were packed together in Patrick Tierney's trap with a woolen plaid tucked cozily around them that Eileen remembered their unfinished conversation. "You never told me about your observation."

"Oh, that." Mollie waved her hand in dismissal. "It wasn't anything really. I was just thinking how very like Sean you are."

Eileen's expression settled into the cool, implacable lines it assumed when something wasn't clear and she needed time to sort it out. There must be a reasonable explanation for the unease she felt at the unfamiliar sound of her son's name on the American woman's lips, for that look in her eyes and the slight, nearly imperceptible color in her cheeks.

The only one she came up with was unacceptable to her. Sean was the only child left to her. Kerry was birthed easily, a calm child, placid, easily satisfied. Not Sean.

When he'd grown up with a mind that matched her own, when she watched him balk at senseless cruelty, when his questions became too advanced for the teachers at the island school, and when he came back to

Galway, Eileen knew his path would be somewhere else. While others settled in, his road was alone. Marriage and children held out no appeal. Now here he was, a bachelor saddled with three small children, burying himself in nappies by day and words by night.

She took another quick, surreptitious look at Danny's sister. The girl's face was averted, her profile outlined against the deepening dusk. Mollie Tierney was lovely, slim and straight, with the golden coloring and delicate features of her mother. But she was different, too, with a sweetness and charm Eileen had never observed in Emma. From the comments of her neighbors with children still at school, those qualities carried over into her work as well. Eileen decided she could like this young woman.

But was a pretty face and sweet disposition enough to mend a family? Eileen wasn't willing to risk her son or her grandchildren for a nebulous *possibility*. Drawing a deep breath, she forced herself close to the edge she normally avoided. "I'm wondering how you persuaded Sean to break away from his writing. He's been quite busy lately."

She watched Mollie pull a wheat-colored strand of hair away from her mouth, noticed the sudden rapid pulse in her throat and the careful way she collected herself, gathering resources from deep inside. Her clear blue eyes, warmed by a touch of green, Patrick's eyes, flickered once, twice, before settling on Eileen's face.

"I'm sure he is busy, Mrs. O'Malley," she said carefully, "but there are times when your family comes first. There isn't anything Sean wouldn't do for his family. I'm sure you know that."

Eileen did know it, but she was more than a little sur-prised that Mollie did. *Just how well does Mollie Tierney know my son?* She pushed the disturbing thought aside. Mollie was a sophisticated young woman, far too sophis-ticated for Inishmore, and too intelligent to repeat the heartbreak of her own parents' story.

13

$\mathcal{S}$ean jogged the last quarter-mile to the cottage, stopping at the bridge to tie his shoe and finger-comb his hair. He wasn't going to have anyone accuse him of tardiness, not tonight, not with Mollie going to such trouble to gather everyone together.

Mollie. He formed the name on his lips and smiled. He'd underestimated her. She was a determined lass, nothing like he'd expected that day she first walked in on him. What would they have done without her? What would he have done without her?

The cottage looked like something out of a Thomas Kincade painting. Every window glowed with light, and on the door was a pine wreath decorated with a large red bow, a hint of Christmas. Before he could knock, Caili opened the door, shrieked, and threw herself into his arms. He gathered her close and breathed in the aromas of sage, meat juices, apples, and cinnamon wafting from the kitchen. His head swam. Releasing his niece, he leaned against the door jamb to steady himself and watched her run back into the kitchen.

Instantly Mollie was at his side, her hand on his arm, worry creasing her brow. "Are you all right?"

He nodded. She was very close. The top of her head reached his nose, and the clean scent of her shampoo replaced the food smells. The room, a small hallway for coats and boots, separate from the kitchen, was unusually warm.

He shrugged out of his jacket, conscious of Mollie's fingers easing the sleeves away from his shoulders and down his arms. He heard her voice, low and soft. He watched her turn away to hang his jacket. Every moment was slow, intensified. He noticed the shape of her arms, the smooth length of her neck, the warm toast color of her jumper. Like Adam with his forbidden fruit, he knew he should stop, move into the next room, shift his thoughts, but the need for a woman, a warm, ministering woman who had answers he'd never dreamed of, held him in a desperate grip.

Christ, help me. This was Mollie, Danny's sister, but she was also a woman, a lovely woman, with long slim legs and hair loose and smooth and caramel-colored, falling to her shoulders. He remembered how it felt to have her in his arms, his hands settling on the dip at her waist, his cheek against the top of her head. Longing shook him. He couldn't help himself. "Mollie." His voice was rough and choked, the emotion raw on his face. He touched her shoulder. He would go no further, not unless she came to him, not unless she wanted it, too.

She turned, a question in her eyes, hesitated for the briefest instant, and then walked into his arms. Thank God.

He'd gone without for too long. The simmering need that a man, overly young for months of celibacy, carried within him ignited. He shuddered, damned his lack of self-control, and, twisting the silky strands of her hair in his hand, he pulled her head back and set his mouth on hers, hard.

He'd intended nothing more than to assuage his raging hunger, to feel once again the nearly forgotten intimacy of lips and teeth and tongue. But the sweetness of her response shook him. She would not allow him to take her mindlessly, greedily, with no thought for her own pleasure. Gently she coaxed him with light fingers and tender kisses, with murmured words and gentle exploring hands.

When his mouth softened and his hands slipped under the wool of her jumper, roaming her back, kneading the silken skin, he heard the tiny sound in the back of her throat, and his heart leaped. How long since he'd really wanted a woman, not just her body but *all* of her? Releasing her mouth, he pressed her head against his shoulder, buried his face in her hair, and listened to the ragged rhythm of their mingled breath.

"Sean." The word was muffled in the wool of his jumper.

"Shh. Not now." It was too soon to break the spell.

She rested against him, clean, damply warm, smelling of flowers and soap.

"Sean." This time the voice came from behind them. "Mollie." Emma's voice, not close yet but soon.

Reluctantly he released her and stepped back. She stared at him, her eyes deeply blue, slate, the rose deep in her cheeks, waiting . . . for something. He touched her cheek. There would be no apology, not this time. Words had no place for what had just happened between them.

She opened her mouth to speak, changed her mind, and closed it again. Turning, she led the way into the kitchen.

Emma stood at the stove, peering into a large baking pan. She nodded. "There you are. Caili said you'd come. The others are in the living room."

Sean greeted her. "Hello, Emma. You're looking grand." He meant it. She appeared to have shaken the lethargy that Mollie was so worried about.

She looked pleased. "Thank you. I'm glad Mollie persuaded you to join us. Your mother's here, too."

Mollie hadn't said a word. He looked inquiringly at her. "Will you join me?"

She wet her lips. Her voice was breathless, the words halting. "Go ahead. I have a few things to do in here."

He frowned and forgot Emma. "Mollie—"

She interrupted him. "There's ale in the refrigerator, or wine if you prefer it."

Conscious of Emma's presence, he smiled and shook his head. "Nothing for me, thanks. I'll wait for dinner. Caili will drink her milk if I have a glass as well."

His niece's name had the desired effect. Mollie relaxed.

"You have a small tyrant on your hands, Sean O'Malley. I hope you realize it."

He grinned, relieved. "I know it."

The scene in the sitting room reminded Sean of long evenings at home when he was a child growing up in his parents' small cottage. Marni and Caili were seated across from each other, bent over a checkerboard lying open on a small ottoman. From the triumphant look on the little girl's face and the stack of markers in front of her, he knew Marni was allowing her to win.

Near the cozy turf fire, Patrick and Eileen shared the couch and a pot of tea. They were deep in conversation. His mother's face was flushed. Gray-black hair curled softly around her forehead, and the lines of her face were not so pronounced in the soft lamplight. Sean could see by the position of her hands that, for the moment, her painful condition had eased.

He crossed the room and leaned over to kiss her cheek. "Hello, Mam."

"Sean." Her face lit with pleasure. "You came, finally. I'm so glad."

"Of course. Did you think I wouldn't?" He shook Patrick's outstretched hand and pulled another chair closer to the fire.

"I've been inviting you for weeks," his mother said. "You're always working."

She had invited him, to the Sheas' house or the O'Learys', never home with just his family. He'd refused her. The talk would turn to Kerry, the Irish penchant for calling up the dead and invoking in them qualities they hadn't had in life. He wasn't ready for that. Maybe he would never be.

"Uncle Sean." Marni looked up from the board. "I need shoes for dance."

It meant a trip to Galway. His heart lifted. No one on the island crafted shoes for the step dancing required of all children in primary school. "I'll see about it next week," he promised.

Inevitably, Patrick asked, "How's the writing?"

"It's grand," Sean replied. "Except for a bit of trouble with the second act." He smiled. Patrick was only being polite. He had no interest in the writing of plays. "I'll work it out."

Patrick nodded, accepting Sean's answer as he appeared to accept all things. What went on behind that complacent mask? What demons interrupted the smooth flow of Patrick's seasons, and how could they be enough to cause a man to drink himself into oblivion? Danny's death, Sean could understand. Yet, on the surface, Patrick had taken his son's loss with the same dispassionate formality with which he accepted the inconvenience of snow in October. True, his wife had left him, but that was years ago, long enough for the wound to heal into a painless scar.

Sean yearned for that time to come, when thoughts of Kerry didn't leave him bone weary, immersed in a helpless kind of guilt that interrupted his sleep and wiped away all desire for food, companionship, or pleasure of any kind, except one, the one his frustrated subconscious wouldn't let him forget.

His mind returned to the kitchen and the woman whose arms had provided a haven he'd only imagined could exist with another human being. That the comfort was forbidden weighed with him, but only to the extent that it would affect her. Sean knew Inishmore, and he knew Ireland. He could no more take up with an American woman, a teacher, no less, than he could eat meat on Friday or pass up the smear of ashes on his forehead signaling the beginning of Lent.

The island was small enough for disapproval to run

through villages and devastate lives. He didn't want that for Mollie, nor did he want it for Kerry's children. The memory of Mollie's scent tugged at him, as did the wary, vulnerable look in her eyes. He pushed it away. There would be no seduction, no matter how tempting, and anything more was out of the question. He'd had enough loss. Sean wasn't willing to risk his heart again. He would tell her so when the time was right.

His mother had asked him a question. He could tell by her lifted eyebrows, her parted lips. She worried about him. She had a right to. He leaned forward. "I'm poor company tonight. I'm sorry, Mam. I didn't hear you."

"I said if you care to look through boxes, I've shoes from when you and Kerry were small. There might be a suitable pair for Marni in the bunch."

Sean caught his niece's eye. She'd heard her grandmother, and, from the slight scowl on her face, he knew she was having none of it. "No, thank you," he said smoothly. "Marni's worked hard at the dancing. She deserves her own pair of shoes."

Marni relaxed, and Caili swept the last of the markers from the board. "I won!" she shrieked, clapping her hands and running to her uncle.

"Easy, lass," he warned her, settling her on his lap. "You want your aunt to invite you back, don't you?" He looked around. "Where's Luke?"

"Right here." Emma walked into the room holding the baby. His cheeks were pink. He cooed when he saw Sean.

Sean held out his arms. "I'll take him, Emma."

She hesitated. "You've already got quite a lapful. Mollie's nearly finished in the kitchen. She doesn't need me."

She was reluctant to give up the baby, but so was Sean. He needed Luke's chubby softness close to his chest. His writing had absorbed him. He'd seen too little of Kerry's children the last few weeks, especially Luke who slept for long hours at a time. "That would be grand," Sean said smoothly. "Let me have him for a minute while you find a chair."

"Play with me, Grandma," Marni said. "I need a partner."

Bless Marni. The child was uncanny. Somehow she seemed to know exactly where to apply the salve.

Emma brightened, handed over the baby, and sat down on the floor, crossing her legs like a girl. "Will you be black or red?" she asked.

Marni grinned. "Black."

"I'm a very good player," Emma warned her.

A tiny smile tugged at the corners of Marni's mouth. "I hope so, Grandma."

Patrick laughed. "Marni's not so bad, either, Emma. You'll need your wits about you or the game will be a short one."

"I'll keep that in mind."

Sean stared at them. They were actually teasing each other, the years of hurt wiped away by the healing presence of the grandchildren they shared. He felt lighter, as if something heavy and dark had been lifted from his shoulders. Because of Mollie and the way she'd pulled them all together, this might turn out to be a family after all.

Luke had tired of his uncle's lap and was seriously

fussing when Sean heard the clink of glasses and silver coming from the dining room. Handing the baby to Emma, he excused himself and walked into the eating area. Mollie was laying out the table. "May I help?" he asked.

"Yes," she said, smiling with her usual confidence, as if the scene between them in the storm room had never happened. "You can finish setting the table while I bring in the food."

The meal was as delicious as it was unusual. Roast turkey wasn't unheard of on the island but never accompanied by the array of pumpkin, sweet potato, and cranberry dishes she'd prepared.

"Thanksgiving always was Mollie's favorite holiday," her mother observed. "Even as a little girl she could hardly wait to come home from school the day before and help me start dinner."

"Is that what it is, Thanksgiving?" Patrick asked.

"Close enough," said Mollie. "We're a few days late, but I don't think it matters."

Caili looked up from her cranberries. "What's Thanksgiving?"

Emma and Mollie looked at each other. "You're the teacher," Emma said. "You tell her."

Mollie dabbed at her mouth with her napkin, sipped at her water, and began. "Every year in November families gather together and eat certain foods, turkey, cranberries—"

"Pumpkin pie," interrupted Emma. Like Mollie, she was partial to pumpkin pie.

Mollie smiled. "And whatever else they like. We do this in memory of the first Thanksgiving, several hundred years ago, when the American Indians and the first European settlers gathered to celebrate their harvest after the long, hard winter the year before. It was a very difficult time. They were grateful to be alive, so they had a feast, invited all their friends, and gave thanks to God."

"That's a nice story."

Sean couldn't help himself. "Everyone wasn't so friendly a few years later," he muttered under his breath.

"Sean," his mother reproved him.

"Excuse me?" The color was high in Mollie's cheeks.

He could have bitten his tongue off. "Never mind."

"No, I want to hear what you said."

This wasn't the place. He shouldn't have brought it up. But if she insisted, he did know something of American history. As in Ireland, the English had conquered, then exterminated the native tribes. "You only told half the story. In less than two hundred years the Native American population was reduced by millions due to war, starvation, disease, and outright annihilation."

"I'm not disputing that," she said reasonably, "but Caili asked me about Thanksgiving."

Sean was ashamed of himself. "So she did. I apologize."

Marni, who'd tensed at the first sign of conflict, relaxed. "What's annihi-, anni—"

"Annihilation," Sean finished for her. "It means to destroy something completely."

Satisfied, she gave it up and applied herself to her candied yams. "This is good, Aunt Mollie. It tastes like dessert."

"It's Grandma Emma's recipe," Mollie said. "Save

room for some pumpkin pie. There's nothing she makes that can top that."

Emma demurred. "I'm not nearly the cook that Patrick is. Do you still like to cook, Patrick?"

"I can put together a fair stew," he admitted, "but I haven't attempted anything more in a long time."

Surprised, Sean glanced at Patrick. Kerry had never mentioned her father-in-law's culinary talents. Perhaps all that ended when Emma left him. He felt a pang of remorse. Danny Tierney's childhood had been a difficult one, and his children had suffered for it. Kerry, a nurturing mother, had been the nucleus of the family. She had asked remarkably little of her husband, understanding and accepting his shortcomings.

Sean looked across the table at the girl who had it all. No wonder she appeared so collected, so capable, compared to her brother. While Mollie was eagerly anticipating her mother's Thanksgiving dinner, Danny had frantically worked to hide all signs of his drunken father, waiting outside in the freezing cold until the pubs closed to bring him home, getting his own meals, hiding bottles, washing, cleaning, squeezing in the minimal amount of schoolwork required to earn his leaving certificate. Why, Sean wondered, hadn't he gone to California with Emma?

Sean was conscious of Mollie's eyes on his face, watchful, anxious. Once again he was ashamed. What had Mollie Tierney ever done but love Kerry's children, invite him to dinner, and comfort him when there was no other comfort in all the world? She couldn't be blamed for her life of privilege any more than Danny could help the deck he had been dealt or Kerry's untimely death. Neither was Emma the culprit. No one had the right to condemn a woman for leaving a loveless marriage. He saw that now. It was harder to forgive Patrick. He had insisted on keeping Danny on the island and at the same time fallen down in his duties as a parent.

Caili sat beside him. Sean nudged her shoulder and held out his glass of milk. Then he drank it down. She did the same. They smiled conspiratorially at each other. For the first time since Kerry's death, Sean was happy, not the giddy kind of happiness he'd once felt when he was young and all of life was before him. This was a contented kind of pleasure, the kind a man felt when his priorities were set and his world in order. He would make it. The children would make it. They would all go on.

Across the table, Mollie smiled at him. He smiled back. Next year she would be gone, but what she'd accomplished would stay with them, with Patrick and the children and with him. Sean would always be grateful to her for that.

The next moment all thoughts of happiness disappeared. He heard it first and knew it for what it was, a shrill, ominous, wailing siren heralding an island disaster. It pierced the comfortable clamor of dinner-table conversation, a sound that would paralyze the fishing community of Inishmore.

All except Mollie froze in their seats.

"What is it?" she asked, bewildered. "What does it mean?"

Sean's eyes met Patrick's. Both men pushed their chairs away from the table and stood. Sean's voice was grim, controlled. "Something's happened, Mollie, something serious. When I know, I'll call you." He looked at the girls' rosy-cheeked, worried faces and smiled encouragingly. "Chin up, lassies. There's always a solution. I'll be back soon."

Both Caili and Mollie managed a smile that disappeared as soon as the men left the room.

14

$\mathcal{K}$laus Vandenbrock opened the door of his cabin and sat down heavily on the bed. He pulled out the flask that was his mainstay, swigged down enough to chase away the cold that hounded him, and replaced it in his jacket pocket. Then he stretched out on the narrow bunk, crossed his arms behind his head, and closed his eyes. Sleep. He needed sleep. Why couldn't he sleep? Maybe when the ship reached Liverpool this damned insomnia would leave him.

Robert Staples's voice crackled over the radio. "We're closing in on something, Captain."

Vandenbrock didn't bother to sit up. Reaching for the radio on his desk, he pushed the transmit button and spoke to his third mate. "What does it look like?"

"Land, sir, on either side of us."

The man was mad. The coordinates were far wide of any land mass this far north. Staples was an American, young, enthusiastic, but overly cautious. It was time he got his feet wet. "Can you handle it?"

"Aye, aye, sir."

"Good man," said Vandenbrock. Replacing the radio, he closed his eyes and willed the alcohol to do its job.

He had no idea how long he slept. But there was no mistaking the exact moment he regained consciousness. The shudder woke him, a long roll that threw him from the bunk, followed by the harsh grating sound of metal giving way to rock. Instinctively he looked at the clock. Ten minutes after midnight. Terror chilled his brain. He could neither think nor act.

He sat on the floor in frozen impotence, staring stupidly at the porthole, struggling to push the cobwebs from his mind. Twenty years of experience wiped away in a tidal wave of horror. He knew what it was. No one who'd captained oil tankers for as many years as he had would confuse it for anything other than a tear in the hold. Given the sound and impact, the hit was large enough to release thousands of damaged barrels of oil into the ocean.

Rising too quickly for a man who'd passed out in an alcoholic haze, he banged his head on the cabinet. He swore fluently, damning Staples and the rest of his crew to watery graves. Rubbing his head, he climbed awkwardly to his feet and tried to think, his only hope that the ship had struck something adrift in the water, an abandoned boat or a lost buoy. God help him if his coordinates were wrong and Staples really had seen land on both sides.

Eight hours later, with the blinking red lights of the Irish harbor pilot pounding a stiletto-sharp rhythm against his alcohol-sensitive pupils, hope was no longer a realistic term relevant to the disaster in which Vandenbrock found himself. Against his will, he'd been forced to submit to a blood test. His alcohol level was .061 percent. Maximum permissible levels for the operation of a commercial vessel did not go beyond .040 percent.

So far he hadn't been arrested. Transom hadn't responded. Most likely they were consulting their lawyers. Not that it mattered. His career was over. The irony of it struck him. Staples would move on with a slap on the wrist, while he would be fired, more than likely never work a commercial vessel again.

More hours passed. Dawn lit the sky, bit by bit, first darkly blue, then pearl gray, and finally silver. Pale fingers of light pierced the clouds and separated, bathing the ocean in a wash of gentle gold, a beautiful day off the coast of western Ireland. Staring out his porthole at the black slick of crude coating the water, Vandenbrock felt his stomach churn. Already birds dove through the rainbow-colored sheen, rising from the water coated with oil.

Lurching from his bunk, Vandenbrock found the door to the bathroom, flipped the light switch, and barely managed to make it to the toilet before heaving up the contents of his stomach.

Two days later Sean stood on the deck of the harbor pilot's boat and stared at the nine-hundred-eighty-seven-foot Transom tanker listing at an unnatural angle amidst a circle of buoys. Response teams had been slow to reach the disaster, and so far only skimmers and conveyer belts to lift the oil off the surface were evident. The technique, widely used because it was least destructive, was also the least effective. Sorbents, removing the oil with sponges made from diaperlike substances, would come next, followed by burning and high-pressure hosing, which, in Sean's opinion, did more harm than good. Areas left alone to be weathered by winter storms ended up with more life than those cleaned by high-pressure hosing. "How many barrels so far?" he asked.

Graham Greene, the harbor master, narrowed his eyes. "Two hundred forty barrels so far and still counting. I would say the largest slick has spread to nearly thirty square kilometers inside a two-hundred-square-kilometer area of smaller slicks. Another million barrels of oil are still on the ship. They'll be siphoned off to another vessel."

"Why is it taking so long?"

Greene shrugged. "No one's worried. The seas are calm. Transom is claiming responsibility. The captain's been fired. Who knows?"

"The ship has shifted," Sean observed. "It looks bad. If we don't step in, the rest of the oil will be lost into the sound."

Greene looked at the sky. "We've a few days yet, if the weather holds. Then we'll need all the help we can get." He looked at Sean. "Are you in?"

Sean nodded. "We're all in, Graham. We've no choice."

That night Luke woke with a howl. Exhausted from worry and too little sleep, Sean changed the baby, climbed back into his own bed, and tucked his nephew in beside him. Luke's chubby fingers curled around his thumb, and soon he was asleep, a small bundle of delicious warmth on a cold winter night. Sean molded his body around Luke's baby shape and tried to sleep over the whistle of the wind. It was a sound he'd heard all his life. Ordinarily he would have drifted off immediately, but heavy winds meant high seas. The Transom ship with its million barrels of oil still hovered perilously nearby, and those in charge waited helplessly for cleaning crews, hoping for clear weather.

At nine A.M. it was dark as midnight. Pounding rain and seventy-mile-an-hour winds kept everyone inside. Shops and schools stayed closed. Residents turned up their radios, banked their fires with enough turf to last the day, and settled in to outlast the storm.

Sean stirred the oatmeal one last time before ladling it into bowls for the children. Sensing his preoccupation, Marni and Caili were silent, dutifully lapping up their cereal as if it were ice cream.

The shrill ring of the telephone jarred Sean into action. Handing Luke's spoon to Marni, he reached for the phone. It was Graham Greene. Dispensing with his usual preliminaries, the harbor master delivered the bad news in a clipped voice. "We need you, Sean. Winds hit the tanker last night, shifting it even more. Containment buoys were ripped apart. We can't use a chemical cleaning agent on the oil."

"Where's Transom in all of this?"

"Campbell, their chief executive officer, concedes it's impossible to contain the spill with the equipment they have. Frankly," Greene added, "the opportunity to recover much oil passed with the onset of the winds."

"In other words, it's up to us."

"Aye, and anyone else with a boat. We need to move the booms as far out as fifty miles to save valuable salmon hatcheries. When can you be here?"

He glanced at the table around which his small family had gathered. The girls, pink-cheeked, staring at him with round eyes, were still in their pajamas. Luke waved his arms from his baby seat. Sean sighed. "As soon as I can get someone here. Keep me informed."

There wasn't a prayer of finding anyone for the children, not on a day like this. He looked at the phone and hesitated. School had been canceled. Mollie would be home with Emma. Still he hesitated. She would want him to call. He knew that. But pride and an honest desire not to take advantage of a woman who was in a vulnerable state held him back. Mollie was a giver, and he was very close to the edge of taking what she offered and damning the consequences. Gritting his teeth, he turned back to the children. "What shall we do today?"

Before they could answer, the phone rang again. He sighed and reached for it. There would be no respite today from the worried fishermen whose livelihoods were on the line. "Hello," he said tersely.

"Sean? Are you all right?"

It was Mollie. He relaxed. "Aye. We're fine."

"Do you need me?"

Did he need her? Four simple syllables with a world of meaning in them. "We're managing."

Her voice deepened with amusement as if she knew his thoughts. "I meant today, for the children. Would you like me to stay with them?" Mollie Tierney would be no man's victim. He should have known that.

"You're saving me again, Mollie."

"I'll expect you to be properly grateful."

He smiled into the phone. "Would dinner and a play in Galway be enough?"

He heard her breath catch and the slight, nearly imperceptible tremor in her answer that no one who didn't know her would notice. "I think that would do it," she said.

"When will you be sure?"

"When it's over."

He laughed. "It's a bargain, then."

"A bargain?" Again her voice was low, amused, a woman comfortable with the dance of courtship. "I thought it was a date."

His grin faded. "It had better not be a date, Mollie."

The silence was thick between them. She broke it. "What will it be, Sean?"

"A night in Galway." She didn't answer. "Perhaps a beginning," he offered.

He could feel her thinking. "A beginning would be nice," she said at last. "I'll be over in an hour."

Sean hung up the hone, shaken, his bravado completely gone.

Marni spoke up. "Is Aunt Mollie coming over?"

"Aye," he said, preoccupied.

"When?"

He glanced at his niece rinsing her plate at the sink. "Soon. Hurry and get dressed. I'll finish up in here and bathe Luke."

"Aunt Mollie's coming, Aunt Mollie's coming," Caili sang as she ran out of the kitchen. Marni was more subdued but no less delighted. Her steps were quick, and the smile on her face warmed Sean's heart. If for nothing else, he would be forever grateful to Mollie for the love she showered on Kerry's children.

By noon the winds had died down long enough for the harbor patrol to attempt the waves. From the bow of the harbor master's small boat, Sean stared out at the mousse, a goopy emulsion of oil and water, in disgust. "How in the name of God did this happen? The sound is clearly marked, has been for years."

"Vandenbrock was drunk," Greene said grimly. "The third mate was at the helm. He's a fifteen-year veteran of the Transom fleet but not as a helmsman. He's a mess hand, cleaning rooms, serving dinner. He has no license to operate a vessel of this size. His file shows that he's shaky at the helm and has a tendency to chase the compass. We have the radio reports. The man asked for permission to change channels. A change was authorized. We have no idea why he didn't comply."

"Was he drunk as well?"

Greene shook his head. "No, just inexperienced."

"Have you any idea what really happened?"

"My guess is that he didn't slow down. The longer it takes Transom to deliver its oil, the more it costs. He tried to steam through at full speed. Normally there shouldn't have been a problem. The ship was off-course."

"How much damage do we know of so far?"

"The slick has spread to nearly a hundred square kilometers. We're in trouble, Sean. Most of the more toxic compounds will evaporate in the next few weeks, but a good percentage will wash ashore. We'll have our share of floating carcasses and oiled animals. There won't be a clean fish pulled from these waters for a hundred kilometers."

Sean exhaled. "We've a crisis on our hands, Graham. Without the fish these people won't survive. We've never dealt with anything like this before."

"Pray for a miracle."

Rescue teams had not yet braved the winds to begin the slow, tedious process of cleaning up the island. Pockets of crude oil blanketed the shoreline, and gulls, their wings shimmering, hobbled along the beach unable to fly. Sea lions, barking in dismay, broke through the soupy foam, slithered up onto the sand, and scraped their hides against barnacle-splattered rock attempting to rid themselves of their rank odor. Already the pristine shore was littered with gasping fish, their bellies bloated and black with tar.

On the small pier fishermen bundled in Arans, their faces dour under woolen caps, huddled together, too bereft to do more than stare out to sea and then back at the blackened beach as if they couldn't quite fathom the disaster that had befallen them.

Sean finished speaking into the mini-cassette recorder he carried with him at all times, stuffed it back into his pocket, and approached the largest group of men.

"What does Greene say about it, lad?" asked Liam Kelly, a large man with a day's growth of beard, a ready smile, and that inevitable fan of lines around the eyes that proclaimed his livelihood.

Sean knew there was no point in hedging. Better to hit them with the worst of it right from the beginning and hope it wouldn't get there. "It looks as if the slick has spread to a hundred kilometers."

Collectively the crowd gasped. Again Liam, the unofficial ringleader, spoke. "There won't be a healthy fish in the whole damn ocean for weeks."

They were silent, waiting for him to confirm the damning words. He met the tall man's accusing eyes. "If we're lucky," he said deliberately. "Months is more likely."

"Holy shit, Sean. They've killed us."

The grumbling increased. Sean held up his hands. "We'll make it. We've gone through this before."

"Easy for you to say!" someone shouted. "You aren't a fisherman. What about us? It takes months to get on the dole."

Sean gritted his teeth. "There will be disaster relief. Transom will have to clean this up."

The voices quieted. "How long will that take?" someone else asked.

Sean recognized John Murphy, the voice of reason in a crisis. "I don't know," he said honestly, frustrated as usual by their dependence. Because he was the only one educated beyond the secondary school, they looked to him for answers. It was a role he'd neither asked for nor wanted.

"What do you think?" Murphy persisted.

"Give me until tomorrow morning. As soon as I find out anything, I'll call Liam and he'll call the next man. Each of you will contact someone else so the lines stay free." He appealed to them. "How about it, lads?"

Murphy nodded. "I'm in. You're an island man, Sean. You know what this means to us. I'm willin' to wait and see what you can do." He turned to the men behind him. "In the meantime I'm goin' to see if I can get myself some work on the roads for the winter."

A series of nods and mumbled ayes and half-hearted slaps on the back preceded the gradual breaking up of the crowd. Slowly Sean released his breath. He had no idea who would take on the task of skimming the oil from the surface and cleaning up the beaches. The logical choice would be Transom. But would they admit their blame?

His heart sank at the thought of men on the dole. So far the Arans had escaped the Irish legacy of unemployment that had existed on the mainland for years. Fish and small gardens and, for the last twenty years during the summer season, tourism had kept the islanders adequately fed and sheltered. How long the proceeds from last summer would last depended on individual families. It was already December, and the weather was harsh. He guessed it wouldn't take much longer to run out of whatever surplus they had managed to gather.

He ducked into the small office at the corner of the harbor and reluctantly picked up the telephone. His evening in Galway with Mollie would have to wait. The searing disappointment shocked him and pointed out disturbing parallels he'd never recognized before. His work was all-consuming, leaving little time for personal relationships. The last few weeks he'd tried balancing his deadlines with caring for the children, with woeful results. Now this catastrophe. If Emma Reddington was sensible, she would spirit the children back to California as fast as she could make the plane reservations.

Years ago Kerry had accused him of a single-mindedness

that shut out all needs but his own. He'd disregarded her criticism, preferring to think it was a rare moment when she'd resented the ties that bound her, irrevocably, to the island.

First he dialed his own number. No answer. Next he tried Mollie's cottage. Emma picked up the phone. Even with her American accent she sounded enough like her daughter to jar him momentarily. He asked to speak with Mollie.

Her voice, low-pitched, lovely, competent, steadied him. "How is everything?" she asked immediately.

He sighed. "Not good. The water is polluted for sixty miles. Fishing is completely restricted."

She gasped. "What will we do?"

We. She'd said *we.* It warmed him. "I'm not sure yet. I'm waiting for answers."

"It's all over the news. Transom has fired the captain. It looks as if they're allocating money for the cleanup."

"That won't help the fish, Mollie. The obvious oil deposits on the beaches will be cleaned up relatively quickly, but in the water the oil will sink, float again to the surface, and be redeposited over and over. It will break up into patches of mousse instead of staying in a continuous slick which is easier to skim or burn. All marine animals, including fish, will be loaded with hydrocarbons. The most toxic and volatile compounds will disappear into the air in the first few weeks, but what's left won't be edible for human consumption for years to come."

Her voice dropped to a whisper. "This is a nightmare."

"I agree."

"What can I do?"

"Take care of the children."

"Don't worry."

"Thank you, lass. I'll make it up to you. I promise."

She laughed, and for that small immeasurable instant his spirits lifted.

"I'm counting on it," she said.

He was still smiling when he replaced the receiver.

15

"What in heaven's name has gotten into you, Mollie? I've never seen you like this." Emma, her lips pursed in disapproval, stood at the entrance to the small storm room off the kitchen.

Mollie continued wrapping the muffler around her neck. "Like what?"

"You're being defiant."

Mollie struggled for patience. "Mabry O'Farrell is the closest thing to a doctor we've got," she explained for the third time.

"No one here needs a doctor. I know chicken pox when I see them."

"You haven't seen them all that often."

"Twice is enough to know. Danny had them, and you had them."

"None of the other children in school has chicken pox."

Emma sighed. "Someone has to get them first."

Mollie buttoned her coat and pulled on her gloves. "Then you won't mind Mabry confirming your opinion."

Emma's face was mutinous. "I don't think her diagnosis would be particularly valid, Mollie. She has no medical training."

Mollie fixed her attention on her mother. "You really don't like her, do you?"

"Not particularly."

"Why not?"

Emma shrugged. "She was hardly welcoming when I first came here."

"But she delivered Danny and me."

"Only because I couldn't get to the hospital."

Mollie hugged her mother tightly. "Don't worry. It'll be all right." She stepped back and reached for her hat. "Do what you can to keep the kids comfortable. You're good at that."

Emma smiled half-heartedly. "What shall I tell Sean when he calls?"

"Tell him you think the children have chicken pox and that I've gone to get Mabry to be sure."

"I'm not looking forward to this, Mollie."

"I don't blame you." She opened the door. A blast of cold air hit her full force. She gasped, lowered her chin into the muffler, and stuffed her hands into her pockets. "So, this is December in Ireland."

"It's December on Inishmore," said her mother dryly, "and, according to the weather reports, eighty degrees in California."

Mollie looked back over her shoulder. "Do you want to go home?"

The question hung there between them for a full minute. "Of course not," Emma said at last.

"Good," Mollie replied deliberately, "because we really need you here."

Her answer disturbed Emma. Later, after she'd bathed the girls in corn starch and tepid water, dabbed calamine lotion on their spots, and fed them chicken soup and Jell-o, after Marni, the last holdout, had succumbed to a restless sleep, she realized what it was that bothered her. Mollie had said *we* as if she had aligned herself with the islanders.

Mabry O'Farrell leaned over the twin bed where Caili slept and felt her forehead with the back of her hand. Holding the lamp so that the child was shielded from the light, she carefully lifted one eyelid and then the other before sliding her fingers down the small neck to settle at the pulse point at the base of her throat.

Mollie wondered what Caili, harboring more than her share of imagination, would think if she woke up to see this black-garbed woman with her flowing hair and strange, all-seeing eyes bent over her.

Mabry straightened to her full height, held her finger against her lips, and beckoned Mollie to follow her out of the room. "Emma's right," she said, closing the door behind her. " 'Tis the pox."

"Chicken pox?"

"Aye. Your mother's seen it before. She'll know what to do. Have you told Sean?"

"Not yet."

"He'll need to know, lass."

Mollie leaned against the wall and closed her eyes. "I don't think I can," she whispered.

"Why not?"

"How much more can he take?"

Mabry lifted her chin. "A great deal more than you imagine. Sean is an O'Malley. He isn't one to give up when times are hard. Survival has never been easy on the Arans, Mollie. Those who stay here have adapted to a way of life that seems harsher than most, but it has its own kind of reward, and we take our pleasure in it when we can."

"A terrible beauty."

"You're not the only one who can quote Yeats, lass. Remember that, and don't underestimate Sean. He'll come through and be stronger for it." The harshness left her mouth, and she smiled. "He'll know soon enough without your saying a word. Why not offer him a meal and a pot of tea first?"

"I have to teach tomorrow."

"How long until Christmas holiday?"

"Three days."

Mabry frowned. "Surely your mother will help. I haven't seen her. Is she here?"

"She's tired," Mollie lied.

The old woman's eyebrow lifted. "More likely she wants no part of me. Emma took a dislike to me from the beginning."

Mollie refused to gossip about her mother. "Thank you for coming. Would you like a cup of tea or a snack before you leave?"

"Thank you, lass, but no. There will be others needing comfort after the news they've had today." She turned and headed for the door.

"Mabry." Mollie couldn't help herself. She had to

know. "Do you—that is, can you tell—" She stopped. It was too ridiculous.

Mabry smiled. "When you find your voice, Mollie Tierney, you know where to find me. Perhaps one of these days, when the chicken pox have vanished and things are settled, you'll have time to stop in for a bite to eat and a bit of conversation."

"You know, don't you?"

"Aye, lass. I know. But it doesn't take a genius or a witch for that. You've the face of a flower, so open and clearly marked that anyone who looks can see what's there. When you're ready, come and ask your question, if you're ready for the answer."

Mollie peeked into her mother's room. Emma was reading in bed, her hair pulled up in a pony tail, granny glasses perched on the end of her nose. She looked much younger than her fifty-six years. "You were right," Mollie said. "It's chicken pox."

Carefully, Emma placed the bookmark in her book, closed it, and removed her glasses. "Is she gone?"

"Yes."

"Good."

"Everyone's asleep."

"They'll be restless tonight, and you have school tomorrow. Why don't you go to bed? I"ll listen for them if they need me."

"Thanks, Mom. I really appreciate this."

"Mollie—" Emma hesitated.

Mollie sat down on the side of the bed. "What is it?"

She searched her daughter's face. Mollie looked back at her steadily, honestly. The years had taught Emma wisdom. She rested her hand against the smooth young cheek. "You're comfortable here, aren't you, Mollie?"

"Yes."

"Inishmore can be very appealing in the beginning."

Mollie leaned back on the bed, propping herself up on her elbows. "What happened here, Mom? Why didn't you stay?"

Choosing her words carefully, Emma attempted to explain what she had never really put into words, not even in her most intense therapy sessions. "I've asked myself that question for years."

"And?"

"I was lonely, Mollie, desperately lonely. There wasn't a single person on this island I called my friend. I couldn't talk to anyone. The thought of spending my life in solitary confinement sent me over the edge." She wet her lips and confessed the shame she had thought to keep from her daughter. "I couldn't cope. I'd never felt that way before."

"What about my father? Couldn't he help you?"

Emma leaned her head back against the pillow. "Patrick was the last person I could turn to."

"Why?"

"Because he loved me. Because I felt so desperately sorry for the way I deceived him."

"I don't understand."

"I was a naive young girl when I came to Inishmore, and Patrick was the handsomest man I'd ever seen. Quite simply, I was seduced by our differences, that and a pair of blue eyes and a way of turning a phrase that was irresistible to women far more experienced than I was. I didn't look beyond that. Lord knows what he saw in me.

Probably the same thing. I was an American beauty, pretty enough and different, less traditional than the women he knew. We were intrigued by each other. But it didn't last."

"Did he feel the same way?"

Emma shook her head. "Everything agreed with him quite well. We were in his world. For him nothing had changed except he had a wife and two children waiting at home. He had his friends, his family, the comfort of a way of life he'd grown up with. When I left, I broke his heart."

"Was that the only way, Mom? Couldn't you have tried to make it work?"

"Oh, Mollie." Emma sighed. "I wish I could have given you an intact family. But sometimes the loudest silences in a marriage are those where everything's already been said. Sometimes the arguing becomes so frequent that it's the condition instead of the exception, and there's nothing left to do but retreat to different corners and pray there won't be a rematch."

"I wouldn't have thought the friends and family part would have bothered you."

A tiny smile quivered at the corner of Emma's lips. "Why is that?"

"You aren't exactly the social type. I don't remember your having many friends apart from Dad."

"Everything changed after I came home from Ireland. I'd lost Danny. I couldn't think of anything else. My parents were older. My father wasn't in the best of health, and my mother had her hands full caring for him. I fell into a severe clinical depression. Then I met Ward." She smiled tremulously at her daughter. "He saved my life, and we married. Everything came together after that. That was when I tried to bring Danny to California. But Patrick wouldn't consider it. I can't blame him, after the way I left.

"Ward and I consulted attorneys who told us that our case would be difficult because, legally, by leaving Ireland, I'd abandoned my son. After several sessions I started to decline again. Ward got me to let go of that part of my life and concentrate on what I had. I won't pretend I was the best mother in the world, Mollie. I don't think a mother ever recovers after the loss of a child. But I tried." Tears welled up and spilled over onto her cheeks. "I must have done something right because you certainly turned out beautifully."

"Oh, Mom." Mollie's eyes filled. She sat up and gathered her mother into her arms. "You were a great mother. You've always been there for me. You still are. I don't know what I'd do without you. I need you."

Emma laughed tearfully, shifted out of Mollie's embrace, and reached for a tissue. "You're the most independent person I know. You never really *need* anyone. Still, it's nice to hear you say it." She blew her nose. "What do you have in mind for these grandchildren of mine?"

Mollie settled back on the bed. "I'm not sure. How long do chicken pox last?"

"About two weeks."

"School will be out in a few days. Together we can manage. That will relieve Sean. At last he won't have the children to worry about."

Emma picked at the threads in the comforter. "You've grown fond of Sean, haven't you?"

Was it a trick of the light, or was Mollie's face warmer than it had been a minute ago?

"I'm not sure *fond* is the right word."

"What is the right word?"

"Intrigued, maybe even fascinated."

"That can be dangerous."

"Maybe. I'd like to know him better, but he holds himself back. He doesn't trust me, probably because of the children. I don't think he believes that I would have come here anyway, even if Danny and Kerry were alive."

Emma sighed. "If we're assigning blame, I'm more at fault than you are."

Mollie didn't argue.

"Not that it matters," her mother continued. "If Sean O'Malley can't see that you're not a deceiver, he's a very poor judge of character." Emma clutched the comforter tightly. "Tell me you aren't doing all of this because of some distorted sense of obligation."

A line formed between Mollie's eyebrows. "Doing all of what?"

Emma plowed ahead. "Becoming Kerry's replacement, Patrick's daughter, the children's mother—" She stopped, her bottom lip caught between her teeth, not daring to go any farther.

"Go on."

Emma had never heard that tone in Mollie's voice before. "Just tell me it isn't so."

"If you're suggesting that my feelings for my nieces and nephew and my father stem from guilt, you're wrong."

"Am I?"

Mollie rubbed her elbows. "I've wanted to come here

for years. You know that. I've always wanted to know my father."

"What happens at the end of the year?"

"What has that got to do with anything?"

"I think you already know, Mollie, but I'll make it very clear. If you continue this way, how will they ever manage without you?"

Stricken, Mollie stared at her mother.

Emma relented. Taking her daughter's hands in her own, she leaned forward and kissed her cheek. "Don't worry, darling. I know you mean well. It's not that bad. We'll worry about it when it happens."

"I didn't think," Mollie said slowly. "What should I have done?"

"People have a way of solving their own problems if you let them," explained Emma. "Just as they learn to rely on those who step in to save them."

"I only wanted to help."

"And you have. The children love you."

"Is that so bad?"

"Of course not. But you're not their mother, Mollie." Emma drew a deep breath. "You can't make up for their lost parents. This isn't your home. Your future lies elsewhere."

"I never wanted to replace Kerry. I wanted—" She stopped. How could she explain the sense of purpose she felt for the first time?

"Yes?"

Mollie shook her head. "Never mind. I don't know what I wanted. I'm too tired to think." She scooted off the bed. "Good night, Mom. I'll see you tomorrow."

Emma stared at the door long after Mollie had walked

through it. Not so very long ago she'd been where Mollie was, young and lovely and more than a little fascinated with a blue-eyed, black-haired Irishman. She knew her daughter well enough to finish her sentences for her. Mollie, ever the perfectionist, wanted to do a great deal more than replace Kerry. She wanted to eclipse her. What Emma didn't know was how far Mollie would go to do it.

Sean O'Malley didn't appear as Mollie claimed. In Emma's experience, men with chins like his were rarely at a loss. She'd watched him carefully. He was unusual for an Irishman in that he didn't gravitate to a pub when his world stood on end. Times had changed. Ireland had changed. Maybe the tradition of "a pint all around" was a thing of the past, even on Inishmore.

But Sean was still an islander, even though he'd gone and come back again, even though his heart wasn't set on the island. His ties were strong, strong like Patrick's, strong enough to suck the life from a marriage, especially marriage to an outlander. She didn't want that for Mollie.

Emma reached for the light switch, blanketing the room in comfortable darkness. The island was a wonderful place to raise children but not so wonderful for children who would someday be adults. Her head spun. Maybe her fears were groundless. Mollie was sensible. It was only a year. Surely, after a year, she would see that she didn't belong here.

16

Alice Duncan shifted the load of books she carried higher on her hip and smiled at Mollie seated at the large desk in front of the classroom, if one could call it a classroom anymore. It looked nothing like the room where Mary Ryan had taught for so many years. Slowly, over the weeks, the young American had converted what had once been an austere environment into a cozy room adorned with children's writing and artwork. The desks were arranged in groupings of four around an overhead projector, and in the corner, surrounded by well-stacked bookshelves, sat a rocking chair, huge overstuffed pillows and a carpet remnant, a "reading corner," she called it. "Don't look so distraught, Mollie. We've the chicken pox every year."

Mollie leaned her chin on her hand, a worried crease between her brows. "What if everyone gets them?"

"Most likely we'll have an outbreak in the lower levels. Many of the older children have already had them. I've heard it's better to get them when you're young." Alice changed the subject. "How is Sean holding up?"

"I don't know. I haven't seen him much. He comes to see the children and goes back again. Most of his time is spent at the beach."

Alice nodded. "In an emergency like this, every man is necessary, especially islanders like Sean. He knows the way of things. Is your mother watching the wee ones, then?"

Mollie nodded.

Alice sat down at a student desk. "How is Emma?"

"Tired."

"With three children to manage, I would expect that."

"My mother is the only one who appears to be benefiting from the chicken pox," Mollie observed.

"How so?"

"She's busy and has no time to dwell on what she didn't do for Danny."

Alice lowered her eyes. "And Patrick?" she asked casually. "Is he well?"

"I suppose so. He keeps to himself."

Alice absently drummed her fingers on the desk. Her thoughts were no longer in the present. Mollie continued to speak, and Alice nodded but she wasn't listening. She'd perfected the pretense long ago when the island women, missing their men and with too many dark hours ahead, would draw out their conversation long beyond what was necessary to explain their purpose.

She was recalling the day she first met the black-haired, clear-eyed Irishman called Patrick Tierney. Thirty-five years ago no would describe him as a man who kept to himself. A storyteller perhaps, a man fond of books and quoting the great ones, a hardworking man with a wry wit, a ready wink, and a way about him that drew people in. He'd certainly drawn her in.

Alice had never considered herself impulsive or impressionable. She was sent to Inishmore because of her facility for the Irish language. Five teachers before her, young women from Dublin and Cork, had requested a transfer back home after only a year. The islanders wanted their children educated but maintained a suspicion of strangers and kept their distance. Loneliness and weather sent the teachers scurrying back to the mainland.

Alice was different. In every season Inishmore spoke to her. She loved the power of winter, the slanting, needle-sharp rain, the howling wind, the soft gray days of autumn, and the crisp, cold nights when the mist rolled in, blurring edges and lights until the island looked like something out of a fairy tale. Spring was not to be missed with its burst of flowers, sea lions frolicking on the beaches, white sheets flapping in gentle winds, the smell of a different current, the flocks of birds resting on stained rocks. Fall was lovely as well. A season of silence was fall.

The only season Alice could do without was summer. Summer, with its flocks of tourists, glutted roads, strange accents, crowds in the Superquinn, the restaurants, the lighthouse, strangers climbing the paths to the forts. Summer was the season Emma had first come to Inishmore. She was only a tourist, Alice told herself in the beginning, an American who would go home with the bellowing sound of the ferry's final call. But she hadn't. She'd stayed and married Patrick, bore him two children, and gave up to go home, leaving behind a man so changed no one recognized him.

No, Alice would not soon forgive Emma Tierney, not even for Mollie. When she first learned that Emma's daughter was coming to teach on Inishmore, she had been prepared to tolerate her, to help out as needed, and then to have as little to do with her as was possible for the only two teachers sharing a school on a small island.

But Mollie had surprised her. Her sweetness was deceptive. She had her share of spirit and more than a hint of steel in that spine she unconsciously straightened when approached with a new challenge. Her voice was clear and lovely. Even from across the room it was pitched so everyone could hear, not at all loud but deliberate, with an emphasis on the sibilants. Everyone around her, including her students, was caught in its rhythms.

She was amazingly wise for a young girl, innocent, shamelessly happy over small pleasures, nothing like her mother, who'd never smiled and rarely left her yard to meet her neighbors. Emma Tierney had lived on the island for nearly ten years and never really known anyone. Alice knew that islanders could be hard on strangers, especially those with contempt for their island, and Emma had that to spare. They never forgave her.

Mollie was her own person, neither like Patrick nor like Emma. She was beautiful like her mother in that classic way that made a person stop on the street and surreptitiously stare after her, hoping to have an excuse to look her straight in the face. Alice had never coveted that kind of beauty. It created unnatural expectations and prevented kinship with other women. Classic beauty got in the way and had to be overcome, or others would never really see the woman beneath the face. She suspected that Emma and Mollie had come from a long line of classic beauties. But, with Mollie, one was left with more than the image of her face.

Mollie was looking at her curiously. Alice nodded and smiled as if she'd been attending all along. She gathered her books together and stood. "I'll be leaving now. Don't stay too late. I imagine your mother could use a bit of a breather with the children. If there's anything I can do, let me know."

"Good night, Alice." Mollie's clear voice followed her out of the classroom into the bitter cold of the winter night.

Alice trudged up the long gradual incline toward her cottage. At the fork in the road, she found herself hesitating. Finally she turned to the one on the left, the one leading away from home. The ascent was steeper than she was accustomed to, and at the end of nearly two miles she stood in front of Patrick's red door, drawing in deep, restoring breaths. What was she thinking? Her stomach twisted. But she was here. Alice shifted the books back into her other arm and knocked. Minutes passed. She knocked again. Light glowed through the window curtains. She heard movement behind the door. Suddenly it opened, and Patrick filled the space of her vision. He looked surprised.

"Alice."

"Good evening, Patrick."

He stared at her, a puzzled expression on his face. "Is anything wrong?"

"No. May I come in?"

"Of course." He stepped aside, waited for her to walk past him into the kitchen, and closed the door behind her. "Please, sit down." He pulled out a chair and relieved her of her load of books. "Do you have time for tea?" he asked politely. "I've lamb stew and a bit of salad."

"As a matter of fact, I do have time if you're in the mood for company."

He set the books on the telephone stand near the door, straightened, and stared at her curiously. "Would you care for a glass of something?"

She shook her head. "No, thank you."

His mouth twisted. "I won't be having any if that's what's worrying you."

Her eyes, brown and honest, were level on his face. "I've never been one for spirits, Patrick. Surely you remember that."

The crease in his brow deepened. "*Should* I be remembering that, Alice?"

The wave of red began at her chest and moved upward. She was a fool. She'd always been a fool when it came to Patrick Tierney. Even before Emma, he'd never noticed her, not the way she'd wanted him to. She was plain and he was not. He belonged with a woman like Emma. Like gravitated toward like. Patrick would never see her the way he'd seen Emma.

Ironically it wasn't Patrick Tierney's handsome face that appealed to her, although she couldn't imagine him any other way. Indeed, she would have preferred a package far less attractive. It would have fueled her hope. It was his rough edges that called out to her, along with his unusual compassion and that fragile vulnerability he carried close to the surface at all times.

Alice was a nurturer, and never had there been a man so in need of nurturing. Emma's defection had nearly destroyed him. Alice would have liked to have been the one to pick up the pieces. But as far as she knew, Patrick had shown no signs of needing another woman.

She'd come to that conclusion long before Mollie came to the island. But now Emma had returned. Emma, lovely, confident Emma, a woman who'd never had an awkward moment in her life, who walked with a languid, slow-moving grace, a woman who conjured up images of tea-length gowns with cut-in sleeves, of sun-bronzed, flawless skin and golden hair falling across her shoulders, of crystal flutes, icy champagne and caviar. Emma, middle-aged and still beautiful. Emma, the mother of his children. Did a man ever get past the woman who'd given him children?

She swallowed and smiled. "Normally I don't mind being alone, but tonight I needed company. I'll go if it's an inconvenience. We've known each other for a long time." She left out the unspoken words, that they were the only two single adults of an age on the island, that once, before Emma, they'd shared long conversations and other lonely evenings, sympathetic in their love for books and Irish writers.

"It's a pleasure to have you, Alice," Patrick said formally. "I'm sorry I didn't think of it myself." He moved toward the bubbling pot on the stove, ladled out two servings, and carried them back to the table. He waited for her to take her first cautious bite. "How is my daughter?"

Alice relaxed. "Mollie is lovely. Her only flaw is that she does too much."

Patrick nodded. "She puts me in mind of Marni."

Alice thought a minute. "In some ways," she agreed, "but Marni's circumstances are different. Her life is not at all as Mollie's was."

She saw his mouth tighten and hurried to explain. "Mollie would have been the same no matter where she grew up, Patrick, and Marni, too. Some are born to the breed. Would you change either of them?"

"It's Danny's life I would have changed."

His hand lay on the table. She reached out and covered it with her own. "I'm so sorry."

"I should have let him go with Emma."

"You thought you were doing the right thing at the time."

He shook his head. "I wanted to punish Emma. I thought she would come home after a time. In the end it was Danny I punished, and myself."

The tender lamb felt like steel wool in her mouth. She forced herself to chew and swallow.

He smiled crookedly. "I'm blathering on tonight, Alice. I don't know why. Perhaps because you're here and I don't often have the chance. Forgive me."

She would say it once and then move on. "Danny was another one who was born to the breed, Patrick. There was nothing you could have done to change that. Had Emma taken him, she would have had her share of difficulties as well."

"Danny would have been spared a father who closed down the pubs."

"I won't defend you, but Danny wasn't the only one. Many of my students have parents addled with the drink, but they go on, leave the island, find jobs. More than a few are successful. Danny did none of those things. He found Kerry and settled in to the life he wanted. She could have coped without him but not he without her. The children are more fortunate than most would have been."

Patrick lifted his head. "Sean?"

Alice nodded. "And Mollie. I don't know how they would have managed without Mollie."

He sighed. "I haven't been much help to them, have I?"

Warmed with stew and tea, Alice spoke her mind. "Not really."

She thought she'd offended him, but when she looked up from her plate, his eyes were on her and there was a definite twinkle in them.

"You've been hard on me tonight, Alice. Was that your intention?"

She flushed. "Of course not."

"You've been hard on Emma as well. I'd no idea you disliked her so."

Alice stirred the last mouthful of stew in her bowl. "I don't *dislike* Emma. We just never got on. You were my friend, Patrick. I couldn't be very fond of her after the way she left you."

She felt him look at her, his glance moving over her face, curious, probing. Lifting her chin she met his stare. "If you've a question, ask it."

He smiled. "I wonder why your friendship escaped me, Alice."

"It did no such thing. It was always there."

"Thank you for that."

Embarrassed, she stood and carried her bowl to the sink, where she washed and dried it thoroughly. When her emotions were under control again she turned, leaned back against the counter, crossed her arms, and dared the question that had bothered her since Emma had returned to the island. "Has she changed much?"

"Who?"

"Emma."

Patrick thought a minute. "I really don't know," he said at last. "We haven't seen much of each other. She's older, of course, but still lovely."

Alice blanched. Emma *was* lovely, but she was fifty-six. Age had leveled out some of the differences between them. But perhaps it didn't matter. Perhaps a man always saw a woman the way he remembered her.

"I don't believe I ever really knew Emma," he continued slowly, as if the thought had just occurred to him. "I created a woman in my mind who was nothing like the one I married." He shrugged. "When you ask me if she's changed, I have no answer."

Alice's face softened. "I'm sorry, Patrick. You should tell me to mind my own business."

He shook his head. "You knew her nearly as well as I did. Does she seem changed?"

Alice stared past him, reliving old memories. "I don't think anyone on this island really knew her. I do remember that in the beginning she laughed a great deal and that all eyes were drawn to her. It was as if she colored the room with light. We were caught up in her pleasure, in her beauty and spirit." She left out the rest of it, the jealousy that turned into heartache, the slow realization that Patrick was pulling away, falling in love with a woman she could never compete with.

He nodded. "It was her spirit that attracted me. I'd never met a woman so filled with life and hope and smiles, so unconcerned with practical matters." He stared, unseeing, at his plate. "We had a few good months. What puzzles me is why she stayed at all. I was hardly a catch, an uneducated Irishman with little to offer a woman like her."

"Don't sell yourself short, Patrick. Any other woman would have been happy to have you."

"Not Emma."

"No," agreed Alice, "not Emma. But why should that surprise you? Not many of our own stay on Inishmore. To imagine a woman like her, accustomed to sunshine twenty-nine days out of thirty, adjusting to a place like this, was too much to expect. There wasn't a prayer of the marriage working, Patrick. We all knew it was merely a matter of time. To my way of thinking she lasted longer than most would have."

He smiled ruefully. "Where were you when I needed it explained to me?"

"You were besotted. You wouldn't have listened."

"I suppose not."

"What happens now?"

He looked surprised. "Now?"

"Her family is here now. Perhaps she could be persuaded to stay."

His mouth dropped. "Tell me you're joking, Alice."

"It isn't a joking matter."

He understood her unasked question. "There is nothing left between Emma and me. She's another man's wife and has been for nearly thirty years. What's come over you?"

The words were like cooling ointment on a painful burn. She could rest on those words and save the hard questions, the ones like *How do you feel when you see her?* or *Could you ever love again?* She wet her lips. "Emma always did bring out the worst in me. I'm sorry, Patrick."

Across the room she could see his eyes warm and blue. "You're a good lass, Alice, to be concerned about me. Don't worry so."

Were all men so obtuse, or was it this particular one? "Perhaps I will take a drop of the spirits after all, Patrick, to keep the chill away."

When they were settled in the living room with a pillow behind her back and a blanket tucked around her legs, after she'd taken her first sip of the warm amber liquid, she remembered what she'd been meaning to tell him all along. "There's talk of evacuation in the village."

"There's been talk of it before."

"The water is polluted for hundreds of kilometers. It may take years to recover."

"There are other ways to make a living."

Lord, he was stubborn. She opened her mouth to tell him just how stubborn when something in his eyes made her stop short. He'd been remarkably agreeable all evening long. She wouldn't risk their tenuous new start by opening up a tender subject. Meanwhile there was tonight, a rare and lovely thought. She would savor it.

17

Sean dipped the washcloth into the bathwater and squeezed it over the baby's shoulders. Luke splashed happily and laughed at him. He managed to return his smile, grateful that at least Luke hadn't succumbed to the aggravating childhood illness that had turned his normally cheerful, uncomplaining nieces into temperamental fishwives.

After rinsing the last bit of shampoo out of his nephew's hair, Sean lifted the baby out of the tub, wrapped him in a towel, and carried him down the chilly hallway into the main room to dress him near the fire.

The girls had finally dropped off to sleep, their faces sore and raw against the pristine white of their pillows. He had barely secured Luke's diaper when the doorbell rang. Leaping over an ottoman and a small table, praying that the girls wouldn't wake, he answered the door before the caller rang a second time.

It was Mollie. He breathed a sigh of relief, invited her inside, and closed the door against the cold. She went straight to the baby, kissed both round red cheeks, and began drying the areas Sean usually forgot, behind the ears and between each miniature toe. "I came by to tell you I've thought of something," she said, gently patting the fold of Luke's ear. "What if we file a suit for negligence and liability as well as damages?" She peeked behind the baby's ear, frowned, and looked more closely.

"For what reason?"

"To make Transom Oil responsible not only for cleanup but for the livelihood of the community. We would ask them to pay for interruption of employment."

"Do you know of a precedent?"

"I've asked a friend in America to find out. He said he would call tomorrow if he has anything."

Resentment colored Sean's response. "What does your American friend know about Irish lawyers?" As soon as the words were out he was ashamed. "I'm sorry, Mollie."

She wasn't paying attention. Instead, she'd taken off the baby's sleeper and turned him around, peering closely at his back. "Sean, look at this. Is it what I think?"

He picked up his nephew and examined the small back. Tiny red areolas were forming at the top of the spine. He checked in back of Luke's ears and swore fluently. "How much more do I have to take?"

"The children are the ones who have the chicken pox," Mollie reminded him, lifting the baby from his lap. "It makes sense that if the girls have it, Luke would catch it, too."

He stared at her. "Does anything rattle you?"

"Of course." Avoiding his eyes, she carefully eased the

baby's chubby legs into his knit sleeper and snapped the buttons shut. "There you are, love," she crooned, "all ready for bed."

She knew her way around the cottage. Passing through the kitchen, she picked up the bottle, warm and waiting, in its pan on the stove. She smiled at Luke. "You're not feeling it yet, are you, little guy?"

He smiled back, his lips widening around the nipple for an instant before beginning his meal. Mollie carried him into his bedroom and sat down in the rocker beside the crib. Within minutes the warm milk and the rocking motion worked their magic. The baby's eyelids fluttered and closed. His mouth relaxed, and he slept. She lowered him into his crib, tucked the blanket around him, and kissed his cheek before raising the bar.

For several minutes she stood there, watching him. Luke was a beautiful baby. The symptomatic red sores had not yet reached his face. His cheeks were soft and clear, his eyelashes long and dark against cream-colored skin. Whorls of light brown hair were growing in all over his head, and his hands, open and relaxed in sleep, were long and well shaped.

An ache rose in Mollie's chest. She hurt for Kerry. How tragic that a mother should miss seeing this. Another thought occurred to her, just as sobering. What if she never had children of her own? She was approaching her twenty-ninth birthday. The girls she'd grown up with were married. Most had children. Marriage and children had been her plan, too. Yet she was no closer than she had ever been. She thought of Garrett and dismissed him immediately. Garrett Michaels would never be her husband. She'd told him so, but he stubbornly refused to accept it, insisting that she wait, that too much had happened, that she didn't know her own mind.

If there was anything Mollie knew, it was her own mind. It frightened her sometimes, the images that flitted across it, impossible desires she had no business imagining. One day, when she had the time, when she wasn't teaching or worrying about her mother or Patrick or the children or the condition of the island, she would sit down, allow herself free rein, and examine why she spent a good part of every day thinking and worrying about Sean O'Malley.

She had never met anyone like him. He was complicated, intellectual. His thoughts were quick, his humor sophisticated, his moods unpredictable. He was bound to his sister's children in ways mere words couldn't begin to express. She loved that in him. It wasn't a difficult stretch to realize why that part attracted her so. She was sensible enough to know, by itself, it wasn't enough. He was also rigid, with the kind of inflexibility that saw no way other than his own. It frightened her.

He was back in the living room. Mollie hadn't been alone with him since that night in the room beside the kitchen. He'd asked her to Galway but not for a *date*. For what, then? She took a slow, steady breath, smoothed her hand over Luke's blanket one last time, and returned to the firelit room where Sean waited.

He sat on the couch, staring into the blazing turf fire, his profile backlit by the glowing flames. A lump rose in her throat. She swallowed, confused by the roiling emotions peeling back the edges of her control. She wasn't ready for this. She started to back away. He turned and stood. She stopped. In the dim light she couldn't tell if he was smiling or frowning.

"Mollie? Is everything all right?"

Her voice was air-filled, tremulous. "Yes."

"I've made tea. Will you stay for a bit?"

Her smile was forced. "Yes." She approached the couch and sat down on the other end.

He handed her a cup. "Milk and sugar. That's right, isn't it?"

She nodded and lifted the cup to her lips. She was being ridiculous. That night in the kitchen was a lapse. He'd forgotten it, and so would she. "Exactly right," she pronounced in her normal voice. "How is the cleanup coming along?"

He shrugged. "Slowly. There's a crew from Australia and another from America flying in this week. We can use the help."

"Where in America?"

"Scripps Institute."

"San Diego. That's close to home."

"Aye."

The pot of tea would take forever to empty. Silence, awkward and thick, settled over them.

He broke it. "I'm sorry about Galway."

"Don't be. I understand."

"You've been a tremendous help with Luke and the girls, Mollie. I don't know what I would have done without you. Thank you for everything." There was no doubting the sincerity of his words.

"I love them," she said simply.

He smiled, and her heart skipped a beat. "I know that. You love easily."

She set the cup and saucer back on the table and thought a minute. "No," she said. "I don't. I can count the number of people I love, *really love*, on one hand. That's unusual for someone my age." She challenged him. "Don't you agree?"

He found himself counting—Caili, Marni, Luke, and Emma. Four. Who was the last? Maybe Patrick, but he didn't think so, not yet. She still hadn't completely forgiven Patrick for his defection.

She was waiting for his answer. He gave her the one that first came to his mind. "I think it would be more unusual for someone like you to count those who love her in such small numbers."

He knew the exact moment she understood. Her face flamed. She looked away. "Thank you. That's a lovely compliment."

"You're not comfortable with compliments, are you, Mollie Tierney?"

"I don't remember having any trouble with them," she said stiffly.

"Perhaps it's only when they come from me."

"Why would that be?"

It lay there between them, the unspoken question, out in the open at last. "Because you know the choice is yours."

She looked at him again, at the vertical creases in his cheeks, the slant of his cheekbones, the arch of his brow, and his mouth, kind, male, smiling. She smiled back. It was such a relief to finally say it. "I choose, yes."

Yes. A single word, a wealth of meaning. Carefully, slowly, he reached across the space dividing them, lifted her hand, and carried it to his mouth. His lips were warm against her palm.

Her eyes closed, and her head fell back against the couch. For days she'd tortured herself, rehashing and analyzing, over and over, finally concluding that his kiss had meant nothing more than a momentary lapse not to be repeated. The timing was bad, she'd rationalized. Four months wasn't long enough to know a man's heart and mind, or was it?

She felt him beside her, his hand on her arm, her throat, her cheek. "Mollie," he murmured before his mouth closed over hers, "whatever do you see in me?"

Turning to him, she filled her hands with the wool of his sweater, with the thickness of his hair and the taut, bunched muscles of his shoulders. A million thoughts leaped to life in her brain only to disappear in the maelstrom of rising desire. Was this love, to want and need and tremble with passion, yet to be afraid at the same time? What did he feel for her, this man with his lightning moods and his sliding, crooked grin that stole the air from her lungs and squeezed her heart with a yearning she couldn't explain? It was a question that needed answering, but not now, not when his hands warmed her skin, kneading their way under her sweater, across the bare skin of her back, not when his lips teased her mouth apart and his tongue curled around hers, coaxing her into an intimacy she must have known before but never with him, never like this. Later, much later, she would ask her question, and the others she'd pushed aside.

Sean had known desire, long ago, but he'd forgotten how it could rise up after a long dormancy and catch a man unaware, when it was least expected, when he didn't want it. What he wanted now, as he'd never wanted anything before, was to feel a woman, this woman, beneath him, taking him inside her, cooling the burn, soothing the pain. He wanted to touch the bones of her face, the nape of her neck, the soft roundness of her breast. His mouth was filled with strands of her hair, whiskey-gold in the firelight. Her face was pressed into the curve of his throat. The strength of his hunger shook him. He didn't know wanting could feel this way. Why had it never felt this way before?

He didn't know when it changed, when he knew she would have him without refusal, without the games women played, without the words they needed before giving of themselves. He carried her into the bedroom, grateful that he'd thought ahead to light the fire. Locking the door against interruptions, he undressed her slowly, baring one small section of skin at a time, touching her, kissing her, suckling her until she was naked and shivering and wanting him as much as he wanted her.

She was neither shy nor bold, her quick fingers aiding him in the separating of buttons from their holes and the sliding of zippers and the loosening of laces and all that kept him from her waiting, eager, flame-gilded body. She touched him all over, tentatively at first and then with growing confidence, molding the lines and shape of him with her hands and arms and lips. Her mouth settled on his, and she kissed him deeply.

He pulled back before entering her, to look at her face. What he saw there tugged at his heart. There would be no stopping, no regrets. She was seeing him, seeing through him. Had he ever really looked at a woman at this, their most intimate moment? The answer shamed him.

Keeping his eyes locked on hers, he slid deeply into

her, moving with the rhythms of her body, feeling the warm female flesh close tightly around him. He felt the sound more than he heard it, a small involuntary whimper she couldn't control. She wanted him. The knowledge was powerful, heady. It inflamed him. His control broke, and he surged inside her.

When it was over she touched him on the blade of his cheek and ran her finger over it. "Sean," she breathed. "Oh, Sean." He put his mouth on hers, and she wanted him to leave it there forever, but there were questions to be asked, and if ever they were to do this again, they needed asking.

"How have we come to this place?" he asked in wonder.

"Because of Kerry," she answered. "Kerry brought us together." She turned on her side and propped her cheek up on her elbow. "Tell me about Kerry."

His mouth tightened. He didn't want to go there, not yet, perhaps not ever again. "My mother would do a better job of it."

"I'm asking you."

"There's nothing to tell."

"Of course there is. I want to know her. Her letters were lovely, welcoming. The girls are the way they are because of her. Don't keep her from me. She deserves to be remembered."

He sat up and reached for his clothes, pulling on his trousers and sweater, not bothering with the shirt. "Leave it, Mollie."

"Why won't you tell me?"

"It isn't what you think."

"What isn't?"

"This life—this island—all of it." He ran his hands

through his hair. "I want to put it behind me. I don't want to speak of it."

"Until you do, you won't be healed."

She reminded him of Mabry. "Do you think because of what we've done that you've the right to examine every bit of my life?"

She shook her head. "It's not what we've done, it's how we feel."

"And how is that?"

Her eyes were very bright. He knew he'd hurt her, but he wouldn't take it back. A woman like her could know nothing of what he carried with him.

"You're afraid to love me because of what my mother did to Patrick."

The veins stood out like railroad tracks on the smooth plane of his neck. "It's more than that."

She waited, refusing to make it easy for him.

"Have you asked yourself what it is you see in me, Mollie?"

"Of course I have."

"Have you really? Is your answer an honest one? Because I'm finding it hard to believe that a woman like you would give more than the time of day to a man like me with nothing to offer but a future on an island that's twenty years behind the rest of the civilized world."

"Is that how you see it?"

His jaw tightened. "That's the way it is."

"Apparently you've taken up psychology as well. What do *you* think I see in you?"

"It's not me you're seeing."

"Who is it, then?"

"A father."

Her mouth fell open. She nearly laughed. "Believe me, Sean. I don't consider you to be the least bit fatherly."

"Not for yourself, Mollie."

A tiny furrow appeared between her eyebrows. "I don't understand."

He stood and walked to the window, fists balled in his pockets. "You came here in desperate need of a father. It's my guess that you've been looking for him your whole life. When he wouldn't come to you, you decided to come to him. I'm thinking that without Danny's three children you wouldn't have been nearly as accommodating as you were ten minutes ago."

Mollie recoiled as if she'd been slapped. Her eyes blazed dangerously. "You can't really believe that."

"It doesn't take a genius to see what's obvious."

Without speaking, she found her clothes. Deliberately, unselfconsciously, she pulled on her sweater and slacks, her socks and boots. Then she shook out her hair and stood. "I'll be leaving now," she said without looking at him. "Thank you for the—" She hesitated. "The interlude."

"Mollie." He reached for her.

"Don't." She held up her hand. "Don't touch me. I don't want you touching me."

"Mollie." He was desperate now. "Don't do this."

"Do what?"

"Pull away like this."

"You've just told me what I feel for you isn't real. I've had some psychology, too, Sean, enough to know that people superimpose their true feelings onto others. What you really mean is your attraction for me is nothing more than a desire to provide Kerry's children with a mother."

She couldn't be serious. "That isn't true."

"Isn't it? What if I wasn't the nurturing type? Would you still be interested?"

"Any man with eyes would be interested in you, Mollie."

"Coming from anyone else that would be a compliment."

He could see that she was close to tears. "From me as well," he said gently.

Her voice cracked. "I don't understand you. What just happened here?"

He closed his eyes. "I'm afraid of you, Mollie Tierney. You've turned my life upside down. I don't know what I want."

She laughed bitterly. "When you do, let me know."

With that she was gone. He should have stopped her. When had he ever known anyone like her in his bleak, empirical world, a woman joyful enough to dance in the rain, who poured elegance when she walked, an imprint indelibly carved on his brain, gold-brown hair, eyes like blue smoke, a mouth—

His jaw clamped. He turned back to the kitchen with its sink full of unwashed dishes and a table cluttered with correspondence he couldn't have finished if he had a staff of twelve. This was his world. For the moment, Galway and Dublin, culture and civilization were beyond him. He'd accepted it. If not giddy with his lot, he'd been satisfied, until Mollie Tierney walked into his life.

18

$\mathcal{M}$ollie was angry, with a cold, quiet outrage that settled like a ball of ice in her stomach numbing all other
emotions. She smiled mechanically, taught her students,
answered their questions, and corrected their papers,
negotiating her way through the last days of the school
term on automatic pilot. Only with her nieces and
nephew did she allow a glimmer of her natural warmth
to shine through. She pushed all thoughts of Sean
O'Malley and their humiliating evening together from
her mind. Later, much later, when the incident wasn't so
raw, when she could look at it rationally, she would take
it out, dust it off, and figure out how she'd ended up in
this condition.

Mollie was a realist. She saw no point in hedging or
avoiding the truth. She loved Sean O'Malley, all of him,
the difficult, inflexible, irritating parts of him. And
because of her mother, he was afraid to love her back. It
was so simple and so disastrous. Mollie wasn't skilled at
manipulation. Either Sean wanted her or he didn't. She

wouldn't try to win him over. Instinct told her he wasn't a man easily convinced. But more than that, she wanted no part of coercing a man to love her.

The day before the holidays had been an exhausting one, finishing up the term, organizing the play the children had rehearsed for their parents, supervising the Christmas party, and distributing the monogrammed pencils and candy canes she'd found in Galway City.

She gathered the gifts her students had given her—handmade Christmas ornaments, shell necklaces, soda bread, and amateur watercolor paintings—and packed them into two cardboard boxes. They were too bulky to carry home. She would ask Patrick to drive over in his pony cart and help her carry them. Mollie looked at her watch. It was late, nearly time for tea. The girls were still not well enough to entertain themselves, and her mother would need help with the evening meal.

Reluctantly she looked around the classroom, closing cupboards, sweeping the last of the crayons into a drawer, straightening the apple-shaped pencil holder on her desk. It was time to go home.

She'd managed to avoid Sean on those occasions when he brought the children in the mornings and picked them up at night. It was easier when she was teaching, but now, with two weeks at home looming ahead of her— She sighed, locked the door, and started up the path.

Emma, busy with caring for three small children with chicken pox, had no time to analyze her daughter's mood swings other than to hope she had come to her senses and was anxious to return to her life in Newport.

Christmas would soon be upon them, and Ward was flying in for the holiday.

Stirring the soup Eileen had delivered that morning, she watched through the window, waiting for Mollie to come home from school. It was after four and already dark. Surely she wouldn't stay late on the last day before vacation.

She peered out the window. Was that someone coming up the road? Emma reached for her glasses. It was too dark to make out his features, but he was definitely a man, a stranger. He carried a duffel bag, and, from his stride, Emma knew that he was young. She opened the door and stepped out onto the porch. "Good evening." She smiled. "May I help you?"

"You're not Irish," he said.

His accent couldn't be mistaken. "Neither are you."

He laughed and held out his hand. "Russ Sanders from Scripps Institute, San Diego, California. I'm here to help with the Transom spill."

"Emma Reddington from Newport, California." She released his hand and waited.

"May I come in?"

Emma hesitated. It was one thing to talk to a stranger on the front porch, but to ask him in—

"I spoke with your daughter on the phone," he explained. "There's a housing shortage on the island. Everything is full. They're asking for families to rent out spare rooms."

"Mollie agreed to rent out a room, without even asking me?" Emma was incredulous.

"Apparently so, but if it's a problem—" His expression was troubled.

"No," she said politely. "Of course not. Please, come in." She led the way into the living room. "I was surprised, that's all. I hope you've had the chicken pox."

"I have."

He grinned, and Emma's eyes widened. "Have you met my daughter, Mr. Sanders?"

"Call me Russ. No, not yet. I called her from the tourist bureau."

Emma smiled. "I'll show you the spare room. It's small. I hope you don't mind."

Again he smiled, and her heart flipped. Where was Mollie?

"I don't mind small," he said easily. "More than likely I'll only be here to sleep."

Emma led him to the bedroom on the south side of the cottage. "I'll leave you to settle in. Mollie should be home soon. Tea will be ready in half an hour."

"I'm not much of a tea drinker, Mrs. Reddington."

She laughed. "I'm settling into old patterns. Tea is the early evening meal. We're having roast chicken and potatoes. You're welcome to join us."

"I'll do that. Thank you."

Emma closed the bedroom door and offered up a silent prayer of thanks. Polite, gorgeous, and straight from San Diego. She couldn't have set up a better set of circumstances if she'd orchestrated it herself. If only he was fond of children. Mollie wouldn't want anyone who didn't like children.

Emma looked in on her grandchildren. Caili was recovering nicely. Dried half-circles still marked her forehead and cheeks, but her open sores were gone. Luke's case had never been a serious one. It was Marni who had her grandmother worried. The child was having a difficult time of it. Her temperature was normal. Emma would never have allowed Patrick to bring the children in the trap if Marni had a fever. But she was unusually lethargic and slept a great deal more than a girl her age should. Her moods shifted, and her grandmother despaired of ever seeing the reasonable, even-tempered child she'd come to love.

The table was set and the chicken browned and appetizing in the roaster. There was still no word from Mollie. Emma called the children and her new guest to the table. She considered it something of a test. If Russ Sanders could eat with three red, scabby faces staring at him, he would be a likely candidate for Mollie's affections.

She heard his steps in the hall. Luke lay in his infant seat and waved his rattle. Marni and Caili looked up expectantly. He stood for a minute in the entrance, obviously American, all six feet several inches of him. Then he smiled, and Emma relaxed.

"Hello there." He pulled out a chair and sat down.

"We have chicken pox," Caili confided.

"I can see that. How's it going?"

The girls stared at him. He amended his question. "How are you feeling?"

"Better," Marni said politely

She did look better.

Caili spoke. "My spots are nearly gone. They went away sooner than Marni's."

Without asking, the American began carving the roasted chicken. "Sometimes it works that way. The younger you are, the easier you have it."

"Really?" Marni looked up eagerly.

He nodded. "Really."

"How long do you think it will be until I'm well?"

He finished cutting the last piece of breast meat, replaced the knife and serving fork on the platter, and looked at Marni's face. Gently he took her chin in his hand and turned it one way and then the other. "I would say another week or so will do it."

"How can you tell?"

His eyes crinkled at the corners when he smiled. "There are six children in my family. We've all had chicken pox."

Marni sighed with relief. She picked up her fork and for the first time in days applied herself to her food.

Emma was more than pleased with Mollie's new houseguest. Six children. A large family. Better and better. She glanced at Marni's plate and sighed with relief. The child was actually eating. "My goodness, Marni. Why didn't you ask me? Did you think you'd have chicken pox forever?"

Marni hung her head. Her voice was so soft Emma could barely hear it. "Some people don't always get well. Ciara Feeney didn't."

Horrified, Emma forgot all about her plans for Mollie. She'd heard the tragic story of the little girl with spinal meningitis. She reached across the table and covered Marni's hand with her own. "Ciara was different. All children recover from chicken pox," she said firmly, not caring whether or not it was true. Her reward was Marni's smile.

Emma looked at the clock on the wall. Where *was* Mollie? Before she finished her thought, she heard the front door open.

"Aunt Mollie's home," Caili sang. She dropped her fork and dashed out of the kitchen.

Russ chuckled. "Aunt Mollie must be very popular around here."

Emma smiled. "The girls are fond of her."

Marni corrected her. "We're not fond of her, Grandma. We love her. Everyone does." She appealed to Russ. "She's twenty-eight."

He looked interested. "Really?"

"And she isn't married yet."

His eyes twinkled. "Is that a problem?"

"Don't you think that's rather old to not be married?"

"That depends on your perspective. How old are you?

"Nine."

"I suppose for a nine-year-old, twenty-eight seems old. But I'm thirty-two and still not married. So, you see, twenty-eight doesn't seem that old to me."

"Will you be getting married someday?"

"Probably."

Marni brightened. "Perhaps you'd like to marry Aunt Mollie."

Emma laughed. "Marni, stop. Mollie doesn't need you to recruit a husband for her. She's perfectly capable of finding one on her own."

"Something smells delicious. What are we having?" Mollie stood in the entrance to the kitchen with Caili beside her.

Emma watched Russ's eyes widen in appreciation. He leaned over to whisper something into Marni's ear. "It's chicken," answered Emma. "Sit down and eat before everything's cold. Where have you been?"

"Gathering everything together." Mollie smiled at

Russ. "You must be Russ Sanders." She extended her hand. He stood and shook it, holding it for exactly the right amount of time. "I'm Mollie Tierney."

"Pleased to meet you, Mollie." He waited until she sat down before taking his own seat. "I appreciate the use of your extra room."

She reached for the chicken and potatoes. "I'm glad we could help. What will you be doing first?"

"Assessing the extent of the damage in terms of lost animals should take a few weeks. After that we'll check the oil levels in local waters and the damage to the hatcheries."

"How long will it take?"

"It depends on what we find. Best case, two months. Worst, a year."

Her eyes, blue and cool, met his across the table. "I won't be here in a year."

He grinned. "I hope I won't, either."

Emma watched their interplay. He was definitely interested, but she couldn't tell with Mollie. She had designated personal relationships as off-limits ever since she began to date seriously.

"It's too bad you'll miss Christmas at home."

He shrugged. "I'm used to it. It's been quite a while since all six of us have managed to make it home for Christmas."

"It must be hard on your parents."

He laughed. "There's always a crowd. Two or three missing children aren't even noticed."

Emma looked shocked. "Don't be ridiculous. All mothers miss their children, no matter how much of a crowd there is."

Mollie stared at her. Since coming to Ireland, her mother's personality had completely reversed itself. The sweet, accommodating woman she'd grown up with would never have told a stranger he was ridiculous.

Russ appeared oblivious to her rudeness. "Maybe you're right," he said agreeably. "However, there isn't much I can do about it." He smiled at Emma. "Do you have other children, Mrs. Tierney?"

"Reddington," she corrected him, "and, no, I have no other children, not anymore."

The silence was thick and uncomfortable. Mollie broke it. "My brother died recently."

"Oh, geez." Russ looked around the table, at the girls, round-eyed and solemn, at Emma fighting back tears. "Listen, I'm sorry, I didn't mean—"

"It's all right," Mollie assured him. "How could you have known? It's just still rather raw." She smiled at Caili and changed the subject. "Guess what we did at school today?"

"What?"

"We had a gift exchange. Remember the pencil boxes I bought in Galway and we wrapped to take to school?"

Caili nodded. Her eyes lit up expectantly.

"I took them to school for the party and brought back gifts for the two of you."

Caili clapped and dropped her fork. Diving under the table, she found it and came up smiling. Emma handed her another one. "Where are they?" the child asked.

"In my room. As soon as you're finished eating, you can open them."

"Who would like dessert?" Emma asked.

"What is it?" Marni still had not regained her appetite.

"Red Jell-o," replied her grandmother.

Caili spoke. "I'll have some after my present."

"No, thanks, Grandma." Marni sounded tired. "Maybe later."

Emma began to clear the plates. "There's apple pie, too, if anyone's interested."

Russ brightened. "You've talked me into it."

Mollie laughed. "Good choice. My mother's apple pie is unparalleled."

"I'm sure it is. I haven't had a meal like this since I left home."

"How long has that been?" Mollie asked.

Emma took longer than necessary gathering the flatware. She was more than mildly interested in his answer.

"About six months."

"Does your job keep you away for that long?"

He shook his head. "Not usually. We've only had six major oil spills in the last decade. Two of them, including this one, happened in the last six months."

"What do you do when you're not cleaning up spills?"

"I'm a veterinarian, specializing in marine animals. I research, tag, and monitor animals, provide information to the community."

"What kind of information?"

"There is always some new controversy over maintaining the wetlands. I provide education about the effects of development. Before I can do that, I have to do my homework."

"I don't like homework," Caili interrupted.

"Hush," Marni reprimanded her.

Again Russ grinned, and Emma wondered how Mollie could remain so unaffected.

"When you really love what you're doing, homework isn't so bad," he said.

Mollie's lips twitched. "In the future, I'll make more of an effort not to bore you, Caili."

"I'm not bored, Aunt Mollie. I just don't like homework."

"You're very lucky to have a teacher like Mollie," observed Russ.

"Why?" the child asked.

His voice took on a deeper, intimate note. "Because I can't imagine her boring anyone."

Satisfied that the conversation needed no help from her, Emma disappeared into the kitchen.

Mollie wiped Luke's hand and face and lifted him from his chair. "If you'll excuse me, I'm going to wash him off. Then I'll make coffee and take it into the living room." She looked over Luke's head at the tall American. "You are a coffee drinker?"

He nodded. "I like it thick and black."

"Tonight you'll drink it mild and decaffeinated. The black part won't be a problem."

His smile was a white triangle in his tanned face. "Whatever you say, ma'am."

"I doubt that," she murmured under her breath, and walked the baby down the hall to the bathroom.

19

Mollie tossed in the throes of a troubled dream. Water boiled around a small boat, lifting it to terrifying heights so that it balanced on the crest of the swell and then dropping it into deep caverns dwarfed by sea walls as high as the jagged, dangerous cliffs of Dun Aengus. She couldn't make out the features of the men on deck, but she knew one of them was Sean.

She woke, cold and trembling, and looked at the clock. Four in the morning. Pulling the comforter up to her chin, she stared at the ceiling. The darkness wouldn't lift for another five hours. She dozed. At first she thought the pounding on the door was the beginning of another nightmare, but then her mind cleared and she heard heavy steps in the hall.

Throwing back the covers, she reached for her robe, threw it on, raked shaky fingers through her shoulder-length hair, and ran down the stairs. Russ was already at the door. She reached his side just as he opened it. They stood there together, Mollie in her unbelted bathrobe, hair bed-tousled from her restless night, the tall American shirtless, trousers hastily pulled on, his fly zipped but not buttoned.

Tight-lipped and grim, Sean stood on the porch, looking from one to the other. He spoke to Russ. "We need help. There's a school of porpoises on the beach, slick with oil."

"Wait for me." Russ disappeared up the stairs.

"We need you, too, Mollie," Sean said softly. "We need every hand we can get."

Her hand moved to her throat. She swallowed. "I'll change and tell my mother. It won't take long."

Minutes later, bundled in waterproof slickers, the three of them hurried, without speaking, down to the shore. The scene on the beach drew Mollie up short. Volunteers had already arrived, and small bonfires illuminated the scene. Terrified, she could only stare in horror at the carcasses and gasping animals wallowing on the sand, clinging to their last bit of life. A westerly wind carried the metallic stench of old blood, rotting animals, and kerosene across the beach and up toward the cliffs. Mollie pressed the back of her hand against her nose and clutched Sean's sleeve with her other hand. "Is there anything to be done? It looks . . . too late."

"It is," he said shortly, "for most of them. We'll save a few."

"They can't go back into the ocean. Where will we put them?"

"There's a cove that's nearly clean. It should hold the porpoises for the time being if we're lucky, until we can transport them to clean ocean."

"Why wouldn't it?"

Russ joined the conversation. "Mammals this size need more space."

Mollie breathed in through her mouth. Sean watched her hand leave it, watched her back straighten, and heard the words he knew she would say back at the cottage when he'd asked for help. He'd known her four months. Four months, a year, a lifetime. It didn't matter. He knew her as well as he knew anyone. Another woman might answer differently but not Mollie.

"What should I do?" she asked.

Sean pointed to a section of beach where the largest group of people congregated. Washtubs had been set up on the sand. Human figures, white cloths in their hands, knelt beside the bodies of two inert porpoises, rubbing down the animals in sweeping circular motions. Three small canoe-like boats, curraghs, floated in the surf, and a fishing trawler hovered close to the shoreline. "Those vats are filled with detergent and water," he said. "Before we can put the porpoises in the cove, they need to be scrubbed and rinsed. That's where we need help the most."

Mollie climbed down the embankment and walked across the sand. Away from the beach, cottages were still dark and children slept. Here, on the beach, bonfires choked out the shadows, flame-painting figures, human and animal, illuminating faces, transforming the darkness into an unnatural golden daylight that Inishmore had never before seen in the dead of winter.

"We can use another set of hands over here," a woman called out.

Mollie found a towel and walked toward the American voice. "Lift the flipper," the woman said. "This one's thick with it."

Automatically, Mollie reached for the leathery appendage and extended it. It felt smooth, cool, oil-slick.

"I've got to suction out the blow-hole," said the American. "Is everybody ready?"

Mollie panicked. "For what?"

"We've got to hold him down." Someone else spoke, a man this time, again with an American accent. "He'll think he's suffocating. He's going to struggle." He placed Mollie's hands on the hard skin just below the flipper. "Press here, hard. We'll do the rest."

Mollie closed her eyes and pressed. Under her hands she felt the surge of powerful muscle as the animal struggled to survive. Someone swore. She pushed harder. The awful sucking nose of the syringe continued. Again the animal bucked in a terrifying final attempt to throw off the misunderstood invasion of its body. She found solace in a mindless litany, *Pease porridge hot, pease porridge cold*. Tears coursed down her cheeks. Again the heaving wet animal flesh rose under her hands. She pushed still harder. Her breath came in short, desperate gasps. Finally, the animal lay still, completely spent, while the team of rescuers finished their ministering.

"We're done here," the first woman said quietly. Sighing, Mollie stepped back. Two men hand-signaled the small boat. Working collectively, the team rolled the passive mammal onto a canvas sheet and dragged him to the boat where he was placed gently in the hold. "Why isn't he moving?" she asked.

"He's been sedated," the woman said. "As long as he doesn't feel immediately threatened, he'll lay still until we get him on the big boat and into the clean water of the cove." She smiled. "I'm Beth Bradley from Scripps,

San Diego." She introduced the others, friendly, serious faces with open smiles and American manners. Two of them were already at work on the other porpoise.

She smiled. "Mollie Tierney."

"You're not Irish," Beth said.

"No. I'm from Newport, California, not too far from you. I came to teach school for the year."

"Are you ready to start again?"

"Yes."

Beth nodded. "Follow me. I've tagged the ones that are still alive."

Mollie worked furiously all morning long and late into the afternoon, scrubbing, rinsing, refilling the vats with fresh water, tearing clean strips from wide sterile sheets of cotton. Once, late into the morning, women from the villages passed by with mugs of steaming tea, hot bread, and jam. Gratefully, she eased her aching body into a sitting position and curled her frozen fingers around the mug. She had never been so tired and sore and cold.

Sean sat down beside her. "You've been a trooper, Mollie. Thank you for your help."

Her mind, numb from cold and lack of food and sleep, stirred to life with the bread and tea. She looked around, the scene on the beach sharp and clear in the lead-gray afternoon. "Where is everyone?"

"Everyone?"

"The fishing boats are docked. Why isn't anyone else helping?"

"Alice is here."

Mollie shook her head impatiently. "Why aren't the fishermen here?"

He looked surprised. "Fishermen and porpoises are natural enemies. A porpoise school means less of a harvest. You won't find any island families working to take the food from their mouths."

"They must resent us terribly."

He shrugged. "Not really. Islanders are a pragmatic people, Mollie. They recognize that others have a job to do. Cleaning up the oil is a priority. They want that, too. If it means rescuing a few porpoises, sea lions, and pelicans, they'll go along with it, but they won't inconvenience themselves." He grinned. "You won't be shunned in the village, if that's what's worrying you."

"It isn't, and you know it." She thought a minute. "I'm wondering what they're thinking. All these people, professionals commanding salaries, their expenses paid, to save animals while the islanders ration food in winter. A small portion of the money spent on saving animals would tide these people over for several years."

"Cleaning animals is something we can do when we're not cleaning oil. That's what they're really here for."

"I doubt it, Sean. These people are exhausted. We've been working around the clock. No one will be cleaning any oil until this is finished and they've had some rest."

"I knew all Americans weren't environmentalists, but somehow I thought you would be."

She frowned. "I thought I was, too. It's easy to be an environmentalist when you live in Newport Beach with money and choices. Life looks different from here."

His eyes were serious, the lines around his mouth pronounced with weariness. "I imagine there are many choices in America."

"Yes," Mollie said, surprised that she meant it. All her years of romanticizing had brought her here, to this.

She felt his eyes on her face. Her skin was stiff with salt, innocent of makeup. She'd pulled her hair back and secured it with an elastic twist. She cared what he thought of her, even now. Self-consciously, she licked the salt from her lips and turned away from him to look down the beach. "Where's Russ?" she asked. "I haven't seen him since we came."

"He's working with another group from Australia at Saint Mary's Point."

"More porpoises?"

Sean shook his head. "Birds. The Australians have come up with a method to dry-clean them. It's less stressful and doesn't destroy the waterproof properties of the feathers."

"How do they do that?"

"Finely ground iron powder. The birds are dusted with it and then combed with a magnet that removes the oil and the iron. Oil sticks to iron powder more readily than it does to feathers. Iron powder is cheap and plentiful. It's also nontoxic and a nonirritant."

"How do you know all this? I thought you wrote plays."

He grinned, a flash of humor in the bleakness. "Haven't you heard the old adage 'Write what you know'? What do you think I write about?"

"I don't know any of your plays."

"I didn't think you would."

"What's the name of the one you're working on?"

"*The Beggar of Inishmaan.*"

"It doesn't sound very uplifting."

"You'd be surprised."

Her eyes closed. Maybe she'd offended him. Waves of weariness washed over her. His next words jerked her to attention. "What do you think of him?"

"Who?"

"Your American guest."

She answered without hesitation. "I don't know him very well, but he seems pleasant enough. The girls can't get enough of him."

"What about Emma?"

Mollie laughed. "A man who does dishes? My mother thinks he hung the moon."

"Do men not do dishes in America?"

"I imagine it's the same as here. Some do, most don't."

She left the rest of her thought unsaid, the unasked question, *Do you do them?*

"I do dishes on occasion, when I can no longer find the kitchen counter," he offered.

She smiled. "That's fairly typical of men. Even when they marry, women do most of the cleaning."

"But it wouldn't be your arrangement, would it, Mollie? Is that what you're saying?"

She looked at him then, at the light in his eyes, at the sharp clean blade of his jaw. "No," she said deliberately, "that's not what I'm saying. Everyone's circumstances are different."

He relaxed and stared out to sea. "It's difficult," he admitted, "to do it all."

"You have us," she reminded him, "for now."

"Thank God for that."

She changed the subject. "Russ said this could last as long as a year."

"We'll see oil residue here on this island for ten years."

"What about the cleanup? Will it take that long?"

"Probably not. Most of what we can do will be finished in the next three months. The rest is up to Mother Nature. Storms, wind, rain all have their part to play. We're fortunate that this happened now before the summer. We've some bad weather ahead. That disseminates more of the oil."

"What about the fish? Will the men be able to go back to work?"

He shook his head. "Not this year."

"Have you given any thought to my suggestion?"

"The lawsuit?"

She nodded.

"I've mentioned it to Graham. When this dies down a bit, I'll have more time to look into it, but it really isn't my area, Mollie."

"It isn't mine, either, but someone has to do it."

"And you've decided that someone is me?"

"Who else?" she asked.

"Someone more directly involved."

"Sometimes the most qualified person isn't one who is directly involved. Besides, we shouldn't wait too long."

"Why not?"

"Litigation takes time, Sean. These people need money."

He was looking at her again with an expression she couldn't read.

"What is it?" she asked.

"You could do it."

Mollie shook her head. "I don't know anything about maritime law."

"It was your idea."

"It wasn't exactly a stretch," she protested. "Any logical person would have suggested a suit for damages."

"Not here. These people don't think like that. Most of them are suspicious of outsiders. If they have experiences with the law, they aren't positive ones."

"Would they go along with it?"

"I think so, if it meant their survival." He smiled at her. "The difficulty will be deciding who should benefit. If it isn't everyone on the island, I wouldn't pursue it. That would cause more problems than the oil."

"I agree. Everyone suffers from a poor economy. I think everyone should benefit."

"Will the solicitors think so, I wonder?"

She sighed. "I'll have to ask them, won't I?"

He nodded. "You will."

She rested her chin on her knees. "Did you know all along that I would do it?"

He grinned, and the relaxed happy look of him turned her heart over. "I know you're persistent and intelligent. I know you've resources people here have never heard of."

"Do you realize," she said softly, "that you separate yourself from the people here?"

"Surely not."

She said nothing.

Curiosity made him ask. "What makes you say that?"

"You refer to your neighbors as 'the people here' or 'the islanders,' never 'we' or 'us.' "

He thought about it. She was right. "I'll have to work on that."

"It isn't a criticism, Sean, just an observation. I wondered why, that's all."

"You brought it up. You must have a theory."

She stood and brushed the sand from the back of her legs. "It's just something I noticed. I really haven't given you much thought lately."

He watched her walk away from him, her body falling into the swinging, athletic gait he'd come to associate with her alone, a colt in slow motion, young, confident, not at all Irish. For hours she'd worked like a laborer without complaint, and still she went back for more. He'd meant to tell her to go home, sleep. But, as always, she took his mind and twisted it, wrung it out and stretched it until it went somewhere he'd never intended for it to go. She no longer looked like Emma. She was nothing like Emma. A woman like her could steal the soul from a man, and when she left him there would be nowhere else in the world for him to go.

She hadn't given him much thought. She was lying. He knew her. He felt as if he'd always known her. She fancied herself in love with him. But that would go away once she was gone. He had no doubt it would go away if he asked her to stay.

The group from Scripps was breaking up now, all Americans, all competent. Even now the shiny, confident look of them set them apart. They worked in shifts, like an organized machine, taking turns on the beach, cleaning birds, skimming oil, relocating sea lions, communicating in the friendly serious language of men and women summoned to a common calling. He was grateful to them, all of them. More than that, he liked them, especially Russ Sanders, the tall American with the friendly smile and a ready wit that reminded him of Patrick.

He'd been the last to come. There was nowhere else to put him but with Mollie and Emma. Sean knew Mollie would like him. They were the same. It was easier when people were the same.

Despite his ten-year absence, Sean was an islander. The fatalistic acceptance of a world shaped and purged by wind and rain and a hard-edged sea was in his blood. He frowned, impatient with the direction of his thoughts. It was better this way. In the end they would all go home, and the island would settle down again. He thought of the men without work and the harsh winter to come. Perhaps Mabry was right. Mollie wasn't one to sit by and let things happen. Perhaps she would leave her mark on Inishmore after all. Knowing her had changed him. He recognized it now. He asked himself more questions, posed more what-ifs in his mind. What it all meant he didn't know yet.

Squinting into the meager December sunlight, he could barely see the outline of the mainland. Inishmore had always been home. He couldn't imagine an existence apart from it, and yet his life was improved when he was away. He stood and walked back toward the sudsing tubs. There was still the oil, three sick children at home, and a play waiting to be finished.

20

Huddled in an Aran sweater, her hands stuffed into the deep wool pockets, her body braced against the force of the wind, Emma stood on the edge of Dun Aengus cliff overlooking the sea. This had become her favorite spot on the island. Strange, how time changed one's perspective. Thirty years ago nothing on Inishmore had pleased her. All she could think of was the cold, not the crisp, clear cold of a winter night in Boston or New York but a thick, damp, miserable cold, not actually wet but too far from dry ever to feel comfortable.

All the islanders felt it. They would say, "There's a wicked damp in the air," or "My feet are gone damp in my shoes," but it never appeared to bother them. Only Emma shivered and froze and sought out seats near whatever turf fire was available. Only Emma had worn three sweaters and two pairs of socks and wrapped her babies so tightly their cheeks were always flushed and they screamed in protest.

She'd hated it here, this stifling, ocean-locked land

where one could walk from one end to the other in two hours' time, where the fog hung thick as gray blankets over the cliffs and the fierce wind reshaped the land almost as quickly as day changed into night. She'd hated the people with their identical blue eyes and their smiling, cordial faces and their placid acceptance of birth and death and all that came between. She'd hated the way they slid into their language, low, husky, guttural sounds that came from somewhere back in their throats and appeared to require no movement whatsoever from mouth and lips.

Eventually she'd come to hate Patrick, seeing the same face, the same eyes, hearing the same voice that she heard in all the serious, inbred islanders she could ever talk to or befriend. She forgot that once she'd loved him, that his black hair curled around his ears, and that his voice, whiskey-soft and lilting, had charmed her into his arms, his bed, his life. She'd gone away, emotionally at first, pushing him from her in the only way she knew how, with words. They came from her mouth, ugly, blaming, until there were no words left at all. She refused to speak or to eat or to move with any purpose around the small cottage that was Patrick's home, the home that would never be hers.

Finally, when he could take no more of it, he told her to leave, without Danny. Those weeks when she struggled between staying and leaving, when her mind hung by fragile threads, when Mabry had spoken in that whispery, crackling voice that froze her with fear, Emma lost what was left of who she was. She'd gone away with Mollie, a baby who had no memory of the island or her father.

Now it was different. With the advantages of age and wisdom, Emma could see that Inishmore had its own kind of beauty. The scrub, the twisting stone fences dividing the land into patches of green, the sheep thick on the roads, and the churning clouds were part of a disappearing charm that drew swarms of tourists year after year, season after season. Not this season, of course. Winter wasn't a time when people left their home fires for the wet cold of Inishmore. Winter was a season of silence when fog hung thick over the island and every footstep down the twisting cliff paths was a challenge. A rare, clear day like this one was an occasion to celebrate.

Emma had left the children with Mollie. They were healing quickly now and sleeping later than usual. She looked at her watch. There was something she needed to do, something she'd put off for weeks, but first she would visit Danny.

Bordered by stone fences, the road to the tiny church twisted its way down to sea level. The ocean, calm for a change and visible on all sides, reflected blue skies and friendly wind.

She made her way past the randomly erected gravestones, hundreds of years old, chipped and precariously balanced, their letters nearly worn away by weather and lichen, to the newer part of the cemetery where Danny lay buried beneath the rich limestone.

Emma stood for a moment staring down at the mound of dirt that was all that remained of her child, her firstborn. A woman knew nothing of the roiling emotions that came with the birth of a child until that child was born and the tiny warm weight of him was curled against her breast. A woman remembered her first child differently from the others, the soft folds of delicate skin, the whorls of fine hair, the baby scent that lingered on blankets and diapers and towels. There was something about a first child that a mother watched more carefully, paid attention to more fully, accounting for the first smile, the first steps, the first word in a way she never would again. It wasn't that she loved the others any less, but the first one was her blueprint, her debut to the world.

Something moved behind her. The barest slip of shadow crossed the pale gray of the headstone. Emma stiffened. She didn't want company, not here, not today. Everyone on the island knew who she was and whom she'd come to mourn. She waited for the intruder to go away. Instead a voice, a whispery crackling voice, interrupted her. "*Dhia Duit, a* Emma."

Three decades spent on the other side of the world disappeared as if they'd never been. The words came back to her. "*Dhia es Muire Duit, a* Mabry."

"*Conas ta tu?*"

Emma glanced at the old woman. "*Go maith.*"

"*Buiochas le Dia.*"

Her fists clenched. "Why do you say it like that?"

Mabry fixed her piercing gaze on something in the distance. Emma was about to repeat her question when the woman spoke. "I've often wondered if you could tolerate it here with us, even for a short time."

"Should it matter?"

"Everything that happens on Inishmore matters."

Emma pushed the air out of her lips in a deprecating sigh. "Most of the world is unaware this island even exists."

"If they didn't know of us before, they do now."

"Because of the oil spill?"

Mabry nodded. "Aye."

Emma stared down at the grave. She wanted to be alone. Short of coming right out and saying the words, she didn't know how to make the woman leave, and so she remained silent.

"I followed you through the village," Mabry confessed. "There is something I should say."

Emma waited.

Mabry's right hand closed over her left fist. "I'm very sorry, Emma. I wish—" She stopped.

Emma refused to help her.

"I don't make things happen. I only see them."

"No, Mabry," Emma replied coldly, "you predict disasters. People change the course of their lives because of what you tell them."

"Is that such a bad thing?"

"Why not ask if it does any good?"

"Be fair, Emma. Patrick kept your son from you. I had little to do with it."

"You said he would be miserable away from the island. He believed you. Everyone on this island believes you."

"You went away and never came back."

"Do you blame me for that?"

Mabry shook her head. "Your mind is your own. No one can make such a judgment."

"Patrick made it soon enough," Emma remembered bitterly.

"He was a man in a difficult place. Danny wasn't an easy child, and with no mother to raise him—" Mabry shrugged. "It wasn't pleasant for Patrick, either, Emma."

"He told me not to visit, that no island hearth would welcome me."

"Patrick nursed his pain for a very long time. There were one or two who might have taken him on and been a mother to Danny, if he'd shown the slightest interest."

"Don't say he was so in love with me that he never looked at another woman," Emma said scornfully. "I won't believe you."

Mabry spoke carefully, measuring out her words. "It would be more accurate to say he was disappointed in his marriage. It made him leery of women altogether."

"Is that why he's never remarried?"

"Possibly."

"Has he ever told you that?"

"Patrick isn't one to volunteer what he's thinking, Emma. You should know that."

She knew nothing of the sort. Her mouth tightened. It didn't matter now. But she was still curious. "How do you do it?" she asked.

"Do what, lass?"

"How do you know everything before it happens?"

Mabry smiled. "Why has it taken you thirty years to ask me such a question, Emma Tierney?"

"I don't believe in the Sight."

"Then you won't be interested in my answer."

"You can't expect any sane person to believe such a thing."

"We islanders don't claim to be sane, lass," Mabry said gently. "What I came to tell you was that you were right to go. You didn't belong here. You don't now. Not many do, not even those who begin their lives here."

Emma wet her lips. The question burned on her tongue, but she refused to ask it. Mabry O'Farrell would not have the satisfaction of rearranging any more lives. "Goodbye, Mabry."

The old woman's mouth turned up in the ghost of a smile. "You can rest easily, Emma. Mollie doesn't belong here on Inishmore any more than you did. She has the advantage because she knows it."

Emma gasped. "How could you know—"

"No vision brought me such news, if that's what you're thinking."

"Then how—"

"I listen, Emma, and I watch carefully. That's all the witchcraft I have within me. I need no sorcery to read what is in a mother's heart after one child has already been lost to her."

Mabry did have an odd way of knowing things ahead of time. Emma had read a number of biographies about people like her. Despite her skepticism, her heart lifted. Mollie was safe.

"What about the children?"

Mabry straightened, pulling her shoulders back. The smile left her mouth. "They are Sean's concern," she said coldly. "I'll be going now."

Emma watched her walk away, a straight figure without a hint of stiffness, dressed in black. A strange pounding began in her heart. "Do you see everything, Mabry O'Farrell," she whispered, "or is your Sight selective? Can you control it, or does it come over you unannounced?"

The day was unusually clear. Patrick watched her walk the last quarter-mile up the winding path to the cottage where he'd lived for forty years, where he'd brought her home for the first time, his new bride.

Looking at her now, moving purposefully up the road with long athletic steps, he couldn't imagine what had come over him. She was slim and blond and attractive, more so now at fifty-six than when she was at twenty because most women her age were not so well preserved. But the warmth that had once spilled from her smile was gone. She no longer laughed with her eyes. Emma had lost her spark and with it the glow that set her apart.

Patrick shook his head sadly. For years he'd imagined her as he remembered, a woman unlike any other. But the Emma Tierney he'd created didn't exist outside his imagination. Perhaps she never had, or perhaps the stark living on the island to which she could never acclimate herself had changed her into a shell of the woman he'd met, married, and shared two children with.

What could she want with him, she who avoided even the simplest contact? He wanted to open the door, to meet her in the natural sunlight. No. Better to wait until she knocked. He would invite her in, offer her tea. The small courtesies would relax him, help him forget the last time she was here.

She knocked firmly. He walked through the kitchen to the door and opened it, feigning surprise.

"Hello, Patrick." No hesitation here.

"Emma."

"May I come in?"

He stepped aside. "Of course."

She walked past him into the warm firelit room. He watched her look around, taking in the same potbellied stove, the oak table and chairs, the sideboard his mother had left him, the modern refrigerator.

Her voice was awe-tinged, her eyes wide, blue, wonder-filled. "You haven't even arranged the furniture."

He shrugged. "Why change something if it suits you?"

"For the sake of variety."

"I've never been one to need variety."

Her cheeks flamed. "No. I suppose not. May I sit down, Patrick? I've come to ask you something."

He pulled out a straight-backed chair from the table. "Will you share a pot of tea with me, Emma?"

She sat down. "Yes, thank you."

She didn't offer to help, and he was grateful for it. The familiar rituals of boiling water, warming the pot, measuring leaves, and setting out milk and sugar steadied him. She wanted to ask him something, did she? What could she possibly want after all this time?

Emma had never kept him waiting, and she didn't know. She drank her tea black without sugar, a preference that made the back of his tongue curl in anticipation of her every bitter swallow.

"I want you to tell me about Danny," she said unexpectedly. "I need to know what he was like at the different stages of his life."

He stared at her. "Why now?"

"Nothing is ever right anymore. I can't rest, and I can't go home without knowing more than I do. You kept him away from me. That was your choice, not mine." She spoke clearly, pointedly, her eyes fixed on his. "It was your mistake. This is your penance."

"Are you for playing the part of my confessor, Emma?"

She shook her head. "It's not you who concerns me, Patrick. I'm a mother, a mother whose child was kept from her. You did that to me. For thirty years I kept silent because of my own guilt. Now I want answers."

Emma was hurting, was she? He was no stranger to heartache, most of it on her account. He wasn't saint enough that the news of hers didn't please him. Still, he'd loved her once. The past tense of the thought took him by surprise. It was true. He no longer loved her. The moment had slipped by him without his even realizing it. She was Danny's mother, and she deserved to lay him to rest. "What would you like to know?"

Her eyes lit up. "What was his favorite color?"

"He never said anything about a favorite color."

"What about his favorite meal, his favorite book?"

Patrick looked startled. Did women know these things? "I have no idea, Emma. Danny and I didn't discuss such things."

Her laugh was brittle. "Mothers *notice* those things, Patrick. They don't have to discuss them."

He slowly chewed a biscuit that he'd set out with the tea. "Perhaps I'll be of less help to you than you thought."

"What was he like in school?"

"Difficult," he said without thinking. "From the time he was small, he was always in one scrape or another."

"Did he have friends?"

Did Danny have friends? He hesitated. It came to him, suddenly, that he didn't want to add to Emma's heartache after all. "He had a few, although he wasn't the sort people take to easily."

"Was he a good student?"

He thought a minute. "He was bright enough, I suppose. Reading and figures came easily, but studying didn't interest him. His marks were satisfactory, but there was never a question of his going on to university. Education would have been the way out," Patrick said without sympathy. "It's the way for many who have no desire to live out their lives here. But Danny never wanted out." He watched Emma chew on her bottom lip. He wasn't satisfying whatever need she had to learn about their son. How did one account for the life of a child to a mother who'd never known him? Was there a way to do it properly? "The best thing he ever did was marry Kerry O'Malley. She steadied him. He drank less."

"Did you tell him that?"

His mouth twisted. "I didn't have to tell him, lass. He knew it himself. Besides, who am I to offer advice, a man with no experience at holding a marriage together?"

She flushed. "You might have tried. You might have said that's how you knew."

He shrugged. Outside, birds circled in confusion, reformed their phalanx, and flew away. "When did you start drinking?"

He sighed. Here it was, the inevitable question, the one he knew she would ask even though he hoped she would not. "I was always a drinking man, Emma. I put it aside while you were here."

"If you did it for me, why couldn't you do it for your son?"

How could he explain without appearing as if he blamed her, for blame her he did not? Reaching across the table, he took her hands in his own. She did not pull away. "Try to understand, Emma. I didn't make a decision to drink or not to drink. I simply hadn't the urge to drink during the years you were with me. Later, after you left, long after you left, I drank more and more. It was a gradual thing. I did not wish to stop. Those were difficult years for Danny and me."

Her eyes were wide, gray-blue, haunted. "Why did you keep him from me, Patrick? You couldn't have believed Mabry."

"Ah, but I did believe her, Emma. Mabry is more often right than wrong. But I did not keep Danny and you apart because of it." He released her hands, stood, and walked to the window.

"Why, then?"

"Anger," he said simply, resting his head against the cold windowpane. "I was angry with you for so long it was part of my life. I wanted to hurt you, and Danny was my weapon."

"You hurt him as well, and you hurt Mollie. She missed not having a father."

Turning, he looked at her, sitting at his table the same as if thirty years had not passed since the last time she had done so. "I went to California, not even two years after you left me. Did you know that?"

She shook her head.

"I went alone to the address you wrote on the back of Danny's letters."

Her expression was troubled, innocent. How long would it take her to understand?

"You were living in a grand house with more rooms than a hotel." Still she looked at him, unashamed.

"It was Ward Reddington's house. You were living in Ward Reddington's house with my daughter."

The color rushed to her cheeks.

"I came to see if there was any way we could be a family again, and you were living with another man, after less than two years."

"Oh, Patrick." Her laugh was part shame, part exasperation. "You didn't understand." She shook her head and looked down at her hands. "I'm so sorry that I didn't make you understand that I wasn't coming back, not ever."

"It no longer matters."

She looked up, surprised. "Really?"

He smiled. "Aye."

This time her laugh was one of relief. "Maybe there's a chance for us."

"For our family there's a chance, but not for us, not together." It had taken him a great many words and three decades to say it, but there it was.

She smiled, and this time she reminded him of Mollie. "I'm glad I came."

He grinned, remembering why he'd been so taken with her all those years ago. "I'm glad, too, Emma." He turned serious again. "But I'm not glad of why you came."

She stiffened. "What do you mean?"

"Luke and the girls are Irish, not American. Their parents were Irish. Sean is an exceptional young man. We don't always see things the same way because he never cared much for Danny, but he loves the children and he can provide for them. He's young. He'll marry someday. The woman he marries will know the children come with him."

Once more he took her hands. "Admit it, Emma. Your husband can't be happy about raising three young children when it's nearly time for him to retire."

Emma flushed. Patrick was remarkably astute. Either that, or the situation was so obvious anyone could assess it.

"You've the legal right," Patrick continued, "but I want you to think about what I've said. It won't be like it was with Danny. No one will keep the children from you."

Emma tried to resurrect the edge of the bitter anger that had taken hold of her when she first heard that Danny had died. But she couldn't. The hurt was there, but the rage was gone, and if she looked at it truthfully, she was better for it.

"I'll think about it," she said.

21

$\mathcal{M}$ollie watched Mrs. McEwan hold a handkerchief to her lips, close her eyes wearily, and lean her head back against the torn upholstery of the *Aran Seagull*. She didn't really know Fiona McEwan. The woman was older. Her children had grown and left the island, but on her way to school in the morning Mollie had waved to her as she swept the front steps of her small cottage.

Fishing inside her purse, Mollie produced a roll of peppermint Lifesavers, leaned forward, and touched Fiona's shoulder. "Would you care for a mint? They might help."

"It's kind you are, Miss Tierney," she said, "but nothin' helps the seasickness. I'll be feelin' grand again once we reach Galway. The ocean is all which ways today, isn't it?"

Mollie smiled. "Will you be coming back tonight?"

"No, lass. I'm to visit my sister in Ballyshannon, thank God. I'll not be braving the trip for another week or two." Once again she pressed the handkerchief to her mouth. "I think I'll step outside for a bit of fresh air. Sometimes that helps."

Mollie watched her stumble down the aisle and disappear through the flapping plastic curtain that led to the deck. She settled back, unbuttoned her coat to absorb the heat from the grate directly above her, and stared out the scratched glass window at the rolling gray sea. Garrett had given her the name of an attorney in Dublin who specialized in maritime law. Over the telephone Daniel O'Shea had completely disarmed her. Mollie's experience with lawyers was limited, but she was sure most of them didn't answer their own phones or make appointments. Mr. O'Shea did both, and he'd agreed to meet her in Galway, a four-hour drive from Dublin.

At first she'd been skeptical of an attorney who appeared to have time on his hands, but Garrett assured her he was competent and even renowned. Better still, he worked on a contingency basis. Now her hope was that he would help. "Please, say you'll help," she whispered fervently, fogging the window with her breath. Closing her eyes, she deliberately pushed aside the tangle of relationships in which she'd found herself since coming to Ireland.

It had all been so simple before. Life flowed like a lazy, slow-moving river, no rapids, no flooding, just a steady, harmonious progression with her mother and Ward, her friends and Garrett. No, she amended, not Garrett.

Even so, the picture was a tranquil one, no surprises, no highs, but certainly no lows. Mollie was beginning to understanding the value of tranquility, the kind in which life-altering decisions had no place. And yet what kind of life would it be without children, sticky-fingered, wide-eyed, so innocent and precious her heart hurt to watch them sleep?

She avoided her next, obvious question, the one about the man who would have an equal interest in those children. It was still too close, too personal to take out her feelings, brush them off, and inspect them. She would do that later, when time and more distance than twenty-six miles across the sea to Galway, had leveled them out.

Galway on the cusp of Christmas a gasp of color in the wintery grayness. Red bows and green garlands draped invitingly over street lights and shop signs. Silver and gold bells hung from every door, and the strains of popular carols faded in and out as customers came and went, opening and closing doors behind them. Inviting smells wafted from bakeries and tea shops. A dusting of snow covered the streets, and to Mollie, who had never seen a snowy Christmas, the Irish city looked like something out of a Dickens fairy tale.

Buttoning her coat up under her chin, she wrapped her muffler loosely around her neck, stuffed both gloved hands into her pockets, and walked away from the bus stop toward High Street. She had never been to the restaurant where the attorney suggested they meet, but he'd assured her that it was a popular one in Galway.

She found it easily, a small shop with frosted windows, crisp curtains, and a welcome sign over the door. Mollie hung her coat and smiled at the friendly waitress who nodded at her from behind the counter before looking around. Several tables were occupied, including one with a man whose face looked as if it belonged on a Marlboro billboard. He was finishing off a substantial breakfast. Mollie took a quick look at his faded denims, plaid shirt, and hiking boots and immediately disqualified him. The lawyer from Dublin had obviously not yet arrived.

Choosing a table by the window, she folded her arms, prepared for a wait. The road from Dublin wasn't always predictable in winter. Mr. O'Shea might be more than a few minutes late. Accepting the inevitable was something she'd come to terms with since arriving in Ireland. It wasn't only the roads that were unpredictable. The Irish had a different conception of time than Americans did. Hours of operation were posted but not necessarily followed, especially in winter. A shop with a nine o'clock opening might have its doors unlocked by eleven, and if the weather was bad or there was a horse race in the vicinity, the proprietor might decide not to open at all. Pharmacy hours were unusual, too. Prescriptions were called in to the local chemist day or night, and if he had gone fishing or taken a few days off, it remained unfilled. Banks were open on Wednesdays. Bakeries, butcher shops, libraries, and the post office operated on the whim of whoever was in charge of the key. Only the pubs could be counted on, and the churches. Rain or shine, their doors were open until well after midnight during the week and ten on Sundays.

Gradually, Mollie had come to accept these quirks as part of Ireland's charm. Settling in for what might be a lengthy wait, she stared out the window, at people hurrying by, stamping their feet and blowing on their hands. Winter in Galway.

Daniel O'Shea watched her for a bit. He knew who she was the instant she walked through the door. She was a woman who stood out, not pretty, just beautiful, the kind who would make a man do a double take and stumble. Garrett Michaels had described her essentials perfectly. What he'd left out were her other qualities, the intriguing ones that became obvious after only a few minutes. Mollie Tierney was indeed tall, attractive, and blond, but she wasn't Irish, at least not a hundred percent, and definitely not Catholic Irish. Irish women approaching their thirtieth birthdays did not look twenty, nor were their bodies the kind found in health-club advertisements. She'd shed her coat, revealing a conservative sweater and slacks, but it wouldn't have mattered what she wore. It was the woman one noticed, not the clothing. She walked as if she were comfortable inside her body, an alluring walk, the kind that left grown men weak.

She'd turned away from where he was sitting, leaving only her profile visible to him. Her hands were on the table, one on top of the other, perfectly still. She'd smiled at the waitress, nodded at something she'd said, and turned to look out the window, absorbed in the scene outside. Unlike most Americans, she didn't check the watch on her wrist or even look around the small restaurant after her first cursory glance. She simply waited and watched. Even after the waitress brought her a pot of tea, she left it, continuing to gaze out the window completely engrossed in the images, as if she couldn't get enough or by some miracle her sight at been restored and she was seeing it again after a very long time.

Daniel finished his toast, crossed the floor to stand before her, and held out his hand. "Miss Tierney? I'm Daniel O'Shea."

She looked up. He was gratified to see the look of surprise on her face. Masking her initial reaction, she shook his hand and motioned him to the chair across from her. "Please, sit down. Thank you for coming all this way so early."

No mention of his unorthodox clothing. No coyness or flirtatiousness in her manner, not even a hint of self-consciousness. Perhaps women like her had no need of such devices. "How can I help you, Miss Tierney?"

Now she would ask him to call her Mollie. It happened every time, the first step, the subtle segue into the personal. He wouldn't hold it against her. The leap to using Christian names was a common practice in a new, informal world. He would call her Mollie, and she would call him Daniel.

She came right to the point. "You're familiar with the oil spill on the Aran Islands?"

It was front page news for the entire week. "Of course," he said politely.

"Then you know that the fishing industry has been completely decimated. Men are out of work, and it's December."

Keeping his eyes on her face, he waited for her to explain her connection with the fishing community of Inishmore.

"I want you to represent them in a personal damage suit against Transom Oil."

Daniel frowned. "Who, exactly, would I be representing?"

"The men of Inishmore and their families." She frowned. "I assumed Garrett explained all this."

"To a degree." He leaned forward, elbows on the

tablecloth. "There is some precedent for suit in this case, Miss Tierney. The *Valdez* oil spill has been recently settled, but it isn't something that happens overnight. That judgment was ten years in the making. Your friend in America suggested that the families on the island needed compensation much sooner."

Her face paled. "Ten years?"

"Aye, and they were lucky the oil company didn't appeal. Otherwise it would have been longer. Often it's the heirs who collect, Miss Tierney, not the actual victims."

He watched her wet her lips. Garrett Michaels said she was smart. She would sort it out quickly, and then he would find out why she had taken on a cause with no hope of personal gain.

She didn't disappoint him. "Why did you come all the way from Dublin to tell me this?"

His heartbeat accelerated. "There's another way, but it won't bring millions in compensation."

"We don't need millions."

His voice changed. "We?"

"The fishermen and their families, all of us." She waved her hand. "Without a living wage, a great many of them will be evacuated."

He still didn't understand. "Surely you know your teaching job is secure, at least for the year. It doesn't matter whether you've fifty students or a handful. The government is committed to providing an education for the children of the islands."

She stared at him, bewildered. "What does my job have to do with anything? I'm in no danger of starving, no matter what happens."

Daniel was thoroughly confused. It was time to ask the direct questions. "What is your interest in this, Miss Tierney? Why are you the one approaching me?"

"I was born in Inishmore. My father lives there. I have two nieces and a nephew who mean a great deal to me, and I have the time to help."

Daniel had kept his eye on the Aran oil spill waiting for just this occasion, wondering if and when someone from the island would contact him. It wasn't the issue that had taken him by surprise, it was the messenger. "In other words, this is personal?"

He watched the color rise in her cheeks, watched her look away. He waited.

"I don't need money, Mr. O'Shea. I'll be leaving the island at the end of the school year." She met his glance once again. "This isn't about me. Do you need a retainer to take on the case?"

"Good Lord, no!" She'd surprised him. "There will be money enough when it's over."

"Are you so sure we'll win?"

He grinned. "Absolutely."

"How long will it take? These people need compensation immediately, and they don't want any part of the dole."

"I'll meet with the attorneys for Transom Oil. It's possible, with a bit of persuasion, that they'll agree to pay a portion of the damages in payment plans to the affected families."

"When would that be?"

"Three months if all goes well, maybe six on the outside."

He could see her disappointment. Mollie Tierney had an expressive face. "I'm sorry, Mollie, but that's the best I

can do." He meant it, just as he meant to break through
the formality that characterized most of his first inter-
views. He liked her, more than he imagined he would.
Garrett Michaels had not impressed him. Mollie did.

"Is there anything to be done?"

"Evacuations aren't as terrible as they sound. Most
people find relatives to help them settle in. The economy is good. Jobs are easier to find than they've ever
been. Their government stipends will hold them over for
a while."

She moved her hand in a brief, emphatic motion of
denial. Her eyes were very bright. Daniel had the dreadful sensation that she was about to cry. He reached across
the table and covered her hand. "Mollie—"

"The economy is good for skilled people," she said,
her voice choked with unshed tears. "They won't settle
in. The island is all they know. Everyone who is capable
of leaving already has."

"I don't understand."

"Inishmore's population has remained stable for centuries because it can only sustain a limited number of
people. Children grow up knowing they'll leave. They
prepare for it, all except those who can't or won't
because of temperament or preference or ability. Many of
them aren't of an age to begin again. Those are the people who face evacuation, Mr. O'Shea. What we're looking at is a tragedy."

"I see."

She looked down at her untouched tea. "Thank you
for your time."

He raised his eyebrows. "Now wait a minute. You
aren't giving up, are you?"

"I still want you to continue with the suit, if that's what you mean. These people deserve something, even if it's after the fact."

"Good. I'll need information, numbers most of all, income averages, expected time the men will be unemployed, who else the oil spill is affecting, restaurants, merchants, that sort of thing."

"I don't know any of those things, but I can give you the name of a person who does."

He pulled out a tablet of paper and a pen from his shirt pocket.

"Sean O'Malley would be the best place to start."

Surprised, he looked up. "I attended university with a Sean O'Malley from Inishmore. He's a playwright, a rather well-known one. Could it be the same man?"

"There's only one that I know of on the island."

"Surely he's not one of those who isn't capable of beginning again."

Mollie smiled for the first time during their meeting. "He's one of the other ones."

"Ah, the temperamental ones who stay out of preference."

This time she laughed, and Daniel, who normally remained as personally removed from his clients as possible, was conscious of a strong desire to make her do it again.

"I don't think it's preference. He really has no choice."

"Do you know him well?" he asked casually.

"Yes. My brother and his sister were married."

"Were married?"

"They died."

"I'm terribly sorry."

"Thank you." She reached for her purse. "What happens next?"

"I'll contact Sean O'Malley." He removed the bill from the table. "Never mind about your tea. We're not so liberated here in Ireland."

Again she laughed. "I've noticed."

"Do you approve, or are you one of those women who fights to open her own doors?"

She thought a minute. "I enjoy the small courtesies," she said carefully, "but I also think people should follow their dreams, no matter what their sex. It goes both ways, don't you think?"

She was lovely and unusual and completely earnest, and he probably would have agreed to anything she suggested. Collecting himself, he nodded. "A grand philosophy, very sensible."

Her mouth curved. "Goodbye, Mr. O'Shea."

Too soon, she was standing up, pulling on her gloves, reaching for her coat. "Are you alone in Galway for the day?"

"Yes. I have Christmas shopping to do."

He was sensitive enough to recognize a dismissal. Standing, he held out his hand. "It was a pleasure meeting you, Mollie."

"Thank you. I'll tell Sean you'll be contacting him."

He watched her walk through the door. Then he settled back for one last cup of tea and a brief rerun of their meeting. It was something he always did before he took on a case, assessing the liabilities against the benefits, the defendant's case against the one he would bring to the court, lining up in his mind the arguments on an imaginary clipboard.

Mollie Tierney would definitely be an asset. Young but not too young, well spoken, educated, and attractive. The courts were sympathetic to women like that, and they liked Americans. She would definitely be one of his strongest assets.

From what Daniel remembered of Sean O'Malley, he would be one as well. A quiet bloke for the most part, reserved but not self-conscious, bright, with a crooked grin and a dangerous, understated charm capable of reducing its recipient to a state of fawning dementia. Yes, Sean O'Malley would be another asset. Daniel wondered if he'd changed. He pushed back his chair, gathered his belongings, and stood. It was time to find out.

22

Russ Sanders smelled like pine trees with a touch of spice. Mollie, circling the dance floor of the community center in his arms, inhaled deeply to be sure she'd gotten the combination right. The aftershave was something called Poison or Poseidon. She couldn't remember which.

Despite their straitened circumstances, the islanders had generously donated what they could to the celebration. Long white-clothed tables groaned under the weight of ham, bacon, and beef. Tantalizing aromas of roasted potatoes and fried chips, soups, bread, scones, and cakes wafted from the kitchen. Foil-wrapped paper bells sat on smaller tables that had been pushed back from the wooden floor to make room for the dancers. Red and green streamers hung from the rafters. Wreaths made of paper, berries, and dry twigs decorated the walls, and an enormous nativity scene covered the length of the entire banquet table. The barren limestone of Inishmore did not provide for Christmas trees. Mollie missed the clean pure scent of pine.

Seated in orange plastic chairs against the wall, women, past the age of dancing, nodded and gossiped while men of the same generation gathered at a corner of the bar downing Guinness and watching the grainy television screen. Young people crowded the dance floor. Sweating bodies swirled to the sounds of drum, flute, banjo, and accordion music, blurring into blue clouds of cigarette smoke. A *cruínniu* at Christmas was an all-important event on the island.

Russ was tall, but Mollie could still see over his shoulder. Sean had taken to the floor with Caili. He lifted her against his chest so they were eye-level. Her small gamin's face was alight with laughter as her uncle dipped and swayed to the melodic music of the local band.

She watched him lean into the little girl's neck and whisper something into her ear. She saw him look at her, his face alive, on the verge of a laugh, his eyes warm with love. Mollie felt the tightening in her chest. She knew what it was, this breath-stealing feeling, as if the fiddler had increased his tempo and the sedate dance had become the wild toe-pointing, heel-kicking Irish jig she loved to watch but hadn't the courage to try for herself.

Forcing her eyes away from the man she wanted, she smiled at Russ. He was easy to be with, a pleasant companion, a witty conversationalist, the perfect tenant. Her mother approved of him. Emma fed him gourmet meals, refused his help in the kitchen, and suggested opportunities where he could be alone with Mollie, all of which he accepted with appreciation and good humor.

The fiddler's fingers flew across the strings. The tempo of the dance increased. She pulled away, and he dropped his arms immediately. "This one isn't for me," she said. "Let's sit it out."

Obligingly, he followed her back to a table where the group from Scripps had gathered.

Beth, the marine biologist Mollie had met on the beach, moved over for the two of them to sit down. "This is nice," she remarked when Mollie had settled in beside her. "I was miserable when I found out I wouldn't be home for Christmas, but this makes up for it." She lifted her Guinness in a salute. "Cheers. Do you miss being home?"

"I miss the convenience," Mollie replied, "but my family is here. That makes all the difference."

Beth nodded, her attention focused on the dancers. "How do you feel about your brother-in-law?"

"Excuse me?" Mollie stammered.

"He's single and gorgeous. Would you consider setting us up?"

Mollie's fingers tightened around her glass. Deliberately, she kept her expression neutral. "I don't think he's in the market for a relationship right now," she said carefully.

Beth nodded. "I know that he recently lost his sister and he's caring for her children, but I've heard that you have to snap up the good ones right away or someone else will beat you to it."

"What makes you think Sean is a good one?"

"Are you saying he isn't?"

"Of course not." What was she saying? "I didn't realize you knew him well enough to make that kind of judgment."

"I don't," Beth said agreeably, "but look at him out

there with the little girl. A man like that has to be one of the good ones."

Instead Mollie looked directly at the attractive American woman. Dark hair and eyes against cream-colored skin were a lovely combination. "I'm afraid you're on your own where Sean is concerned. I met him for the first time in September. That isn't long enough for me to orchestrate his love life."

Beth laughed. "All right. I'll do the best I can to throw myself in his path now and then."

Mollie sipped her drink. Her stomach burned with roiling emotions. She forced herself to ask the question. "Do you think you could really live here permanently?"

"Good Lord, no!" Beth appeared genuinely shocked. "Whatever made you think I'd consider it?"

"What about Sean?"

The woman's eyes widened. "I want to go out with him, Mollie, not marry him."

Like red flags, the angry color rose in Mollie's cheeks. "In other words," she said tightly, "you want to spend time with him, sleep with him, possibly make him fall in love with you, and then leave him."

"Whoah, Mollie. Relax." Russ's calm voice cut through her diatribe. "I don't think Beth meant that at all."

"No?" Mollie kept her eyes on Beth's face. "Tell me what Beth meant."

"I didn't mean to offend you, Mollie." Beth's tone was troubled, conciliatory. "I had no idea your feelings were so involved. I'm sorry."

Mollie spotted her niece as she crossed the room, weaving her way through the dancers. She smiled warmly as Marni approached the table and spoke to Russ.

"Hello, Mr. Sanders. I've come to ask Aunt Mollie to sit with us for a while. I hope you don't mind."

"Not at all," Russ said heartily. "I'll come, too, if it's all right."

Mollie slipped her arm around the little girl's shoulders. "This is my niece," she said to Beth. "Her name is Marni. The little girl on the dance floor with Sean is Caili." She nodded toward Emma, who stood on the other side of the room, holding Luke, tapping her feet to the music. "That woman is my mother, and she's holding my nephew. My feelings are definitely involved."

"I'm sorry," Beth apologized again.

Mollie studied the troubled, pretty face of the American girl and relented. "So am I. I'm being rude. Please, forgive me."

Beth brushed the words away. "Forget it. There's no harm done."

Russ started to get up, but Mollie laid her hand on his arm. Her smile didn't reach her eyes. "Please, stay here with your friends. I'll see you later."

He watched her walk away, a thoughtful expression on his face.

Beth nudged him. "If I were a betting woman, I'd say you didn't have a chance in that direction."

"The race isn't over yet."

"It's a race, is it?"

"Yes."

She lifted her glass. "May the best man win."

Russ grinned. "And I thought we were friends."

Beth burst out laughing. "If we weren't such good friends, I'd be after you myself."

"Thank God, I've been spared that," Russ said fervently. "You go through men like water."

Mollie lifted Luke's limp weight from her mother's arms. "You look like you need a break."

Emma nodded. "It's amazing how he can sleep through this noise." She tucked a stray strand of hair behind Mollie's ear. "Are you having a good time?"

"Yes," Mollie lied. "Are you?"

"Actually, I am. it's a pleasure to see the children well and enjoying themselves again. What happened to Russ?" she asked casually.

"Nothing."

"I saw you dancing with him. You make a lovely couple."

Mollie rested her cheek on the baby's head. "Do we?"

Emma sighed. "I wish I knew what you're looking for, Mollie. You're nearly thirty."

"Are you trying to get rid of me?" Mollie teased.

"I just want you to be happy."

"I am happy, Mom. Don't worry so much. I have a few years left before I'm past hope."

"Of course you do. I simply don't understand why you're so fussy. What on earth could be wrong with Russ Sanders?"

"Nothing. He's just not for me, that's all."

"How do you know? You haven't given him a chance."

Mollie opened her mouth and closed it again. How did she know? There were a hundred reasons, but the most obvious one was walking toward her this very minute. She watched him cross the floor. To Mollie, it was as if everyone else had faded away and he was the only one left in all the noisy, smoke-filled room.

What was it about a man that made a woman's knees go weak and her heart pound and every rational thought in her brain turn to mush? Sean was funny and unassuming and intelligent, but so was Russ. Sean had the children, and she loved them. But she would have wanted him without the children.

"Emma." He nodded his head at her and reached for Luke. "I'll take him, Mollie. You don't want to be missing the dancing, and neither does Russ."

He'd noticed. "Russ has plenty of partners to choose from," she said, handing over the baby.

"But not the one he wants." Sean settled the sleeping baby against his shoulder.

"Why not give Patrick a turn with Luke?" Emma suggested. "He was quite good at it when the girls were small. That way you can dance with Mollie."

Mollie's face flamed. "I don't think—"

Sean interrupted her. "Will you wait for me, Mollie, while I find Patrick?"

"There's no need," Emma said. "He's at the far table with your mother and Alice Duncan. I'll deliver this young man to him." She took the baby and left them, standing alone together.

"Will you dance with me, Mollie?"

He was complicated and vulnerable and filled with surprises, and just now there was nothing she would refuse him. "Yes." The single word, husky and low, was all she could manage to say.

He took her hand, his fingers curling around hers. Every sensation was heightened, the dampness where their palms touched, the strong line of his shoulders under the soft wool of his sweater, the straight, clean blade of his jaw, blending into the bones of cheek and chin, and, when he turned to take her in his arms, the clean soap smell of his skin. The top of her head brushed the tip of his ear. If she turned just so, his lips would touch her forehead.

The music was slower now, the beat melodic, smooth, romantic. Mollie closed her eyes. His arms tightened around her, and all that was left of her awkwardness disappeared. She felt boneless, her body molding to his, filling in the spaces between thigh and hip, chest and waist. He said something, his breath warm against her ear, but she paid no attention, her senses saturated with a combination of desire and need, her mind refusing to go beyond this moment, this man.

Suddenly she felt a blast of cold. The music sounded far away. She opened her eyes. They were just outside the door, no longer dancing. Sean's arms were still around her. Surprised, she looked up. What he wanted was clear enough in the tense, thin set of his lips and the hard, narrowing eyes. She wanted it, too. They stood there, bodies touching, arms entwined, neither one wanting to move first, a standoff. She searched his face, her eyes missing nothing, settling on his mouth.

He was the first to soften. She saw the curve of his lips, saw reason replace the wild look in his eyes, saw the gentle decline of his head as it lowered to touch his lips to her forehead. She found her breath and lost it again with his words.

"Do you have any idea what you do to me, Mollie Tierney?" he said, his voice a whisper, laced with a hint of regret.

She couldn't speak, wouldn't speak. There was no answer she could make that wouldn't break the magic.

Gently, he pulled her close against his heart, wrapped his arms around her, and rested his cheek against hers. Minutes passed. Her blood pounded in cadence with his.

"Warm enough?" he asked.

She nodded. There was no room for words, only warm arms and hard lines, soft wool and clean-scrubbed skin. It was enough, more than enough, if only he would stay.

He pulled away too soon. Forever would not have been long enough. Mollie gathered what remained of her poise and forced herself to look at him. His eyes were pale, the irises thin and colorless in the white moonlight.

"You're a comforting sort of lass. Has anyone ever told you that?"

Comforting. He thought of her as comforting. She wanted scorching, sensual, tempting, unforgettable. "No," she said, "and it doesn't sound very complimentary."

"Oh, but it is," he said softly. "It's a grand compliment for someone like yourself."

She was curious. "What does that mean, someone like myself?"

"Surely you know what a man thinks of when he first sets eyes on you."

She shook her head.

His voice dropped, warmed, the words sliding off his tongue like warmed whiskey. "You're the kind of woman a man aspires to, Mollie, the kind he holds up as a standard to measure all others by."

She would say it and get it over with. He knew her mind anyway. "I would rather be one of the others."

His eyes twinkled. "Would you?"

"You know I would. I don't offer myself to just anyone."

He was serious again. "I know that."

She didn't want it to end, this delicious, temporary taste of forbidden fruit, but it was cold and getting colder by the minute. Soon others would notice their absence. She glanced at the door. Particles of light danced in long rays, illuminating the dusting of snow on the ground. "We should get back."

"Aye."

She turned to go, but his hand on her arm stopped her. "I promised you a night in Galway."

"Never mind. It's all right," she said quickly.

"I'd like to take you to Galway, Mollie. Will you go with me?"

She looked at him, at the black pupils taking up the color in his eyes, the black hair falling over his forehead, and the clean, perfectly cut symmetry of his mouth. He would hurt her, badly. She knew it as surely as she knew the tide would be out in Curwin Cove in the morning. "Why?"

"Do we need a reason?"

"Yes."

He thought a minute. "Christmas presents. I need help with Christmas presents."

She laughed. The mood was broken. "All right. If you can find the time, I'll help you with your Christmas presents."

He held the door for her. "I'll find it."

The cottage was lonely without the children. Mollie added several squares of peat to the fire and rubbed her arms.

Emma joined her on the couch with a cup of tea. "I had a very nice time," she said.

Mollie smiled. "Me, too."

Emma set down her cup and looked around. "It's empty without Luke and the girls. I miss them."

Mollie stretched out, resting her head on her mother's lap. "We'll see them tomorrow." Emma's fingers played in her hair. "You like Sean, don't you, Mom?"

The fingers stilled for a moment. "Of course I do."

Mollie heard the hesitation in her voice. "But?"

"I do," Emma insisted. "I like him without reservation."

Mollie sighed and closed her eyes. "I don't think he would have danced with me if you hadn't forced him into it."

Emma remained silent.

"Why did you do it?"

A full minute passed. Finally she answered. "There's chemistry between you. It's clear to anyone who cares enough to pay attention. Even the children sense it. But chemistry alone isn't enough. It's the everyday living that makes a relationship work, as well as similar values and shared backgrounds. The sooner you realize how different you are, the better. The only way to find that out is for the two of you to really know each other. You're intelligent, and so is he. You'll both see it once you wade through the attraction."

"What if we don't?"

"You'll face some heartache."

"Why are you so sure it couldn't work?"

"I know this island, Mollie. There's nothing for you here. You haven't made a single friend since you've been here. Your life is caught up in your job and the children and Sean. You haven't seen a movie or gone to the theater or even to a bookstore. You can't take a class or hear a lecture or go to a concert unless you count whoever's playing at one of the local pubs."

"There are bookstores all over Ireland."

"You know I'm right. Don't think I don't understand your attraction to Sean. He's a very appealing man, and he has the children."

"What do they have to do with it?"

"They're part of the package, and they adore you."

Mollie sighed. "That's what Sean said. He thinks I want him because of the children."

"Good Lord. It's come to that already?"

"If you're asking if he knows how I feel, the answer is yes."

"Oh, Mollie." Emma's eyebrows rose in dismay. "It gives him a tremendous advantage. How could you do such a thing?"

Mollie hid her face in the folds of Emma's sweater. Her voice was muffled. "It just happened. I'm not myself when I'm around him."

Emma stroked the heavy, honey-gold hair spilling into her lap. "I've never worried about you before," she said softly. "It's an odd feeling."

"Don't worry, Mom. I'll be all right in the end."

"It isn't the end that concerns me. It's all the stops along the way."

Mollie yawned and closed her eyes. It was late. The evening had turned out much better than she expected.

23

The small commuter plane seated eight, two single-file rows of four seats on either side of the narrow aisle. Mollie swallowed and sat down behind the pilot. Sean took the seat across from her and smiled bracingly. They were the only two passengers.

"Six minutes, Mollie. That's all it takes, and we'll be on the mainland."

"It's so small."

"Large or small, planes fly on the same principle," the pilot assured her as if comforting frightened Americans was part of his job. Straightening something over his head, he pulled on several levers, adjusted his head-phones, and the plane roared to life. "Fasten your seat-belts," he shouted above the din.

With shaking fingers, Mollie managed the clasps. The plane bounced down the bumpy runway toward the sea. She closed her eyes, concentrating on the movement. They were moving faster now, gathering momentum for that final, climactic thrust when the wheels left the ground and somehow, miraculously, the silver, bullet-shaped body propelled itself into the air.

For Mollie, every flight was the same. Normally she wasn't a particularly fearful flier, but she hadn't ever gotten used to the idea that a heavy body, a combination of physical materials, metal, plastic, fabric, and wire, filled to capacity with people, could actually stay up in the air. It was an aerodynamic miracle she refused to take for granted.

She felt the tilt of the plane and, only a minute or two later, its leveling out. The engines were louder than she remembered. Cautiously, she opened her eyes and peered out the window. The ocean was terrifyingly close.

Sean leaned across the aisle. "We're nearly there," he said.

"So soon?"

"It's a six-minute ride," he reminded her.

She felt better.

"There." He pointed to a spot outside her window. "That's the landing strip. It's a bit rocky going down."

Her fingers clenched around the armrests.

He grinned. "We haven't lost anyone yet, Mollie, but we can take the ferry back if you'd rather."

"Could we?"

He whistled under his breath. "This really bothers you, doesn't it?"

She looked at him curiously. "What about you?"

"The odds are with us."

Their landing was surprisingly smooth. Mollie followed Sean to the terminal, where he engaged the man at the gate in conversation and came away holding a set of car keys.

"Did we need to rent a car?" she asked.

"It's a loan. Robbie Anderson is a friend of mine. We'll drop the car with his wife when we're in town."

Connemara's brush and wild grass in the dead of winter was tobacco-gold bogland, flat plains with silver lakes and pools of fresh rainwater, a contrast to the green limestone of the Arans. Occasionally a small cottage no bigger than a shed with a thread of white smoke escaping the chimney interrupted the landscape.

"It's so empty," Mollie said, her voice reverent.

Sean kept his eyes on the narrow road. "All of the West is like this. The land can't support more than a few." He glanced over at her and grinned. "You don't get out much, do you?"

"No. I don't. I should do more of that. It would be a shame to spend a year here and see nothing of Ireland."

He nodded. "Donegal and the north are worth the drive. Most tourists visit Cork and Waterford. They're lovely, but the real Ireland is to the west and north."

"I'll keep that in mind." She rolled around the idea of leaving Ireland. A month ago it had stirred to life an ache in her stomach. Now it was different. She pushed the thought away. "How far is it to Galway?"

"Another ten minutes or so." A frown marred the space between Sean's eyebrows. "I'm new to this, Mollie. I've never bought an entire Christmas before. Caili isn't a problem. She's Kerry all over again, not bashful about what she wants, but Marni's not so outspoken. She's a bit too old for dolls. At least I think she is," he said help-lessly.

"She likes to read," Mollie offered, "and she's artistic. We'll find enough to make her smile." Without thinking, she reached across the space that separated them to touch his arm. "Don't worry. Marni's still a little girl, and she isn't hard to please."

He covered her hand briefly with his own. "I'm counting on you."

Mollie bit her lip and turned to look out the window. The signs in Irish and English pointed them toward Salthill and Galway. Sean took the road toward the bay. Expensive homes with large windows, many advertising bed-and-breakfast accommodations, faced the sea.

"How far away is your house?" Mollie asked.

"We passed it a few minutes ago."

She looked at him, surprised. "I'd like to see it. Why didn't you say something?"

He ignored her question. "If there's time, I'll give you a tour on the way home. Your mother tells me that Salthill is like Newport."

Mollie looked at it with her mother's eyes. It did look like Newport. The boardwalk with concession stands closed for the winter, the wide sidewalk for biking and jogging, the ferris wheel, the gift shops, and above it all, set back on lawns with panoramic views of the island, spacious well-kept homes that would fit nicely into Spy Glass Hill, the neighborhood where Mollie had grown up.

Sean followed the road past the old Claddagh houses to the north end of the city, drove across the bridge, pulled into a multilevel carpark, and found a space. Galway was the largest city in the West, and Saturdays were busy.

Mollie buttoned her coat and reached for the door handle, but Sean was already there. He opened the door and helped her out.

"For a man who doesn't own a car, you have lovely manners," she teased him.

"Actually, I do own a car, but I don't need it on the island. As for manners, isn't that how it's done in America?"

"Not often enough. It was a lovely gesture. Thank you."

He smiled at her. "You're very welcome."

The shops, brightly lit and decorated for Christmas, were warm and welcoming. Immediately, Mollie found a cable-knit sweater for her mother in a soft blue, a nubby tweed jacket for Patrick, and an Irish wool cap for Ward. A muffler for Alice, a delicate teapot for Eileen, and toys for the children were purchased in less than two hours.

The door to Kenny's Bookshop rang merrily when Mollie followed Sean inside. She looked around in amazement. Familiar with the large chain bookstores popular in California, she had expected the world-famous Kenny's to be the same. Instead, it looked more like a public library with rows of wooden shelves and hardcover books, their spines facing out. Small hand-written signs indicating the genres were tacked to each shelf. Oils painted by local artists adorned the walls, and a winding staircase led to a second floor with more books and a reading room. Mollie, whose idea of heaven was an afternoon with a book, was immediately attracted to the shelf of Irish writers. Her eyes were drawn to the first editions. She pulled out a volume of poetry written by Yeats.

An hour later Sean found her seated cross-legged on the floor, with two piles, one small, one large, in front of her. "Find anything?"

She looked up guiltily. "What time is it?"

"Time for lunch. Did you find anything for Marni?"

She nodded. "And for Caili and Luke."

"Luke? Isn't he a bit young for reading?"

"He's old enough for someone to read to him, and it will be good practice for the girls."

Sean looked doubtful. "Won't he tear the pages?"

Mollie held up a picture book with stiff cardboard pages. "Not these."

He took it from her hand. "How long have we had such things?"

"Long enough for you to know about them. Don't you read to the children?"

"Of course I do. But we have real books with paper pages. I've never seen anything like this."

Mollie took the book back. "If you don't want it—"

"I didn't say that. I do want it. I've just never seen anything like it, that's all."

"I can buy it for him," she offered, "if you're watching your budget."

"For Christ sake, Mollie," he said, exasperated. "I'm not so poor that I can't afford to buy a book for my nephew."

"Are you always so irritable when you're hungry?"

She heard the sharp intake of his breath. His left eyebrow quirked dangerously. Keeping her expression bland, she braced herself. Seconds passed. His lips twitched. "Has anyone ever told you that you're a saucy lass?"

"All the time." She kept a straight face. "In exactly those words."

He pulled her arm through his. "Shall we buy these books and find something to eat before I murder you?"

"Definitely."

The restaurant sat on the curb of a quiet street, small with dark wood floors and wingback chairs arranged in intimate groupings around round tables covered with white cloths. The waiter led them to a seat near the fireplace. Mollie stripped off her gloves and rubbed her frozen hands.

Within minutes bowls of hot pureed soup, brown bread with pats of butter, and two foaming glasses of Guinness appeared before them.

She raised her eyebrows. "Do you come here often?"

"When I have a reason. I thought you'd appreciate something different from the usual pub fare."

She tasted the soup. "It's delicious."

"You looked like you needed warming."

The soup was followed by slices of roast beef, parsleyed small potatoes, and a mix of perfectly cooked carrots and green beans. Sean ordered another two glasses of ale and a pot of tea.

By the end of the meal the rosy glow that began with the first taste of her soup extended to all parts of her body. Mollie leaned on her elbow and stared into the blue-tipped flames of the fire. She was incredibly content sitting in the semidarkness filled with food, surrounded by warmth.

Sean's voice was buttery soft. "What are you thinking?"

Mollie looked at him, at the triangle of white teeth and firm lips, at the way the lines deepened around his mouth, softening the hard angles and planes of his face, at the blue-green eyes with their sweep of dark lashes and the tiny crow's feet fanning out from their corners, evidence of too much wind and sun on Irish skin. Time stopped. She heard the drip of water in the outside gutters and the sing-song siren of a police car, the ringing of church bells signaling afternoon mass.

The edges of the world outside the restaurant were muted by a soft mist, and somewhere in the kitchen, she recognized the yeasty aroma of rising bread. Suddenly she felt exposed, her nerves sharp and vibrating, her eyes burning and stretched inside their sockets.

She found the words and said them, knowing it was a risk. "I'm wondering if you have any idea how attractive you are."

She saw his hand clench, and watched the sudden tightening of his jaw.

"That's a grand compliment coming from a girl from California."

"Yes," she said evenly. "It is."

"Perhaps this wasn't such a good idea," he said.

"I was thinking the same thing."

"Can we salvage it?"

"That depends on what you mean."

He laughed harshly. "You're quick, Mollie Tierney. I'll give you that one."

She waited silently.

He shook his head and swore. "It isn't that I don't want it or, God help me, that I'm not tempted, but it's a dreadful risk. Can you understand that, Mollie? If you would only understand that, we could—"

She interrupted him. "We could what, Sean? Sleep together? Love each other? Say goodbye in June? No, thank you. I don't want to end up with a broken heart."

"Better that than raise the hopes of three children who don't deserve another loss."

"Why do you keep saying that?"

"Because it's true. Can you live on our island, Mollie, or even in Ireland? Can you give up the world you're accustomed to?"

"Not permanently. But I'm not opposed to spending time here."

"That won't work for me."

"Not even if there was enough incentive?"

"No."

She leaned forward. "Why not? You're an educated man. You aren't limited to living on Inishmore. Once the children are grown, they won't stay if they're to make anything of themselves, especially now. Every fisherman on the island will be leaving, every family with young children. Who will Luke and the girls grow up with?"

"The island is their only stability just now. They've lost everything else. It's not the first time the island's been evacuated," he said. "Even if the children do leave, it will be to Galway or Dublin, not California. That isn't so far away they can't come back to visit."

"My point exactly."

"You don't understand, Mollie. I've spent years away from the island. I encourage everyone to try it, but I don't want to live in California."

"I'm not asking you to *live* in California."

"My answer is no."

She reached for her water. Her hand shook. It was hard to swallow. Carefully, she set down the glass. He didn't see it, the blind selfishness of his decision, the happiness he was throwing away because he wouldn't compromise.

She opened her mouth to continue her argument when it hit her, the revelation that silenced her and left her staring miserably down at the napkin in her lap. She was an idiot. Worse, she was a presumptive idiot. He wasn't in love with her. What he meant and was too polite to say was that he didn't care enough. There was no reason for him to make concessions. What he wanted was an affair. He was a man, after all, a man who found her attractive. But he wasn't in the market for anything permanent, not with her. Warm waves of humiliation washed over her.

Mollie turned toward the fire, grateful for the heat, hoping he would think the color gilding her face was the result of her proximity to the flames and two glasses of Guinness. Rain splashed against the windows and drummed on the roof. "It's time to go," she said quietly.

"The wind is fierce. We'll wait a bit for the weather to let up. Our ferry doesn't leave until four."

No mention of showing her his home, of closing the distance between them. "Will it run in bad weather?"

He smiled, and her heart flipped.

"This isn't bad weather, Mollie. If the ferry closed down every time it rained, it would never run."

She did it every time, emphasizing their differences, revealing to him how inadequately prepared she was to live in his world.

Robbie Anderson's wife was a pleasant woman with a round freckled face and twin daughters who looked exactly like her. She wouldn't hear of them taking the bus back to the ferry terminal. Piling her daughters into the car with the presents, she squeezed into the backseat beside them, insisting that Sean drive and Mollie sit beside him while she talked incessantly from the time they left Galway until they reached Rossaveal.

Mollie was grateful for the diversion. Nothing more was required of her than an occasional monosyllabic answer. She was miserable. The ferry ride loomed before her and then her mother's inevitable quizzing. The solitude of her own room had never seemed more appealing.

Dutifully she murmured her thanks. Burdened with a mountain of presents, she was unable to wave goodbye to the Andersons. Sean purchased their tickets. Relieving her of most of the bags, he led the way up the gangplank into the cabin, deposited the packages on another seat, and sat beside her near the window. Immediately the engines roared to life.

Somehow she managed the journey, smiling at times, responding when appropriate, even managing enthusiasm for the Christmas holiday only three days away. She was emotionally exhausted when they pulled into Kilronen Harbor. Patrick's pony trap waited in the wet darkness. She could barely make out her father's outline leaning against a piling. No one had ever looked more welcoming.

"I've come to drive you two home," he said, looking surprised and touched at her fierce hug.

"Go ahead without me," Sean said. "I've a few things to attend to." He rested his hand on Mollie's shoulder. "You take the packages. We'll divide them up later. Thank you for the day. I enjoyed it very much."

Without meeting his eyes, she nodded. "Good night."

Mollie watched him walk into the mist until it swallowed him completely.

"Are you all right, lass?" Patrick asked.

Her reserve broke. Tears welled up in her eyes and spilled down her cheeks. She shook her head, and a hiccuping sob worked its way up from her throat. She opened her mouth, but the words wouldn't come, and she could only shake her head helplessly.

"There, there, love," Patrick murmured, gathering her into his arms. "Cry if you need to. It's all right."

"I don't want to go home," Mollie sobbed.

"Then I'll not take you there. You'll come home with me, and we'll sort it out. Nothing's impossible when two heads work together. You'll see."

The soothing words eased some of the ache, and before long Mollie was seated inside the trap, her legs wrapped in a woolen blanket, her feet warmed by a hot brick, listening to the comforting sound of her father's voice urging his pony over the narrow roads of Inishmore.

24

*P*atrick Tierney looked at his daughter's swollen face and said nothing until she was comfortably tucked into his easy chair, a blanket around her legs and a cup of tea in her hands. He was fairly sure he understood the nature of her discontent, but until she put it into words he would not presume upon her privacy. After adding more turf to the fire, he sat down across from her and spoke of other things—his grandchildren, the holiday to come, the gifts he had purchased, the food he would contribute. When he had reached the last reserves of his conversation, Mollie's tears were spent.

"I'm sorry," she said.

"Don't be. We all get blue from time to time."

She stared into the fire.

"How was your journey to Galway?" he ventured.

He loved the way her cheeks colored, not rosy pink like an Irish woman's but softer, like ripe peaches.

"I shouldn't have gone," she confessed. "I knew when Sean asked me that it would only make things worse."

Patrick let her talk. He knew with Mollie, as with Emma, it would help.

"Mother said," she continued, "that exposure would help. She said if we spent time together, our differences would divide us, and the attraction I felt for him would fade."

"Did she now?" He would not criticize his former wife, but Emma had her own way of seeing things. There was no crime in looking at the world through the narrow tunnel of her own vision, not unless one disregarded the possibility that there might be another way. Some attractions might fade with exposure, but love, true love, deepened. Only lately had Patrick realized that love could last, unshaken, across decades, despite obstacles thrown in its path. "Perhaps if you had years, your mother's advice would apply."

"That's what Sean said. He's convinced I would lose interest like Mother did." Horrified at her insensitivity, she looked at him. "I'm sorry."

"No need to apologize for the truth. All that's in the past. It no longer has the power to bring pain." He smiled. "I think it's more likely that Sean's nature is a cautious one. He's wondering if he could ever be sure any woman would stay true in these times. I understand that his adjustment from the island to the mainland wasn't an easy one. Perhaps he's doubting his own judgment."

"He said I could never live here permanently."

"Could you?"

Mollie hesitated. "I don't know."

Patrick leaned forward, elbows on his knees, eyes blue and kind and earnest. "Don't be trying to change the measure of a man, Mollie Tierney. That was your mother's mistake, and look what it brought the two of us. Sean has the children to think of. Until that's settled, he won't be leaving Inishmore. Unless he comes around to your way of thinking on his own, there will never be peace or happiness between the two of you."

"It's hopeless, isn't it?"

The lines around Patrick's eyes softened. He reached across the space between them and squeezed his daughter's hand. "I don't think you'll be wanting a life on this island, lass. There's no future here, unless you intend to open a restaurant or a lodging house. The young people are leaving us. There's opportunity on the mainland, computers and such."

Mollie laughed through her misery. She'd used similar words to try to convince Sean. "I'll keep that in mind."

Patrick nodded and leaned back in his chair. "Tell me of the news from Galway."

For another hour or so, Mollie warmed herself by her father's peat fire. The knot of tension in her stomach relaxed, and her depression lifted. The world looked rosier in the small room lit with the soft glow of sweet-smelling turf. Regretfully, she looked at her watch. "I haven't even called Mother."

"She knows I went to fetch you," he assured her.

"I should be going."

"Aye." He set down his cup. "I'll hitch up Brownie, and we'll be off."

It was seven o'clock when the pony trap pulled up to the door of Mollie's cottage. Every window was dark. Only the porch light glowed through the mist.

Patrick helped her down, unloaded the packages, and

handed them to her. "It looks as if you'll have to fend for yourself, Mollie, my girl. I should have thought to offer you a bit of something to eat."

She kissed his cheek. "I'll manage. Thank you for the ride and the conversation."

He tipped his hat. "It was my pleasure."

The door wasn't locked. Mollie turned the bolt and, without flipping the light switch, made her way up the stairs. Russ's door was closed. He kept odd hours because of his schedule, but her mother's door was cracked open and the reading lamp was on. Mollie knocked gently.

"Come in." Emma's voice was groggy with fatigue.

She stepped into the bedroom. "I'm home."

"How was it?"

Mollie shrugged. "Enlightening."

"Are you all right? You look as if you've been crying."

"I'll be fine with some sleep. How were the children?"

Emma laughed. "Exhausting. I don't think I've fallen asleep this early in years."

Mollie crossed the room, leaned over, and gave her mother a quick kiss. "Christmas is only three days away. Do you realize that this will be the first Christmas I'll spend with both my parents?"

Emma was silent for a minute before answering. "I don't want to spoil your pleasure, Mollie, but don't forget that it's the first Christmas the girls will spend without Danny and Kerry. There will be some difficult moments."

"We'll have to keep them busy."

"I'm counting on you for that." Emma brightened. "Ward called before you came home. He'll be here soon."

"Does he need a ride from the airport?"

"No, just from the ferry. I'll meet him."

"Good night, Mom." With a sense of relief, Mollie opened the door to her bedroom and closed it behind her. She wasn't tired as in needing sleep, but her mind was weary and her eyes burned. Kicking off her shoes, she stepped out of her slacks and sweater, pulled aside the covers, and climbed into bed.

The smell of bacon woke her. She turned to look at the clock. It was after eight in the morning. Mollie swung her legs over the bed, found her robe and slippers, and walked downstairs to the kitchen.

Russ bowed to her with a flourish. "I've made pancakes."

Mollie pushed the hair back from her face. "I can see that. Where's my mother?"

"She went into town for groceries. I told her I'd take care of you."

"Where did you learn to cook?"

"The same place you did. In my mother's kitchen."

Mollie sat down at the table, picked up a piece of bacon, and nibbled at the edges. "Was she a good cook?"

"Terrible." He grinned. "Mom's idea of a good meal is canned fruit cocktail dumped over cottage cheese. It was learn to cook or starve."

Mollie laughed. "You're joking."

"No. I'm not." He set a plate of perfectly browned pancakes in front of her. "There's no maple syrup on the entire island, but butter and powdered sugar are almost as good. There's jam if you prefer."

"This is fine," Mollie said when she'd finished swallowing the first mouthful. "It's better than fine. It's delicious."

"Thank you." He sat down across from her and poured himself a cup of coffee. "Is the way to your heart through your stomach, Mollie?"

His voice had changed, lowered, gone serious. She looked at him. "Why would you want to know the way to my heart?"

"Isn't it obvious?"

"Not to me."

"I must be losing my touch."

"Don't," she said evenly.

"Don't what?"

"Complicate things. It's nice the way it is. I feel comfortable with you, but that's all."

"Is there someone else?"

"On this island?"

"What about Sean O'Malley?"

"Sean has no romantic interest in me."

"That isn't what I asked."

She turned her attention back to her pancakes. "What are you asking?"

"Do you have any interest in him?"

"You're confusing me with Beth."

"Am I?"

She stood and walked to the sink, where she rinsed her plate. "This isn't the way to my heart, Russ. Don't badger me."

"I'm trying to figure you out, Mollie. You say you're not interested in taking this any further, and yet you won't tell me why."

She turned around. Her hands found the pockets of her robe. "Does there have to be a reason? Not every woman is looking for a man, or maybe I just don't think of you that way. It's possible to know that about a person right away."

He was silent for a minute. "I suppose it is."

"I'm sorry."

He smiled. "I'm sure you are."

He really was very nice. "I'm truly sorry. I don't want to hurt you."

"Don't think twice about it," he said lightly. "It hasn't gone as far as that."

"Thanks for breakfast."

"You're welcome." He changed the subject. "A few of us are getting together at Clancy's tonight for a Christmas party. Will you join us?"

"Can I let you know? I have a few things to do, and I don't know how long they'll take."

"There's no pressure, Mollie, and if you're thinking it's a date, it isn't intended that way, either. No one's really organized it. Whoever shows up is welcome."

She nodded. "Are you working today?"

"Every day, until the job is done."

"Don't worry about the kitchen. I'll get dressed and clean it up. It's the least I can do."

"Thank you," he said again.

Cold air swirled about the large figure of Colin Keneally as he stood on the threshold of the Tierney cottage, twisting the brim of his hat between his hands. The burly fisherman was slow to speak and slower to move except on the water-slick deck of his fishing boat. There the man fairly crackled with energy. Today, with the icy north wind at his back, he moved and spoke with his usual onshore hesitation.

"I've come to see if anything's changed."

Sean crossed the floor of the small room, reached around the big man, and closed the door. He gestured to a chair. "Will you have something to warm you, Colin?"

"Aye, a wee dram it will have to be, Sean."

Sean disappeared into the kitchen and came back with a bottle of whiskey. He broke the seal, poured a generous amount into a tea mug and a much smaller portion into a paper cup. He handed the mug to Colin and sat down across from him. "Miss Tierney has contacted a lawyer. He'll be coming to the island to talk with us the day after Christmas. We'll know more then."

"Will there be any money for us to hold out the winter with, Sean?"

"I don't know. Sometimes these things take time."

The man's large fingers, torn and scarred from rope burns and fish hooks, tightened around the mug. "We don't have the time, Sean, not unless the fishing bans are lifted."

"That won't happen. If the fish aren't allowed to repopulate, you'll starve in the years to come."

"Better than starving this year."

"I'm sorry, Colin, but I wouldn't count on it," Sean repeated.

The fisherman turned the cup around in his hands and watched the whiskey swirl like liquid amber in his cup. "My mother's sister has an inn in Roscommon. She needs a man to help out around the place. There's room for Mary and the children."

"You've lived here all your life. Your home was your father's and his before him. What will happen to it if you leave?"

Colin shrugged. "I've no choice in the matter. At least I've a place to go, and my children will have food in their stomachs this winter. There's many who won't."

"What about the dole?"

"The dole won't feed nine children, Sean. There will be more than a few who will tighten their belts before another month passes."

"Don't give up yet. Wait and see what the lawyer says. We'll meet with him at the community center. He'll figure something out."

Colin drained the last of his whiskey, set the mug on the floor, and stood. "More likely he'll tell those who have a place to go to get out while they can."

Sean watched the man leave. Colin was right. All lawyers were the same. Daniel O'Shea would be no different, not the Daniel O'Shea he remembered, a hot-tempered, ambitious young Irishman out to make a name for himself. O'Shea only took the big cases, the precedent-setting ones that made the papers. He wouldn't have the news they wanted. He would do what it took to win, earn his fee, and cut what losses he could.

What gnawed at him was that Colin would consider leaving the island. Colin was a Keneally, a family name as old on the Arans as O'Malley. Keneally with their distinctive red-gold heads and square jaws were once sprinkled across the Arans as numerous as the unmortared stone fences that criss-crossed the rocky fields. Now Colin, Mary, and his children were the last to hold the original name. There were Connellys, the anglicized version of the old name, but only one family of Keneallys, and now they were leaving.

Two of his girls were the same ages as Marni and

Caili. He could still hear Mollie's words. *Once the children are grown, they won't stay. Every fisherman on the island will be leaving, every family with young children. Who will Luke and the girls grow up with?*

She was right. Others would follow suit. Large families would go first, and then the others would follow until Inishmore would resemble a retirement community, quaint villages where only the elderly lived, and every summer tourists would come to swig Guinness, ride bicycles, hike to the forts, buy Aran sweaters, eat in the restaurants, and catch the ferry back to the mainland. A few would stay the night to hear traditional music in the pubs and talk to the natives, hearing the Gaelic lilt in their voices, listening to the tales of how it had once been, imagining the ruthless struggle for survival depicted in the O'Flaherty film continually showing at the tourist center.

Slowly, one pebble at a time, from the steady conversation of the original thatched cottages, due to lack of interest and the expense of repair, to the satellite dishes displayed on roofs all over the island bringing in CNN and rap music, the foundation of everything he'd known was being shaken loose.

$\mathcal{M}$ollie breathed in the fog-drowned air and continued walking down the road away from town. She missed the piney smell of Christmas. On Inishmore, the holiday was a bedlam of sensory stimulation, smells and food and music, but no wreaths, no garlands, and no ribbon-bedecked Douglas firs or Ponderosa pines. The day was a holier one than in California. Every islander had his nativity scene proudly displayed, and the three churches on the island, their bells clanging, offered mass on the hour. Nothing was open, not a single pub, not even the smallest convenience store. Other than families making their way to and from the services, the roads were quiet.

Mabry O'Farrell, dressed in her usual black, dug in her garden for winter herbs. She waved and called out as Mollie walked by. "Would you care to come in for a cuppa, love?"

Mollie shook her head, thanked her, and moved on. Farther down, an elderly woman, clumsy in her wellies, her head covered with a red scarf, filled her buckets at a roadside spring and struggled to carry them home. Buckets of water meant a dry loo and no running water.

Two boys, Alice Duncan's students, scraped periwinkles from rocks along the shore, and Colleen Seoighe, her head down and carrying a covered plate, nearly bumped into Mollie. She backed away apologetically. "Here I am, wool-gatherin' again." She laughed. "I'm sorry, Miss Tierney."

"Merry Christmas, Mrs. Seoighe."

Colleen nodded. "Happy Christmas to you, too, lass. And are you appreciatin' your holiday from the children?"

"Definitely."

Again the woman laughed. "I know. All six of mine are here. There isn't a moment to breathe. I'll be on my way now. Say hello to your mam for me, won't you Miss Tierney? My husband says we'll be leaving after the new year, and I don't know whether I'll be over to see her before then."

"I will," Mollie promised, and continued on her way, pondering the irony of her mother's cultivating friendships on the island now that she was a temporary visitor. There had been none all those years ago when she was a bride. Acceptance on the island was slow, the people too honest for superficial smiles.

Mollie had no clear idea of where she was going, only a sense that guided her up toward the cliffs of Dun Aengus, where the view, once the mist separated, was unobstructed.

The wind was up when she reached the broken steps of the old entrance to the fort. She climbed them, pulled herself up, and stood in the flat grassy expanse of what

had once been a courtyard. Walking toward the precarious edge, she stopped a good six feet away from the sheer
drop and looked out over the sea. Most of the fog had
burned off. The muddy color had disappeared from the
water. Sean had told her that ninety percent of the oil
would have evaporated by now. Everything looked just as
it had the first day she'd stepped onto the pier, except
that empty fishing boats bobbed in the harbor and stoic-
faced fisherman in yellow oilskins no longer hauled their
long black curraghs down to a fickle sea.

The ferry, a white silent streak in the grayness, was
still a distance from the harbor. From her spot hundreds
of feet above the water, all was silent except the
screaming of gulls circling above her head. They hadn't
yet come to terms with boats that never left the dock,
men who no longer fished, a pier scrubbed free of
entrails.

Caught up in thought and solitude, she didn't hear
him behind her. The sound of her name blended with
the wind and the cries of the birds. The first she knew of
his presence was the strength of his arms circling her
from behind, holding her against him, warming her,
breathing hard.

She closed her eyes. "Are you following me?" Her
voice was faint above the howl of the wind.

"I am."

"Why?"

"I couldn't help it."

Her heart pounded. It would be so easy to turn, to
bury her face in his chest, to give herself up for a too
brief time to the feel of his hands on her skin and his lips
moving against her mouth. But then what? The last time

she'd indulged herself, the ache that came after was worse, much worse, than anything she'd known before. Mollie knew what he wanted. She wanted it, too. More than once she'd argued with herself that sex might be the way to keep him. Men compromised themselves over it all the time, throwing away lifelong, gone-stale marriages for newer, livelier, younger women, uninhibited enough to experiment in bed.

Then reason would kick in, and the rational side of her brain would remind her that sex without love was never the answer. More importantly, she had enough pride left to want the man she loved to want her back without having to trap him into it.

She pulled away and turned to look at him. He wore a thick cable-knit sweater under his jacket. Above it his eyes were clear blue with a hint of green—ocean-colored eyes. His twisted smile tore at her heart and weakened her resolve.

"There's a storm coming," he said gently. "I didn't want you caught up in it."

"You don't have to worry about me."

"It's too late for that."

Be careful, she mentally chastised herself. *Don't read something that isn't there.* "I needed some time alone," she said out loud.

"Do you need that often, Mollie Tierney?"

She thought a minute. "Yes."

"Are you able to manage it with all we're asking of you?"

She nodded. "An hour or so usually does it. It isn't so much that it interferes with anything."

"Kerry didn't like being alone."

Mollie turned away. "I thought we weren't going to talk about Kerry."

"I don't remember saying that."

She wouldn't remind him. It would bring up other memories of that night, their lapse, and the crossing of a line that should never have been crossed. "Maybe I misunderstood you."

He was silent. She watched his eyes move across her face and settle on her mouth. "You're nothing like your mother, you know," he said softly. "At first I thought so. You have her look about the eyes and mouth. Sometimes the way you smile. But now I see no resemblance at all."

"I'm not my mother, Sean. We're two different people."

"Aye." His voice was husky, choked.

They stood there, inches apart without touching. Black clouds boiled above them. The wind whistled past, bounced against the cliffs, and echoed back again. "It's going to pour," he said.

"Can we make it back?" Already she felt the drops on her head.

He took her hand. "Come on."

Mollie followed him away from the precipice to where a tiny domed hut was sheltered by a rock and mortar wall. The entrance was the size of a window.

"It's bigger than it looks," he said, "and if the current generation of schoolboys is anything like we were, it's probably furnished with pornography and a blanket or two."

Dropping to her knees, Mollie crawled inside. Instantly the noises of wind and rain diminished, and she was swallowed in darkness. "I can't see anything," she called back.

Sean was right behind her. "You'll adjust." A small pinpoint of light permeated the darkness. "I have a flashlight."

It was enough to look around. Grass, long dead but still soft, had been scattered like a carpet on the ground, and in the corner, magazines were neatly stacked. There were no blankets, but inside the thick walls it was warm. She sat down, leaned back, and crossed her legs. "Do you think it will last long?"

She couldn't make out his features, but his voice in the darkness was teasing. "The worst of it will be over soon. If you don't mind a wetting, we should be home in plenty of time for you to cook my Christmas dinner."

"If your heart is set on food, you'd better hope that my mother will have most of it finished by the time we get back." She changed the subject. "Where are the children?"

"I left them with my mother to watch television. She ordered a video of *The Nutcracker* some time ago. It arrived the other day. Patrick will bring them back in time for dinner."

"It's strange, isn't it, how everyone is getting along so well?"

"They've nothing left to argue about."

"What do you mean?"

He thought a minute before answering. "When people's lives are connected and every move one makes affects the other, as in a marriage, there's a tremendous amount at stake. Arguments are inevitable. Your parents' futures are no longer tied together. There's no point in arguing or in making the other move in the same direction."

Her voice was a paper-thin whisper in the dry darkness. "How convenient for them."

She felt his hand on her arm, friendly, comforting. "You don't still hope they'll reunite, do you, Mollie?"

"Of course not."

"Good. Because it's a childish wish and not worth entering your head. Patrick is better off looking in another direction for love."

"You mean Alice Duncan?"

"He could do worse."

Suddenly she was angry. "You have it all figured out, don't you?"

"I beg your pardon?"

"You know exactly what will and won't happen. Is everyone on this island like Mabry O'Farrell, or is it just the two of you who can predict the future?"

"I've only stated the obvious, Mollie. I know nothing of the future."

Ashamed of her outburst, she said nothing, staring at the pinpoint of light in front of her. Every sound was magnified a thousand times. Her breathing was shallow and loud. Self-conscious, she inhaled deeply, trying to slow it. She reached for a magazine and held it under the light. When she saw the erotic pose of the scantily clad woman on the cover, she tossed it aside.

He broke the silence. "If I've offended you, I'm sorry."

She didn't trust herself to speak. What was happening to her? She was frustrated, confused, out of control.

"Talk to me, Mollie. I can't see your face. Please tell me what you're thinking."

She was conscious of his shoulder pressing against hers. "Nothing," she said shortly. "I'm not thinking of anything." She wanted to forget who they were and what they'd said, forget that one day, months from now, she would leave and never return.

"Your nose is growing, Mollie Tierney."

Suddenly it was all too funny. She was Mollie Tierney, privileged, attractive, intelligent, and, if she was completely honest with herself, more than a little spoiled. Not once had she experienced the humiliation of sitting out a dance at a junior high mixer or staying home on a weekend night for lack of a date. Invitations had always come easily and with them the confidence of knowing she was one of the preferred. "The golden girl" were the words printed under her picture in her high school yearbook. She had to travel eight thousand miles to find a man who wasn't interested in her, and the irony of it was that he was the only one she'd ever really wanted. Her sense of the absurd battled with self-pity and won. She laughed.

Immediately the tension in his shoulder relaxed. "You had me worried," he admitted.

"Tell me what *you're* thinking," she countered.

He hesitated.

"I won't run away."

It was his turn to laugh, to rest his hand on her thigh. This time she knew it was a bit more than friendly.

"I'm thinking that I'm alone out of the rain in a warm, dark shelter with a beautiful woman." His voice had dropped, and his hand moved in circles across her leg. "I'm thinking that I don't want this to be another wasted opportunity."

She held her breath.

"I'm thinking that if I move first, she'll be terrified,

run out into the wet, and I'll lose the lovely warm thing there is between us."

Mollie didn't stop to think. She only knew what she wanted and that she'd waited an endless length of time to satisfy her wanting. Her hand found his cheek and slid beyond it to the back of his neck. Drawing his head down, she kissed him.

A sound, a mixture of relief and pleasure, rose up from the back of his throat. His arms wrapped around her, and he deepened the kiss. It was frantic at first, hard and searching, as if he'd forgotten what kissing her was like, but then his mouth gentled, coaxing her to share in the tasting and probing and curling of tongues. He lifted his head to breathe and utter her name. "Mollie."

She heard the lilt at the end. It was a question after all, and she answered it with a slight nod, a movement of her cheek against his, and the quick separating of the first shirt button beneath his sweater.

He kissed her again, slowly this time, a gentle caress of lip against lip, the murmur of words she didn't understand and, with them, a leisurely, thorough exploring of her body, the swell of breast, the curve of hip, and, when she lifted slightly to accommodate his hand, the rounded cheek of her bottom.

Mollie found her own pace. There was no hurry. The rain pounded against their shelter, showing no signs of abating. His body was leaner than she remembered and hard, very hard. His breath came harshly against her ear. One hand had slipped under her sweater and was moving slowly, purposefully, toward her breast. The other had worked off her slacks. She could feel the softness of his worn jeans against her bare legs.

She couldn't see his face. Shifting to the side, she felt the weight of her breast fall into his hand. Lifting her sweater and bra out of the way, he lowered his head and circled one peak and then the other with his tongue. She gasped and held him to her, kissing his cheek, touching her tongue to the inside of his ear.

His hand moved to the front of his jeans. She helped him ease the buttons from their holes, helping him tug the clothes from his hips, and pressed her palm against the bare, hard front of him.

"Mollie?"

Again the question, the wonder in his voice, the desire for her alone.

"Yes," she whispered, her hands sliding down the length of him, jutting angles, hard planes, fitting against her.

Supporting himself on both hands, he linked his fingers with hers and moved over her. She refused to close her eyes when he entered her. She wanted him to remember who he was loving, whose body he was joining with and pleasuring, who he would think and dream of in all the long and lonely nights to come. She wouldn't say the words, not because she didn't feel them or because she was afraid he would draw away, but because she couldn't face the emptiness of not hearing them in return.

It wasn't new, and yet it seemed new, this moving together, the matching of rhythms, the feverish building heat, the wanting more while holding back to heighten each moment, to prolong the pleasure, the give and take of body and soul, heart and mind, for an interlude so brief and yet so profound.

Here, cocooned in warm darkness with sheets of rain falling around them, Mollie learned about desire. Desire that speeds the blood and slows the breath and squeezes the heart in a dangerous slamming rhythm that removes all reality except the present and the person and the moment when the earth moves close to heaven.

He came quickly, explosively, a man gone too long without release. She held him against her, searing into memory the shuddering weight of him, the salty taste of his skin, the smooth muscles of his back, the strength of his arms, and the delicious warmth of what they'd shared.

Mollie had never loved a man before. She knew with the same quiet conviction with which she came to all her conclusions that she loved this one. And she knew that it wouldn't go away. She would live on this island, if only she could have Sean O'Malley. All she had to do was convince him she meant it.

"The rain's stopped," she said softly.

He propped himself on one elbow and looked down at her face. "Do you want to leave?"

"I don't ever want to leave," she said honestly, "but soon they'll look for us."

Reluctantly, he sat up and reached for his clothes.

Mollie watched him dress, loving the quick, efficient way he moved. He finished tying his shoes and looked back at her. His eyes narrowed, and he drew a deep, long breath and exhaled. "You're the loveliest sight in all the world, Mollie Tierney," he said softly. "I wonder if you know that."

Strangely unselfconscious, she held up her arms. He reached for her, pulling her against him. This time she knew what he liked and what aroused him. Her kiss was lingering, a promise of more to come.

"I'll wait outside, or we'll never get home," he said, regret strong in his voice. He backed away through the entrance.

She dressed quickly and crawled out through the opening. The rain had stopped.

Sean stood on the edge of the cliff facing the sea. "Look." He pointed out the shimmery outline of a crescent moon in the afternoon sky. "It's going to be a clear night." His arm slipped around her waist. "A slipper-footed moon is a wishing moon, lass. Wish on it if you like."

Mollie wished.

"What did you wish for?"

She looked at him. "Do you really want to know?"

"I do."

"Will it come true if I tell you?"

"I have no idea."

She would tell him anyway. "I wished for you to fall in love with me."

Expressionless, he stared at her. Then he smiled, that quick twisting of his mouth. "Wish again, lass," he said gently. "We won't have another moon like this for a month."

"Why again?"

He flicked her cheek with the back of his finger. "Because you've no need to waste a wish."

26

Sean left her at the junction of the road. "I'll go home and clean up before I come for dinner."

Mollie nodded. "The girls want to help with the table."

He laughed. "More than likely they want to inspect the gifts. Your mother said four o'clock. Does that suit you, Mollie?"

"That would be fine," she said, as if they were discussing the weather, as if nothing at all had passed between them.

Sean knew why. He knew how vulnerable she was and how much it had taken to leave what they'd shared at the place where they'd left it. She was brave and proud as well. She'd told him once how she felt. He knew she couldn't tell him again, nor would she make demands. Mollie wasn't like that. It was one of the many qualities he loved about her.

Hands in his pockets, Sean climbed the slight grade toward home. He thought of Mollie all the time. All the while he was staring at his computer screen and trying out the words, layering his scenes, deliberating stage directions, waiting on hold for someone to answer the telephone, preparing meals for Luke and the girls, she was always on his mind. The smell of her perfume, her laugh, the lovely multihued gold of her hair came to him at the oddest moments. He loved her. He hadn't believed it was possible to love a woman the way he loved Mollie. It terrified him.

He wanted her gone because he couldn't stay away. Sex hadn't cured him. Once he thought it might. Now it shamed him that his thoughts had even traveled in that direction. Not that it wasn't satisfying, an understatement if there ever was one. It wasn't Mollie's body that drew him. It was her ability to endure, to take what was mundane or inevitable, even tragic, and turn it around until it was something more, something possible, hopegilded. He couldn't bear to see that quality disappear, and it would after a few short years on an island, waterlocked from the rest of Europe, an island where there were no shopping malls, where sheep crowded country roads, where men fished and smoked and woman watched the telly and knitted away their winters, where rain poured down in buckets and there was no escaping the cloying smell of wet wool.

Ireland was no place for a woman like Mollie, and Newport, California, was no place for a man who taught Irish history and wrote Irish plays. That wouldn't change, and neither would his resolve to spare his sister's children further pain. Come summer, Mollie would go home. They would miss her, but not so much that they wouldn't recover, provided she remained Aunt Mollie, as long as he didn't bring her into his home, as long as he didn't believe she could be a part of his future. The state of his heart was another matter. He would leave that one alone for now and enjoy his Christmas dinner.

Alice Duncan pulled her coat tightly around her. "I still think it's odd that we'll be having Christmas dinner at your ex-wife's home, Patrick. I don't feel comfortable at all."

"It's my daughter's home," he reminded her, "and it's the first time in twenty-eight years I've shared Christmas with her."

Alice relented, and the expression that softened her face whenever she looked at Patrick came over her again. "You're right, of course. I should be grateful I've been invited."

Taking one hand from the reins, he covered hers and squeezed it gently. It was nothing short of a miracle that this woman, decent, warm, educated, had loved him for all these years. "Mollie likes you," he said simply.

"I wonder if Emma does."

Patrick shrugged. "We've not discussed it. It doesn't matter. Emma isn't part of our lives, Alice. Her approval isn't necessary."

"Have you told Mollie?"

"Not yet. But I'm sure she knows. Not much misses our Mollie."

Alice settled back against the padded seat, and once again Patrick marveled at how easy it was when you measured up in the eyes of a woman who really loved you. How easily life flowed. He resolved to make up the years they'd missed starting immediately. His family would be gathered. He would announce their plans today.

He looked at Alice, at her sensible haircut, at the roundness of her cheeks, at her sturdy figure and capable, square hands. This was the woman he would look at across his breakfast table for the rest of his life. She smiled at him. He felt a surge of happiness. Clucking to Brownie, he urged the pony over the rise and onto the gravel driveway of Mollie's cottage.

They were the last to arrive. Mollie opened the door and took their coats. She led them into the living room, where strains of "The Little Drummer Boy" sounded from the stereo speakers. Sean and the girls were intent on entertaining Luke. Seated in chairs pulled close to the fire, Eileen and Russ were in deep conversation with a handsome older man who could only be Ward Reddington. There was no sign of Emma. Mistletoe hung over the doorway. Patrick stopped directly under the arch and, in front of everyone, took Alice in his arms and kissed her thoroughly on the lips. She blushed and laughed.

Mollie's eyes were wide with surprise, but her manners were beautiful, a credit to Emma. "My goodness. What a lovely way to start the celebration." She kissed her father on the cheek and then leaned over and did the same to Alice. "Do we have more to celebrate than Christmas?" she murmured.

"I'm not—" Alice stopped, tongue-tied, and looked at Patrick.

"We do," he said promptly, "but our news will wait. Where is your mother?"

"In the kitchen." Mollie dipped a ladle into the punch bowl, poured out two cups, and served them. "I'll introduce you to Ward, and then I'll go check on her.

Help yourself to the starters, but don't eat too much. Mother's outdone herself. She's never had a crowd this size, and she's in heaven."

Emma was stirring gravy with one hand and opening the door of the oven with the other when Mollie walked into the kitchen. "Would you check on the turkey, Mollie? I've turned it so the thermometer is in the back, and I don't want to leave the gravy."

Obediently, Mollie found the oven mitts, pulled the bird out, and checked the temperature. "It's done," she said.

"Take it out and let it stand," said her mother. "We'll eat in about thirty minutes." Smiling, she focused on the gravy. "Is everyone here?"

"Yes." Mollie hesitated. "Alice seems especially happy."

"She's very nice," Emma observed. "Don't you think so?"

"Uh-huh." Mollie dipped the basting brush into the meat juices and painted the sides of the turkey with long, casual strokes. "She's lived here a long time."

"She was here before I came," said Emma.

"Did you know her very well?"

Emma measured out a quarter-cup of wine and added it to the gravy. "She was your father's friend before we married. Neither of us saw her much after."

"How well did you know her?"

"Well enough, I suppose." Emma thought a minute. "I wonder why she never married."

The turkey glistened with juices. Mollie continued to baste. "Maybe because the man she wanted was already taken."

Emma turned off the flame under the gravy and gave Mollie her full attention. "Are you trying to tell me something?"

Mollie bit her lip. "I think they're seeing each other."

"Who?"

"My father and Alice."

"Do you mean as in dating?"

Mollie nodded. "It may be more than just dating."

"Does that bother you?"

"I don't know. I suppose not." She looked at her mother. "It shouldn't."

"But it does?"

She took a minute to answer. "Yes," she said, embarrassed. "It does."

"Have you thought about why that is?"

"I haven't had time. I just found out."

Emma smiled gently. "Everyone is entitled to some happiness in this life, Mollie. Your father has been alone for nearly thirty years."

"It's just that—" She stopped.

After removing the basting brush from Mollie's fingers, Emma set it on the counter, turned her daughter around, and rested her hands on her shoulders. "You expected, after all these years, to have him to yourself, and now you'll be sharing him with Alice."

"That's not it," Mollie protested.

"Isn't it?"

"Not exactly. I didn't expect to have him *all* to myself. I knew there were Danny and the children."

Emma waited.

"A woman is different," Mollie finished.

"How?"

"It isn't that I don't like Alice, but she isn't family."
Mollie was close to tears. Ashamed, she turned away. "I
know I'm being childish and terribly selfish."

"I don't think so," Emma said softly. "You've been
amazing. I'm proud of you. If anyone is to blame for your
not having known your father all these years, it's Patrick
and me."

It was more than that, but Mollie left it alone. There
was no point in worrying Emma. She worried too much
already. Her pointless matchmaking attempts had proven
that. She changed the subject. "Shall we take everything
to the table?"

Emma nodded. "Call the girls. They'll want to help.
You decide where everyone sits." She hesitated. "If you
don't mind, Mollie, I'd like you to seat Ward at the head
of the table. This has got to be awkward for him."

Mollie smiled. "Don't worry. Ward will be fine, Mom.
He always is as long as you're around."

Warm was the word that leaped to Mollie's mind
when she looked at her family gathered around the large
dining table. For as long as she could remember
Christmas meant Ward and her mother, just the three of
them. They would sleep late in the morning, have a
leisurely breakfast of cinnamon rolls and coffee, open
gifts, walk along the estuary down to the shoreline and
back, eat dinner, linger over coffee, and go their separate
ways, Mollie to visit friends and Ward and Emma to an
evening movie.

It was the children, Mollie decided, looking at the
bright eyes and expectant faces of her nieces. They were
incredibly well behaved considering the number of gifts

in the living room with their names on them. Children made all the difference. There was something about children and Christmas that made sense.

She glanced across the table at Sean. His lips were clamped around a green bean, and his eyes twinkled down at Caili. Quickly, the little girl positioned her lips around her own bean. As if in response to some secret cue, they simultaneously slurped them down. Caili squealed with laughter.

"Sean," his mother admonished him. "Don't be playin' with your food. What kind of example is that for the children, and with company about? Shame on you."

Sean grinned. "I'm sorry, Mam."

Eileen's lipped twitched. "You're not sorry at all," she said. "Everyone will think you were raised in a pigsty."

Mollie laughed. "Don't worry, Mrs. O'Malley. Sean's manners are beautiful in public. He isn't at all embarrassing."

"Thank God for that," muttered his mother under her breath.

"When can we open our presents?" Caili asked.

"When you've had your dinner," replied Sean. "Every bite."

Caili looked doubtfully at the huge plate Emma had filled for her. Her lower lip trembled.

Sean relented. "Don't worry, lass." He began dividing the food on her plate. "There now. This should keep a tiny mite like yourself filled up until breakfast. Can you manage this?"

Caili's smile returned. She nodded and applied herself to her food.

Content in his chair, Luke banged a wooden rattle on the tray. Mollie watched Marni move a goblet out of danger and marveled, once again, at the child's maturity.

"Everything is delicious, Emma," Alice said. "Thank you for inviting me."

"You're very welcome. Mollie helped with the cooking."

Russ shook his head in mock regret. "Don't try to marry her off, Mrs. Reddington. It won't work. Trust me."

Sean's fork stopped in midair, halfway to his mouth. Mollie's face reddened.

"Shame on you, Russ Sanders," Emma replied playfully. "As if Mollie needed help finding a husband."

"Thank you," said Mollie. She looked pointedly at Russ. "Just because I'm immune to your charms doesn't mean I'm not interested in marriage altogether."

Russ pounded his fist against his chest. "Cruelty, thy name is Mollie."

Patrick interrupted. "As long as we're speaking of marriage, I have an announcement."

All eyes turned toward him. Fingers of ice clutched at Mollie's heart. *Don't* she pleaded silently. *Not here, not yet.*

Alice flushed and looked down at her lap.

"I have asked Alice to marry me, and she has agreed."

There was a moment of shocked silence. Emma spoke first, her voice warm and accepting. "Congratulations, Patrick. What wonderful news."

Ward reached across the table and held out his hand. Patrick took it. "It is wonderful news, Patrick," he said. "What a surprise."

"It's rather sudden, isn't it?" Eileen asked.

"We've been friends for years," replied Patrick, "and we're no longer young."

Alice looked at Mollie. "You haven't said anything, Mollie."

She smiled and hoped it looked natural. "I'm happy for both of you."

Alice relaxed. "That's a relief. I prayed that you would feel that way."

"Will Miss Duncan be our new grandma?" asked Caili.

Patrick smiled. "In a manner of speaking."

Marni spoke this time. "What shall we call you, Miss Duncan?"

"Alice is fine with me," she said. "I know it will take some getting accustomed to."

"Will you still be our teacher?"

"I will."

Marni frowned. "I don't think we can call you Alice at school."

"No," agreed Alice. "Mollie is your teacher. What do you call her at school?"

Marni thought a minute. "I don't call her anything."

"I call her Aunt Mollie," Caili said.

Patrick interrupted them. "You'll do whatever makes you comfortable. We've had mothers and fathers teach their own children here on the island. It makes no difference when it comes to learning."

"Will you have a ceremony?" Russ asked.

Alice and Patrick looked at each other. "We've spoken of going to Dublin," said Patrick. "We'll have a civil ceremony at the government building. I've a bit put aside. We'll wait until the summer when Alice has her holiday from school. That way we can plan a visit somewhere."

Summer. Mollie relaxed. Summer was months away. She would have time to acclimate herself to the idea of Alice and her father. Across the table, Sean caught her eye and smiled. The memory of what they'd shared earlier and her own resolve rose inside her chest. The ache of what it meant for Alice to have a place in her father's heart lessened. After all, change was a good thing. She smiled back.

Russ pushed back his chair and nodded at Emma. "Thank you for an excellent meal. I've got to motor to Inishmaan to relieve some of the others for a few hours, but I'll be back." He rested his hand on Marni's head and then Caili's. "There are some packages in the living room for the two of you from me. Don't wait to open them. I may be late."

"The trip isn't a long one, but there's a storm watch," Sean warned him. "It could be dangerous."

"I won't try coming back if it looks bad."

Sean frowned and would have said more but thought better of it.

"Russ is nice," observed Caili after he'd left the dining room.

"Yes," Emma said. "He is."

"Do you think he's nice, Mollie?" asked Caili.

"Yes," replied Mollie, "and now I think it's time to open presents."

Russ forgotten, the girls leaped from their chairs and ran into the living room. The adults followed, Emma, Ward, and Eileen first, then Patrick and Alice. Mollie waited for Sean to unbuckle Luke from his chair and carry him into the living room.

"They're right, you know," he said conversationally. "Russ is quite nice."

"He's more than nice. He's perfect."

"He's interested in you."

"I've never encouraged him."

"Sometimes that doesn't matter."

"He's intelligent and rational," she explained "He'll move on easily, especially when he finds someone who appreciates him."

The baby reached out and grabbed a handful of Mollie's hair. They stopped, and Mollie held Luke while Sean worked open the small fists. She felt his breath against her ear. "Do you think the same can be said for everyone?"

She lifted her chin and looked directly at him. "I think I've passed the stage of moving on easily."

"You and I, perhaps," he agreed, "but not the children."

Mollie knew what she wanted. She also knew the odds against it happening, but she wasn't ready to give up, not now, not after today. Maybe whatever was between them wasn't enough to make him change his life, but it meant more to him than he knew. Mollie resolved to make him know. She wasn't a martyr. She wanted no part of an unequal partnership where one loves more than the other. Relationships like that always seemed sadly pathetic to her. But if it was a matter of opening one's eyes, of showing him the possibilities, that she could do. It was only the beginning. If Alice, a woman in her middle fifties, could find happiness, so could she.

27

Sean turned on the reading lamp beside his bed and leafed through the gold-edged pages of the volume of poetry Mollie had given him for Christmas. William Yeats, a first edition. Where could she have found such a treasure? He remembered their conversation at Kenny's Bookshop. She must have purchased it there. He was surprised that Kenny had let it go to anyone other than a collector. Mollie had powers of persuasion that amazed him. She'd gathered their scattered family together, managed to talk Daniel O'Shea into coming to Inishmore, and now a rare first edition.

He read the lines she'd noted with faint pencil marks. He smiled. She was partial to Yeats's love poems. The stirring ballads of revolution were left spotless. *Come live with me and be my love, and together we will all the pleasures prove.* He ran his fingers over the famous words. Strange, how people were all the same. Even a wealthy Protestant like Yeats yearned for a woman he couldn't have. Although, Sean remembered, he did marry her in the end. Sean wondered if Mollie knew the story and then decided she must. She was a teacher, after all.

Leaving the book on the nightstand, he turned out the light, pulled the comforter over him, stretched out, and clasped his hands behind his head. Rain and a wild, roaring wind battered the windows. The girls, accustomed to the weather of their native island would sleep through it, but Luke might wake. It took years to adjust to the wailing sound that fisherman attributed to lost silkies.

A nagging anxiety he couldn't quite place kept his mind alert even as his tired eyes closed. Maybe if he slept, it would disappear by morning. Tucking the pillow closer to his cheek, he turned over and deliberately tried to relax. Slowly the tension eased. His mind drifted. His breathing normalized and he slept.

The wind had gentled but a steady rain still drummed on the roof when Sean's alarm blared to life. Groggily, he reached over and turned it off. There was no hurry. It was the day after Christmas. No one was expecting him anywhere and he had enough work to keep him busy. Propping himself up on his elbow, he pulled the Yeats volume from the nightstand and began to read. There was a time, during his university years and later, when he'd read Irish authors daily, the real ones, Synge and Behan, O'Flaherty and Heaney, the ones who had introduced the world to the realities of growing up poor and Catholic, in English-occupied Ireland.

Yeats was a paradox, a poet, born and raised an aristocrat, with an appreciation for the common man. In many ways he was like Mollie.

The telephone jarred him from his thoughts. Quickly

he picked it up before the second ring. He needed a few more minutes of solitude before the children descended upon him.

"Sean?" The harbor master's deep voice carried a note of alarm.

"Aye, Graham. What can I do for you?"

He came right to the point. "We've an emergency on our hands. There's no word of the American, Russell Sanders. Two of his colleagues expected him last night. It looks like he took the boat out shortly before the worst of the storm hit. He didn't return it to the slip. Can you tell us anything?"

Sean swore under his breath. "Russ had dinner with my family last night at Mollie's cottage. He left before eight."

Graham's voice was grim. "There's another storm coming in. We need men who can handle the boats. Can you help us, lad?"

"I'll be there," Sean said shortly and hung up.

Sheets of rain pounded down on men in yellow slickers and thick rubber-soled shoes as they gathered on the pier for assignments. Graham Greene's instructions left no room for questions. Last night's wind made it impossible to predict where the boat might have drifted. All they could do was search.

Sean climbed into a thirteen-foot Calibogie with a small mast and tied-in sails. He preferred a sailboat with an outboard motor to a straight cruiser. One never knew when a motor would quit. Sails were his insurance policy.

"Turn your radio on," Greene shouted, "and report in every thirty minutes."

Sean nodded, reached down, and pulled the cord. The motor roared to life. Greene lifted the ropes from the pilings and threw them on deck. Sean twisted them into an expert coil, knotted and secured them to hooks on the deck. Bending his head, he stepped into the cabin and took the wheel, checking to see if everything was secured. The open ocean would be a challenge compared to the relative calm of the harbor.

Keeping his eyes on the instruments, he fiddled with the radio, found the right station, and flipped on the controls. The Loran was useful for more than just finding fish. He shrugged out of his slicker, hung it up beside him, and sat down, keeping both hands on the wheel. Calculating the timing of Russ's movements the evening before, he made mental adjustments to the route the harbor master suggested he take.

Russ left Mollie's house after eight o'clock the night before. If he'd gone straight to the harbor without stopping, he would have been on the water by half past eight. Thirty minutes would have placed him at the pier of Inishmaan with time to spare before the worst of the storm set in. But his coworkers claimed he'd never arrived. He must have stopped somewhere before leaving the island. Sean racked his brain. Where could he have gone for the two hours it had taken for the storm to whip itself into a dangerous fury, and why would he have remained on the boat in such weather in the first place? The only other explanation was that he had miscalculated his coordinates and overshot the island, an easy thing to do when visibility was zero.

Too quickly the island shore disappeared, and Sean was shrouded in a cloak of gray. Gray ocean, gray mist, gray sky all blending together in a world with no beginning or end, no horizon, no relief from the frightening netherworld color that terrified anyone unfamiliar with western Ireland.

Sean checked his compass again, rechecked the Loran, and adjusted his position. In less than a minute he was off-course, evidence of a fierce wind and a dangerous current. Again he readjusted, pulling hard on the rudder and holding it in position instead of setting the automatic device. As a precaution he reached for the thick belt attached to a hook on the cabin wall, wrapped it around his waist, and secured it to the pin beneath the rudder. A troubling notion occurred to him. Russ Sanders was a Californian. He'd claimed to be an experienced sailor. Sean wondered just how experienced he was when it came to navigating the Atlantic.

Graham Greene's voice crackled over the radio. Sean lifted the radio and held it to his mouth, keeping a tight hand on the wheel. "I'm holding steady," he said into the mouthpiece. "I'll check near Nugent's Inlet. There are two or three safe harbors he might have found."

"A new storm's approaching," Greene cautioned him. "Don't be a hero, Sean."

He replaced the radio. A wave of water the size of a barn rolled toward the boat, demanding all of his concentration. Grimly he maintained his hold. The Calibogie was a flat-bottomed vessel, virtually unsinkable, but it would turn as much as three hundred sixty degrees in rough waters. Sean didn't relish hovering upside down for any length of time before the boat righted itself again. It wouldn't take more than ten minutes for the cabin to fill with water.

It occurred to him that he didn't have a will. A year ago he would have laughed at the idea. But now, after Kerry, it made sense to him. The children would go to Emma, of course. He would have preferred Mollie. The girls loved her, and she was the right age, more so than his mother, Emma, or Patrick. But what a burden for a young unmarried woman. And what a handicap. What chance would she have for children of her own? Who would want a woman, even a woman as lovely and warm as Mollie was, with three young children not her own?

That left Emma, their legal guardian, designated by Danny and Kerry Tierney. Emma was relatively young. She had a husband, and she adored the children. They would grow up in California. Best of all, they would be close to Mollie. Emma was the logical choice.

A part of him, the logical part, had already posed the question: if Mollie was the optimal choice for the children, why not ask her to marry him and secure the best mother they could possibly hope for? The other part of him, the romantic, hot-blooded Celtic side of him, yearned for a woman who wanted him for himself, a woman who would stand beside him wherever his path led, with or without the children. Sean knew Mollie loved him. He knew the attraction between them was powerful. They'd danced around it long enough to stir the embers into a blaze that threatened to consume both of them unless it was satisfied. But why did she love him? Would she love him if he wasn't caring for her brother's children? The questions nagged at him.

Ten years ago he wouldn't have concerned himself with such absurdities. He would have snapped up Mollie Tierney in an instant and been grateful for the opportunity. But experience and a jaded wisdom had left their mark. He wasn't so quick to believe that once you married a woman, she was yours, unequivocally, forever.

Another wall of water washed over the boat. Sean heard the groan of mast against wave, felt the give of the sturdy little boat and anticipated the sway of the deck, a full forty-five degrees this time. His hands strained against the rudder, holding it steady, a few degrees lost, not much but enough. He dared not release a hand to adjust the instruments. By his calculations he should be very near Inishmaan. On a clear day it would be no more than thirty minutes. He had been out twice as long now. Cold seeped through his jacket. His fingers felt numb. Where was the damned island? It was past time to check in with Graham. If only the wind would let up.

He glanced at the Loran. The Calibogie looked like a tiny twig tossed about by moving mountains. But now there was something else on the screen, and it looked very much like a boat, and it wasn't moving even in the middle of the squall.

The wind turned. Sean braced himself. The water was moving in both directions, cresting over the deck and cabin, crashing in on the boat. Sean heard the crack of the mast. The rudder spun out of his hands. He felt the surge of the mighty wave, the crest lifting the boat higher and higher. The deck lurched beneath his feet. His stomach heaved. He pitched forward, and his head struck the wood of the instrument panel. He was conscious of pain and blackness and then nothing.

Barefoot, Mabry O'Farrell stood outside her cottage, facing west. Something was terribly wrong. She could feel it in the taste of the wind and the pounding surf, in the strange heat coming up from the ground warming the soles of her feet. Where was Sean O'Malley and that likable young American with the lovely grin? Why must her sight fail her when she needed it most?

Like an angry banshee, the wind screamed in her ears pulling at her hair and clothes, twisting the wool of her scarf, stinging her eyes and her lips and the sharp bones of her face. She paid no attention, her gaze focused on something beyond the grayness, beyond the scope of ordinary mortal vision. There was nothing pleasant in the scene that appeared like a distant landscape before her eyes. Change, in Mabry's experience, was rarely pleasant, not in the beginning. It took time, becoming accustomed, forever leaving behind the old and embracing the new, before it was welcomed. She had never been one to adjust easily, even now, when the death of her island was imminent.

The truth of it was she was afraid. Age had overcome her, and the time for new beginnings was long past. She had never been away from the island, never felt the need once the possibility existed. What better life for an old woman than this melding of sky and sea and wind and rock? The island had shaped her, given her wisdom and longevity. Mabry knew, with a certainty she had never felt before, that the end of her life was closing in on her. The ebb and flow of the tides and the pulse of her blood shared a rhythm. Without the one, the other would cease. How could she make them understand, these skeptical, sacrilegious children of this modern world, that she must stay, that she and the island shared a life source that couldn't be severed?

Frustrated, she muttered a Gaelic curse. The wind tore the sound away. Where were the visions when she needed them most?

Mollie walked from the stove to the dining-room table, where her mother and her nieces played Monopoly. Luke lay on a blanket on the floor babbling and waving his arms and legs. It was her third round trip. Each time she was about to sit down she found she'd forgotten something else, a spoon, a napkin, the sugar bowl. Finally it was right. She sat down and poured milk into the cups with trembling hands, half a cup for each of the girls, a splash for Emma and herself.

Forty-three hours had passed since Russ Sanders had left Kilronen Harbor, and there was still no sign of him or his boat. The harbor master was not optimistic. Every member of the rescue team had returned to shore when the second storm hit, every one except Sean. That was yesterday morning. The storm had raged for thirty straight hours, hitting barely an hour after he had left the harbor.

Graham Greene had tried to reassure her. He spoke to her in the kitchen, keeping his voice low so the children wouldn't hear. "Sean knows these waters better than anyone. He's probably found shelter in a cove."

"Have you had radio contact?" Mollie asked.

Graham hesitated, his kind, ordinary face too honest to dissemble. "I'm afraid not, Mollie, but it doesn't necessarily mean that he's hurt. More than likely it's a mechanical failure. That's not unusual in a storm the size of this one."

She kept her eyes wide, refusing to blink, keeping the tears at bay. "Call me as soon as you know anything."

He patted her shoulder awkwardly. "Of course."

That was early this morning. There was still no word. Mollie filled four cups with tea, reversing the ratios for the girls' cups. She added two biscuits to each of the saucers and passed them out. Then she folded her hands and stared unseeing at the Monopoly board with its three silver markers on St. James, Boardwalk, and the Reading Railroad.

Somewhere else people went about the business of living, paying bills, laughing, sharing cafe mochas and conversation across a table. Somewhere else children jumped rope and played with Christmas toys and skateboarded on the boardwalk beside white sand and blue oceans. Somewhere else women shopped in covered malls and skied down pristine slopes and ate popcorn in movie theaters with plush high-backed seats. Somewhere else friends met for lunch in trendy restaurants with tables by the window, linen napkins and gleaming silver and bone china cups with saucers. Somewhere else lives were predictable. Men left at eight and came home at five-thirty, played with their children, ate dinner, watched television, and made love to their wives. Somewhere else, but not here, not on this island where men fished during the days and drank away the nights and women knitted and stared at the horizon and endured.

"Mollie." Emma's voice broke through her thoughts. "The worst of the wind has stopped. After tea why don't you take the girls to the post office and drop off the mail? They need a break, and the fresh air will do you good."

She looked at her mother, at her blessedly familiar face with its gently pointed chin, new lines of suffering around her eyes and a tiny furrow denting her forehead. She had lost a son, her husband had returned home, and yet she was here, playing board games with her grandchildren, hurting for her daughter, graciously inviting her ex-husband's fiancée to their holiday dinner, welcoming her into the family.

Somehow Sean managed it as well. His last few months without his twin sister had faded into the wake of years of memories, of the beginning of a life shared, childhood pleasures, adolescent secrets. He'd survived her death, the blackness, the final parting, a devastation so deep that the very word *pain* was a gross understatement.

At first Mollie didn't recognize the emotions that rose from the pit of her stomach and spread out to her extremities and up into her throat, rooting her to the chair and freezing the muscles of her throat. It was something she'd never experienced before. Then it came to her. *Terror.* This icy numbness could be nothing else but sheer terror, the kind that comes when life is threatened and the adrenaline pumps hot and pulsing through the veins. What if Sean O'Malley was lost, a victim of the Irish Sea like Danny? Could a reasonable God allow this family another tragedy? Could she look into the clear, trusting faces of her nieces and explain that Sean would not be coming back to them? How could she go on knowing that her life and the world would continue without Sean O'Malley in it?

She couldn't do it. She simply couldn't walk down to the post office with the children and pretend that nothing had changed, that Sean was working in his office and would stop by later to collect them, to coax Marni into a smile, pull Caili's curls, and tickle Luke on the sensitive spot underneath his chin.

What was wrong with her that she couldn't endure what others had? Was there a weakness in her, an accident of birth that lowered her pain thresholds, leaving her unable to cope?

Marni was staring at her. Mollie swallowed and wet her lips. "I think I'll go upstairs and lie down for a while."

Emma looked at her, the line in her forehead pronounced. "Are you ill, Mollie?"

"I'm not sure. Maybe."

Caili walked around the table and leaned against Mollie. "I'm sick, too, Aunt Mollie. Can I sleep with you?"

Mollie hesitated. She wanted to be alone. Words formed on her lips. Then she caught sight of the little girl's anxious green eyes and relented. "All right, love."

They climbed the stairs together. Mollie fluffed up the pillows and turned back the comforter. She helped Caili remove her shoes and climb into bed. Then she lay down beside her. The little girl rolled against her, tucked her thumb securely into her mouth, and stared at her aunt. "Shall we pray for Uncle Sean and Russ?" she whispered.

Mollie swallowed hard. "It wouldn't hurt."

Caili closed her eyes, clutched Mollie's hand, and recited a prayer in the guttural, back-of-the-throat Irish that the islanders reverted to in times of great emotion.

Mollie envied them their language, their traditions, their communion with the elements, their deep faith in God, and, most of all, their ability to endure. Even this child with her drooping eyelids and her body curled into a fetal position against her side understood that she was powerless to change the whims of fate and therefore accepted them. Prayer. There was power in prayer. Mollie closed her eyes, wrapped her arms around the small body tucked against her own, and prayed.

28

"Mollie." Her mother's voice pulled her from the haze of sleep the following morning. "They found Russ's boat. He's safe."

Safe. Russ. The obvious question formed in her mind. She opened her eyes. "Sean?"

Emma shook her head. "Nothing yet. Russ anchored his boat in a sheltered bay and waited out the storm. We can only hope Sean did the same. We'll know more when the weather clears."

"Is Russ home?"

"Yes. He's just eaten a huge breakfast, and now he's sleeping."

Mollie groaned, rolled over, and looked at the clock. "You did all this yourself, and it's only six o'clock."

Emma pulled the comforter up and tucked it around Mollie's shoulders. "Go back to sleep. There's no need to get up yet. I just wanted you to know."

Sleep. She wanted her to sleep. Emma's cure for everything, sleep and a glass of water. Mollie hung on the depths of despair. The hollow feeling was back in her stomach, and her eyes burned from the tears she'd held back the night before. Sleep. She would sleep. Time would pass. Sean would be found, and this nightmare would fade into an annoying memory.

She woke, much later, to clear skies. Stretching, she swung her legs over the bed, found her slippers and robe, and walked to the window. Water dripped in a steady rhythm from the rain gutters. Overhead, hungry gulls circled and screeched their outrage. The oil spill had diminished their food supply. Through the glass Mollie could smell the sea. Even though there was very little marine life left in the waters around Inishmore, it stilled smell of fish.

Outside her room, in the hallway, the telephone rang. She held her breath and waited. Minutes passed. Nothing. She exhaled, looked longingly at her rumpled bed, and decided against it. Emma would need help with the children. There were nine days of vacation left. Maybe she could take the girls away from the island for a holiday, to Galway or even Dublin. They would visit the shops on Grafton Street, order tea and pastries at Bewley's, see the Book of Kells at Trinity, all the touristy things that people did, things the girls had never seen. Marni would like that.

Firmly suppressing the notion that it might be impossible to go anywhere because Sean O'Malley would be pronounced lost at sea and once again the island would be gathered for a funeral, Mollie carried her clothes into the bathroom, turned on the water, and stepped into the shower.

*　　*　　*

Both girls were unusually subdued when Mollie joined them for lunch. She helped her mother ladle tomato soup into bowls, slice grilled ham and cheese sandwiches into fourths, and carry everything into the dining room.

It was comfortably warm. Luke slept soundly in his cradle, his small chest rising and falling with every breath.

"When will Russ wake up?" Caili asked, her voice hushed.

"Probably not until tomorrow," Emma replied. "He hasn't slept in a while. He needs to catch up."

"When will they find Uncle Sean?"

Mollie's heart thumped in her chest. She felt dizzy, and her breath shortened. Gripping the edge of the side-board, she stared out the window. What did one do when brought up against such a question, plainly asked, with-out the softening of polite language? Powerful words, Mollie decided, were plain words. Polite people said "passed away" instead of "dead," "discomfort" instead of "pain," "substance abuser" instead of "drug addict" or "wino," "unflattering" instead of "ugly." It took a child to lay the truth out before them, the horrifying reality of what might be. Mollie waited for Emma's answer, for the reassuring denial that would give them all hope.

The silence stretched out, connecting them with invisible threads. Mollie turned to face them, two little girls and a woman who'd aged a decade since she'd returned to Inishmore, all of them waiting for her answer. She wet her lips and spoke gently. "Soon, I hope. You can be sure that everyone is doing all they can to help."

"Mabry says sorrows come in threes," said Marni.

"That's ridiculous," Emma sputtered, "Mabry is an interfering old—"

"If she's right," Mollie cut in, "we've already had our three. First your mother, then your father and the oil spill."

Marni brightened. "You're right. Mr. Greene will find Uncle Sean, Caili. We've already had our three."

Mollie changed the subject. "Why don't we take a short holiday, just for a day or two, while there's still time before school starts again?"

"Where shall we go?" Caili asked.

"Dublin," replied Mollie. "Have you been there?"

Marni scrunched up her face and thought. "Perhaps, when I was a baby, so I'll not be remembering it."

"I've been there," Caili volunteered.

"You haven't," Marni corrected her. "Neither of us has."

Emma hesitated. "Do you think it's appropriate, Mollie, at such a time?"

"We can wait in Dublin as well as here. The girls and I can catch the plane this very evening and be there in less than an hour. We'll shop, walk around, take in a change of scenery, and be home the day after tomorrow."

"This is a small island," her mother warned her. "What might be acceptable in Newport may not work here. It may appear disrespectful."

Mollie smiled at her nieces. "There's ice cream in the freezer. Why don't you two dish up four bowls and bring them back here for dessert?"

Both girls slipped from their chairs and raced into the kitchen.

Mollie waited until she heard the refrigerator open.

"Is it disrespectful to give two little girls a few hours of happiness before their world caves in again?"

"I don't think so, but others may."

"If Sean is—" She couldn't bring herself to say the word *dead*. "If he isn't coming back," she amended, "we won't have to worry about anyone's disapproval. The children will go back with you to Newport, and I'll finish out the school year and come home."

Emma sighed. "You're right. It's not as if Dublin is on the other side of the world. Take the girls and try to forget all this for a bit. It certainly isn't helping Sean for us all to be sitting on pins and needles for the phone to ring. I'll watch the baby and look after Russ. If anything develops, I can always call you."

It took less than an hour to make the arrangements, another to pack, and by three o'clock, Patrick had arrived with his pony trap to carry them to the small commuter airfield. The pilot was the same one who had flown her to Galway before Christmas.

He grinned. "So, you've conquered your nerves, have you?"

Mollie laughed. "I have."

"Shall we go, then? The flight should be a smooth one."

Mollie buckled the girls into their seats and sat down in the row across from them.

Caili's eyes widened, and she stared at her aunt in alarm when she heard the engines turn over.

Mollie smiled bracingly. "I brought some coloring books and crayons. As soon as the plane is in the air, you can pull out your tray and color. It won't take us long."

The plane lifted. Mollie held her breath. "My ears feel funny," complained Caili.

"Hold your nose and blow." Mollie pulled a pack of gum from her purse. "Chew on this. Sometimes it helps."

Within minutes the plane had leveled, and both girls were chewing and chatting happily. Mollie leaned her head back against the cushion and stared out the window. Only a few minutes, and Inishmore and its tragedies would be behind them. By the time they returned— She wasn't delusional. Two days meant everything. If Sean's boat was still missing, the search would end. He would be lost at sea, and those who were left would adjust.

For Luke and the girls the changes would be enormous. For herself . . . she wouldn't go there, not now, not on this tiny plane with nowhere to hide.

Number 31, the guidebook-recommended bed-and-breakfast near Saint Stephen's Green, was spacious by Irish standards. Two connecting rooms with a balcony looked out over a tree-lined garden, empty now that it was winter but no less welcoming. Downstairs a modern living area with sofas covered in a royal blue material, arranged in a square, faced a large fireplace glowing with peat. Shelves filled with books lined the walls, and a huge vase of pink and blue azaleas dominated the rectangular coffee table in the center.

The girls were hungry. After consulting a map, Mollie tucked an umbrella under her arm, took them each by the hand, and led them out the door toward the Temple Bar area, where Gallagher's Boxty House offered rolled potato pancakes filled with meat and vegetables, fish and chips, hamburgers, and whatever else would never be found in Kilronen.

Within minutes she'd found Grafton Street. The pedestrian boulevard was a shopper's paradise. Street musicians sang and danced while fingering whistles, fiddles, harmonicas, and a kind of bagpipe Mollie had never seen before. Vendors hawked the *Big Edition*. Shops, catering to those with Christmas cash, were brightly lit, frocked in ribbons, bells, and holiday finery. Bewley's, a larger and far more grand tea and coffee house than Galway offered, fairly swelled with people.

Mollie followed the street around Trinity College Green and turned left on Aston Place.

"Look, Auntie Mollie." Marni pointed to their destination with her free hand. "Gallagher's has a queue."

"That's because the food is delicious," replied Mollie. "You can wait a few minutes, can't you?" She lifted Caili's chin. "Can you wait, Caili?"

The child's eyes were huge and round in her small face. She nodded. Mollie knelt down beside her. "Are you all right, love?"

Caili whispered something unintelligible.

Mollie picked her up. "Tell me again, in my ear."

Again Caili whispered. Mollie smiled. "Dublin is the largest city in Ireland. Most of these people live here, and a few, like us, are visiting. By tomorrow afternoon you'll be used to crowds."

"We've never been farther than Galway," Marni explained.

"Galway can be crowded, too," said Mollie.

Marni looked dubious.

Setting Caili on her feet, Mollie led them to the end

of the line. Around them conversation, laughter, and cigarettes were passed back and forth. Mollie listened intently. The city atmosphere, the people, and the lights energized her. Accents were different here in Dublin, crisper, more English than those from the west of Ireland.

Inside the restaurant was dim, warm, and boisterous. Service was pleasant and efficient. Marni groaned with delight when she bit into her bacon and cabbage boxty. Caili's awe had disappeared, and she managed to eat half of her hamburger and a good number of chips before pushing her plate away.

"May we have a pudding, Aunt Mollie?" she begged.

"You can't possibly still be hungry."

Caili shook her head, and her curls danced. "No, but I want a different taste in my mouth. May we have a pudding, please?"

"I'll have to roll you back to the hotel." Mollie signaled the waiter. "Let's see what they have."

Mollie ate two bites of the trifle Marni couldn't finish and watched in amazement as Caili licked her ice cream dish clean. "You're amazing. One would think you'd never had ice cream before."

"We didn't have it much at all before you came," Marni said. "Da said it was too dear and not at all necessary."

Not for the first time, Mollie wondered if she would have had anything at all in common with her only brother. "Are we finished?"

Both girls nodded in unison.

The streets were not quite as crowded as they had been earlier in the evening. Mollie stopped to let the children watch a puppeteer, then gave each of them half a punt to drop into his cap.

They continue down Grafton, around Saint Stephen's Green to Lower Leeson Street and Number 31. Mollie inserted the key into the wooden gate and held the door for the children to step into the courtyard.

Mrs. Flannery, a narrow woman with an angular haircut and features that belied her cheery demeanor, greeted them. "Did you have a lovely meal, my dears?"

"We did," replied Caili. "Marni and Mollie had boxties, and I had a hamburger and chips." Her eyes rolled, and her voice dropped conspiratorially. "We even had a pudding."

"My goodness." Mrs. Flannery's hands flew up in mock amazement. "You lucky girl. I'm sure you're filled up to the brim."

"I am," replied Caili, "and Marni, too."

Mrs. Flannery laughed and patted Caili's cheeks. "Will you be wanting the tea tray sent to your room later in the evening, Miss Tierney?"

"Tea, all by itself, sounds perfect. I'll call down after I put the girls to bed."

"What would you like to see tomorrow?" Mollie asked after tucking the covers around Marni.

"I want to see the General Post Office where the revolution started and the bullet still in the wall. We've heard it so often in school."

"What about you, Caili?"

"The zoo."

Mollie spread out the map. "The post office is on O'Connell Street. It looks like the zoo is on the west side of the city near Phoenix Park. We'll take a taxi." She looked up and smiled. "We'll have plenty of time for both." She kissed Marni first, then Caili. "I love you. Good night."

Caili, her thumb wedged into her mouth, was nearly asleep. Leaving the door between their rooms slightly ajar, Mollie switched off the light and sat down in the chair beside her bed. She looked at the phone. There were no messages. Her mother hadn't called. Nothing had changed on Inishmore. Once again despair swept over her. Here with the children, eating out, visiting the city, she could manage because she could forget for a while. What would it be like all alone on the island until June, with her mother and the children gone?

Clouds, the color of dark ash, rolled in during the night, threatening rain. Undaunted, Mollie pulled out her umbrella and, after a full Irish breakfast of eggs, bacon and sausage, tomatoes, toast, juice, and tea, bundled up the girls and headed for the taxi queue.

The old-fashioned black automobile that pulled up was a treat in itself. Caili's gasp of delight when the car rolled forward and moved with the flow of traffic startled Mollie until she remembered that her nieces hadn't ridden inside an automobile more than half a dozen times since they were born. Outside of minivans, there were few cars on the island, no repair shops, and only a single gas station. What would they make of California freeways and seventy-mile-an-hour speed limits?

The west end of Dublin wasn't the usual tourist haunt. The zoo was virtually deserted, and the three of them were able to work their way quickly through the snow leopard compound, the penguin and ape exhibits, the reptile house, and the aviary. By one o'clock Mollie was more than ready to stop for food and rest her feet before venturing down O'Connell Street.

The post office was a functioning government building as well as a historical monument. The front window, complete with its embedded bullet, carried a description of the 1916 battle that resulted in independence for the twenty-six counties of the Republic of Ireland. From there Mollie pointed out the statue of revolutionary David O'Connell, presiding over the junction of the bridge, before making their way over to Lower Abbey Street and a taxi queue back to the hotel.

"Look." Marni pointed to a large, colorful poster behind glass on the wall behind them. "Isn't that Uncle Sean's play?"

Mollie turned and froze. They were standing in front of the famous Abbey Theater, the National Theater of Ireland, where works by Synge, O'Casey, Friel, and Leonard had premiered. There, among the famous portraits of past and present writers, was the marquee advertising an evening performance of *The Rose of Tralee* by Sean O'Malley.

The Abbey Theater. He was accomplished enough to have his work performed at the Abbey, the theater of William Butler Yeats and Lady Augusta Gregory. Never once had he implied that he was more than marginally successful. He'd been reluctant to stop and show her his home in Galway. He worked in a cramped bedroom office in his sister's tiny cottage on Inishmore. Mollie was confused. Why would he allow her to believe he was no more than a starving artist when only the greatest of

Ireland's playwrights had their work performed at the Abbey?

Another thought occurred to her. When had she ever asked him if she could read something he'd written? When had she expressed more than a cursory interest in his work? The answer to both questions shamed her. Suddenly it was very important that she see his play.

A taxi pulled up beside them. Mollie slid into the back seat beside her nieces. Tomorrow they would fly back to Inishmore. But there was still tonight. The play started at eight o'clock. After dinner she would tuck the girls into bed and take Mrs. Flannery up on her offer to babysit.

The children were exhausted. After Mollie kissed each soft little cheek, she pulled Caili's thumb from her slack mouth, closed the door to their room, and dialed the phone number of her cottage on Inishmore. All lines were down because of the storm.

Frustrated, she hung up, buttoned up her coat, and ran down the stairs to tell Mrs. Flannery she was leaving.

29

Sean O'Malley waved to the pilot, pulled up the collar of his jacket, and ran into the terminal of the commuter airfield. Twenty-four hours of straight rest and a hot meal had completely revived him. All that remained of his ordeal was a slight headache from the blow to his head and an aversion to water that he didn't believe was temporary.

It amazed him that everything had suddenly become so crystal-clear. The possibility of losing his life had a dramatic effect on his perspective. Mollie's face was his first coherent image when he'd regained consciousness. It stayed with him, sustaining him, throughout the hours he'd waited for rescue.

He loved her. He'd always loved her. Forty-eight hours clinging to half a boat in a heaving ocean had clarified that emotion for him. Now all it took was for him to tell her, to convince her that he'd been foolish, to explain the reasons for his caution, to woo her, if she was skeptical, into his arms and his life, permanently.

Emma had wanted him to call immediately, but there was no phone service off the island, a result of the storm. He decided to fly to Dublin and call from a phone booth near the Green. Number 31 was on Lower Leeson Street.

A woman with a pleasant voice answered on the first ring. "Miss Tierney is out for the evening," she said. "Shall I tell her you've phoned?"

"This is Sean O'Malley. She has my nieces with her. Would you mind if I stopped in to wait?"

"Sean O'Malley?" The woman's voice rose an octave. "The playwright Sean O'Malley? The one missing in the storm?"

"The same."

"My goodness, Mr. O'Malley. We're very glad to have you back with us. You're certainly welcome here at Number 31. Miss Tierney has gone to the Abbey Theater to see your play. You might want to catch her there. I'm caring for the girls, but they're asleep now."

"Thank you. I'll do that."

He needed no introduction at the Abbey. The theater was dark and the play well into the third act when Sean took his seat in the back row. His eyes adjusted, and he looked around. The room was nearly three-quarters full, not bad for a play that had premiered nearly two years before. He settled back to wait for the curtain call, the lights, and, now that the blinders had been removed from his eyes, the sight of Mollie's face when she first recognized him.

Mollie stared at the stage, completely immersed in the story, the characters, and the rich humor of the dialogue that surrounded and enhanced the tragedy of the plot. It could never have been anything else but an Irish story. She felt foolish, selfish even, caught up in the idea that there were more Irish in America than in Ireland and that immigration was a way of life for them. Why hadn't she seen that Sean was connected to his country in the same way as any of the authors who made the required reading lists in Irish literature classes? He needed the inspiration of Ireland and the world where he'd grown up to do what he loved.

Mindlessly she clapped as the actors took their first and then their second bows. The auditorium lights were on, but they were still dim, in keeping with the old-fashioned tone of the restoration. It was soft light, friendly light, very like the candlelight of the eighteenth century, flattering to the hair and complexion.

Still caught up in the complicated structure of the play, Mollie collected her program, purse, and coat and turned to walk up the aisle. She was one of the last to leave. Casually, accidentally, her glance fell on a lean, dark-clothed figure standing in the last row. Her heart jumped. It couldn't be. She shook her head to clear her vision.

He walked toward her. Mollie dropped her program. Her purse and coat were next. Pulse racing, she stood frozen, her breathing forgotten, until he held out his arms. Finally, daring to believe, she ran up the aisle and threw herself against his chest. Wrapping her arms around his waist, she gathered the wool of his pullover in her hands and clung.

Words were unnecessary. Later she would ask what had happened and how he could appear before her, apparently unscathed, when all the world had given him up for drowned. Now it was enough to touch him, to smell the cold December night he'd brought with him, to run her hands up and down the nubby fabric of his sweater and underneath to the smooth, soft cotton of his shirt, then up to the sharp bones of his face and the faint edge of beard beneath his skin.

What was left of the audience ignored them, making their way up the aisle, dividing around them, keeping their eyes downcast, minding their own business, unusual for curious Dubliners. When they were alone at last, Sean lifted Mollie's head from his shoulder. "I haven't kissed you yet." He touched her cheek. "I never thought I'd kiss you again."

She lifted her lips.

It started tenderly, cautiously, a gesture of reverence. But soon it was more, a drowning, a swallowing, hands and arms and tongue coming into play, the kiss of a man who knew he was going down for the last time. "Jesus," he muttered. "Let's go home."

"The girls are at the hotel."

"We'll get another room."

"I have another room."

Mollie followed him up the aisle, out the door, and into the backseat of the taxi waiting outside. She heard Sean converse with the driver and tried to pay attention, but her mind wouldn't work. He was alive and he was here. She was the one he'd come to.

Mrs. Flannery peeked out of the kitchen and waved.

"How were the girls?" Mollie managed.

"Not a peep out of them."

Sean introduced himself and continued up the stairs. Mollie held tightly to his hand. Careful not to make noise, she turned the knob and stepped inside. The door between the rooms was slightly ajar. Sean stepped in the smaller bedroom and sat down on the side of the bed his nieces shared. Gently, he rested one hand on Caili's head and the other on Marni's.

The look on his face tore at Mollie's heart. She stepped back to give him some privacy and removed her coat and gloves. Her hands were trembling. What now? What did his coming to Dublin really mean?

She waited, counting the minutes. It seemed an eternity before he came back into her room.

After closing the door behind him, Sean locked it and stepped in the light. From across the room she could see the color of his eyes, the clear, water-locked color of them, sometimes blue, sometimes green, more often something between the two. He wore his twisted grin, but there was something different in his smile. Dear God, let it be what she thought it was. Somehow she remembered to breathe. She watched his eyes move to her mouth and narrow. The wanting rose in her throat, crowding the air. Was it possible to want someone so and pretend otherwise. The space between them sizzled with tension.

She swallowed and sat down on the bed. "Tell me what happened to you."

He shrugged. "There isn't much to tell. Shortly after I left, I hit my head and blacked out. When I came to, the boat was listing, and half of it was gone. I hung on until the rescue boat came."

Mollie shivered. "You were lucky."

"Aye." He sat down beside her and touched her face, her hair, her eyelids, following with his lips. "Very lucky."

"How did you find me?"

"Your mother gave me the name of your hotel. I called from the Green, and Mrs. Flannery told me you were at the Abbey."

She sighed, closed her eyes, and rested her head on his shoulder. Just now, she could hold no more.

He ran his hand up and down her arm. If only this moment and this mood would last forever.

His voice was husky, the words sincere, unschooled. "I want to make love to you, Mollie. I've thought of nothing else since Graham pulled me into his boat."

She had a million questions, but they could wait. Everything could wait, for now. She turned to find his lips, firm cool lips that pressed against her mouth, opening, welcoming, drawing her in, readying her for his hands sliding down her zipper, baring her shoulders, her breasts, slipping off the rest of her clothes and then his own. The feel of his arms dizzied her, cool flesh against warm, his murmured words and seeking mouth exploring the column of her throat, the junction of her shoulder, the pulse where the blood drummed, the slope of one breast and then the other, circling with his tongue, sucking, hard.

Completely aroused, Mollie let her instinct prevailed. Sliding her hands across his shoulders and down his back, she paused at the dip between waist and hip, her fingers lingering on the bunched muscle beneath the skin. This part of a man was so definite, so hard and muscular, so completely masculine.

"Don't stop," he whispered, lifting his mouth from hers. Had there ever been a time when he hadn't wanted her, from that very first day she'd stood on Kerry's front stoop, hair a twisted tangle of wheat and honey, lips parted in a movie-star smile? She seemed too good to be real. She was still too good to be real, but this time Sean knew better. This time he wouldn't turn away. This time he wouldn't refuse the treasure offered him.

He felt her mouth open against his chest. Her hands were on his backside, warm, urgent. She was ready for him. He kissed her deeply. Without releasing her mouth, he parted her thighs with his leg and entered her. The slight intake of her breath nearly undid him. He stopped moving. The scent of her skin, the silky hair, the soft, hot flesh closing around him were an onslaught of sensation, coming too soon after his battle for survival. For the first time since he was a boy, Sean lost control. The heat mobilized, pulsing through him, from his body to hers, a debilitating release of desire and need, fear and love, an affirmation of life.

Later, much later, when the fire had burned low in the grate, when he'd kissed her palms, her belly, her breasts, and the smooth insides of her thighs, when he'd found the place between her legs and touched her with his fingers and his tongue until she was spent, when he'd pulled the covers around them and they lay in spoon fashion on the large bed, his hands cupping her breasts, he asked her, "What did you think of it?"

"Of what?"

"The play."

Mollie closed her eyes and thought a minute, composing in her mind exactly the right words that would make him realize she understood. Words that would tell him she knew his story was far more than the plot, and his theme was always Mother Ireland.

Letting the covers fall to her waist, she sat up and looked at him, at the blue of his eyes, the black hair that fell across his forehead, and the high, clear bones of his cheeks. He was pure Celt, born to the breed. "It made me realize how well you understand people and how very Irish you are." A wave of color stained her cheeks. "I'm sorry that I didn't see one of your plays sooner. It would have settled things for me."

He frowned. "What do you mean?"

"You're in love with Ireland, Sean," she said softly, "with her tragic history, her greenness, her beauty, and, most of all, the voices of her people. This is your home. I understand that now. You should never leave it."

Reaching out to her with gentle fingers, he traced her cheeks, her chin, the shape of her lips, the blade of her shoulder, the lovely soft curve of her breast.

"Are you giving me up, lass?"

Her head fell back on the pillow. She pressed her fingers against her eyelids, holding back the wetness, and nodded.

He moved over her again, entered her, matching his rhythm to her breathing and then to the soft gasps of pleasure coming from the back of her throat. Her rise was slower this time, deeper, more profound, in keeping with the slow-growing intensity of his rhythmic thrusts. When she climaxed, she felt a completeness, a giving and receiving of body and spirit, of a kind she had never known before.

Mollie knew she would love again. It was inevitable. Somewhere in the world walked a man who waited for her, a man she would share a life and children with, a man by whom she would be pleased. She was a woman easily pleased, one who loved laughter, who measured the success of her life through small pleasures lived in a hundred small moments during the course of every normal day. She would not be a martyr and mourn Sean O'Malley forever. There would be a time when this ache in her heart had passed, when the memory of her year in Ireland would be a faint smudge on the canvas of her life, when another man and his children would take up the space in her heart. It wouldn't be the same, not ever, but it would be enough.

All that lay ahead in the nebulous future. There was still tonight to live through and all the nights ahead until June when she could go home.

She must have slept. When she woke the room was dark. She was very conscious of Sean beside her, the warmth of his body pressed against her, his smell on the sheets, the stickiness between her legs because of him, because of what they'd done together. Mentally she chastised herself. How could she have slept? Their time was so short.

Sighing, she turned over and ran her hand up his thigh, past the jutting bone of his hip to rest on his chest. He covered it with his own.

"Are you awake, love?"

Love. He'd called her love. "Yes."

"A Calibogie is unsinkable," he began conversationally.

"Oh?" Her brain struggled from its last vestiges of sleep to follow him. The boat. He was talking about the boat.

"Did I tell you that it cracked down the middle?"

"No."

"It did. There was nothing, no motor, no sail. All I could do was hang on and hope for rescue."

"And you were."

"Aye. Two days later."

She kissed his shoulder. "You were very lucky."

"It changes a man's perspective when death stares him in the face. Nothing else matters but staying alive."

"I can't imagine."

He shifted to look at her, the eyes close and colorless in the darkness. "My priorities have changed, Mollie. I promised myself that if I survived I wouldn't let you go."

At first his words didn't register. When they did she began to tremble. "What are you saying?"

"I want you stay in Ireland with me. Can you do that, Mollie? I won't ask you to give up your home entirely. We could work something out, part of the year here, part in California."

"On Inishmore?" she asked.

"In Galway. I've a home there. It's large enough for all of us."

For all of us. Mollie's head spun. What was he asking? Sean was wonderful with Luke and the girls. He was educated, literate, capable. His mouth and hands made her blood run hot, but was it enough?

"Am I too late, Mollie? Did I wait too long to come to my senses? Am I wrong in thinking you love me?"

She shook her head, very conscious of the swell of his arm beneath her cheek. "It isn't that," she whispered.

"What is it, then?"

She sat up, covering her breasts, tucking the sheets beneath her arms. "I love Luke and the girls, but I want children of my own."

"I'll give you children."

Frustration sharpened her voice. "Are you asking me to marry you?"

"Of course. What did you think I was asking?"

"You never said the words."

He reached for her, his hands clasping her arms above the elbow, drawing her down against his chest. His hand cradled her neck, rubbing the soft skin beneath her hair. His voice against her ear was soft, amused, the words firm and assured. "I love you, Mollie Tierney. I'm not a rich man, but neither am I poor. I've a mortgage on my home, but I can afford to support a family even if I never sell another play. A playwright isn't a movie star. It gives me a very good living, but I'm not wealthy, not like a doctor from Newport, California."

He lifted her chin and looked into her eyes. "Will you be my wife, Mollie, live with me, bear my children?" He kissed the lobe of her ear. "Please, say yes."

The words were old-fashioned, sentimental, perfect. Still, there was a vague, unsettled question she couldn't shake. "Would you be asking me if you hadn't gone looking for Russ and nearly lost your life?"

Sean knew the words he was about to utter would determine the course of his life. He began slowly, wanting her to understand what had always been in his heart and what had prevented him from acting upon it. "I would have asked you, Mollie, but perhaps not now. I would have argued with myself that you were an American, accustomed to a life of sunshine and comfort. I would have reminded myself that your mother had left Ireland and her husband, taken her child, broken a man's heart. I would have let you go home, suffered your absence for a goodly length of time, and then I would have gone after you."

"Are you still worried about all those things?"

He shook his head. "I did a great deal of thinking while floating in the open ocean. We won't be living the austere life of a fisherman's family on Inishmore. I have friends in Galway, professional people you'll be comfortable with. We'll go to California whenever you like.

"You're probably wondering if any of this has to do with the children. I've come to a decision about that, too. If your mother takes them with her, I won't like it. But neither will I fight it. She is their legal guardian. They have nothing to do with how I feel about you." His voice grew husky with emotion. "The alternative is life without you, Mollie, and nothing is worth that. Marry me, please."

Smiling, she turned her head and pressed her lips against his chest. "Yes," she whispered, "I will."

30

Caili broke away from Mollie and ran up the rock-lined path to the cottage, where Emma waited on the porch. Throwing her arms around her grandmother, she announced, "Auntie Mollie and Uncle Sean are getting married. We're going to live in Galway for a time and another time in California with you."

Emma lifted the little girl into her arms. "My goodness." Her eyes moved beyond Caili to Mollie and Sean walking up the path with Marni between them. "You've certainly brought some interesting news. Have you gotten it right, I wonder?"

"She has," said Sean firmly. "Mollie has agreed to marry me. I hope you'll allow the children to be with us in Galway for part of the year. The schools in Ireland are very good."

Emma smiled, set Caili on her feet, and hugged Mollie. "That sounds like a wonderful idea. Congratulations to the two of you. Have you decided on a wedding date?"

"Soon," said Sean.

"Not too soon," Emma said quickly. "Mollie is my only daughter. I'd like her wedding to be special. It's difficult to put a wedding together in a short time."

"We're going to be married here, Mom," Mollie said gently, "on the island."

Emma's face fell. "What about your friends at home?"

"We'll have a reception in Newport later," Mollie explained. "We're going to have the ceremony in the church where Sean was baptized and where Danny and Kerry were married." She squeezed her mother's hand. "It's what we both want."

Emma smiled tremulously. Her eyes were very bright. "I'll pray for sunshine."

Sean released his breath, and Mollie laughed.

"Don't think you won't have a crowd," Emma warned them. "Daniel O'Shea has negotiated a settlement with Transom Oil. Nearly all the families involved will have a generous income until fishing is approved again. You're responsible for that Mollie, everyone is very grateful to you."

Sean groaned. "The entire island will expect to be invited to the wedding." He glanced hopefully at Mollie. "Are you sure you don't want a quick ceremony in Dublin and a Paris honeymoon?"

"Quite sure," Mollie said firmly.

This time it was Emma who breathed a sigh of relief.

Two years later

Sean pushed aside the contents of his suitcase, cursed under his breath, and looked guiltily at the four-poster bed where Caili lay on her stomach coloring.

"You said a bad word, Uncle Sean," she announced.

"So I did. You won't be telling your Aunt Mollie on me, will you, lass?"

"Not if you tell Annie to let me stay up until you get home."

"That's a hard bargain, my love. You know we won't be back until the wee hours of the morning. I'm sorry, but I can't do it."

Caili sat up and crossed her legs. "Why are you mad?"

"Who's mad?" Mollie walked into the room, and Sean caught his breath in appreciation. How did she manage it? A little nothing of a dress. Understated elegance. Everyone would look at her and know why the flavor of his work had changed, acquiring mystery, a different kind of edge. They would also know why his nights were never long enough. "I can't find my cuff links," he stammered, caught up, even after a year and a half of marriage, in her rhythms, counting the hours until he would have her alone again in the quiet darkness of their bedroom, cool silky skin wrapped in cotton sheets.

She found them, as she always did, effortlessly, smiling conspiratorially at Caili. "Annie's here, love. Why don't you ask her if she wants some tea?"

Caili collected her crayons and slid off the bed. "Maybe she'll let me stay up until you get home."

Sean held his breath.

"I doubt it," Mollie said, slipping her arms around her husband's waist. Waiting until Caili left the room, she whispered into his ear. "What would you do without me?"

"God help me if I ever have to find out," Sean said fervently, turning to kiss her. "Is everyone ready?"

"My mother and Ward will meet us at the theater. Alice and my father are in the suite with your mother, entertaining our babysitter." She reached up to straighten his collar. "You look wonderful. Are you nervous?"

"Premieres always make me nervous."

"The critics have yet to disappoint you."

"There's always a first time, Mollie. My run of luck can't last forever."

"I'd call it talent."

Once again he kissed her, lingering in the softness of her lips. "You're not exactly impartial."

"I've seen the play, Sean. You have nothing to worry about." She tugged at his hand. "Let's go down. The car must be here by now."

"How is your father taking all this?"

"He's amazingly calm. It's Alice who can hardly contain herself. Thank you for inviting them, Sean. They'll never forget a night like this."

"He's your father and the children's grandfather." Gently, he rubbed his hand across her flat middle. "Have you told them yet?"

She shook her head. "I wanted to wait until tonight at dinner when we're all together."

"Four months, and you're still not showing."

"It's completely normal, according to the doctor. I have gained weight."

"Three children are a lot of work. Maybe we should relax this summer, let your mother take them with her."

"I'll be fine," she reassured him. "You worry too much."

"I love you."

"I'm counting on it. Now, we really have to go or we'll miss the first act."

The Rolls-Royce threaded its way through the hemmed-in traffic crowding the front of the entrance of the Abbey Theater.

Alice stared out the window at the throngs of people waiting outside. She clutched Patrick's arm and nodded at Sean. "You must be thrilled at such attention."

Sean loosened his collar. "It's a bit nerve-racking, actually."

Eileen smiled at him. "Will it ever change, do you think?"

Sean laughed. "Perhaps, when it doesn't matter so much. Right now I've a family to support with another—"

Mollie pinched his arm. "Look," she interrupted. "Isn't that Mother and Ward?" The Rolls pulled up to the curb, and Emma waved.

Grateful for the diversion, Sean stepped out first and helped his wife and then his mother.

A reporter broke through the corded-off area. "Do you consider this to be your finest piece, Mr. O'Malley?"

Sean favored the man with his smile. "I do, but I always feel that way about my latest work. Let's wait and see what the reviewers say."

An usher led them to a private box slightly above the stage. Sean waited until everyone was settled and comfortable before seating himself. He reached for Mollie's hand.

Keeping her eyes on the stage, she smiled at the predictable nature of her husband's habits. Who would have thought this man, so leery of commitment only a short time ago, would turn into such a devoted husband and father? He was a complicated man, far more complicated than she'd realized, but maybe every new bride felt that way about the man she married. It was a toss-up, really, the successful merging of two people to create a family. Mollie hadn't quite figured out why some unions worked and others didn't. She hadn't spent a great deal of time analyzing her marriage. She was far too busy, too content, and too incredibly happy to spend a great deal of time on the why of it all. Maybe someday she'd go back to teaching, but not now, not with three small children and another on the way. Besides, she loved being home while Sean worked in his office a few doors away. She especially loved it when he read his scenes to her, particularly the challenging ones.

The lights dimmed. A collective hush of anticipation fell over the audience. The curtain rose. As usual with Sean's plays, it began with an event that elicited a gasp from his audience, followed by a series of flashbacks weaving past and present to develop the nature of the characters. Dialogue was his specialty, and the witty ripostes for which he was famous were greeted with appreciation by a friendly applause.

Gradually, as the play progressed, his grip on her hand relaxed, and Mollie knew he was satisfied with his achievement.

Dinner at Chapter One in the basement of the Dublin Writers' Museum on Parnell Street was superb. Mollie, finally finished with her morning sickness, ordered the spring lamb and parsleyed potatoes. She refused the wine and the traditional champagne toast.

Over dessert, a delicious sherried trifle which Mollie also refused, Emma leaned across the table. "You've skipped the wine all evening. Do you have something to tell us, love?"

Mollie blushed. Under the table, Sean's hand gently squeezed her thigh. "Yes," she said, smiling at her family. "In November, Sean and I are going to have a baby."

Amid the congratulations and waving champagne glasses, Mollie's glance met her husband's and her breath caught. She knew that look and what it meant. Now she had the perfect excuse. "I'm a little tired," she announced. "If you don't mind, I'll say goodnight now."

Sean stood beside her and slipped an arm around her waist. "Take your time. We'll take a taxi back to the hotel and see you in the morning."

Mollie rested her head on her husband's shoulder. "Do you think the girls will still be awake?"

"Caili will be," Sean predicted. "She wraps Annie around her little finger."

"Will she be happy about the baby, do you think?"

Sean smiled. Already Mollie's sentences were ending with questions, a peculiarity of Irish dialect. "She'll be thrilled."

"Are you thrilled, Sean? Really?"

He kissed the top of her head. "I've no words to tell you what you've brought into my life, Mollie O'Malley. I'll just say that my cup runneth over."

Satisfied, Mollie closed her eyes and gave herself up to the rocking motion of the taxi as it made its way back down Parnell Street toward Saint Stephen's Green. Soon, very soon, morning would come and they could go home.

Mabry O'Farrell stood on the cliffs of Dun Aengus and looked out over the sea. Rare June sunlight lit the cloudless sky and the water to a shattering, electric blue. A wave of gulls screeched overhead, and in the harbor several small, single-manned fishing boats motored their way toward the dock. It was a start, a small one, but a start nonetheless.

She pulled the newspaper she'd picked up that morning out from under her arm and scanned the front page of the theater section until she found what she was looking for. Then she reread it. It took more than a minute. Her eyes were fading, even in the brilliant light of a June morning. Words like *brilliant* and *inspired* leaped up at her. Appropriate words to describe the thoughts put into words of a man like Sean O'Malley.

Mabry thought back to the wedding that had taken place nearly eighteen months ago. It was an island event. No one had dared miss it. Sean was one of their own, but Mollie was their savior. Strange how things worked out. Mabry was feeling her age.

Sighing, she folded the paper and turned toward home. A small figure, nimble as a goat, ran up the path, breathing heavily. "What is it, Christie?" Mabry asked.

"Da sent me," the child explained when she caught her breath. "It's Mam's time. He says to hurry."

Mabry's fatigue disappeared. Her step was light as she hurried down the path to her cottage. The age-old birthing ritual called out to her. Once again she felt the pulse of the earth beneath her feet, the pull of the tides in her blood. Soon, very soon, she would bring another islander into the world.